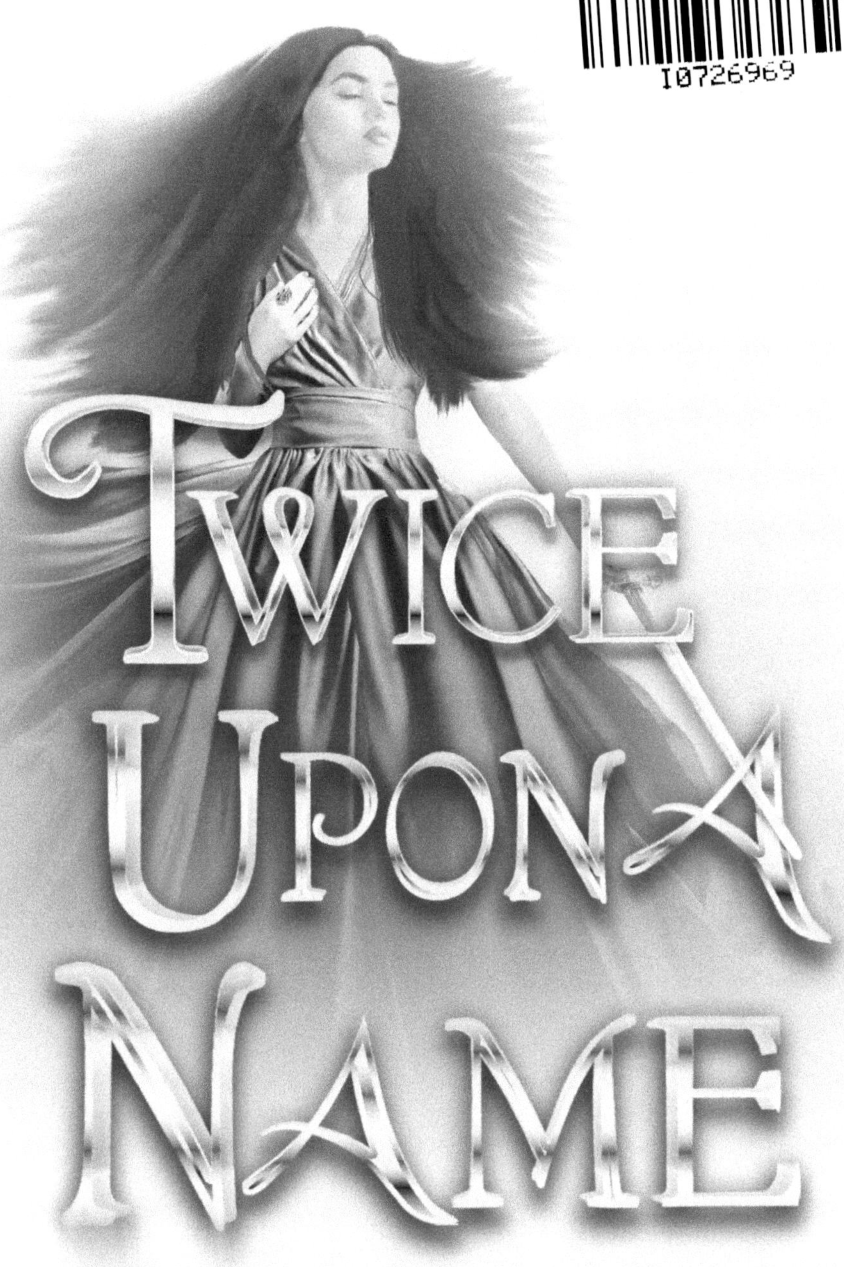

Twice Upon A Name

Bronzewood books
Eden Prairie, MN

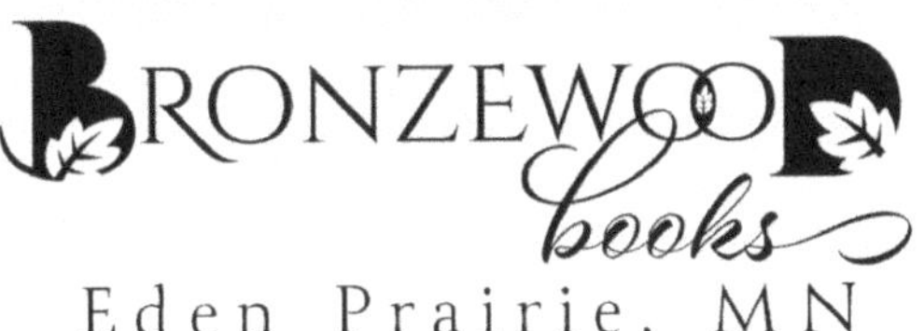

*To all the teachers
who infuse their pupils with a love of books
and an enjoyment of life*

Contents

Time, Untangle This

Susan Stradiotto
& Sky Sommers

Finally, having recovered from being tossed about the Illyrian Sea on little more than a branch, Tarryn Silverwood made her way toward the pier in search of passage home, to the Isle of Midnight. Tarryn glanced about nervously. Of all the Twelve Islands, the Isle of Sixes was no place for anyone of the nobility to land. It was the most rundown of the southernmost islands. The dress she'd acquired on her father's account was a mite too short and more than roomy in the chest, but the seamstress offered her a bit of stuffing to hold the thing up. It was as passable for a lady—the daughter of the Marquess of Silver Woods, no less—as it could be.

Days, or perhaps more than a fortnight had passed since she *should have* attended Lady Glenna Ironraven's presentation to society. The ball would have also been an opportunity to discover if anyone had seen her brother, Tyronnen, who left home in search of a way to resolve their family's financial distress. Instead, the boat she'd chartered from her home on the Isle of Midnight to the ball on Tenth Isle smashed against a boulder and left her afloat. Tarryn hoped to reach Lord Ironraven and be able to explain away the absence of any Silverwood retinue at the most celebrated event of the season. Her family couldn't afford a tarnish on their name. If Tyronnen had not been able to secure good fortune or if a similar fate had befallen to him on his voyage and he was now lost in the tempestuous Illyrian Sea, then their name was all Tarryn had left.

Father's health was fading too fast. She was only supposed to be away for one evening. One! Worries over her father and what would become of the Silver Woods if neither she nor her brother returned had Tarryn tied in knots, but there was little she could do alone. It wasn't just about tending to the books. Caring for their lands and providing for their people was too much for an eighteen-year-old lady with little experience in such matters. Tarryn needed to find her brother. Two heads were better than one.

Although, her first matter of business was to find passage north from the most rundown town of this rundown island.

Tarryn's hopes, however, faded fast as she ran down the street toward the docks. All the ships, save for one, were pulling away. Naturally. It was mid-afternoon, and few sailors would dare to cross the Illyrian Sea by starlight.

The docks creaked when Tarryn stepped onto them, but they held her weight. She lifted her skirt and ran for the last remaining ship. Tarryn had to gain passage and convince the captain to help her, but all she had to offer was her father's name.

An old woman sat at the entrance to the boat, wearing a rough spun and shapeless dress, cleaning a fish over a pan.

"Pardon," Tarryn said.

The woman looked up from her work. One eye sized Tarryn up from head to toe while the other remained closed, that side of her face set in a permanent scowl as if it would never relax.

"How much is the fare to the Isle of Midnight, please?" Tarryn asked, to maintain propriety. Of course, she didn't care, and her father would find a way to repay the captain of the vessel whatever fare he desired.

"No, no, that'll never do," said the woman, wiping her nose on her sleeve. "That won't do at all. The capt'n won't let you on board looking like that."

"Why?" Tarryn surveyed her prim and proper dress in baby blue and twirled her parasol by its handle, hoping the stuffing didn't slide or else she'd look like a lumpy mattress. "Am I dressed inappropriately for a sea voyage?"

The woman spat at Tarryn's feet. "You're a lady, that's why!"

To her own chagrin, Tarryn jumped away and emitted a quite unladylike squeak. "Is that to say the captain hates women?" Tarryn frowned.

"Captain Starrytide says 'tis bad luck for the ship to have women aboard. A curse in the eyes of Mac Lir." The woman stood, closed off the gate, and dragged her stool over to block the way.

Tarryn scoffed. What God would be so rude to say only male passengers could travel by sea, and women were to stay home? Backward island! Tarryn clenched her teeth. There was no other option; she had to get on that ship. "What am I supposed to do? Send the missive to the dragon riders? Or hijack a Pegasus?"

"Dragons'll eat ya before they ferry ya, and good luck catching that horse mid-air." The woman grunted and returned to her fish.

"Very well, what do you suggest?" Tarryn planted her parasol on the deck. "Because one way or another, I am boarding that ship."

The woman cackled but didn't look up. "You ain't going nowhere tonight unless yer a man, dearie, er if yer useful on a ship." She pointed her knife toward a barely legible sign. But she made out the words: *cabin boy wanted.*

"I see," was the only thing Tarryn could say. She peered up at the sun. "When does this Captain—what'd you say his name was?"

The woman sighed. "Starrytide."

"Oh." Tarryn's eyes stretched. "OH!" He was the legendary night sailor of the Illyrian Sea. Well, at least that bought her some more time. He wouldn't leave until the sun had set completely.

She ground her teeth. *Blast it, Ty, where are you? I hope Father can handle things until I can find you and we can get back.*

Tarryn squinted at the grungy sign until an idea blossomed. To gain entry on the ship, all she needed to do was become a *he* by nightfall. She could handle that. The hair would have to go, but it would grow back. Her family's lands wouldn't save themselves.

An hour later, Tarryn returned wearing scratchy brown pants, a shirt that she could barely stand to wear because of the stench, and a floppy hat. She'd chopped off her hair at the chin and drew the curly ends of the hat over her face. With all the puffy skirts and parasols gone, she looked much younger than her ripe age of eighteen. She spotted the fishwife and wondered exactly how many fish that woman cleaned in a day, not to mention where she put them all.

Now or never. If I can fool her, I can fool anyone.

Approaching the woman, she hunched a little and said, "M-Ma'am? Where'd I find Cap'n Starrytide? Uh, puh-lease and thankee."

The woman barely glanced at her. "Come to offer your service, lad?"

Lad? She thinks I'm a boy! Tarryn coughed to stifle her smile. "Aye."

"Thatta way." The woman put the fish pan down and moved toward the rope blocking the gangway. "Cap'n's last boy ran off. Or did he get fired for not keepin' his nails clean? Dunno." She opened the rope for Tarryn to cross and gave her a lopsided smile.

She had fooled the first sentinel, so there was hope. Onboard the ship, she paused.

"Up there, boy." The woman pointed her knife.

Tarryn took a step toward the ladder up to the highest deck when she heard a musical baritone. Or it would have been if it weren't marred by yelling and swearing.

"Move it, mutts! Another cabin boy stolen away!" The voice came nearer. "Can't keep any of the good ones."

Ah, so he didn't run off and wasn't fired. The last one was stolen?!? What kind of ship was this?

A hand landed on Tarryn's shoulder and spun her around.

She bit the inside of her cheek to keep from squealing as she whirled about. She coughed to cover her surprise and kept her chin tucked low. She said in the lowest voice she could muster, "Cap-Captain Starrytide, sir?" Everybody on deck stopped in their tasks, alerted by an unfamiliar voice.

"You? Who are you?" The captain narrowed his eyes at Tarryn.

Tarryn blurted out words before she lost her nerve. "Captain Starrytide, sir? I saw you needed a cabin boy. I've come to apply."

"What?" one swabbie started, "Not another—"

Thunk, his mate swatted him upside the head with the mop.

"Your name, boy?" demanded the captain, leaning onto the railing.

Tarryn cleared her throat and gave him her twin brother's name. "Tyronnen, sir."

"Tyronnen you say? Tyronnen what?"

Tarryn's eyes flew open wide. *I can't give him my last name. Everyone would recognize Silverwood.* "Wood . . . Woodwight, sir." She gave the name of one of her maids from back home. "Tyronnen Woodwight, sir," she added with a nod for punctuation. "Ty for short."

"Tyronnen." The captain gave her a once-over with a dangerous glint in his eye. "Indeed. And what jobs can you do, Ty?"

All around them, the seasoned seamen stifled their giggles.

Tarryn did her best to ignore them and whatever they found so funny. "Anything you trust me with, sir. I'll clean, cook, even write, if need be. Sir." She bit her lip, then stopped herself. Her brother would never bite his lower lip.

"Cleaning and cooking? Female chores." The captain's voice was gruff, but it had a bit of a lilt, now that he had stopped shouting. Tarryn shivered. Somehow, his tone verged dangerously close to wicked.

"My mam taught me, seeing as there was no girl in the house. Comes in handy for the odd jobs," Tarryn managed, proudly sticking her chin up just in time to see another man standing above them. She doubled over in a feigned coughing fit, because this man she recognized.

Duke Braddon Sagewolf, ruler of the Twelve Isles, second only to the King of Illyria, and the most eligible bachelor in the peerage. He stood there with the grace of his station, his hair perfectly styled, his black tunic impeccable, with a golden wolf embroidered on the breast, fierce gray-gold eyes that seemed to see right into her soul. That and a sharp jawline.

How in the world was she going to fool *him*? The voyage shouldn't be long. Maybe if she avoided the man, her disguise would keep? She was sure the man had met her twin brother at court a few times in the past when Father had taken Ty along. They weren't identical, which would help her disguise, but her manner had to be flawless around him.

"Indeed," the captain said again. "Ty, was it? Well . . ." The captain came and put his arm across Tarryn's shoulders, and she quivered inside. Were all men at sea on such familiar terms with each other? "Your Grace, it looks like we have the good fortune to have acquired a new cabin boy." He squeezed Tarryn's shoulder. "Introduce yourself, Ty."

Tarryn grunted. "Uh, Ty Woodwight." She shortened the name to what she called her brother casually. Surely, Ty wouldn't have gotten casual with the Duke to have let his nickname slip.

The captain smirked and winked at her.

Tarryn kept her eyes focused on a rung of the ladder up to where Duke Sagewolf stood. It was growing dark outside, and the swabbies around the boat were pulling in some lines and winding up others. They'd be on the sea soon, and Tarryn hoped this ship was a better bet than the last one she had hired. Every couple of seconds, she allowed her eyes to flit upward until the duke caught her looking.

"That's an interesting name you have," he said. "And you didn't bow at the mention of my station. Interesting."

Immediately, Tarryn put a foot back and bowed low, keeping her spine straight, squeezing her eyes shut. *Please. Please. Please, don't recognize me.*

When she stood, the duke waved a hand in the air. "No matter. All these subjects from the Isle of Sixes are . . . simply uncouth."

Tarryn tried not to react to his dramatic and flippant observation. She didn't disagree, but she'd never say it so outright. An assumption that she originated from this isle, although erroneous, was a good one.

The duke's footsteps retreated, and Captain Starrytide said, "As it happens, it is I who needed a cabin boy, but I'll be sharing you with the duke on this voyage. You better do as you're told by both your masters. It is a privilege to have him sailing on my ship, you understand?"

Pinching her lips together, Tarryn nodded.

"Have you worked on ships before?" the captain asked, pinning her with his stare.

Tarryn gulped. "I . . ." She swallowed. "No, sir, I have not."

A slow wolfish grin spread across the captain's face. "Then let me inform you about your new job. Since you said you can write, you'll occasionally write letters, but moreover, you're here to serve the duke and me. Cabin cleaning, serving meals, and of course, warming our beds, if so required."

Tarryn paled. "Warm your beds?" She whispered and took a step back. Even if Starrytide thought her a boy, this didn't sound right.

The ship's men erupted in manic laughter, but one look from the captain silenced them. *What had she gotten herself into with this complete cad?*

"Not that way, boy. You just take the place of a warm water bottle or coal pan. And then *you* get out before *I* climb inside."

"Oh." Tarryn's shoulders released. *I can be a human coal pan. No problem.* "Yes, sir. I can read and write and clean and bring your food."

"And . . . warm my bed." Devilish sparkles danced in the captain's eyes.

"And warm your bed up for you, sir, yes," she said and got a snort in return.

"And the Duke's bed, should he so require," the captain added.

"Yes. That, too." *Although I bet that wolf would rather brave the cold sheets than let a mongrel boy muddy them.*

"Very well, you're hired. Are you going to ask about your wages?" The captain inclined his head at her.

"I'm sure whatever you paid your last cabin boy plus ten percent would be fair," Tarryn shot off and straightened. If he didn't want to pay more, he shouldn't have announced his last cabin boy had been poached.

"Dougal!" came a shout from above, and Tarryn's gaze jerked upward, and caught the duke's. The captain whipped his head around as well. *Starrytide's given name was Dougal?* A radiant grin spread on

Duke Sagewolf's face. And perhaps Tarryn was imagining it, but his canines seemed to elongate. "We'll stop by the Tenth Isle. Our new cabin boy has a quite pleasing look at him. Ty, he said? Perhaps he can help me on my mission to court Lady Glenna." He marched out of sight.

Captain Starrytide clapped Tarryn on the shoulder, sending her stumbling. As she righted herself, he shouted to someone behind her, "Clean out the tub so we can prepare a bath! And find something decent for the boy to wear." He smirked at her then. "You're going to need to look and smell a whole lot better to meet the daughter of Lord Ironraven."

As the ship lurched away from the dock, Tarryn's throat went dry. What in the world had she gotten herself into?

By the time morning arrived, Tarryn could barely hold her head upright. When she'd gone to warm the duke's bed at midnight, she'd fallen asleep with the warm and spicy smell enveloping her senses. Who knew this seasoned war veteran wouldn't mind a stranger warming up his bed? Tarryn suspected the lavender bath she had endured had something to do with it. The duke woke her sometime in the early hours of the morning to kick her out. She'd been so flustered she hadn't even looked him in the eye, but he'd chuckled when she had shot from his cabin like a bullet. For the rest of the night, Captain Starrytide had her cooking and cleaning until one man on the deck yelled, "Tenth Isle, starboard!" The captain had strutted over and wrinkled his nose before he sent Tarryn off to a private room to take another cold bath. It woke her up for a while, but her eyelids grew heavy again as she stood shivering on deck while they moored the ship. Tarryn sighed. *Why can't we sail straight for the Twelfth Isle, why the tarrying? Provisions? More crewmembers? A leisurely stroll for the duke on dry land?*

As soon as they had the lines tied off, Captain Starrytide flew into action. "Toby, Drew! Lower the tender and join me on my errand."

"Woodwight!" Someone barked and Tarryn jumped, not placing the name she'd given to the captain and the duke just yesterday. Shouted not in Starrytide's baritone, but a tenor. And though it barked that name, the voice had something smooth and enticing in the undertones. Tarryn sucked in a breath, realizing *Woodwight* was *her* only after Duke Sagewolf came to a stop beside her, close enough for her to feel his body heat.

"Cabin boy. I need you to run an errand for me." The duke presented her with an ornate box. Keeping her eyes lowered, she reached to open it.

"That's not for you to see, Woodwight."

Tarryn jerked her hand down to her side.

The duke continued, "It's for you to offer to Lady Glenna on my behalf. Your job here, Woodwight, is to—shall we say—woo the Lady."

Tarryn's eyes, still downcast, went round. She couldn't find words to converse with him, but did all the men speak in such suggestive ways? Beside her, he smelled of familiar spice, the comforting smells she'd fallen asleep to the night before. Of ginger, but also clean, like the Silver Woods after the rain. She held her breath to resist inhaling him deeper or thinking how much it made her want to lean into him.

"Give Lady Glenna the gift and tell her I would have her company for an evening meal before Captain Starrytide sails us back to the Midnight Isle. Can you do that, *Woodwight*?"

She nodded. Why did he keep repeating her last name? Did he know?

"I'll have a proper and verbal response, please," Duke Sagewolf commanded.

Tarryn turned to him, and bowed, once again keeping her back leg bent, her spine ramrod straight. Like all the good gentlemen at court. As she did, the lush texture of the fabric and the majestic golden wolf on the duke's breast made her fingers itch as if they wanted to feel the royal garments.

"Yes, Your Grace," Tarryn said in as deep a tone as she could manage. It sounded somewhat like her brother, but hoarser. If she was to set foot on this isle, she could find someone to ask about her brother. And once she had found him, they could find another boat to hire, dispense with all this charade, and sail back home.

Tarryn stood before Lady Glenna Ironraven with the box on display and her eyes downcast. This was not how she'd planned on meeting the marchioness for the first time. They should have met a fortnight ago, at Glenna's coming out ball. And they would have, had it not been for the storm and the wreckage of that flimsy boat-for-hire. With a satin-gloved hand, Glenna lifted the lid, and her hand went to her mouth as her eyes widened. Must be a precious token, indeed. If anyone on the Twelve Isles could afford a gift of finery, it had to be Duke Sagewolf, the most sought-after man in the social circles, the . . .

Stop it, Tarryn. You must find Ty and go home to Father. With father's illness, Tyronnen needs to return to help me run the house and lands.

Tarryn inhaled slowly through her nose. "Do you find the gift to your liking, Lady Glenna?" she asked, imitating what she believed was her brother's tone of voice.

"The duke really shouldn't have. I simply can't accept it and you know why. It is, though, the most beautiful gift I believe I've ever received!" Glenna reached for Tarryn's face, and she continued to speak before Tarryn could squeeze in a word. "As beautiful as is its bearer." Glenna batted her eyelashes at Tarryn.

"No—"

The lady placed a gloved finger over Tarryn's lips, shutting down the forthcoming explanation. She closed the box, took it from Tarryn's hands, and prattled on. "I'm so happy you've returned, but you do look different, my dear Ty. More slender. They didn't feed you while you've been running errands? Or did you forget to ingest a few morsels because you were busy daydreaming?"

Why would a lady care if a cabin boy was fed well? And Ty? Did I introduce myself? Tarryn screwed up her face, unable to remember giving out any name at all.

Glenna placed the box on a side table, and turned back to Tarryn, sauntering over in a manner that brushed her pink, lace-trimmed skirts back and forth against the marble floor. "Although, I must ask why you would bring me a gift from another man?" Glenna pouted.

"Pardon," Tarryn said as Lady Glenna reached her arms up and gripped Tarryn's shoulders, "um, Lady, uh Gl—"

"Shhh." She placed the satin-covered finger over Tarryn's lips again and ran her other hand down the side of her face. "Tongue-tied around me. How quaint! You, sir, surprise me with your innocence . . ."

Lady Glenna went on, but Tarryn stopped hearing the words. Her heart sounded like a corps of drums in her ears, and her eyes darted back and forth as she tried to figure a way out of the situation. Clearly, she had done a fine job of deception with the lady—enough to warrant her believing Tarryn was her brother. And not to her benefit this time. Because it appeared these two had met.

Tarryn tried to speak again, but the objection came out as a murmur behind her pinned-together lips.

"Yeesss." Glenna tilted her head and peered up at Tarryn. "You, I still think, are much more my type than the old duke. If you make me choose, my love, then my heart, nay my very soul has already chosen you."

Tarryn blinked at Glenna several times. *Wait, what? Love? Chosen me? No. No way! What had Ty gotten himself into? And when? Although a love match with Lady Glenna might just be the ticket to save Silver Wood. But still . . . Now I have to be the stand-in? And what if Ty has perished in the waves?* Tarryn couldn't afford to let go of her ruse with Glenna. Or the captain and the duke. She became wrapped up in how to get out of Lady Glenna's parlor as her brother's potential fiancée babbled on, something about high cheekbones and fae-like features. Tarryn cursed her height and the sharp lines of her face, traits everyone who hailed from the Silver Woods had, her family more so than most. The features suited her brother well, and they were likely the reason she could pass herself off as a man—albeit a wispy one—but she definitely didn't want to be mistaken for him before these sweet nothings and confessions progressed.

Lady Glenna leaned closer until her breath fanned against Tarryn's chin.

Tarryn shook, then spun away. "I believe you must be mistaken, My Lady. The gift is—"

Just then, Captain Starrytide stepped into the door and stomped his boot heel onto the wooden threshold. A clap echoed off the marble in the parlor and silenced them.

Tarryn slipped and let her voice return to its normal higher pitch.

"Captain Starrytide, what brings you on shore and up to the Ironraven Keep?"

"Aha!" barked the captain, pointing at Tarryn.

She hollowed out her throat and lowered her chin—something that seemed to help keep her voice in the right octave. "Captain Sta—"

The captain stomped his foot again, and she and Glenna started. Glenna fell silent—a manner that seemed extremely out of her comfort zone.

Starrytide took several long strides across room and leaned back against the peach-colored, brocade-covered wall, bending one knee and heedlessly planting the sole of his boot on the pretty wall.

Glenna sucked in a breath. "Captain . . ." She lowered her eyes to his offending position.

"My apologies, Lady. I'm accustomed to the ship, you see." He lowered his foot. "As for our impostor here."

Glenna's hand flew to her throat. "How dare you swagger in here and accuse my betrothed of—"

Betrothed? When? Was this before or after the ball? Tarryn bit her lips, aching to find out.

The captain held up a hand. "I'm speaking of my cabin *boy*, Lady Glenna."

Tarryn's stomach clenched, and she thought she might throw up on the pretty peach rug under her feet. She breathed deeply and swallowed a few times but couldn't force herself to speak.

The captain beat his fist against the wall three times, and Duke Braddon Sagewolf entered the room. Glenna fell into a curtsey to the ruler of the Twelve Isles. Tarryn hesitated, not able to immediately decide what act of deference to offer His Grace. Eventually, she gave a courtly bow.

The duke tilted his head and nodded once. He still wore the black and gold tunic, with his head held high and one hand resting over the wolf snout on his breast. The very place Tarryn imagined his strong heart beating within his chest. Heat rushed into her cheeks.

"Woodwight," Duke Braddon mused. "Your name stuck in my mind as odd when we first met yesterday."

Tarryn opened her mouth but the duke held up a finger, forestalling her words.

"And you had this very familiar look about you." He sauntered slowly around the parlor. "I had to wrangle my memories to place you, and wouldn't you know it?" He stopped next to Tarryn with a knowing look on his face. "There seemed to be something clogging the halls of my mental library. No matter how many faces and names I ran through, I couldn't resolve the puzzle."

"Your Grace, permit me to explain," Tarryn started, still keeping her voice lower than it would be—than it *should* be.

Glenna slapped her hand at her side, and Duke Braddon wagged his finger. "Uh-uh. I love puzzles. No, no, allow me play this out, will you?" He scratched his chin.

The sound of his fingers running over his stubble made Tarryn want to run to him and confess everything, but a stern look from the captain kept her fixed in place. Then the captain's eyes drifted back to Duke Braddon, and he smiled.

Am I going to get an earful over borrowing the Woodwight name? Was it someone they knew and held dear? Tarryn tucked her hands behind her back, intertwined her fingers, and squeezed hard. It steadied her for a moment.

The duke continued, both pacing and riddling out his so-called puzzle. "So, I couldn't rest and stayed at the bow of Starrytide's ship for long hours after we set sail. Eventually, the good captain joined me and offered me a gentle reminder where it was that I had come across the name Ty."

Ty? Not Woodwight? They knew she was not Ty?

"Do you know what he said to me?" the duke asked her.

Tarryn swallowed and jerked her head back and forth. "No, Your Grace." Her voice crept back toward normal, but the sound was so soft, she doubted he heard the difference. The gig was up. She was caught. The question was how much shame were they going to put her through in front of Lady Glenna.

The duke turned around, facing the captain. "Shall we replay our conversation, Dougal?"

"Oh, what fun that would be, your Grace." The captain pushed away from the wall.

Glenna let out a little peal of delight. "Ooh. Theatrics!"

The captain gestured to a nearby piece of furniture. "Here. Let us treat the chaise longue as the bow."

Will I ever be able to show my face in honest society again? What would happen to Ty's involvement with Glenna? What would happen to Silver Wood? Tarryn wanted to cry. She sniffed back the burn in her nostrils, holding off her tears by sheer will alone. For once, she felt thankful for all the courtly training her father had insisted upon. It paid off in spades at the moment.

Duke Braddon strolled over and leaned onto the back of the chaise, pretending to gaze out over the sea and motioned for Starrytide to begin.

The captain stepped up to his side. "Your Grace, have you met Lord Ironraven's new minister of finance?"

The duke furrowed his brow and faced the captain. "I have not."

Starrytide mimicked taking a drink from an imaginary tankard. "In that case, have you met Lord Silverwood? The family that lives in the woods north of your castle. I mean the younger one. One of Lord Silverwood's children. Lord *Tyronnen* Silverwood."

Duke Braddon glanced up and back at the captain, his eyes growing wide. "Tyronnen. That's a memorable name. I do believe I've made the acquaintance of one . . . *Tyronnen* Silverwood. Your cabin boy on our last voyage. Sharing a first name and a face with your *new* cabin boy."

The captain nodded once and smiled wide. "Given that Lord Silverwood is rumored to have twins, perhaps our cabin boy is not who we think *she* is."

The duke gasped.

So did Tarryn and Glenna. Tarryn staggered back, unable to let go of her disguise while Glenna stared at her in disbelief.

Captain Starrytide raised one hand high in the air and bellowed, "Tyronnen Silverwood?!"

Two voices answered "Yes," one slightly higher in tone than the other.

Her brother stepped into the room, and Tarryn's hands flew up to cover her mouth and catch her squeal. Tears filled her eyes as she whispered, "Ty?"

"Tarryn!" Her brother crossed the room and took her hands in his. "I was so worried about you."

"And I, you. You've been here managing the Ironraven finances? Have you heard from Father? You . . . we need to return to the Silver Woods."

"I know. I've been working to set aside enough to make our estates prosperous again."

Glenna stepped between them, pushing the twins apart, and she looked from one to the other. "You," she turned to Tarryn.

Tarryn's cheeks flared again, and she tried to say "I'm sorry" with her eyes.

But Glenna turned her back and faced Tyronnen. With more singsong, she said, "And you, dearest." Glenna put her hand on Ty's cheek and stepped closer.

"Ahem!" The captain and duke cleared their throats at the same time.

Starrytide joined the others at the center of the room. "Lady Silverwood, you've put my ship at risk by your presence. I'll have to journey to the Isle of Hands and pay homage to Mac Lir to keep her hale to sail the Illyrian Sea by the stars."

Tarryn shrank before him. "Sir, I only needed passage so I could find my brother. Our father is ailing and I needed him back to see to our lands." Her voice sounded weak, even to herself.

She peered over at Ty, who seemed now to only have eyes for Lady Glenna. Despite the situation, it brought a small smile to Tarryn's face. They must have become well-acquainted over the past fortnight. Perhaps this foretold a lovely courtship that would bring them to the Silver Woods as the next Marquess and Marchioness. A fortune's fool, her brother had managed to find love and care for their family fortunes in one fell swoop.

But where did that leave her?

Duke Sagewolf turned to her and bowed. "Lady Silverwood, may I use your given name? After all, nothing endears people more than a joint voyage, don't you think?"

Tarryn's heart stopped, and for the first time, her eyes wandered up to meet the duke's. They were gray with hints of gold, lupine-like indeed, but they welcomed her too. There wasn't a hint of malice in them. He really did mean not to hold her stealth against her nor reveal the level of their endearment or that she had spent the night in his bed. The duke patiently waited for her to speak.

"Tarryn. You may call me Tarryn, Your Grace," Instead of a bow, she now offered him a curtsey.

"Call me Braddon, please." He chuckled. "That was another thing that gave you away, Lady Tarryn. Those of common birth have never been taught to curtsey like a lady or bow like a lord, but you . . . you executed your bows with a perfection that almost surpasses my own."

Tarryn closed her eyes and sighed. She'd never fooled anyone, had she? Now, she just needed to pick up the pieces of the reputation His Grace and the Captain were willing to let her keep. At least the family estate was safe. Probably. Hopefully. If Ty married Glenna.

The duke held out a hand to her. "Lady Tarryn, may I ask where you put the coffer I provided you?"

Tarryn's eyes went wide. "I gave it to Lady Glenna on your behalf, as requested, Lord Braddon." Tarryn savoured his given name as she said it and found she quite liked it.

The duke bowed his head to Glenna. "My apologies, Lady Glenna, but the gift inside is meant for the lady I would like to court."

Glenna never looked away from Tyronnen as the duke spoke, but she flipped her gloved hand toward the side table. "It's there."

Duke Braddon Sagewolf offered Tarryn his hand and led her to the table. He opened the lid of the box. Inside, on a bed of purple velvet, rested an emerald necklace with diamond accents. The duke lifted the necklace and worked the clasp. "At the end of my tour of the Twelve Isles, I was planning to visit Lord Euan Silverwood to declare my intent to court his daughter. The tales of her loveliness, her grace, and her sharp mind have trickled throughout the clans on the Isle of Midnight."

Tarryn blushed again, this time as a recipient of flattery rather than a victim of guilt.

"I will beg your father's permission as well, but do I have yours, Tarryn?" He whispered her name so only she could hear.

Her own name, spoken with the omission of her title sent a sweet flutter through her insides. Tarryn nodded and turned so Duke Braddon could place the necklace about her neck. "Thank you, Lord Braddon."

"Just Braddon." The duke smiled at her and Tarryn felt her worries finally lifted.

They returned to the others, where Tyronnen and Glenna were whispering to one another in hushed tones, and the captain wore a self-satisfied smile.

"Captain Starrytide," the duke said, "since your superstitions have already been triggered, might I pay you double to sail us, along with Lord Tyronnen back to the Isle of Midnight? It should fund your trip to the Isle of Hands where you can make your amends to your sea god."

Tyronnen demurred. "My sister has a fine mind for numbers too. Perhaps one day, she'll make a fine Minister of Finance, if not for Lord Ironraven, then for Your Grace? Tarryn, do you think you can give father our good news and I might stay here for a while to request Lady Glenna's hand in marriage?"

Tarryn opened her mouth, but Braddon placed a hand on her arm. "If it is well with you, Lord Tyronnen, I can assign someone from my treasury to attend your father's affairs until you can return. I'd rather introduce Lady Tarryn to the Castle of the Isles and at court. After we pay your father a visit and I ask for her hand in marriage, of course."

Tyronnen smiled at Tarryn. "Of course, Your Grace," he said and bowed to the duke.

Braddon took both Tarryn's hands in his and looked into her eyes. "Are you amenable coming with me? Or would you prefer a longer courtship?"

Tarryn's chest swelled, and a smile pulled at the corners of her lips. She never imagined how, in the span of a night and one morning, she'd be holding hands with Duke Braddon. Seeing how Ty was betrothed to Lady Glenna after mere weeks, she didn't think present company would think badly of her for rushing. She didn't want to seem too eager, though. Even though Braddon's scent was making the butterflies in her stomach flip cartwheels. "I will accompany you to your estate via Silver Wood and we can discuss the practicalities of the nuptials."

The duke smiled at her and squeezed her hands.

"Well," Lady Glenna declared, regarding the group gathered in the parlor at Ironraven Keep. "I must say what an epiphany this fine morning has turned out to be!"

SIREN SONG

MEADOE HORA

Nathaira's fingers drummed the side of her leg as she leaned against the pillar. Her blood pounded from the long swim, and the cool breeze off the sea brushed her wet clothes, sending a ripple of goosebumps up her arms. But that's not what made the cauldron of nervous energy in her stomach boil over.

For a year, she'd watched from the rocky outcropping as the ships came, bringing equipment and materials to rebuild the crumbling theater. It wasn't easy to persuade her sisters to stay quiet, to allow the ships to pass, but when she heard what the grand opening performance would be, it was worth it. Now, musicians, players and singers had replaced most of the construction workers. The muses flitted in and out, sprinkling ideas, plot twists, and melodies into the artists' imaginations. Who better to tell the story of the Impassable Sirens than Nathaira's mother, Melpomene, the muse of tragedy herself? Now, the mother who left them to their fate could be the one to save them. If only Nathaira could get inside and convince her.

Music from the rehearsal poured out of the new theater, and Nathaira had to stop herself from humming along. She would never sing. She knew the destruction that came from singing. Voices bubbled over the small patio overlooking the sea, followed by the shuffling of footsteps as a small group of dancers burst through the door. In the opening under the patio where the sea met the land, Nathaira pressed herself into the cold stone, making herself small and quiet.

Listening to the women chat and tease each other gave Nathaira a pang. It was never that way with her sisters. Even before Demeter cursed them, her three sisters were a unit, bound by their ethereal beauty and their sweet voices, so like their mother's. Nathaira stood apart, awkward and tongue-tied, a duckling next to swans. When her sisters were chosen to be Persephone's handmaidens, they left Nathaira behind. She was alone. Maybe it would have been different if their mother had stayed, if they hadn't resented the boundaries Nathaira set to keep them safe. She'd given up everything to take care of them and they barely noticed. As she watched the dancers giggle together, she wondered if this was how it could be with her sisters after she cured them. If they would smile at her without baring their teeth.

"Did you see that ugly crown she brought? It's covered with feathers. I don't know why everyone's going on about it," one performer said. Nathaira's ears perked up.

"It is hideous," another agreed. "But she said it's made from their actual feathers. So, I suppose it lends a certain authenticity." A voice over the loudspeaker summoned them back inside, leaving Nathaira hungry for more details about the crown.

As they shuffled off, Nathaira's heart raced. Could it be true? Could her mother have been so foolish as to bring the real crown here? Of course she could. Her mother saw the crown as a trophy of her victory, her prize from when the Muses beat the Sirens in a singing competition to amuse the gods. Melpomene wouldn't acknowledge it for what it was, the clipping of her daughters' wings.

Nathaira couldn't believe those girls had called the feathers ugly. She always thought them beautiful, a mark of favor from the gods. After Persephone ran off with Hades, Demeter was frantic. She gave the feathers to Nathaira's three sisters, who served as Persephone's maidens, so they could fly to search for her. When Nathaira's sisters couldn't find Demeter's wayward daughter, a furious Demeter turned them into the feared Sirens, cursed to use their beautiful voices to lure sailors to their deaths. If someone heard their Siren song and lived to tell about it, the Sirens would die. Not being chosen to tend Persephone spared Nathaira from the curse, but her fate was still tied to her sisters. Every day without their feathers weakened the Siren songs. It was only a matter of time before they were too weak to lure a sailor. Then Nathaira would be alone.

An idea began to take hold. The feathers in the crown still carried Demeter's magic. If she could get the crown and return the feathers to her sisters, maybe it could make them whole. Then she wouldn't even need to talk to her mother. She could do this herself.

Nathaira took a deep breath. She wondered if her mother was in there now, showing off the crown, putting it somewhere safe. Her mother was Melpomene, the muse of tragedy, formerly of singing, but tragedy suited her better. She loved a bit of drama. Not that Nathaira had seen much of her lately. Since leaving Nathaira behind to care for her sisters, her mother had moved on to more interesting things. Nathaira liked to think it was because she knew they were in good hands, but she suspected it was because Melpomene didn't want to be bothered with her cursed daughters.

Despite the anger she felt toward her mother, when Nathaira saw her glide into the theater, it took all her self-control not to run to her. Instead, she stayed put, held her breath and watched her mother flirt with the director, the musicians, and the writers. Like hunting sailors, it was important to wait for the right moment.

Nathaira rubbed the warmth back into her arms and waited for an opportunity to slip inside, find the crown, and get out before anyone spotted her. Though she might have to come back to see her mother's face when she realized it was gone.

Hours after the sun disappeared into the sea, the fingers of the moon stretched across the water, and the theater went silent. When the last engine faded away down the driveway, Nathaira crept out of her hiding place under the overhang of the patio and climbed over the edge. Up close, the transformation was even more breathtaking. Bright flowers spilling out of hanging baskets brushed stone that was once black with soot, but now gleamed white. She walked up the steps to the doors. To her surprise, the handle turned. Without pausing to question it, she slipped into the foyer.

Its beauty stole her breath. The oldest in town, the theater had survived raids, fire and time. Now, it stood, a sparkling phoenix risen again from the ashes, an elegant mixture of white marble, gold accents and artistic flourishes. She looked down at her bare feet on the shiny marble and wood floor, an intricate mosaic of the sun that reflected the soft light from the twinkling glass chandelier overhead. She didn't belong here.

Relax, she told herself. You are the governess of the Sirens, the fearsome hunters of the sea. You can do this. Steeling herself, she darted across the foyer and slipped inside a door marked Restricted, which opened into a curved hallway lined with doors that wrapped like a horseshoe around the stage. In this row of dressing rooms, practice areas and offices, where would her mother stash the crown?

After several locked doors proved a disappointment, she found one that clicked open. Nathaira stepped inside a large, high-ceilinged room with folding metal chairs lined around a floral-patterned rug. In the back, where the arced rows met, sat a circle of shiny copper kettle drums. A shiver rippled through her body, and without thinking, she grabbed a black jacket draped across a chair and put it on. Pulling the jacket tight around herself, Nathaira felt drawn toward the drums.

Unable to resist, she ran her hand across the smooth surface of the center drum and picked up the mallets resting there. She liked the way they felt in her hand, solid and powerful. Expecting a frightening, thundering boom, she smacked it on the wide surface of the drum. The sound was a dull thud. She released the other mallet closer to the edge, but that wasn't right either. After a few tries, she found the place on the drum where the sound was warm and vibrant. It sang through her arms. As she thumped the mallets, teasing out the various tones and timbers, she lost herself in their song and didn't notice the click of the door opening.

"What are you doing here?"

She dropped the mallet. Heart in her throat, she opened her mouth to respond, but nothing came out. The man walked toward her, irritated and brusque. He noted her jacket and when she didn't respond, asked, "Wait. Are you Samantha?"

"Sam . . .?" she repeated, not sure she heard him correctly over the blood pounding in her ears.

"Sam then," he said. "You're late. Practice ended for the day, and since the other percussionist was on time, he claimed the timpani." His gaze leaped from the drum to her face, still frozen in a weird, panicked smile. "Probably for the best. If you're on time tomorrow, you can play the cymbals. Can you do that?"

She nodded.

With a pointed look, he held the door open. Nathaira took the signal and ducked out, jumping as the door slammed shut behind him. After walking her to the front door, he disappeared back into the building without a backward glance. When he was out of sight, she walked around the building to the back, folded up the jacket, and stuffed it into her hiding place before diving into the water.

The next morning, she was there hours early, partly because excitement kept her from sleeping and partly so nobody would see her climb out of the sea. It also gave her time to dry off. Holding the jacket tight around herself, she paced outside, waiting for the others to arrive. This was a bad idea. What if the real Samantha showed up? What if she made a fool of herself? But she needed to look for her sisters' feathers and this was a way inside. And what if she got to play those drums again?

The man who found her the previous night saw her lingering outside. "Ahh, Sam. Good. Though you shouldn't wear the jacket for rehearsals. Keep it with the rest of the uniform until it's time to perform," he said, and introduced himself as an assistant to the musical director.

Embarrassed, she trailed after him, standing awkwardly as he unlocked the door to the music room. Right away, her attention snapped to the drums. Though she longed to play them, she didn't dare. Instead, she picked a folding chair near the drums and waited. Soon, people arrived, many in pairs, carrying instrument cases and sipping coffee. None acknowledged her. Conversation happened around her as she fidgeted stiffly in her chair, self-conscious of her ill-fitting, scavenged clothes.

A scruffy guy with dark, unruly hair smiled at her. "You must be my partner," he said, holding out his hand. "I'm Jonas, percussion."

She took his hand. "N-Sam. Nice to meet you."

"Your hands are freezing," Jonas said. Nathaira snatched her hand away. "I didn't mean . . . Anyway, let's go get our stuff. Come on."

She followed him to the closet at the back of the room and took the round case he handed her. He carried a small box containing smaller instruments back to the carpeted area. Taking a folder out of his backpack, he organized sheet music on the stand in front of them and started to run through what she'd missed yesterday. He spoke fast, and she had no idea what he was talking about, but she nodded as if she did. Her heart pounded with her fear that every reaction would reveal her deception.

Her part, he told her, was easy. Since he had already claimed the beautiful drums, she only had to work the cymbals and the smaller instruments. When she unzipped the cymbals from their case and crashed them together, she jumped back at the noise. Stifling a smile, he cocked his head. His eyes, she noticed, were the color of sea foam, the melting point between green and blue. She looked at the floor, aware she'd done something wrong.

"I don't have much experience with cymbals," she mumbled, embarrassed.

His brow furrowed. "You're holding them too tightly. They need room to breathe. Here." Cheeks burning, she handed over the cymbals. "Hold one steady, bring the other around in a circle, and brush it. Let it ring."

She tried again, gentler this time, trying to match what he'd done. The crash rang out, bright and true. Jonas smiled and her shoulders relaxed. Maybe she could do this.

The musicians scrambled to their seats as the conductor burst through the door. Nathaira sat rigidly next to Jonas, watching him for signals and following along, crashing her cymbals when he glanced at her. She kept waiting for the real Sam to walk through the door, for someone to stop her, to call her out for being a fraud, but it didn't happen. Then she relaxed and melted into the music. The day flew by and when practice ended, the songs danced through her. She didn't know music could be like this. To her, songs meant destruction, but when the orchestra played together, it sang like joy, like belonging.

As rehearsal ended, she realized she'd been so wrapped up in playing, she'd forgotten to look for the crown. That couldn't happen again. She couldn't let the Siren song of the orchestra distract her from her true purpose.

Over the next two weeks, she was the first to arrive and the last to leave, spending most of her time with Jonas and the orchestra. In stolen moments, she explored the theater looking for her mother's crown, but if it was there, it wasn't in a prop room or hiding among the costumes. She'd even checked the director's office under the pretense of delivering notes from the conductor. Nothing.

Nathaira threw herself into the orchestra, practicing her parts and when she could, Jonas's too. She loved the jangle of the tambourine and the crash of the cymbals, savoring the moment when it all came together, and noise became music.

Her favorite part was the quiet after rehearsal ended, when everyone went home. That was when Jonas taught her the timpani drums. She knew all of this was a lie, but when she held the sticks, it didn't feel like she was pretending. It felt right. The show was a community performance, a celebration for and by the community who made the theater's restoration happen. Later, the touring opera companies would fill these halls, but for now, it belonged to regular people with regular jobs. Jonas must have suspected there was something off about her. She didn't know anything. But he never asked. He just patiently opened up her world. She lost herself in it, the vibration of the mallet, how it rang when she got the correct tone and especially, the way Jonas lit up when she played something well. She ignored the jolt that shot through her body when his hand brushed hers and the twist of guilt in her gut every time he called her Sam.

One night, when she'd gotten home, the rocky island she shared with her sisters was eerily quiet. They were always singing or chattering, but tonight there was nothing. Through the salty breeze rustling the leaves, Nathaira caught the sound of someone weeping and she tore up the path. The fire had died to embers and her formidable sisters huddled together, looking small and hollow. With a raspy voice, her sister Leucosia explained that the worst had happened. "One got through."

Panic squeezed Nathaira's throat. She squeaked, "Did they hear your song?"

Leucosia shrugged. "We couldn't tell."

Guilt washed over Nathaira. She was so wrapped up in Jonas that she hadn't noticed the absence of shipwrecks, how supplies came and went with no issues. While she played music and blushed under Jonas's careful gaze, her sisters were dying. And she was no closer to getting their feathers back.

When she arrived at the theater the next day, she was determined to find the crown before it was too late. Her sisters needed her, and she was all they had. Nathaira had always been the governess of the Sirens. Without them, who would she be?

Now, clutching her wooden blocks, Nathaira held her breath as she peered through the opening in the curtain at the performers on stage. Since not every song required cymbals, she volunteered to help with sound effects. Her box of instruments lay open at her feet, and she watched, waiting for her cue to knock the blocks together, trying not to worry about her sisters.

"Someone's coming," a breathy voice called from the stage. In the pause that followed, Nathaira clomped her blocks together in the pattern she imagined horse hooves to make. It was exhilarating. She exhaled, a little amazed that nobody had stopped the action to tell her she'd done it wrong.

Moments later, a makeshift carriage lumbered onto the stage, and Nathaira almost dropped her blocks when she saw who emerged. Her mother swept out of the carriage, beaming like a queen. The iridescent feathers of the Sirens spilled down her back and glowed in the stage lights, as if lit from within. Nathaira's heart stopped. Then it pounded. She pressed back into the curtain to avoid her mother's eye. Leave it to her mother to insert herself into the play as Queen of the Muses. After the scene, Nathaira clung to the shadows, watching her mother glide offstage and into the main dressing room. When she emerged again, her head was bare.

This was it, Nathaira thought. Her chance. Mind whirling, she tried to come up with a plan, but her options were limited. She could wait until nightfall and return for it, but that would be too late. Her mother and the crown would be gone. She couldn't very well swipe it off her mother's head during the performance. Could she? No. It had to be now.

Nathaira paused. She'd have to take the crown and disappear, which meant she would never see the show or hear it all put together. All of her hard work, the hours she spent learning the music, would be for naught. She knew every word to the songs, every drum beat and cymbal crash. And then there was Jonas. Jonas, who had stayed late and taught her the instruments he loved and showed her that music wasn't a curse. It was a gift. She had repaid his kindness with lies. Guilt washed over her. Still, leaving was a betrayal of everything they'd worked on together. This life wasn't hers, she reminded herself. It was Sam's. Wherever she was. Her sisters' pale faces came into her mind, the emptiness in their eyes as they wasted away in their cottage by the sea. That was where she belonged. If her sisters died, she failed.

Steeling herself, Nathaira waited until she heard her mother's lilting laughter float down the hall to the director's office. When the door clicked shut, Nathaira stole out of the shadows. The performers were all by the stage, huddled, working on a dance. They wouldn't need her sound effects. It was now or never.

She slipped into the door marked with a gold star and scanned the cozy room, the plush couches and soft, patterned carpet. Scarves hung tossed over the corners of lighted mirrors and shoes lay kicked underneath makeup tables. On the opposite wall, floor to ceiling shelves held boxes stuffed with things Nathaira couldn't imagine. She moved toward them, trying to think like her mother. That's when she saw the room divider in the back.

Nathaira knew instantly it was her mother's area. It was exactly what she would like - with the other performers, but separate, a level up. A plush leather chair sat across from a single vanity overflowing with flowers, whose sweet scent fought with the citrus tang of perfume. When she opened the wardrobe, she couldn't believe the crown was just hanging there like a regular hat, discarded like it didn't matter. She ran her fingers across the feathers, still brilliant and soft after all these years. They hummed beneath her fingers. She emptied the garbage on the floor, put the crown inside the bag, and tied it shut.

Throwing the bag over her shoulder, she cracked the door and peeked out. It was clear. Swallowing hard, she stepped into the hallway. Blood thumped through her ears. She'd only gone a few feet when she heard, "Sam! What are you doing? You're supposed to be backstage."

She should have run, but she froze. As she turned toward the director, her mother's sharp intake of breath filled her with dread, and Nathaira shrank under her angry gaze. The director looked confused, glancing between them. "What's that?" he asked, pointing to the bag.

Nathaira's pulse pounded in her ears and her mouth went dry. If she tried to speak, she wasn't sure what would come out. She blinked at him as her mom snatched the bag from her hands and looked inside.

"Nathaira! How could you?" Melpomene wailed. Muse of drama, indeed.

"I need it, Mother. They need it," she hissed through clenched teeth. "A ship has gotten through."

Her mother's hard, blue eyes locked into hers and a flicker of understanding passed between them. Maybe she would do the right thing and give it back.

The director frowned at Nathaira. "Sam, what's going on here?" And then he turned to her mother. "Do you know each other?"

Nathaira watched, waiting for her mother to respond, hoping she would protect her, shield her like a mother was supposed to. The performers, musicians, and stagehands were filing into the hallway. Nathaira could feel their eyes picking her apart. Ignoring them, she pressed on, talking only to her mother.

"They're dying."

"Sam?" Jonas's voice, like an arrow. "What's going on?"

She couldn't meet his soft, familiar eyes and lie to him, so she didn't turn.

"Sam?" her mother repeated, her voice like a starlet on stage. "This is not Sam. She's been lying to you. A ruse to steal this, a priceless heirloom." She whipped the crown out of the bag to the shocked gasps of the crowd. She loved an audience.

"No," Nathaira cried, her shame warming to anger.

"You deny it?" her mother said.

Silence.

Her mother's smile cut like a blade. "I didn't think so. They relinquished them, Nathaira. The muses won, fair and square. It's not my—"

"Did you even hear me?" Nathaira interrupted, her voice shrill. She would not cry. "They're dying. A ship got through. This is their only chance. They're being punished for the games of the gods, something they have no control over, and you do nothing."

Shocked by the outburst, her mother gasped and looked at her daughter as if seeing her for the first time and whispered, "They're monsters."

Nathaira straightened her back but held her gaze. "They're your daughters. Please," she said, softer. "I'm your daughter."

Her mother stuffed the crown in the bag and thrust it at Nathaira. Dismissing her with a wave, she said, "Fine. Take it."

Nathaira clutched the bag to her chest and ran down the hallway, away from the prying stares. Unable to hold them back, tears brimmed in her eyes and rolled down her cheeks.

"Wait." Jonas's voice made her pause, but Nathaira didn't turn.

She couldn't face him. He was her only friend, probably the only one she'd ever have, and she'd done nothing but lie to him. Humiliation burned. "I'm sorry," she called before bursting through the back door. Footsteps thumped behind her as Jonas called for her to stop. She ran across the patio, where she'd first heard the dancers gossiping together, and dove over the edge.

The shock of the water and the swim back to her island cleared her mind. When she found her sisters, they barely lifted their heads. They looked half dead already. Thrusting the crown at them, she ran for food and water. When she returned, she coaxed food into their bellies and color returned to their faces. As her sister Leucosia tore apart the crown, Nathaira told them everything. The feathers, still ripe with magic, found their way back home. When her sisters spread their wings, they were intact, luminous, and strong.

In the days that followed, Nathaira's sisters were different. They included her in their games and brought her pretty rocks from the sea. It was as if, like their mother, they'd truly seen her for the first time. In stolen moments, Nathaira would drum on the rocks with sticks and tell herself this was enough, that she had what she wanted, and it didn't matter she wasn't at the theater for the opening night.

Nathaira was picking through the wreckage of a small delivery boat when a tiny boat crested the horizon. Delighted, her sisters called to each other. When the first honeyed notes of their song found her, Nathaira leaned in, enjoying their beautiful voices until she glanced at the speed boat and saw a familiar curly head.

"No!" she screamed, jumping up and running down the beach. She shouted and waved her arms, desperate to get her sisters' attention, to get them to stop. Like a fish on a line, the boat sailed straight for the rocks. At the helm, Jonas was still, a lazy smile across his lips. Panic swirled. She scrambled across the rocks, yelling his name, yelling for them to stop.

From her perch, her sister Leucosia's sharp gaze snapped to her, and she wailed, a high-pitched eruption. The song stopped. Her sisters had listened and stopped their Siren calls before it was too late. Nathaira screamed Jonas's name. Confusion flashed across his face and then panic as he noticed his boat beelining for the rocks and corrected course.

Relief as Jonas guided his boat to the shore softened the embarrassment that burned through Nathaira. Then she looked closer. No ear plugs or headphones. "What are you doing here? You could have died," she yelled. She glanced up and saw her sisters perched on the jagged rocks, watching. A smile flickered over Leucosia's face.

Jonas looked sheepish. "You didn't come back to rehearsal. Your mom, I guess? She told me where to find you."

But not how to protect himself. Nathaira had so much to tell him, to apologize for, but no idea where to begin. "The show . . ." she started.

He waved her away. "It's fine. We miss you, though. We open next week, you know, and nobody else has your flair for crashing the cymbals." He grinned at her, a smile that cracked her open.

Aware of her face reddening, she looked at the ground.

"But that's not why I'm here," Jonas continued, raking a hand through his hair. "I was wondering if you wanted to come see my band play tonight."

Nathaira's mouth dropped open as she blinked at him in disbelief. "Your band?"

He nodded. "Rock mostly, some covers. Mostly originals. I play drums. Obviously."

"Yes," Nathaira said. "Yes, I would love to."

His sea-foam eyes sparkled. "If we leave now, we can get something to eat and be there early to set up. If you thought the timpani drums were cool, you are going to love my rig."

He held out his hand, and she took it. As the boat slipped away, her fingers drummed the seat. Jonas reached over to still them. His hand was warm over hers and as they sped off, all she heard was the song of the wind.

Meadoe Hora

Meadoe Hora is a writer, working mom, dog rescuer, and lover of beautiful words. She writes books for teens with strong female leads and classic mythology. She is the author of Ariadne's Crown and the Furious Legacy series. In addition, her work has appeared in Chicken Soup for the Soul, Sweatpants and Coffee, and numerous websites. You can find her at www.meadoehora.com. She lives in the US (WI) with her family, two spoiled basset hounds and a black lab who may or may not be a hellhound.

Fine Meadoe online here:
https://meadoehora.com/

The Lies of Lady Roseberry

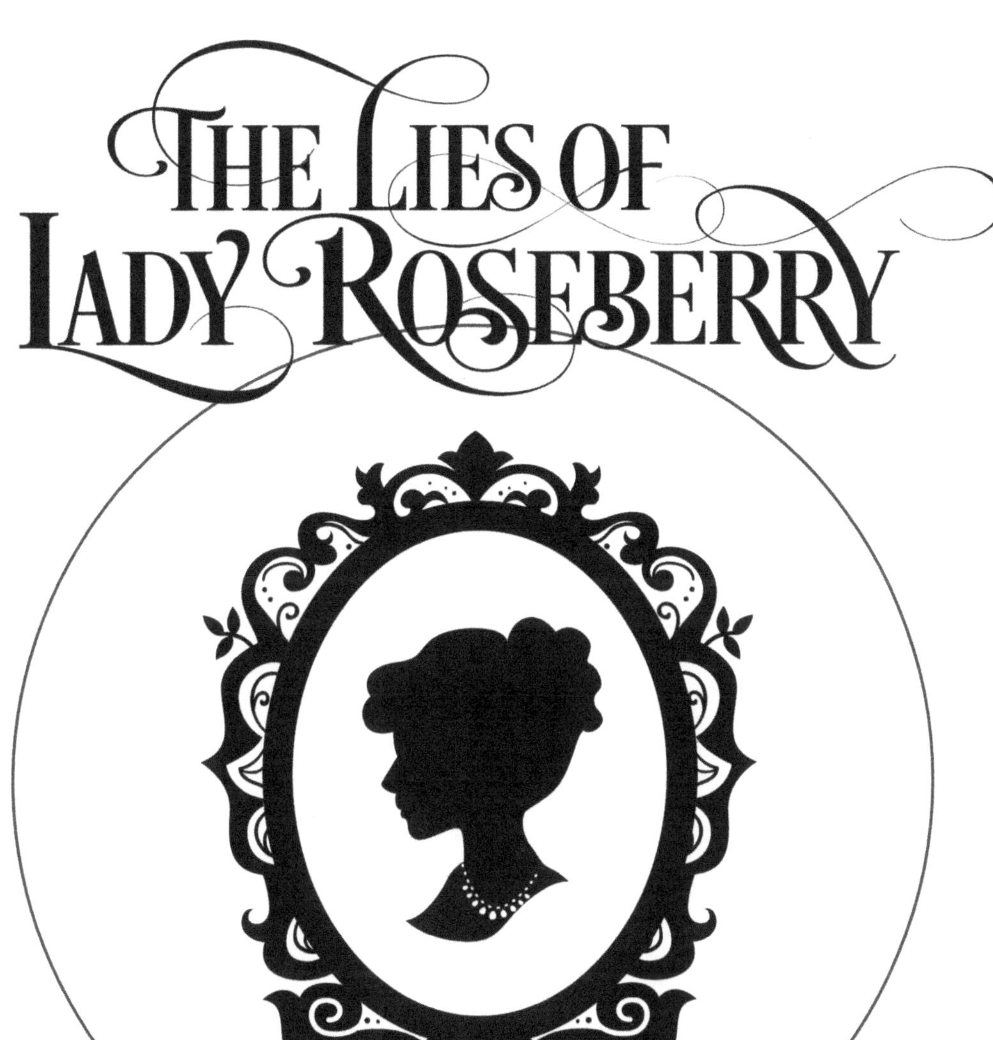

ALICE IVINYA

It was very inconsiderate of the sun to be so bright and cheery on the morning of my execution. The light made harsh sharp lines through my cell window.

Prince Allerick pressed his forehead against the bars, distress clear on his face. He was drawn and pale, his hair disheveled, a shell of the man he had been a fortnight ago.

"Rosie, I'm so sorry. After everything . . . I'm sorry."

I hugged my arms against the cold and walked close enough for his breath to tickle my cheeks between the rods of cold steel. "It's not your fault. I am the one who is guilty of treason. You shouldn't be here." I stopped talking to drag in air before my voice cracked completely. "You should go."

He rubbed his face, his eyes reddened and his skin pale. "If there was anything I could do . . ."

I wound my fingers around one of his wrists. "There is one thing." I bit my lip and looked down. "I would like my execution to be private. Here in the cell. Just me and the guard. I don't want to face all those crowds." I threw a worried glance at the window before looking back at the prince. "Can you do that for me, Rickie? Please, I'm so scared." I let a single tear leak from my eyes.

He clenched my cold fingers in his, a wild desperation in his eyes. "I will go to my father and plead for this at once. Even if I have to bribe the guard, I will make it happen."

I sniffed and nodded, wiping my eyes with my sleeve. "Remember me from before all this happened. When we were happy."

He nodded and squeezed my hands a final time before staggering from the prison, barely keeping his composure.

As the door slammed shut, I sagged in relief. My task was almost complete.

And he didn't suspect a thing.

I tugged off the ridiculous silk dress that frothed with lace and left it crinkled on the chair. Underneath I wore a plain woolen dress of brown with a simple leather bodice. I unpinned my blond wig from my head and uncoiled my bun of dark hair. It had been wound tight enough to give me a constant headache the last two days.

I hid the greasy roots with a bonnet from my bag that shielded my eyes. It matched the plain shawl that hid the old burn scar on my collar bone. Next, I returned to my bag and changed my makeup to dark eyes and bright red lips that danced along the border of respectability. It always made the nobility's eyes slide away from me quickly.

I couldn't help a smile. It felt good to be me again. Or as close to me as any costume I wore.

The whistling of the jailer announced his arrival, and I finished packing everything except the dress. I nodded to him as he approached. A professional demeanor was the easiest way to deal with guards. "Is everything as planned?"

He blinked as he eyed me up and down. "If I'd not been sure which cell I'd put you in, I'd have never guessed you were the same person."

I raised an eyebrow and blinked slowly. "That's the point. Will you let me out? The prince will order you to dispose of Lady Roseberry quietly. He may even add a bribe to mine."

The guard squinted at my ears. "Those earrings. I want them too."

I sighed and made a big show of handing over the emerald and diamond earrings. I'd guessed he'd want something else at this vital moment. The earrings were fake anyway. Better he asked for them than more money.

He unlocked the door slowly, enjoying my impatience.

"The dress is in the corner ready for your evidence. You'll never see me again."

The guard nodded. "And if you have any more last-minute visitors to your cell?"

I shook my head. "Nobody else cared about me." I held out my hand and shook his meaty fingers. "It was a pleasure doing business with you."

My words were a lie. I hadn't enjoyed doing business with him the least, and I'd met some foul characters the last few months. Still, the plan had been a success. The prince's engagement had been broken off by his scandalous attraction to the mysterious Lady Roseberry. The fiancée was out of the picture. Such a shame Roseberry had then attempted to murder the queen when she had refused her blessing. Now she would hang.

And cease to exist.

I reached the stairs washed in the golden sun. The queen's life had never been in true danger from me, but the easiest way to leave high profile jobs was to die. Especially when some fool with a lot of money thinks he's in love with you.

And today was the end of seven months' work, all wrapped up beautifully.

It was time to go home and bask in my achievements. And gold. There was always time to bask in hard-earned gold.

I slipped out of the dungeon on silent feet and into the bustling courtyard. Outside scaffolding was being erected where I was supposed to be hanged, and a man was arguing with a steward. Probably telling him to dismiss the gathering crowds as there would be no show today.

Sorry to disappoint you all.

Instead, a body in my dress would be hung up in my cell, courtesy of the guard. Nobody important would want to look too close in case it offended *royal sensibilities*. And that would be the end of fair but malicious Lady Roseberry.

I hurried through the streets to the Yew Tree Inn, eager to be home. Earl Appan's man would be there with my gold. Then home to my family. Or the closest thing to family I had: The Forbidden Children. My Children.

We all started as orphans, desperate for food and lodgings and people who cared whether we lived or died. And life at the Children's house wasn't bad. Of course, I had always been the best and so had received all the luxuries. And two years ago, Poppy, former Sovereign of the Forbidden Children, had handed the title onto me.

Today I had shown, yet again, that I was worthy of the title. I would lead the Children into greatness. I had fooled the entire royal court and gained enough money to feed us for a year. And that meant better clothes, food, training resources, and a better future. It meant security for those who had had little.

I ducked into the smokey gloom of The Yew Tree and spotted Earl Appan's man paying at the bar and placing his hat on his head, one of the silly velvet ones with a feather the Earl made his servants wear. I frowned. I wasn't late. Why was he leaving already?

I waited as he retreated from the bar and caught him by the door, tugging on his puffy coat. "I'm here. Didn't you see me?"

He frowned, prying his arm from my grasp, and looked me up and down. "How did you get changed so fast?"

Words escaped me for a moment. "I got changed in the cell. Now my job is complete, and I would like my money."

His eyebrow twitched and then he barked a laugh. "Do you take me for a fool? I just paid you five minutes ago. Don't think I'm falling for your costume change."

Paid me five minutes ago? Another of the Children?

I gripped the velvet of his coat tighter. "Who did you pay? What did they look like?"

He gave me a strange look. "I paid *you*. And you should be grateful for such a sum. Now you agreed to never approach me or the earl again, so good day to you."

He tipped the front of his hat and strode out of the inn.

He paid *me*? Impossible. The only people who knew about my deal and knew what I really looked like were the Children. Surely none of them would dare double cross me.

Unless the Earl's servant had been lying? But no. I could read a person's face too well to be fooled by that.

So who had dared impersonate Ivy Rapturefly, Sovereign of the Forbidden Children, and steal her money? Seven months of hard work's money!

Well, one thing was sure, I was getting it back. I was the best and always had been. If I could fool a kingdom and win the heart of a prince, surely, I could find this person too. I would not let this imposter get the best of me.

I pulled the shawl over my head and checked my knives were in place before walking back into the street.

I would view this as any other job. I would collect as much information as I could, evaluate the risks, and strike with everything I had.

The person who was pretending to be me might have disappeared into the city underbelly with my money. Or maybe, just maybe, they might be pretending to be me for longer . . .

Which meant they would have returned to the house to steal everything else from me.

It was the best chance I had. I could only pray they were that stupid.

The Forbidden Children's manor was in the riverside district, a respectable area with a low crime rate and low guard presence, perfect for us whether we walked the street as nobles, workers, or beggars.

I snuck through the gap in the thorny hedge, ran across the lawn we used for combat practice, and climbed the trellis to one side of the house. The sun was stubbornly not on my side, still glaring down as morning turned to afternoon, and throwing sharp shadows across the garden. However, so far there was no sign that I had been seen.

I crept to a window and peered into the dressing room. Empty. That was strange. Normally at least one person was sewing a costume in there. I unsheathed my thinnest knife and slipped it between the window frames to flip the latch. Never did I think I would have to break into my own home.

Inside, the noise of shouts and cheers and smells of roasting food drifted up the stairs from below. They were celebrating.

The imposter must have indeed come here and had fooled them all. The children would only celebrate my victorious return this loudly. None of the other jobs were anywhere near as high profile as mine.

The imposter was not just after my money, but my status. My Children. When I finally got my hands on this person I would . . .

Footsteps sounded on the stairs, and I slipped behind the door as they passed.

No matter. I would have this misunderstanding cleared up in no time. Whatever the fool was doing, they were clearly good, but now they would find they were way out of their depth.

I crept out of the room and stood on the edges of the floorboards so they didn't creak. Slowly I made my way down the landing and around the curve in the stairs so I could see below. They were having a party all right. They even had out the wine and ale. That would be to my benefit.

I slipped closer, peeking down between the banisters every few steps.

I saw her.

Long, dark, wavy hair. Tan skin. Dark eyes. My favorite red dress. How dare she wear my dress? I didn't recognize her because, from this distance, she only looked like me.

It didn't make any sense.

Children were crowding around her on all sides, flinging their arms around her and begging to hear more about her victory. Bitter jealousy twinged in my stomach.

I backed to the wall and calmed my heart. This intruder wouldn't win because she had overlooked one simple but vital thing.

I was the best.

I snuck up two floors to my room and was surprised to find my desk had been rearranged. What had the intruder been up to?

I went to my walk-in wardrobe to find my second red dress that was very similar to the one being worn downstairs. I always had two copies. Too many of my dresses got destroyed when I had to do quick costume changes.

Let's see who would outplay the other at being me.

I had just finished lacing up the back straps and adjusting my knife, when I heard a soft footfall behind me.

I froze. I could only hear the sound of my breathing. Slowly I turned to the door and found a face smiling at me. My face.

I stared at the person who looked *exactly* like me as she swept her eyes up and down, completely relaxed. It was like looking in a mirror.

The corner of her lips tilted up. "Did you really think I didn't expect you to come here? I thought you were meant to be clever." She even sounded like me.

No wonder the Children had been fooled.

I squinted. "Who are you?"

She laughed, throwing her head slightly to one side. "Why, I'm Ivy Rapturefly, the best actress the world has ever seen." Her smile widened. "A more poignant question would be, who are you?"

I folded my arms, impatience starting to override curiosity. "You know who I am, now get out before I tell the Children."

She tapped her chin. "Ah, but what makes you think they'll believe you over me?"

"Every act is flawed."

She raised an eyebrow. "Is it?" She pulled down her collar to reveal the burn scar. An exact image of my own.

My mouth dried as my heart started to pound. There was only one explanation for this: magic.

Magic of any sort was rare, I had only seen it once or twice at court, and this had to be the most powerful kind.

"What do you want?"

"It's not nice, is it, when someone else's games ruin your life?" Her face became serious. "You destroyed my life, now I will destroy yours."

A cold finger ran down my spine.

"Who are you?" I repeated. The words came out as a whisper.

The woman lifted a finger to her necklace and twisted a central ruby which glowed slightly in the candlelight.

Her face was no longer mine.

It was the queen's.

My stomach plummeted. This was not good. This could mean the end to everything.

As if to confirm my fears, the queen's expression was one of barely reined in rage. "Did you really think you would get away with damaging our kingdom? Not to mention breaking my son's heart. He was happy with Lady Isabella. They were a good match and in love. Now he is little more than a husk."

I licked my lips, annoyance rising in my chest that I was the one taking the fall for this. I had done an incredible job of a difficult challenge and had come too far to lose everything. I would not go down easily. "You can't blame me for that. Blame Earl Appan. I was merely his tool." I wiped my hands on my skirts. "I am not morally responsible for any of it."

The queen scoffed. "Is that how you sleep at night?"

"Well, yes actually. Terrible people pay me to do terrible things. Their morality is none of my business. My conscience is clear." I stepped forward. "How did you find out about me?"

Her eyes narrowed. "As soon as you appeared in court, it was obvious your eyes were on my son. Naturally, I investigated you. I can take on many forms, many faces. All this necklace needs is part of you to copy you. A hair, for example. That was harder than I anticipated, since your blond hair was fake. That only raised my suspicions.

"It was your feeble attempt at poisoning which really tipped me off. It was clearly never meant to be lethal. Then it was hardly difficult to guess who had hired you. There was one man who wanted Allerick's engagement to be called off more than any other. One who has his own sights on the throne. When I finally found a strand of brown hair, I learned what you really looked like, and who you were. I followed Earl Appin's servant to the inn and took the money. Then I merely had to pretend to be you before one of the Children recognized me and accompanied me here to a most delightful party."

She removed a money pouch from her belt and tossed it into the air. "So, this is the cost of somebody's life nowadays."

I rolled my eyes. "I broke his engagement. I didn't ruin your life."

The queen took three swift steps forward until her face was inches from mine. "He has lost the woman he loved, and he blames himself for the supposed death of the woman he *thinks* he loved. You have no idea what you have done. My husband, the king, is dying. He planned to hand over the throne the second my son married Lady Isabella. But now Allerick won't even leave his room."

My mouth dried. "I didn't know about your husband." That made this much more serious. But could I really be blamed for information that wasn't available for me?

"Of course not. Nobody knows except me, the doctor, some close servants, and now you. Allerick needs to be strong and secure so he can take the throne as soon as possible. As it is, we may provoke a succession war. There is a rift with Isabella's family. Allerick is doubting his ability to rule. He no longer trusts himself since he fell in love with somebody who turned out to be the sort of person who would kill his mother. He feels like he can't judge character or act rationally."

I chewed my lip. What a mess.

I spread my hands. "This is Earl Appin's fault. You should be saying all of this to him." This mess couldn't be laid at my feet. The Children wouldn't survive it.

The Queen's eyes narrowed. "Oh, he will *hear* from me, I assure you. But first, if you want your Children back, you will fix this mess."

My heart sank. "How? I can't pretend to be Lady Roseberry again; she's just been executed."

The queen twisted her necklace, her face morphing back into mine. "If Allerick isn't settled, secure, and engaged to Isabella in two days, I will keep your Children, and you will never see them again." She walked to the window. "And if you speak to any of them before the end of this arrangement, my guards will come and arrest every person and burn this place to the ground."

For the first time in a long time, I felt a quiver of fear.

⸻

LADY ISABELLA WAS SICKENINGLY PERFECT.

Raven hair, emerald eyes, pale skin, and a frame that curved in all the right places.

I mean, she had been no match for the charms of Lady Roseberry, but that was because she'd never learned to flirt or lie.

I was used to forming and breaking up relationships, but never before had I played matchmaker to reform one I had broken. I was good at my job. Isabella and Allerick now loathed each other.

But I was the best. So I would figure out a way.

And here I was, back in the castle, a place I had hoped never to return.

I smoothed down my servant outfit, my face devoid of makeup, and my hair waxed back into a tight bun. I looked nothing like Roseberry. I entered Lady Isabella's room and curtsied.

"Good morning, my lady. I have been assigned to you today since Clarissa is sick. I am Lusha."

I'd locked Clarissa inside her room with a note saying the queen would pay her a reasonable sum if she stayed quiet all day.

Isabella frowned. "Is she alright?"

I nodded. "Stomach bug, my lady. The physician suggested she rest."

She turned back to the mirror. "Please do my hair."

I slipped her a letter I had forged and started to weave her locks into a complex style. Isabella snapped the seal with a paper knife and cast her eyes briefly over the note supposedly from Allerick apologizing and inviting her to dinner. She tossed it into the fire.

"The cheek of him," she muttered under her breath. "She's only been dead a day and he's already running back to me. It's pathetic."

"He's going to be King," I murmured. "You would be Queen."

Isabella froze and turned around to me. "Who on earth do you think I am? Some power-hungry manipulator?"

I bowed my head. "Sorry, my lady."

She turned back, and I returned to braiding her hair. "No, I will find somebody kind, charming, gentle. Somebody who won't drop me for the next court beauty. I have no further interest in Allerick. He made his decision and didn't turn out to be the man I thought he was."

I kept my expression blank. This might take longer than the queen had given me.

There was a knock at the door, and I hid my smile. I placed the last pin and went to open it. A servant buried under a huge bouquet of lilacs, Isabella's favorites, entered and placed them on the table with another note "from" Allerick.

I admired them. "Goodness, my lady. They smell wonderful. I'm guessing His Highness really wants you to have dinner with him."

She glanced at them, and I only read annoyance on her face. "Send them back at once."

I bobbed a curtsy, hiding my disappointment, and scooped up the flowers. I hurried through her door and dumped them in a random room. There hadn't been a trace of appreciation or forgiveness in her face, and that worried me. I had worked hard to make them hate each other, after all, and done an exceptional job.

At this rate the queen was going to return to quite an expensive bill. Served her right. But I guessed she would be less forgiving if nothing I tried worked.

A man in royal livery was waiting for me in the corridor. I'd convinced the prince's servant to try and get him out into the gardens today for his health. As I approached, he shook his head.

"He's dressed. To be honest, I was worried we wouldn't even get that far."

Great. That wasn't going to help me at all. I slipped a note into the servant's hand. "This is from Lady Isabella. Please keep it discreet. It may cheer him up a little."

The servant looked skeptical. "I doubt he's in the mood to read anything. He blames himself for all the events of the past two weeks. But I will pass it on."

I thanked him and returned to Isabella's room.

"It's a lovely day today," I said brightly. "The sun is warm and the breeze is cool. Perhaps you would like a turn in the gardens?"

The gardens were overlooked by the prince's window. If he wouldn't come out of his own accord, at least he could see Isabella from afar.

The lady's eyes narrowed as she turned to me, and my heart sank. I was being too obvious.

"The queen put you up to this, didn't she? I bet you're one of her maids. Well, you can tell her, I have no interest in her son. In fact, I'm fed up with being pulled and pushed around in this place." She stood up. "I'm leaving for the countryside tomorrow. Tell her I've had enough."

I struggled to keep my expression neutral. "Yes, my lady." I bobbed and left her room.

I flopped to the floor, hidden behind one of the heavy curtains, and leant against the wall. It wasn't working. I thought I could trick people into doing anything I wanted. But I couldn't undo what I had already done. Now, when it mattered more than anything else, I had failed. And it could mean a succession war.

I tipped my head back against the wall and stared at the gilded ceiling. I was tired. So tired. I hadn't slept all night preparing for today, and the night before that had been in a cold cell.

I should be warm and relaxed with the Children, eating roast meat and drinking sweet wine.

Instead, I was here, learning that mending things is much harder than breaking them.

I supposed I had one option left. I could go to Allerick and Isabella as Roseberry. I would take off my wig and explain it had all been a trick. Maybe then they would forgive each other. Or at least talk. And Allerick would stop blaming himself for my death.

But then I would be at their mercy. Worse, they would know my real identity. Word would get around. Nobody would ever hire me again. It would be the end of my career. And, I would have to step down as Sovereign of the Children.

I had never apologized for anything in my life. To do so now would mean losing everything and that was beyond frustrating. I didn't want to admit I had been wrong to do this. It was Earl Appin's plan; he was the villain here. Why should I take responsibility?

But in helping him, I had potentially caused a succession war. Destroyed the confidence of our future king to rule. And I had most certainly been part of that . . .

I ran plans and schemes through my head, desperate for another way. But I knew, deep down, that real forgiveness often needed the truth. If they were to have a strong marriage, I had to undo the mess that would otherwise stay with them forever. They each believed so many lies.

To save the Children, I would have to destroy myself.

But this was about more than the Children. This was also about saving the kingdom.

So maybe it would have to be me who took the fall. The Children could continue without me, it was so painful to admit that.

I took a deep breath. Allerick and Isabella were good people. His mother was plain scary. Earl Appin was a piece of work. And me? Well, I had always just been . . . nothing. A shadow. Somebody who never really existed. A tool for others.

Maybe it was time that changed.

I pushed myself up, feeling sick, and strode to Allerick's room before I could change my mind.

I opened the door and dropped a deep curtsy, letting my bonnet shadow my face. "Your Highness, her Majesty the Queen wishes to speak with you urgently in the blue drawing room."

Allerick looked up from his desk, though there was no sign that he had been reading or writing. There were deep shadows under his eyes. "Really?"

"It is most urgent. She insists."

He rubbed his eyes. "Tell her I will be there shortly."

Next I visited Lady Isabella's room where she was packing her trunk by herself and relayed the same message to her.

When I was confident that they were both going to the drawing room, I retrieved a blond wig from my bag hidden in the servant's quarters, and quickly replaced my makeup for the pastel colors Roseberry had worn.

I waited behind one of the heavy curtains for them both to enter the room, first Isabella, then Allerick.

At once I heard them start to squabble. Isabella sounded furious about the trick. I had to be quick, or she might storm out instead of waiting for the queen.

I took a deep breath, my palms sweating, and sealed my fate.

I stepped into the room with my head high: Lady Roseberry back from the dead.

Allerick gasped. Isabella screamed, pressing gloved hands to her mouth as she fell heavily into a chair.

"Good afternoon," I intoned in Roseberry's deep, luxurious voice. Then I shed my wig and pulled off my dress to reveal the servant outfit below and replaced my bonnet.

"Lusha?" Isabella had turned pale. "What is the meaning of this?"

I discarded the bonnet and apron and wound down my hair, combing it out with my fingers while my heart pounded.

I struggled to meet their eyes, the sensation strange. "I have something to admit to you both. Lady Roseberry never existed. I am a con actress. I was paid to break up your engagement. I will leave you to determine by whom. But the damage that has been done is too much. I wish to undo it." I met Allerick's eyes. His face was utter disbelief and shock. "You never failed to save my life. Nor did I ever truly try to kill the Queen. Our love wasn't real." I gestured to Isabella. "Yours is."

"I don't believe it." Allerick's face was only paler. "But . . . if I can be fooled so easily, I have no right to be King. No right to anything."

Isabella glared at him. "And you can't truly love me if you would go after a flirtatious pretty face and so break our engagement, whether she is real or not."

I held up my hands. "I lied to both of you. I poisoned you against each other, painting pictures of each of you that aren't true. I beg both of you to get to know one another again. Discover the truth of matters." I lifted my eyes to Allerick. "And I truly believe you will be a good king. You were lonely. That was why it was easy for me to deceive you. I seemed to fulfill your needs. But I think Lady Isabella can do a far better job than I ever could, even as Lady Roseberry. She will be your rock."

"And what of you?" Isabella's voice was cold.

My mouth dried. This wasn't pretend. This was real.

I lowered my head and spread my hands. "I am at your mercy. Admitting this to you reveals my identity and so loses me my job. I won't deceive anyone again. If you wish to let me go, I will travel away from this country and start afresh somewhere else. I won't ever return." I lifted my head. Isabella was still glaring at me. I licked my lips. "I am sorry." The words felt strange, heavy and light at the same time.

Isabella looked at Allerick, and they shared some sort of non-verbal exchange.

The prince turned to me. "Go far away then. And don't let us see you again."

I bowed low and turned to the door as the couple leaned toward each other. Isabella spoke first, quiet and curious. "Does this mean . . . did you ever kiss Sophia Halland?"

Allerick choked a shocked laugh. "Goodness, no. And, er, do you really wear perfume made of other women's sweat just to attract me?"

Isabelle burst out laughing. "Ew! And I'm guessing you don't still sleep with a teddy bear?"

Oh dear, that one was actually true.

I slipped out and closed the door. I took a deep breath, a weight lifting from my shoulders. It was over. I had done as the Queen had asked. More. The rest was up to them. If they could learn to forgive, the succession would be restored.

I had saved the Children. But I had revealed myself to Allerick and Isabelle and so had lost them in the process.

Because as much as it broke me to admit it, the kingdom was more important.

But then, maybe it wasn't a bad thing being free of the games, the pressure. Hiding myself so deep down, I formed no attachments, and felt nothing. I didn't know who I was.

I looked out the window. I would go east. And, this time, I would be myself: plain Ivy Rapturefly.

Alice Ivinya

Alice is a USA Today bestselling author. She is also an award winning international and Barnes and Noble bestseller.

She lives in Bristol, England. She is wife to Sam, mummy to their toddler and owns the best dog in the world, Summer. She has loved fantasy all her life and loves dramatic stories with deep meanings behind them and happy endings. When she's not off galavanting in other worlds, she loves walking the dog and spending time with her church family.

Find Alice online here:
alicegent.com

POISON QUEEN

R.S. WILLIAMS

FIONN

Fionn's heart pounded in her chest as she hid the contraband she'd smuggled across the border. *They saw me. I know they saw me. I must hide it.* She cursed as she knocked a glass jar containing a batch of Dimikka Elixir to the floor. It smashed on the ground, producing a short hissing sound as the white smoke dissipated.

Ignoring the bout of adrenaline flooding her body, Fionn removed one pebble and kept it to the side. She removed the false back on the third shelf and stuffed the rest of the moonstone pebbles inside before concealing them again. They were a delicacy of the Unseelies and banned by the Seelie Queen nearly six years ago. Despite the risks, only moonstone pebble dust could make the Dimikka Elixir more potent, to be used as an antidote. Without it, she would not be able to fulfill her shipment.

After her father died, Fionn took it upon herself to carry on the work as the official royal apothecary. The king and queen had never met her, and she assumed they thought her father was still brewing the elixir for them.

Fionn took a deep breath. Even if they had seen her smuggling contraband, the royal family would not do anything. At least that was what she told herself. Who else would be able to make their elixir? It healed almost any wound, with the exception of rare fae-creature poisons and fatal blows.

Once hidden, Fionn turned to the center of her room. Brewing in her pot was the next batch of Dimikka Elixir. It only needed one last ingredient. Grinding the pebble to dust, she added it to the pot of golden liquid and added another log beneath the pot. A few minutes and the elixir would be complete, her shipment fulfilled and ready for collection.

Fionn jumped as her door crashed open, reaching out to protect the pot. A burly man carrying another stumbled in. He dropped the man he carried as she said, "be careful."

The burly man bent over, catching his breath before he looked up and said, "You better be a healer. Save him."

Not a request.

She stepped forward and the burly man flinched. "What happened?" Fionn asked, bending down to the man on the floor. Touching his head, she felt the cold sweat on his forehead. Fionn stuck a finger under his nose. Though faint, she felt the warmth of his breath, which was a blessing. "He's still alive."

"We were attacked near the border."

Fionn raised an eyebrow. Her eyes moved to the man on the floor. He was wearing the uniform of the Seelie guards.

"I'll need more than that. If I don't know what happened, I don't know how to treat him," Fionn said. She fumbled about with the unconscious man's clothes and found a clear liquid oozing from a small cut on his right hip. She scooped up a bit in her hand and sniffed it. *Poison.* "How did he get this?" She rolled him over and showed the cut to the other man.

"Fighting, I guess. We were sent over to spy and got ambushed on the way back," the man said. He moved away and looked out the window, staying near the side to avoid anyone outside spotting him.

She frowned. *Clearly not fond of sharing information.* Without knowing exactly who, or what, had poisoned the guard lying on her floor, Fionn would only be able to administer a general remedy in the hopes that it would break the fever.

Her eyes landed on the Dimikka Elixir reserved for the royal shipment. Though it wouldn't save him, it might keep him alive long enough to get him the antidote. It came with the risk that his fever could get worse, as she didn't know what substance was killing him. Not having a better option, Fionn grabbed a cup from her kitchen and prepared the liquid, then poured some into the unconscious man's mouth and helped him swallow.

After a few gulps, the man opened his eyes and coughed, spluttering the concoction over himself. "Ah, where am I?" The guard scrambled to his feet. His eyes landed on her. "Who are you, and what did you do to me?"

"For goodness sake, Patrick, calm yourself," the man by the window said. "She saved your life."

Patrick bowed his head. "Thank you, Miss . . ."

"Fionn. Just Fionn, and I only gave you extra time. We need to get you to a healer to get an antidote."

"What did you give him?" The burly man pushed off the wall and stepped closer, snatching the cup from her hand. He sniffed it and smiled. "I knew there had to be something more. No one lives this close to the border and survives." He slammed the cup down on the table.

Fionn flinched and stepped backwards.

"You must be the poison expert my father sent for," he continued.

"The queen. We must get back to the queen," Patrick said. At first it was barely a whisper, but then it grew until he released her from his grip and fell to the floor in a coughing fit.

Fionn hesitated, but the other man came to Patrick's aid. He hooked Patrick's arm around his neck and held him up.

"No, Your Highness, I will be fine."

Your Highness? This is the prince? "I-I will make some more for the road. He will need a few doses to make it back."

"Then pack provisions. You'll be coming with us."

"What?" Fionn dropped the cup and shook her head. "No, no. You have the wrong person."

The prince raised an eyebrow. "Are you refusing an order from your prince?"

Fionn swallowed. Her eyes darting around the room to find an excuse to stay where she was. She couldn't leave before the shipment was collected, yet she couldn't refuse the prince either.

Patrick's knees gave way. "We must return with haste. The queen . . ." He coughed again.

"We have no choice," the prince said. "My father sent for you, therefore I cannot leave you here. The Unseelie were expecting us. We have a traitor in the court. Now, make what you need and help me get him back to the palace."

Fionn nodded and got to work. First, she decanted the pot of elixir into bottles and placed twelve of them in a bag, along with a note which she would stash in the drop site she used to communicate with the royals.

Once she was finished, they helped Patrick onto a horse outside. As she mounted her own horse, a young boy ran down the road towards them. His arms flailed around as he shouted.

"The queen is dead."

ELREN

Alone on the balcony that connected to his room, Elren sighed. He'd been standing there for almost an hour now, trying to avoid heading down to the wake. Why his father had insisted on a grand gathering after the queen's burial, Elren didn't know.

What he did know was that he hated wearing black. Blue and green suited him much better, and mourning was something he didn't have time for. Elren needed to find the traitor in his court. He wanted to tear them limb from limb for giving Patrick and him false information. For Patrick almost losing his life and for killing his mother. He swallowed hard and looked down at his hands.

"Prince Elren?"

He twisted at the sound and almost grabbed the young woman by the throat.

"Anita, you should know not to sneak up on me when I am deep in thought."

She stepped back wide eyed. "Apologies, Your Highness. I came to advise that Miss Bluegate is waiting for you." Anita looked at the floor. They didn't speak for a few moments before she elaborated. "The poison expert. She's waiting for you. Lan and Calver are also waiting to report their findings."

Right, the woman I found that father sent for.

"Of course. I'll be right down." He moved past her and stopped as he caught sight of himself in the mirror. "Do I look as ridiculous as I feel?

"You look like a grieving son, Your Highness." Anita moved to the door and opened it, waiting for him to walk through.

He strode through the hallways with his head held high. Though he was a grieving prince, that didn't mean he would let anyone see his emotions. They made him appear weak, and he wouldn't give the Unseelie spy any reason to send word back to their court that the Seelie prince was weak.

Servants moved out of his way, bowing their heads as he passed. Elren hesitated at the doors to the great hall. His father would be inside, dressed in black and kneeling in front of his mother's coffin. The funeral was over, but tradition gave the family a private ceremony.

Elren took a deep breath and nodded to the guards. The doors opened, and he strolled inside toward the king.

His father finished muttering, but Elren caught the last few words. "This can't be the child of prophecy."

Elren touched his father's shoulder, and the king looked up at him. His father's eyes, usually full of kindness, were sunken. Elren swallowed hard.

"Where is everyone?" Elren asked after a few moments of silence. "I thought you'd invited the High Lords and their families to join us?" He looked around, avoiding his father's gaze.

"I did, but you were right. They can mourn, or not mourn, my precious Larissa however they like. This should be for you and I." The king wrapped an arm around his son's shoulder. "Bringing the High Lords here when we have no idea who committed this crime seems dangerous at best."

Elren nodded. "It did cross my mind. We were found too easily by the Unseelies. Someone here must be a traitor."

"That is why I wanted the poison expert. The guards said you brought her with you?" King Warren stepped back and waved his arm. The guards at the far end of the hall opened the doors.

Two guards escorted the young fae woman into the room. She seemed uncomfortable, her eyes staring at the floor.

"Father, is this really necessary? She saved Patrick, after all."

The woman pulled her arms free of the guards and flattened her dress. "Considering you are asking for my help," she said, directing her comments to him, "this seems a poor way to start."

Elren pressed his lips together. Had he known she was so feisty, he might have left her back in her little home. Yet something about her ignited parts of him he thought long forgotten.

"Miss. Bluegate—"

"Please, call me Fionn." She frowned at him, then curtsied and added, "Your Highness."

Elren cleared his throat. "Fionn, my father requested that you aid us in finding my mother's killer and therefore we have asked you here to hear the guard's report. As the poison expert, we were hoping you might be able to give us some answers."

Fionn nodded but didn't say anything further.

The guard on the right, Lan, nodded his head. "Your Majesty, as already discussed, the queen was poisoned. We believe it was the Unseelie."

King Warren stroked his chin. "You suspect them instead of someone in our own court?"

"They all dislike you," Elren said. "It could be any of their High Lords, or their king. Who here would dare to stand against you?"

Lan shifted his stance and lowered his eyes to the ground. "Well . . . you asked us to investigate the queen's last few days. We spoke to her handmaids, Lady Balfia and Lady Raisel."

Fionn cleared her throat. "I really don't think I should be here for this," she muttered.

"You're an expert on poisons, are you not?" He hadn't meant his tone to be so sharp. "Listen to what they have discovered and then tell us what you need to do."

"I'd need to examine her, unless someone already got a sample of the poison?" Fionn swallowed hard.

Elren folded his arms, his magic flaring on his fingertips, causing the vines running along the walls to grow a few inches. "Lan, continue. You spoke to the ladies of the court my mother frequently had luncheon with. What else?"

Lan still had his eyes on the floor, his fingers twitching at his sides.

"Calver? Are you willing to say what Lan clearly won't?" Elren waited a moment before adding, "Or should I lock you both up and get someone else to continue the investigation?"

The king sank to his knees on the mahogany floor. "I'd understand if they had poisoned me, but why her? Why Larissa?"

"I think I can answer that," Fionn said.

Elren turned to see the poison expert standing on the small step next to the queen's coffin. "What are you doing? Get away from there!" He rushed towards her and reached for her arm as she leant into the coffin.

As he touched her, she pulled her arm back, bringing the cloth covering the queen's belly.

Mother was pregnant? I haven't been away that long.

"Father, did you know this?"

"That your mother was with child? Yes, I did."

His eyes landed on the guards. Both of them glanced at one another, the coffin, and then back to the floor.

"Oh, for the love of the crown, spit it out. Now," Elren demanded.

"She was having an affair," Calver blurted. Lan slapped him on the shoulder and all eyes turned to the king.

Elren spun on his heel and crossed the room in two steps. He felt Fionn's eyes on his back, but he didn't care. How could this man accuse his mother, the Queen, of having an affair? "Say that again?"

Calver gulped. "I said—"

"I know what you said."

"Elren, don't. It's alright," the king said. He shook his head and sighed. "I knew. I knew about the affair. Though who it was with escapes me."

"If I may," Fionn said, interrupting the momentary silence. "I have a sample of what I need. You have someone to find, and then once we know what and why, we can locate the who."

Elren had to admit the plan was logical. "Fine. I'll take you to the alchemy lab. It should have everything you'll need." He turned to Calver and Lan. "You two escort my grieving father back to his rooms." Elren stepped closer, and the guards flinched. He shook his head and beckoned them closer to allow him to lower his voice. "If you can, find out what my father knew about my mother's . . . lover." The word tasted like dirt in his mouth.

I hope it doesn't turn out to be his crime of passion. Elren took Fionn by the arm and nearly dragged her out of the hall.

FIONN

After being left alone in the alchemist's laboratory for almost half a day, it had crossed Fionn's mind to try and leave the Seelie Palace. The poison's effects were . . . unlike anything she'd seen before. Were it not for her curiosity about it, she would have attempted to escape.

Huffing, she slammed the failed test on the table, spilling the black liquid, and looked at her sample. One test left. The test no self-respecting apothecary would carry out because the source of such poison didn't exist.

I have no other choice.

She shook off the feeling that her father would be turning in his grave and picked out what she needed. Eye of newt, crushed. Dust from a white whelp and . . . Fionn looked around the room. The final ingredient she needed would be the petal of a Bloombrant. One of the only plants that can counteract the poison from a Popdel.

A Popdel. Really? Her late father's words echoed in her mind. She slid off her stool and moved over to the shelves, scouring them intently. No Bloombrant. Not even a single petal.

She pulled her arm back and knocked off a jar of black twigs. "Dammit." Bending down, she gathered the twigs together and looked for something to place them in. She managed to find an empty jar and popped the twigs in. When she went to place it back, a glistening of silver caught her eye.

Bloombrant petals, though pink in color, had a silver dusting that shone in a certain light. Fionn's eager fingers reached forward and grabbed hold of it. There was a whole jar full of them.

She rushed back to the table as the doors opened and Prince Elren entered the room. Ignoring him, she dropped the petal into the mixture and waited.

"Any progress?" the prince said, closing the gap between him and the table.

Fionn ignored him. Her eyes trained on the mixture as it slowly turned from clear to . . . Oh, my. The mixture was blue, and green, and then blue again.

"Impossible," Fionn said, stepping back from the table. "Who has a Popdel? They should all be extinct."

Elren cleared his throat. "Sorry, did you just say a Popdel? The most poisonous fae-creature known?" The prince scowled at her. "Don't be so preposterous."

"Every other test failed. This is the only one that has worked," Fionn said calmly.

She moved the vial into his eyeline and lifted it up. The blue-green changing liquid glistened.

"Popdel." The prince's frown deepened. "Well, do you have any left?"

Fionn shook her head and swallowed hard. *What does he want more for?*

"Pity. Well, we can lie to him." He stepped back and rolled his shoulders, relieving the tension in them. "Come. We are going to meet my mother's lover."

Fionn hardly thought a poison expert should be the one interrogating the queen's lover. Though from the sour look on the prince's face, she would be better to not question him either.

She pocketed the vial, not knowing if she would need it for some kind of proof, and followed the prince out of the room. Fionn had to quicken her pace to keep up with Prince Elren's strides. They weaved through the halls and descended a staircase at the far end that took them down into the dungeons where she had been held previously.

The cold air made her shiver as they ventured further into the dark underground of the Seelie Castle. Passing some unoccupied cells, they crossed into a large room that housed a table with two chairs and a man chained to the wall.

His hands were bound above his head, his shoes and shirt had been removed, and his head was covered by a bag.

"Is this really necessary?" The words escaped Fionn's mouth before she had time to stop herself from saying them.

Prince Elren spun on his heels. His breath was hot on her face. "He committed treason. Now, stay quiet until I say so."

Fionn gulped and nodded as the prince stepped back and moved toward the captive. He ripped off the hood and Fionn glanced away as she saw the blood on his face. Prince Elren lifted up the man's chin, and he opened his eyes.

She couldn't hold back her gasp as the turquoise colour in his eye caught the light of the torches on either side of him. Unseelie. She tried to step back, but felt the roughness of the wooden table behind her.

"Hello, Alastair. I am—"

"I know who you are, and I know why I am here. Get on with it, Prince. What do you want to know?" The Unseelie spat out some blood on the floor.

Fionn shivered as Alastair's eyes looked up and focused on her. He cocked his head to the side and smiled, his glare boring into her mind.

"I see you brought me a friend."

"She's here to verify what you say. I have questions." Elren slapped the Unseelie in the face, knocking his gaze from Fionn. "Where did you find the Popdel?"

Alastair smiled again, blood dripping down his chin. "Ah. She's a clever little one. Not many people would think to look for an extinct animal."

"Answer my question," Elren said through gritted teeth. "Where did you find the Popdel?"

"I breed them. I know it's against the law, but so are most things I do." He winked at her, and she shook her head.

Fionn expected the prince to react in some way, attack him or release some noise of frustration. Instead, Prince Elren stayed deadly silent. He swayed slightly on his heels and breathed slowly. She could feel the tension in the room rise with every exhale.

"You defiled my mother."

Fionn cringed away from the awkwardness of the conversation. *Why couldn't he have crashed into anyone else's house other than mine? Maybe if the royal family knew about my father, about me, I wouldn't be in this mess.*

"That wasn't a question, Your Highness."

"A Popdel was used to kill her."

She peeked at Alastair. His blasé tone and cheeky smile had vanished, replaced with an ashen face and glazed eyes.

"What? I thought you found my pets in your gardens. Not . . . no . . ."

Prince Elren turned to Fionn. She shrugged at him and he frowned. Stepping away from the Unseelie chained to the wall, Fionn watched as the prince stopped by her side. His hand reached into her pocket and pulled out the vial of liquid.

"You didn't know?" Fionn asked, breaking the deafening silence. "The queen was killed by poison. Poison from creatures you just admitted to breeding. You laughed when we asked you about them. Why?"

"Because I bred them for Larissa. My Larissa. She asked me for something no one else would have."

Fionn rolled her eyes. "A poisonous creature is hardly a worthy gift for someone you love." She sighed loudly, her eyes glancing at the prince who stood beside her. He was still as ice, staring at the confirmation there must be some truth to what the Unseelie spoke.

"They knew. They must've known." Alastair stared down at the floor.

Fionn pressed her lips together, waiting for the answer that she knew was coming.

"If she's gone, that means . . ."

"I'm sorry, Alastair. Both of them are gone." Fionn felt a lump in her throat and tried to swallow it down. "As the prince said, someone poisoned her."

Alastair shook his head. "No. They tried to kill my child and ended up killing the queen. They wouldn't have wanted to do that. They wouldn't have wanted to start a war when they plan on having peace talks."

Fionn glanced back at the prince. He had turned to face her, but his eyes were still on the vial in his hand.

"You keep saying 'they'. Who are you referencing?" Prince Elren asked, his voice all but a whisper.

"King Ander. The Unseelie King and his court."

———

ELREN

Though Elren hated to admit it, the more he thought about the events that had transpired, the more he started to believe Alastair's tale. Still, it took him longer than it should have to summon Fionn. Her continued defiance frustrated him, but his father insisted she join them to meet the Unseelie congregation.

He glanced out of the window. The sun was setting, its last segment barely visible above the tree line. Elren frowned. He'd called for Fionn almost an hour ago. *Where is she?*

The door to his sitting room opened as he turned his back from the window, hoping it was her arriving. He sighed. Only a servant coming to light the fire. *Where is Fionn? She should have been here by now.*

Elren marched out of the still open door and headed towards the room he'd given Fionn. He'd felt it necessary to make up for his father's poor decisions when she first arrived. The suite he'd allocated for her to use until this matter was resolved was located seven doors down from his royal rooms.

It was unusually quiet, save for his stomping footsteps. Elren glanced behind. There wasn't a single servant in sight, and no noise from the bustle of castle life. The hairs on the back of his neck stood on end as he crossed the top of the stairs into the east side of the building.

Fae magic shrouded the hallway. Darkness descended from the ceiling, muffling all noises until his stomps became whispers. Elren's breath quickened as he picked up his pace and almost yanked the handle off its hinges, trying to open the door.

Inside, Elren didn't give his brain time to evaluate the situation. He rushed forward and grabbed the cloak of the man holding Fionn by her neck. Elren yanked him back, and the assailant's arms flung backward, letting her go. Elren threw him down onto the floor and followed him as they both scrambled to stand.

"What is going on?"

"She's immune."

Elren frowned at the assailant's comment. His eyes were not emerald or sapphire, but bronze. *Human. A human attacking a fae. And what was she immune to?* He turned to Fionn, who rubbed her neck and shook her head as their eyes met.

"I would suggest thinking twice before you make a dash for the door, Human." Elren twisted his head around to indicate he could see what the man was planning. "I'm faster and stronger than you." He showed off, darting to the man's side before he could blink, and forced him to sit down on a chair. "Now, Fionn. How about you tell me what has been going on?"

It took her a few attempts to get the words out before she finally made sense. "He tried to poison me. When it didn't work, he attacked me . . . you know the rest."

"Poison you?" Elren raised an eyebrow. *He must have meant immune to poison.*

Fionn shook her head. "He must not have used enough."

"I used plenty. You shouldn't be breathing," the human spat.

Elren backhanded the man. "Speak when spoken to." He readjusted himself after catching a glimpse of Fionn's disapproving look. "How did you know it was poison? No, wait. Why did you let him in?"

"He pretended to be a servant. Brought me wine, water, and bread. Said it was to prepare my stomach for this evening." Fionn pointed to the tray on the table. "Then he attacked me. Screamed something about it not working."

Elren frowned. *The congregation.* They were already late, but taking the culprit of attempted murder would give his father something else to focus on other than his tardiness.

He turned to Fionn. Her brown hair was curled and half pinned back, with ringlets hanging on either side of her face. Her dress was ivory with white flowers that covered the floor-length skirt, leading to a thin strapped top that accentuated her figure with a cinched in waist and embellished belt. She looked . . . stunning.

"Tell me more on the way."

Fionn nodded her head towards the man. "What about him?"

"He's coming with us."

Elren stared at his father as he strode into the hall. The background music stopped. Whispers and gasps went around the room. Marching the would-be assassin up to his father, he made the man kneel before the king.

Glancing over his shoulder to check Fionn was three steps behind him, Elren stepped back, closing the gap. If he could he'd put her arm in his, but they had to at least attempt proper etiquette In front of two kings hoping to discuss a peace treaty. A little ironic, as the assassin had claimed the Unseelie King was behind the whole thing.

"What is the meaning of this?" King Warren said, standing up from his throne. "Who is this man and why have you brought him here?"

"He tried to kill your apothecary," Elren said, fighting the urge to roll his shoulders back. "Had a most interesting tale of events too." He couldn't help but glance at the Unseelie King, still holding the hand of a High Lord's daughter.

"A tale indeed if you saw fit to march him in here like some kind of prized pig."

Elren clenched his jaw and composed himself before speaking further. "He claims King Ander sent him to kill Fionn." He turned his gaze to the Unseelie King, whose face stayed blank and then continued to speak. "He is the second person I have questioned today who has made the same claim."

The room was so silent you'd have heard a pin drop. Instead, Elren heard his father take in a deep breath and then huff it out. King Warren limped down the stairs and when he got to the man kneeling on the floor, he grabbed his chin and forced him to look into his eyes.

"You will speak the truth."

"Yes."

"You will not lie."

"I will not lie," the assassin said, his mind already melded to the king's.

"What were you doing here tonight?"

"I was tasked with eradicating the poison expert. She could expose the Popdels."

The king looked at Elren. He nodded to his father, and the questioning continued.

"Popdels? Who has them? Where were they from?" The king dropped the man's face and stepped back. He'd asked too many questions in succession. The persuasiveness of his voice wouldn't work. "Who has the Popdels?"

The man's head snapped in the king's direction. "Alastair bred them. Then King Ander told me to move them."

FIONN

She tried not to react when Elren gripped her hand tightly as they entered King Warren's study.

"Are you alright?" The prince whispered. She nodded, a smile teasing on her lips as he hovered closer to her.

The king had opted to finish the conversation away from the majority of the congregation after the accusation. Fionn hated the tension that surrounded them and turned her thoughts to something else in an attempt to distract herself.

The prince had placed himself and Fionn off to the left of the room. While the two kings and an unseelie advisor filled the other side.

"I don't really see that this is necessary, Warren," King Ander said, flustered. "I've never seen that man before. He's obviously lying, trying to stop the peace treaty."

King Warren smiled. "Yet he is the second person to accuse you. You must see how that looks."

Fionn squeezed his hand and Elren leant closer to hear her whispers. "We could always give him the poison."

Elren frowned. "As much as I would enjoy that, we can't poison the Unseelie King in front of his advisor."

You can't.

"So we just let him get away with killing your mother?" Fionn sighed. Noticing the prince's jaw clench, she continued. "He—"

"Fionn, I know you're offering to help, but if he dies here, war will follow."

She studied the two men as they argued, throwing accusations back and forth. Question after question was deflected or returned in the same manner. *He did it.* Fionn didn't know why, but she knew it was true. Alastair loved the queen. That she knew to be true, and he didn't know his Popdels had killed her. Which meant someone else had done those things.

She let go of the prince's hand as he stepped forward and joined the argument. Fionn moved to a small side table. It had glasses, a decanter of wine and another with an orange liquid. Taking the top off to sniff it, Fionn pulled back. It had a strong alcoholic scent. Perfect for hiding poison. A clink rang through the air as the bottle tapped the top of the glass. She took the small vial she'd taken from the alchemy lab out from her sleeve and poured some into the three glasses closest to her.

"See, the woman has the right idea," King Ander said. "Let's have a drink, calm down a little. Everything is fine."

"Everything is not fine," the king snapped. "Someone has accused you of killing my wife. My wife, Ander. Not a knight, or a peasant, or some other insignificant person. My wife. The queen. That is an act of war."

"Here," she said, presenting the tray to the king. He took the one furthest away, and she turned to the prince. "A drink, Your Highness?" Elren sighed before he took the second untainted glass. Whichever one King Ander chose, he would drink his own poison.

"Drink, King Ander?" Fionn asked. It took everything in her to not let her hand shake as she stood there holding the tray up.

King Ander took a step forward and eyed the glasses before taking one. "Thank you."

She moved to the advisor, who took the drink without thinking and nodded his thanks. *I will need to drink as well.* Fionn returned to the table, placing the tray down and picking up the final drink.

"What's the matter, Ander?" King Warren asked. "Not feeling the drink now?"

Fionn could feel Elren staring at her. Returning to her position beside the prince, Fionn placed the glass to her lips and drank the entire thing in one gulp. King Ander followed suit shortly after.

"May death come on swift wings." Fionn's voice was barely audible as the whisper escaped her lips.

She knew the Unseelie King had heard her when his glass fell to the floor. He stumbled back, the king's legs giving way, and he landed in a crumpled heap on the floor.

"Fionn!" Prince Elren appeared by her side, an arm wrapped around her waist, and nestling under her arm. He took the weight of her as feeling drained from her legs. Not from the poison. More shock at what she had just done.

I killed the king.

"What did you do?" Fionn knew the king had spoken, but her eyes wouldn't leave the sight of Ander clutching his throat. His body jerked to a stop as he went slack.

"Are you okay?" Prince Elren said as he moved her away from the body. "Tell me you didn't lace them all?" The prince raised an eyebrow. "The assassin was right."

Fionn turned her head as recognition ran across the prince's face.

"Not all of them," she said, turning to look at King Warren. "I knew he wouldn't take a drink from me, so I had to give them to everyone. I-I can't explain it but I know everything Alastair said was the truth. I couldn't let him get away with it." Fionn's eyes fell on the advisor, still holding his drink. "You didn't drink."

"It's alright," King Warren said. "He works for me. Been spying on the Unseelie for years and reporting back to me."

"And now that role is over. Thank you, Your Majesty," the advisor said, bowing his head.

Elren's hands left her arm, and he stepped back. "Wait, if he's been giving you information, and Ander knew about the child, is that how you found out?"

"Yes and no. We both had our dalliances over the years. We agreed to raise the baby as our own." King Warren put his glass down on his desk and sighed. He leant forward and continued. "We had hoped it would be a girl."

"You wanted another child?" Elren asked.

"We thought the child would fulfil the prophecy of the Queen Regent. Half Seelie and Half Unseelie born to rule both kingdoms as one."

Prince Elren coughed. "You really believe in that silly legend?"

King Warren pushed off the desk and stormed over to his son. "That legend is standing right in front of you. Unaffected by the poison she ingested. Poison created by the Unseelies. Poison that killed your mother and the child along with it."

The pair of them turned to her. Instinctively, Fionn stepped back.

"You have no reason to be afraid of us," King Warren said. "The only thing I ask is that you marry my son. Uniting us all."

"But I'm not Unseelie."

The king smiled. "You're not fully Seelie either. You have to be half of both."

I have never met my mother.

"Your silence speaks volumes."

Elren held his hands up. "Wait a minute. Aren't we forgetting something here? King Ander is dead on our land. What exactly are we going to do about that?"

"The Unseelie court hated Ander, and the High Lords were plotting to get rid of him. Zevran here will inform them their plan succeeded. Ander was never going to agree to peace, they'd have killed him upon his return."

Fionn smiled. "It seems you knew the game being played before the players did."

King Warren laughed. "I had my sources, though no one expected the Popdels." He held out his hand. "Now, are you going to give me an answer?"

"Shouldn't she be giving me an answer, father?" Elren said, stepping forward. "Fionn, would you do me the honour of becoming my wife?"

She took a deep breath and smiled, placing her hand in his. "May peace reign."

R. S. Williams

R. S. WILLIAMS is a fantasy author from Somerset, England who lives with her husband, daughter and two cats.

She started writing in her late teens and grew up on a steady diet of books and tv shows feeding her imagination. When she's not writing or reading, Rhianne enjoys watching far too much Netflix, playing video games and going for walks.

To find out more, sign up for the newsletter or follow her on Instagram @authorrhiannewilliams

Find Rhianne online here:
www.authorrhiannewilliams.com

To Walk in Royal Shoes

Marie Reed

Ayomide looked up from his office computer at the chime of the bell on the front door. He glanced at the clock to see that the secretary wasn't due to be back to the office for twenty minutes, and the next client's appointment was ten minutes after that, so his boss wouldn't be back this early either. Ayomide rubbed his eyes, then he stood and went to check who had walked into the lobby.

Walk-ins were rare for this office, and for good reason. The lawyer Ayomide worked for had paid handsomely for a witch to charm the front door to keep humans from noticing it. When Mr. Visnosky opened his firm, people told him he'd lose clients by only representing paranormal cases, but after only a few years, he was the most sought-after lawyer for paranormals in the city.

Ayomide walked down the short hallway to the lobby and saw a short man in a crisp suit studying the painting on the other side of the room. He turned at the sound of Ayomide's steps.

"Kelechi, how wonderful to see you well." The man smiled and opened his arms as if to greet Ayomide with a hug.

Ayomide froze, confused. "I'm sorry, sir, but I believe you're looking for someone else. I am Ayomide Darksaffron, a paralegal working for Mr. Visnosky. Were you asked to meet someone here, perhaps?"

The man laughed, his bright teeth in sharp contrast to his dark skin and black suit. "You've always been such a joker, Kelechi." He walked up to Ayomide and clapped him on the shoulders. "I promised you that I would not let anyone follow you when you left the Hollow Mountains, but you have been gone for years now. It is time to come home."

Ayomide took a few steps back, holding out his hands in front of him as he broke from the man's embrace. "Sir, I have no idea what you are talking about. I've never been to a hollow mountain, and I've never seen you before in my life. I can help you find this Kelechi if you'd like, but I do not know anyone with that name. I'm not sure how much help I would be."

The man now looked at him sternly. "Kelechi, enough of this. I know you wanted to get away before having to take the throne, but you must come home now. I didn't want to tell you this here, but your father is ill. His healers don't believe he has much time left. You must come home now."

Ayomide had had enough. This man was either very confused or seriously disturbed. He kept his hands raised as he walked backward to his office, prepared to lock the door and call the Paranormal Police Department. "Sir, I am going to have to ask you to leave. I am not who you think I am, and I don't think I'll be able to help you. I wish you luck searching for your friend."

Ayomide was halfway through the doorway when he heard the man snap his fingers. Ropes instantly appeared, wrapping themselves around Ayomide's ankles and securing his arms at his sides. He lost his balance and fell to the floor, turning so his shoulder took the impact of the floor instead of his face.

"I've had enough of this, Kelechi. You knew when you left that you would have to return someday. You are the only heir. The Hollow Mountains need you. It is time you accepted this." With another snap of his fingers, both the suited man and Ayomide disappeared in a cloud of smoke.

* * *

WHEN THE SMOKE CLEARED, AYOMIDE FOUND HIMSELF LYING on a cold stone floor, still bound. He glanced around the room. A large unlit fireplace dominated one side of the stone room and an old-fashioned poster bed with thick curtains on the other. He had heard about travel spells before, but they were very difficult to do properly, especially with passengers and long distances. This man must be a powerful witch. Or something else entirely.

Another snap of the man's fingers and the ropes vanished. "Thankfully, it looks like you'll still fit into your old clothing," the man said as he opened the doors of an armoire. He thrust some clothes at Ayomide, who had just started to stand and almost lost his balance again when he caught the bundle. "Put these on so you look presentable for the court. And no more of that nonsense, Kelechi. You're the crown prince. It's time to behave like one."

Ayomide called after him as he walked to the door. "Sir!" The man turned. "I am not your prince. I swear I'm not."

The man sighed. "I will tell the king and queen that you are weary from travel and need rest. I will have you meet with my commander in the morning, who will be able to break whatever memory spell you had done to try to keep me from bringing you home. And then when you are over this decision, I will bring you to see your parents."

"Thank you, sir. I promise you that your commander will prove that I'm not lying."

The man scoffed softly but let the subject drop. "I will have dinner brought to you shortly," he said as he left the room.

Once alone, Ayomide decided to look around. Escape was out of the question; he had no idea where he was or how to get home without the witch's help. He quickly circled the room, searching for something helpful but found nothing out of the ordinary except a good amount of dust. Ayomide ran his hands through his hair. It seemed the prince had been gone for a long time, and he was beginning to suspect that he never planned on returning. How had the witch found him to begin with anyway? Maybe this commander would be more willing to listen in the morning.

He kicked one of the desk legs in frustration and a couple of books tumbled to the floor. Ayomide picked up the top one, surprised that he could read it. Then again, the witch also spoke the same language as he did, so maybe he shouldn't have been surprised. He decided that he might as well get comfortable for now and lit a fire before swapping his dress pants and button-up shirt for what he assumed were pajamas he found in the armoire.

Ayomide took the book, *A Brief History of the Hollow Mountains*, with him to the chair closest to the fireplace, which was now burning brightly. Ayomide's suspicions that the prince had done this on purpose grew. Why would the prince have kept a history book of his own country in his bedroom? Shrugging, he decided that since he had nothing better to do, he might as well learn about this kingdom.

The next morning, Ayomide woke to a loud knock on the door. After he had eaten last night, he returned to the history book, ultimately bringing it to bed. Apparently, he had fallen asleep reading, as it was still open beside his pillow. Sharp pains tore through his neck from the angle he'd fallen asleep in. He got up and walked to the door, rubbing his sore neck. On the other side stood a maid with a breakfast tray.

Ayomide opened the door for the maid, who curtseyed before taking the tray to the table in the sitting area of the room. The witch, who had also been waiting in the hallway, pushed his way past Ayomide to the armoire.

"Commander Azuresmith will be arriving shortly. I spoke to her yesterday, and the spell to prove your identity will require a blood relative. The queen has agreed to attend, so your reluctance to return home doesn't reach the king." The witch spoke from behind the dressing screen. Ayomide assumed he'd once again chosen "appropriate" clothing for him to wear.

"Eat quickly and then dress," the witch continued as he walked back into view. "I will greet the commander and take her to the queen before collecting you." Ayomide nodded as the witch and the maid left the room.

When the witch returned, Ayomide followed him down multiple long hallways and a passage hidden by a tapestry before they came to a small sitting room where two women sat speaking. The older one was clearly the queen; her gold and white dress sparkled with small jewels, as did her hair, dark with streaks of grey, which was braided in an elegant updo. The other woman was dressed much more plainly, and her light brown hair was loose, trailing past her shoulders. She turned in her chair as the men entered the room, then stood and met them halfway.

"Emenike, how wonderful to see you," she said with a smile.

The witch, apparently named Emenike, bowed his head. "And you, Commander. Thank you for coming so quickly."

"Of course. This is a very simple test, but not one I use very often. I will teach it to you." She turned to Ayomide. "I am Callista, Commander of the Impassable Sorcerers. We'll need a few minutes to prepare, and then all we'll need from you is a drop of blood." She pointed him to the now empty chair beside the queen and then walked to a nearby table with Emenike.

Ayomide stood there for a minute, then decided that since he didn't know for sure how long he would be in the room, he might as well sit awkwardly beside the queen who believed him to be her son. He slowly made his way across the room, gave what he hoped was a respectful bow to the queen, and gingerly sat down, trying not to make eye contact.

"You do look exactly like my son." The queen spoke so quietly that

Ayomide barely heard her. He wasn't sure what he could say to respond to that, so he stayed silent. A few moments later, the queen continued. "I cannot decide if I want you to be Kelechi and know my son is lying to continue to avoid us, or that he went to such great lengths to hide from us to search for a lookalike to trick us." She was silent again, sitting stiffly in her chair as if trying to keep her composure, then said, "Neither option shows qualities I would wish for the future king to possess, but we have no other choice for the throne."

Ayomide still did not respond, and the queen didn't act like she was expecting him to. He tried to think of a way to make the situation better, but he thought again about the history book that had been left out on the prince's desk. He could not imagine why the prince would abandon his kingdom without any way to communicate with his parents, especially if he was the only heir. He shook his head. He knew nothing about the prince or why he had left, and it wasn't his place to worry about it. Hopefully, whatever potion or test would prove his identity quickly and he would be sent back home. He had enough of his own problems to worry about. Explaining his disappearance was at the top of the list.

Emenike walked over to Ayomide and the queen, carrying a basin full of a shimmering liquid. The commander followed him. They stopped between the chairs, and Commander Azuresmith turned toward the queen.

"Your Majesty, we are ready for you now," she said. She held out a small needle. "I need you to prick your finger and squeeze a single drop of blood into the center of the bowl." She turned to Ayomide and handed him another needle. "You will do the same. If you are blood relatives, the droplets will combine in the center. If you are not, they will separate."

Emenike held the bowl up to the queen as she quickly stabbed her finger with the needle. A drop of blood fell neatly into the middle of the shimmering liquid, creating ripples. He then held it closer to Ayomide so he could do the same. His drop of blood landed practically on top of the queen's. Almost immediately, the two drops separated and sped to opposite edges of the bowl.

Emenike looked up, astonished. "You are not the prince. But," he pulled a coin out of his pocket, "Kelechi sent me this so I could find him. Why would it lead me to someone else?"

"Did he give this to you before he left?" The commander asked, taking the coin from his hand.

"No," Emenike replied. "He promised to come home every six months, and he did at first. After a year, I was sent this. He said coming home was limiting his travels, so he told me to use this beacon when we needed him."

"Obviously, he had this made after he discovered he had a looka-like," Commander Azuresmith said as she studied the coin. She looked up. "I'm sorry. Emenike did not tell me your name."

"Ayomide Darksaffron, ma'am," he replied.

"Ayomide." The queen spoke. "I am sorry that you were dragged into this. We will make sure that you are sent home very soon."

"Actually, it may be best if he stays, Your Majesty." The commander spoke to the queen, then glanced back at Ayomide. "I have a feeling that Prince Kelechi probably had someone watching you to see when someone came looking for him. Bringing you back home might send him on the run again. Allow me to search the realms for the prince and I will take you home myself when I return to the Hollow Mountains."

"How do you plan on finding my son when he does not want to be found?" The queen had tears in her eyes. "He left us. He abandoned his people. Does he not care about us at all?" She rose from her chair angrily, pulled a handkerchief out of her sleeve to wipe her eyes, and then gestured to the door. "What am I supposed to tell my husband, who may not live to see his son return?"

The four of them stood silently. Ayomide had a feeling that neither of the witches—or sorcerers, as they seemed to go by in this land—had an answer for her. He wasn't even sure how Commander Azuresmith planned to find the prince.

"Your Highness?" he finally asked, breaking the silence. "If you don't mind me asking, what illness does the king have?"

"We believe it is what your realm refers to as brain cancer. He has lost his ability to walk, and his vision and speech have both been affected. He is very fragile and requires almost constant care. No mage or healer has been able to help. And from what I understand, if we were to attempt to cross realms with him, your healers would not be able to cure him either.”

“No, we do not have a cure for cancer. There are treatments, but they are painful and hard on the body. If he is already so weak, I don’t think any of our doctors would be able to help.” Ayomide was quiet for another minute as he thought. “Would it be a comfort to him if he thought his son was home? I wouldn’t want to lie to him, but I could sit by his bedside and, I don’t know, hold his hand and let him say the things he wants to tell his son.” He ran his hands through his hair as he exhaled. “I just . . . he shouldn’t have to worry, and if I can help . . . “

The queen touched his arm, dabbing her eyes with the handkerchief in her other hand. “You are a good man, Ayomide,” she said. “I will consult his healers, but I believe that the comfort of having his son home is all we have left to ease his suffering.” With that, she nodded to Emenike, who escorted her out of the room.

Ayomide turned to speak to the commander. “How long do you think you’ll be looking for the prince? I need to go home. I’m sure my boss is wondering why I left in the middle of the day.”

“If he believes that you have taken his place, he won’t have a reason to suspect I would be searching for him, especially if Emenike also stays in the Hollow Mountains,” Commander Azuresmith answered. “Maybe a few days. A week at most.”

“But they’ll report me missing before then. Why can’t you send me back and then search for the prince?”

“Kelechi’s disappearance affects the entire kingdom,” she explained. “I understand that you want to return quickly, but the Hollow Mountains will fall into chaos if it is known that the prince is missing with the king in such poor health.”

Just then, Emenike returned to the room. He looked out of breath. “The king is awake and would like to see his son. The queen will also be in the room to help with any questions he may try to ask you.” He was silent for a second. “The healers do not believe he has long. Perhaps a few days. It is very likely that Kelechi will not be found before his father passes on.”

“Then I should leave and begin my search,” Commander Azure-smith said. “I will send a message to Emenike when I have news,

Ayomide." She took his hand in both of hers and gave him an almost motherly smile. "Thank you for staying to help."

The commander left swiftly as Emenike led Ayomide to the king's chambers, where the queen was waiting in the main sitting room. She spoke to Ayomide quietly before leading him into the next room. "My husband is receiving a sleeping tonic now, so he will not want to speak much, but he would like to see Kelechi before he falls asleep. I will sit off to the side and let you know if you need to respond to anything."

"Thank you, Your Majesty."

The queen led Ayomide into the king's bedchamber. The room was dark with all but one of the windows covered in heavy drapes. A soft-looking chair had been placed beside the bed, and another was near the open window. The queen led him to the king's bedside.

"Kelechi is here to see you." The queen left Ayomide at the bedside chair and walked to the other, picking up some fabric from the basket beside the chair.

Ayomide looked at the king. It was obvious that he had been a strong man, but the illness had turned him frail. His skin was ashy and wrinkled, hanging loose on his skeletal frame. His dark eyes were emotionless as they focused on Ayomide's face, then twinkled with delight as he recognized him.

"My boy," he rasped, then a coughing fit tore through his entire body. When it was over, the king reached for Ayomide's hand, grasping it with all his limited strength. They stayed that way until the king drifted off to sleep.

For the next four days, Ayomide spent time with the king while waiting for news from the commander. He read aloud from the history books he'd found to pass the time until the king passed in his sleep.

The king's funeral was quickly arranged and quite simple compared to what Ayomide assumed it would be for the ruler of a country. The royal crypt was carved into a cave in the mountain the castle was built on, and only a small number of dignitaries came with the royal family to pay their final respects. A few came up to him and the queen, but most filed silently past them to place a flower on the casket.

One man at the back of the cave caught Ayomide's eye. He was very average looking from what Ayomide could tell, with dark skin and hair, but he still had the hood of his cloak up and kept to the shadowy corners away from the other mourners. As everyone else started to trickle out of the crypt, he stayed.

Ayomide turned to the queen. "Would you like a moment alone? I can escort the stragglers out and wait at the entrance."

"Yes, please," replied the queen, as she dabbed her eyes.

Ayomide left her with Emenike and walked to the cloaked stranger. "My mother wishes to say her goodbyes alone. I must ask you to leave so she can have some privacy."

"Of course," the man said. He began walking toward the doorway but stopped before leaving and took a long look toward the casket at the far end of the room.

Ayomide followed. "I believe the sorcerers will be sealing the king's grave soon. If you would like to pay your respects, I can have them wait a few more minutes." The man hadn't acted like he'd wanted to leave, but Ayomide had no idea who he was. He had briefly met most of the dignitaries at this point, or at the very least the queen or Emenike had told him who they were, but there was something vaguely familiar about this man's shadowy features.

The man was silent for a moment, then replied in a strained voice. "No, I've given up the right to say a proper goodbye." He looked up at Ayomide, the movement pushing his hood back. The shadows retreated enough that Ayomide could see the tears in his eyes. Suddenly, his features flickered, and for a second it was like Ayomide was looking in a mirror: the man now had the same dark brown eyes, angular jawline, and tightly coiled black hair as he. The man's face changed back just as quickly.

It was the prince. Ayomide was speechless.

"Please don't let them know I was here," Kelechi said quickly. "I don't want to come back. I just wanted to say goodbye to my father. I left hoping to find a way for someone else to rule, and when I found you, I knew that this was my way out. But I can't come back."

"But," Ayomide started in a strong whisper. "But I had a life! What right did you have to choose this for me? And your parents! Your mother has been grieving you since she found out you abandoned her, and now she is grieving your father. You would leave her alone?"

"I'm not going to get into the whys," said Kelechi. "I have never wanted to rule and when I had the opportunity to give them their prince back without having to do it myself, I took it." He paused. "I didn't just send Emenike the tracker as soon as I happened to see you. I looked into the work you do, how much you care about the people who came to that lawyer looking for help. You will make a good ruler. You are what the Hollow Mountains need in a king. I am not ever going to be that person." He nodded at Ayomide, pulled his cloak even further over his face, and left quickly.

Ayomide stood stunned. By the time he came to his senses, Kelechi had disappeared. The disguise would have required a mage of some sort, and they'd probably been waiting outside for Kelechi to help him disappear. Again.

Ayomide returned to the hall to see the queen standing with Emenike. Should he tell them that he saw Kelechi? Would knowing he was here help the situation at all, or just reopen the wounds of his abandonment?

"What happened?" Emenike asked as he approached.

Ayomide stumbled over his words as he tried to figure out what to say. "There was someone acting suspicious, so I went to see who it was. I asked him to leave, and he disappeared before I found out who it was."

"Can you describe him? I will inform the guards to keep an eye out."

"Not well. He kept his hood up." Ayomide decided to keep Kelechi's visit to himself. Knowing he was here and left again would not help the situation. Somehow, he needed to let Commander Azuresmith know. "I don't think he'll stay here. He's probably long gone."

Emenike nodded. "We will schedule extra guards and patrols just in case."

Footsteps echoed behind them. They turned to the queen, who had been close enough to hear the end of the conversation. "Extra guards would be preferable until after the coronation. We will need to start discussing plans in the next few days." The queen's eyes were red, her face tear stained, but she held her head high, ready to face her people again.

Ayomide asked, "Should we contact the commander to see if she has any leads? If she returns soon, we should wait for her."

Both of his companions agreed. Emenike said he would send a message to Commander Azuresmith that evening and when he received a response, the queen would begin preparations for Kelechi's coronation. Ayomide couldn't decide if he hoped they would hear from her immediately or not at all. He had agreed to temporarily take the prince's place, but it was looking like this was designed by the missing royal to be a permanent arrangement from the start, and Ayomide couldn't think of an easy way out of the situation.

AYOMIDE SPENT THE MAJORITY OF THE NEXT FEW DAYS IN the library. He had finished the books Kelechi had left on his desk at this point and wanted to know more about the Hollow Mountains. The kingdom had an interesting history, as they had accepted magic users and realm travel early on. It was really different from what he was used to; back home, the paranormal community had to hide their true identities around mundane humans or risk being attacked in the streets.

The library door opened, cutting through the silence. A butler announced Commander Azuresmith's arrival moments before she walked into the room.

"Did you find him?" Ayomide asked her, setting down his book as she sat in the chair next to him and magically lit the logs in the fireplace. Blue flames caressed the wood as it caught.

"No." She sighed. "I believe I was close and then he realm-jumped and I lost him."

"He was at the king's funeral."

Her eyes widened in surprise.

"Not for long," Ayomide continued, "and he stayed near the back with some sort of glamor disguise. I think I'm the only one who knows he was here."

"You didn't tell the queen?"

"No. I didn't think that reminding her that her son doesn't want to see her would be a good idea, especially at her husband's funeral." Ayomide paused, and they sat in silence for a few moments. "He said he doesn't want to rule. He thinks I would do a better job as King."

Commander Azuresmith waited another moment before replying. "That might be for the best. Kelechi was never going to be a good ruler. He made it clear that he didn't want the responsibility, even before he ran away."

Ayomide was becoming tired of everyone making decisions for him. "I had my own plans. I was going to become a lawyer and help the paranormal community."

"Like the man you apprenticed for."

"I . . . yes," Ayomide answered. She was more or less correct, and he didn't feel like getting into explaining how law school worked to an off-realm witch. Or mage, or sorcerer. He still wasn't sure about the correct magic user terms here. "Did you go see Mr. Visnosky?"

The commander nodded. "Yes, right before I returned. In part because I was curious about where you came from, and because I thought Kelechi might go back to that realm if he thought he'd been caught."

"I'm guessing he wasn't there then. So, I have to be here for the coronation, and to rule afterwards, all because you can't find him." Ayomide stood up and grabbed the fireplace poker, shoving it into the logs and making the blue flames jump higher. He let out a deep breath as he watched the fire. "I had plans," he said quietly.

"I know," she replied. "I've also seen what change has come from your disappearance. Your employer is leading a movement to overhaul the entire Paranormal Police Department in the city. They've already found many cases of disappearances, of faked evidence that led to the imprisonment of innocent people. If you were to return to your realm, it might undo the good that is happening."

Ayomide turned away from the fire and to the commander. "So even if I didn't stay here, I still couldn't go back."

She shook her head. "Not without destroying the worldview of billions of people across the realms. Only a small number of us know about how vast the universe truly is."

He stared at the fire again. He knew he couldn't go back home. The truth of his disappearance, with realm-jumping magicians and the existence of multiple worlds, would be too much for the general population to accept; they were still getting used to the idea of paranormals. He could ask to go somewhere new and start over . . . or he could stay here. Become King. Maybe he wouldn't be doing what he had planned to do in his life, but he could still do good here. The people of the Hollow Mountains didn't deserve the mess of not having a ruler. He could stay. He set the fireplace poker back in its stand and turned back to the commander.

"Okay. I will stay here. But the royal advisors should know what happened, and I would like Emenike to be added to them. I'll need a lot of help while I'm learning."

Commander Azuresmith smiled and stood. "You will be a wonderful king, Ayomide. I will go fetch Emenike and then we can meet with the queen to prepare for your coronation, Your Majesty."

Marie Reed

Marie Reed is currently a stay-at-home mom of two who is still trying to figure out what she wants to be when she grows up. She fell in love with books of all kinds at a young age and devoured entire libraries while still in school. A dozen or so years later, she finally finished writing her first short story and is currently working on a full length novel. You can keep up with Marie's reading and writing at:

https://linktr.ee/mariereed

Born to Prove

Dani Hoots

The red haired and bearded man before me stood at the top of the bridge and peered out at the universe. Specks of every color filled the dark and vast universe. One could spend an eternity counting the stars and planets and still not be close to knowing the extent of how big it truly was. The land under my feet shimmered like that of a glass rainbow. I stared at it all in awe as I had never seen anything so beautiful.

A fox weaved between my legs—its fur feeling soft against the bare skin of my legs. Something about the fox felt familiar—as if the two of us had met before. As I glanced at the wonder before me, I realized it all felt familiar. It was as if it were an edge of a memory.

Before I could find the memory that was somewhere deep inside my mind, the man began to step toward me, and watched me as he twirled a large hammer in his hand. As he stared, I wrapped my arms around myself. His crystal-blue eyes felt as if they could see deep into my soul.

"Prove to me your worth, Arian Artuflnose."

Before I could respond—before I could ask who Arian was, something strong ripped me backward and I felt as if were falling into oblivion. I screamed, asking for anyone—anything—to help me.

THE SOUND OF MY ALARM WOKE ME FROM MY SLUMBER. I blinked a couple of times, trying to come back to the real world. That was one strange, vivid dream, and I wondered for a moment if the dream was reality, and this was actually a dream. I knew that wasn't the case, but I still couldn't shake off the feeling that it had meant something—that it wasn't my subconscious processing info from the day before.

I grabbed my phone and scrolled through social media as I did every morning. It was probably a bad habit, but it helped me wake up and get the mental gears going. After liking a few of my friends' photos from last night's party I had skipped out on, I shoved the comforter off of me and got ready for the day.

My first class was, of course, all the way across campus, and it was the earliest class I had all week, which was not a good way to start a Friday. I quickly took a shower, ran some gel through my hair, and put on a simple shirt, jeans, and converse. I had prepped my backpack the night before, so I didn't have to scavenge for all my notes, books, laptop, and pens. I learned to do that after the first two weeks of school.

I hurried past other students in the dorm who also had morning classes as quietly as I could since it was early, and some people were still asleep. Others were not as thoughtful as I was to their neighbors on their floor. I was definitely glad I was on the top floor of the dorm, although that meant I had to take five flights of stairs. I didn't wait for the elevator since it was popular in the morning and because I didn't want to be one of the poor students who got stuck in it, which happened every quarter at least twice.

Once I made it down the stairs, I rushed across the campus, careful not to get hit by the food delivery robots that were sending off breakfast orders all across the area. I thought they were the coolest things I had ever seen and reminded me of the mouse droids from *Star Wars*. I had yet to order from one, however. The college campus was spread out in the middle of a forest, which meant a lot of paths between buildings went through one part of the forest or another. There was one chunk of forest, however, that many claimed was haunted. There were many myths as to why it was haunted, ranging from a supposed murder decades before to claims that the plant life was completely different than other parts of campus. All of them were proven false, however.

Passing by one of the large oak trees, I thought I saw movement coming from behind the trunk. I shifted so I could peer around it, praying that it wasn't some students making out. Instead, I found an orange fluffy tail. I grinned widely. It was a fox. It turned and saw me staring at it and quickly scurried off with a little scream. I couldn't blame it—if a large creature was staring at me when I woke up, I'd freak out too.

Although foxes weren't unheard of in the area, I had never seen one before. I thought about searching around for other creatures but then glanced at my phone. If I didn't hurry, I'd be late for class. I clutched the straps of my backpack and began to jog.

I got to class right before the professor shut the door. He gave me a look as I was a minute late and he did not appreciate tardiness of any kind. I quickly took a seat in the middle of the classroom and pulled out my notebook.

"Now, today we are moving onto the Nordic Region and their mythology. Open up your textbooks to chapter 11."

I pulled out the textbook and opened it up to the chapter. I was met with an art piece of a blond man holding a large hammer and riding a chariot pulled by goats. Something about the photo drew me in. Then I realized what it was—the man was the same man as in my dreams. Under the picture read *"Thor's Battle with the Giants" by Mårten Eskil Winge.*

"Now," the professor began, snapping me out of my memory. I got my pen ready as he spoke quickly. "We will begin our discussion with Thor, the thunder god, warrior, defender of Asgard. He was also associated with agriculture and fertility . . ."

The professor went on and I took as many notes as I could. My soul felt drawn to every word he said. Soon the class finished, and I found myself wishing it would go on for another few hours. I had a feeling the other students did not feel the same way.

I had a bit of a break so I went back to the woods to see if I could find the fox, but I didn't find any traces of the creature. As I was about to leave, I noticed something sparkling on the ground. I bent down and grabbed it. I ran my thumb over the piece of metal to reveal an engraving. It was in a language I didn't understand. If I wasn't mistaken, it was in the language used by ancient Vikings.

I put it in my pocket and hurried off toward my next class. I would try to remember to drop it off at the lost and found later.

Classes finally ended for the day, and I couldn't wait to get back and have my leftover mac and cheese. I would probably watch some TV before working on my homework. It seemed as if homework never ended, and I couldn't wait to graduate in a little over a year.

The sun was beginning to set as I ventured through the woods. It was quiet as many students had already headed to the dorms or to the Memorial Union for dinner.

I entered the woods, keeping an eye out for my little fox friend. As I ventured further into the woods, I felt something shift in the energy. Instead of the forest clearing my mind and giving me a sense of calm, it now made my hairs stand on end. It wasn't the woods I was used to. I clutched the straps of my bag, wondering if it would be better to turn around and go the long way. I shook off the thought. I had been in this forest countless times now. There was no reason to be scared.

It was quiet—too quiet. I peered around, looking for any signs of disturbances but found none. There wasn't even a peep out of any of the squirrels, and I didn't hear any other people on the path.

What was going on? Was this what people were talking about when they said it was haunted? Now that I thought about it, the foliage did appear different. What was once an open forest with evergreens now appeared like a creepy swamp in a fairytale.

Suddenly, I heard a loud noise. I spun around and found the last thing I would ever think of—a large creature one would only imagine in a movie or video game. I collapsed to the ground, staring up at the large figure. It was clear and cool air came off of it as if it were made of ice. It stood over six feet tall and towered over me as I fell back. Its dark eyes stared down at me.

"At last, I have found you." The creature's voice was as cold as the creature appeared.

"What's goin—" I began when suddenly the figure pulled out a large ax with its long, icicle-like fingers and lifted it up. This couldn't be real. There was no way creatures liked this could exist.

I closed my eyes, unable to move. Before I could scream—before the monster could swing its weapon down on me—I heard a bird caw. I opened my eyes once again and found a raven had used its talons to grab the ax shaft and tried to pull it away. It cawed at me as it struggled with the ice giant.

I scrambled back up and ran as fast as I could to get away from the monster with the ax. With how far I had traveled, I should have seen the dorm by now but there were no buildings in sight. Where was I? What was happening?

As I ran, I could hear the raven fight with the icy creature, but I didn't turn back. I had to get out of here.   I had to find help.

The more I ran, the more I realized this was not the familiar forest I traveled through when I was going from class to class. No, this was like something out of a horror film. No matter how fast I ran, I couldn't find the end of it. My heart felt as if it were going to leap out of my chest.

What was I going to do? There was no way I could defeat this creature. I didn't even have scissors in my backpack.

As I thought about my backpack, I struggled to throw it off in hopes it would lighten my load and I could run faster. The raven had stopped attacking the giant ice creature, and it let out a roar as it headed toward me. I reached for my phone and dialed the emergency number.

My phone made a beeping sound. I peered down at it and found I had lost service. How was that possible? I was in the middle of campus.

This had to be a dream. Either that or I had been transported into some fantasy realm, which seemed very unlikely. I blinked hard, trying to force myself awake. This all felt so real, and I had to get out of there.

I tried pinching my arm, but that was no use. I could try to face my fears, so to speak, and fight the monster. If this was a dream, the monster was my fear of failing next week's test or something. I glanced over my shoulder at the creature. No, there was no way I was going to stop and try to fight that. It wanted to kill me.

As I turned back forward, my foot got caught on a root that was sticking out of the ground. I flew forward and smacked down on the forest floor. Luckily there was a lot of moss, but the wind was still knocked out of me.

I spun around to find the creature had gained on me. The monster raised its ax, and I was about to scream when the fox I had seen earlier ran toward me. In its mouth was some type of metal object. As it came close, it tossed the object toward me. I caught it in the air.

Lightning filled the sky and shot down straight to the object I held in my hand. It practically blinded me as the lightning went from the object and into the icy giant. The creature was flung backwards and didn't move.

I stared down at the weapon in my hand. It looked like a hammer—something out of a Marvel movie.

"Is this . . ." I began when the raven that had saved me earlier flew down from the branches. It transformed into an elderly man with a large hat and cloak. Over one of his eyes was an eyepatch.

"It is Mjölnir, the weapon of Thor, yes," the man said as he pulled out his pipe and began to smoke.

I stared at it. I couldn't believe my eyes. Were all the stories real? I shook my head. "I don't understand. How can all of this be real? And why is Thor's weapon in my hands?"

"That is a long story, but Thor is missing and Mjölnir has chosen its new owner in order to find its master. It has chosen you—child of Thor."

I stared at the man. "Child of Thor? What are you talking about?"

The old man took a few puffs of his pipe and then began the story. "Gwyndel Sweetprism, you are the reincarnation of the child of a dark elf and Thor, Arian Artuflnose, just as the pendant you found earlier says. You were given the chance to show the gods who you are, and you have shown that you are honorable and a good person. I have been watching you for many generations and you have never faltered—no matter what life you were living. Now is your chance to show the gods who you are and what you are meant to do. The question is, are you ready?"

I clutched the weapon tight. All of this sounded like it was impossible. I couldn't be the chosen one to wield this weapon, could I? But all of it felt so familiar. I took a long, deep breath as I peered over at my fox friend. He turned his head to the side, as if wondering what I was going to answer.

"I am ready."

Dani Hoots

Dani Hoots is a science fiction, fantasy, and young adult author who loves anything with a story. She has a B.S. in Anthropology, a Masters of Urban and Environmental Planning, a Certificate in Novel Writing from Arizona State University, and a BS in Herbal Science from Bastyr University.

Her hobbies include reading, watching anime, cooking, studying different languages, wire walking, hula hoop, and working with plants. She also loves mythology and has a YouTube channel called "Mythology & Folklore w/ Dani Hoots" where she talks about different figures in mythology and tells old folktales. She lives in Arizona.

Instagram: https://instagram.com/danihoots
Free Book: https://dl.bookfunnel.com/crulacn4p7

Hippolyta Goes Hunting

ALEX STUBBLEFIELD

Hippolyta packed the cart full of herbs, fungal remedies, rare talismans, bitter teas, and tonics. Next to her wares, she packed a bedroll, rope, and a heavy cloak to shield her against the inevitable fog and rain that Hollow Clouds was known for. There was a small pack of rations for her to subsist on. Pickled tongues, tonsils, and eyeballs. Dried meat. A little jar of salt to bring out all the flavors.

"Are you sure that will be enough?" Kei asked.

"There's always the mule, if times get tough," Hippolyta answered with a sly grin.

"You wouldn't—" Kei gasped.

"Of course not!" Hippolyta cackled. "How could I deprive you?" Mule was Kei's favorite kind of meat, though Hippolyta couldn't figure out why. Too tough for her taste.

"When you return, we'll feast."

"I might have to slaughter him and dry the meat before my return journey, but you'll have your portion."

"And the slimes will have theirs?"

"If I don't feed them, they get hangry. You know that." Hippolyta shrugged.

"Which is why I hate when you leave me alone with them." Kei gave a shudder. "I swear they swarm over me while I sleep. Very unsettling."

"They won't touch you." Hippolyta stroked Kei's slippery cheek. His skin was always pleasantly cool and moist. "I won't allow it." Kei shrugged, but Hippolyta could see that he wasn't entirely reassured. Her connection and control over the slimes was strong, but it weakened the further away she was from the Woods.

She clambered up onto the tall seat of the cart. It was challenging to ascend with her stumpy legs and stout body. Kei gave her a push from behind. She gripped the tanned leather reins in her stubby fingers with their chewed-to-the-quick nails and earthy green hue. She swatted the old mule's backside, who lurched forward, and the cart started forth.

"Send word when you get there," Kei called after her. Hippolyta waved a hand behind her in farewell. As a gifted mycologist, she was able to send messages through the sprawling mycelium networks that ran underground all throughout the country. She had tested it before on her journeys with splendid success.

The ground below the cart was soft and spongy, covered with thick moss, completely muffling the hooves of her steed. The rhythmic squeaking of the iron wheels was the only sound to be heard in the Woods. Hippolyta guided her rig expertly through the trunks of the enormous fungi that rose up all around them. She knew which way to take to avoid the bogs, pools of quicksand, and dens of carnivorous amoeba.

The putrid smell of rot was pleasing to her pug-like nose. It smelled like profit. Of her graduating class at her witchcraft school, she was the only one who had mastered the art and science of mycology. Plenty of the other witches had been adept with botany, but she alone had known how to strum the strings of mycorrhizae and send messages throughout an entire forest undetected.

Her fungal network gave her an advantage because it tipped her off when strangers crossed the threshold of the woods. No trespasser got any further into her domain than she allowed them to. She prided herself on keeping the ecosystem of the woods in balance. In return, the creatures of Hottentot listened to her, aided her, and did her bidding. Such had been the way with her slimes.

Kei had not been much different.

The old frog had been her first acquaintance in the Hottentot Woods. She had rescued him from being eaten by a rabid bear. Although Kei was twenty times the size of a normal toad, he had been no match for his aggressor. She was new to the Woods and had needed a friend as well as food. Her magic had allowed her to overpower the bear. She and Kei had eaten a delicious bear stew that night.

Her archrival from her school days, Leonna, had been praised for brewing delicious teas and learning how to ferment them in pleasing ways. Hippolyta's fungal teas were bitter and curdled on the tongue, but their potency and usefulness were beyond anything else her classmates had created. With her concoctions, Hippolyta could heal or kill. Her liqueurs could lure your lover or make you forget your most painful memories. Her work was not delicious. It was deadly.

Hippolyta's dealings with darkness had made her an outcast her whole life, even among her classmates. Hippolyta envied the ease with which witches such as Leonna gained the admiration of students and instructors alike. Leonna was from a wealthy line of accomplished sorceresses and seemed to breeze through all her courses despite her apparent lack of talent. Hippolyta worked her fingers to the bone and strained her eyes, reading late into the night. Leonna hadn't worked for success, so she didn't know real struggle.

Even now, it wasn't as though Hippolyta wished to travel outside of the woods. However, it was her business in the villages that fed them while Kei supplied them a place to live. It was an arrangement that had been working well for quite some time. Kei had shown her around the woods and taught her which of the large mushrooms had hollowed out trunks fit for habitation.

Her business had run out in Hazeltown, and she now turned her eyes north toward the remote village of Hollow Clouds. It was a market yet untapped. The mountain folk, often referred to as Cloudies, were a gentle, private folk that did not often venture down from their elevated reaches. The Hottentot Woods grew between the foot of the mountain and the next nearest village, and that was enough to delay many a practiced traveler. Anyone who wanted to get to Hollow Clouds from Hazeltown had to be prepared to tack on an extra day's journey to circumvent the Woods. No one but the very foolish or very intoxicated ever ventured in, for no one who had, ever ventured out again.

As she reached the edge of her beloved woods, Hippolyta knew there was one thing left to do before ascending the mountain. Although she knew the chances were miniscule of anyone recognizing her, Kei always insisted that she disguise herself when she went into town. The old amphibian had grown quite fond of her, it seemed. Hippolyta pulled a small vial from a chain around her neck. She removed the cork and swallowed the contents down in one gulp. Despite having taken this draft a hundred or more times, she never enjoyed it. An unpleasant rise in temperature overtook her body until all her parts became as malleable as melted wax.

Hippolyta grimaced against the implosion of heat, and she focused her mind as she rearranged her features. There was a limited time to complete the transformation before the internal blast furnace began to cool and her features would start to set into their new array.

The witch's bulbous eyes sank back into her head and her lids closed more fully over them. Hippolyta's wide, full mouth pulled together into a tight, pursed expression, and her cheeks drew in tighter over her cheekbones. She strained her neck to elongate it and sucked in her round tummy to flatten it. The furnace began to cool. Now even her own mother wouldn't be able to recognize her, much less the Cloudies who could have heard whispered rumors about the witch in the woods. She pulled her hair up into a tight bun and covered it with her hood. The fog line started at the foot of the mountains and obscured the rest of the range, except for the tallest peak.

The transfigured sorceress pulled a heavy cloak around her body to obscure the wood witch's telltale green gown. She peered at her reflection in a hand mirror and gave a small, satisfied nod. With her disguise in place, Hippolyta was ready. Priscilla Humphreys was the alter ego that she wore to the markets of Hazeltown and Whitecaps. She was a traveling saleswoman in this guise. Priscilla's story was that all her wares were purchased from wholesalers whom she conveniently didn't name due to proprietary concerns.

Hippolyta had come up with this alter ego during her school years to spy on pesky classmates. While Priscilla befriended the other witches and gossiped with them, Hippolyta was scorned and shunned by those same women. She had been far ahead of the class in her abilities to conceal her identity. No one suspected frumpy, grumpy Hippolyta Gloomspell could be capable of such an advanced feat. She found that their capacity to underestimate her supplied her with a secret advantage.

She had used this disguise to become close with class rival, Leonna. Priscilla learned of Leonna's tricks and tips before she could use them in class and performed them first. With Priscilla's knowledge, Hippolyta was able to sabotage Leonna's love potions and make a fool of her with charmed objects gone wrong. If only Leonna could see her now.

It had been nearly twenty years since Hippolyta had last been to Hollow Clouds. The old mule she relied on struggled up the steeper parts of the trail, and Hippolyta had to feed him some strengthening potions to enable him to finish the journey. The elixirs were just what the poor beast needed to reach the high, wooden gates of Hollow Clouds. Hippolyta doubted if the steed could make his way back down the mountain. Kei would be pleased.

"Just put him out of his misery," Kei had croaked as Hippolyta hooked up her cart to the old beast. The poor creature was humpbacked with age, and it was missing patches of fur. The dark, damp conditions of the Hottentot Woods had not been kind to the mule.

"I'll put you out of your misery," Hippolyta replied with a cackle.

Kei scoffed, but she knew he never took her threats seriously. He had been with her longer than the mule.

She had purchased the mule several years back from a traveler at the Crow's Foot Inn in Hazeltown. The traveler had been a shabby drunk from Whitecaps, who needed a drink more than he did his mule. Hippolyta acquired the mule for a bargain. The drunk was just a bonus. Meat was rare in the woods.

Hippolyta had to listen to Kei complaining for weeks that she would not let them eat the mule, but the minced meat pasties she prepared from the drunk man had satisfied his appetite. She felt the alcohol had tenderized the meat from the inside out.

With a tug of the reins, the cart came to a stop before a sturdy gate constructed out of hewed pine wood. There was a guard tower posted at the top of the gates. A crossbow was mounted there, but it was pointed at the sky rather than the ground. A lithe young man with a brown leather jerkin and matching hunting cap covering his dark, floppy hair emerged from the guard tower.

"Hullo there!" he called. "State your name and business."

"Priscilla Humphreys," Hippolyta called in her sweetest voice. "Headed to the market."

"Right'o!" Without any further questions, the crossbowman hurried back into the guard tower. The large wooden gates swung slowly inward, and Hippolyta and her cart plodded forward. "Have a good day!" The young man called from the guard tower.

Hippolyta flashed a smile at him over her shoulder. *He'd make easy prey,* she thought to herself as she left the gates behind her. More friendly Cloudies waved at her as she moved down the main square. *Yes, I think business will be very good here indeed.* Her stomach grumbled as she swung her greedy eyes to-and-fro, licking her lips.

The town square in Hollow Clouds was much smaller than in the towns of Fair Weather Valley. Here, the mayor was in charge of running the market, whereas, in Hazeltown, the mayor would have never got his hands dirty. This Mayor Glass was a different type altogether.

"Miss Humphreys, here you are," Mayor Glass said as he walked her over to a dilapidated wooden stall. Her stall was wedged between the other vendors, too close for her comfort. "It isn't much, but if you'd like some help with repairs, there is no shortage of lumber smiths and carpenters in Hollow Clouds. Lumber is our top commodity!" Glass smiled cheerily.

"This will be fine," Hippolyta reassured him.

"We're also known for our fine wool! There are pastures on the east side of the mountain." Glass teetered precariously back and forth from foot to foot as he spoke. His white mustache and black hat wobbled with the rest of him.

"And, of course, you'll want to know where the Inn is," Mayor Glass said, nodding to himself. "Stuart keeps a pub across the square and always has a few spare rooms available. We don't get many visitors here," Glass tittered nervously.

"I appreciate your hospitality, Mayor," Hippolyta answered with one of Priscilla's most charming smiles. "I'm sure I'll be alright. I travel often."

"Oh, yes! Well, I'm sure you'll do just fine, Miss Humphreys. Don't hesitate to holler if you need anything!"

Hippolyta pretended to busy herself with unpacking her cart as the Mayor dawdled away. Once she heard him strike up a conversation a few stalls over, Hippolyta whispered a spell that righted the dilapidated stall instantly. She set up the rest manually so as not to draw too much suspicion. She would arrange her wares and then wander over to the Inn to get her bearings. A quick protection spell would make sure nothing walked off while she was gone.

Kei would not approve of her tactics. He warned her that befriending the locals was too risky. She could slip up and tell them something that revealed her true identity. Hippolyta always assured him that she was too smart for that. She needed to be friendly and well-known to the locals. No one would suspect her. No one would be the wiser. The locals often came to feel that they knew her, and that made it much easier to slip into their lives and lure them away.

The pub at the inn would most likely be a key gathering place for the locals. In addition to her conversations at the market, the pub could give her a chance to eavesdrop on others. Townspeople were often superstitious, but also curious.

Glassworks was the name of the Inn. It turned out that Stuart was Mayor Glass' nephew. It was early in the day and there was only one other patron: a middle-aged man with a beard and salt-and-pepper hair. Before him was a stack of papers and a ledger book. Hippolyta felt his eyes on her as she bellied up to the bar.

Priscilla was attractive for a middle-aged woman. This was also part of Hippolyta's strategy. If school bullies had taught her anything, it was that people liked you more when you were attractive.

"Can I buy you an ale?" the salt-and-pepper–haired man asked.

"I prefer mead," she replied sweetly.

"Stuie, one mead for the lady!"

Hippolyta perched on a bar stool, leaving one empty between her and the man at the bar. She took a sip from the mug she was handed and grimaced. Mead was always much too sweet for her palate.

"Where are you from?" the man asked.

"Lots of places," she said, shrugging. "But most recently from Hazeltown."

"Pfft." The man spluttered. "Townies are always saying how much the Valley is better than the mountains. I'm surprised you'd come here."

"I sell my wares wherever business is good," she explained. Hippolyta took another small sip of mead.

"Smart businesswoman," the man said, inclining his head towards her. Then he stooped back over his paperwork.

"What line of business are you in?" she asked.

"Tobin's our schoolteacher," Stuart chimed in. "Always grades his papers here since no kids are allowed."

"And the ale is cold and plentiful," Tobin added with a guffaw.

"Cheers," Hippolyta said, raising her mug. "Teaching is noble work." Tobin knocked his mug against hers.

Later when she was back at her stall, Hippolyta sat back, content with her progress. She had found out that the schoolteacher, Tobin, was a bachelor with no family and an ambitious apprentice. At least if she took him, there would be someone to fill his shoes at the school and not too many family members to miss him. Her targets needed to be forgettable. She didn't want to draw too much unwanted attention to their disappearances or else there might be prying questions and investigations. That was more trouble than it was worth.

Chatting with the young woman at the stall next to her who was selling wool and sheepskins, Hippolyta learned of the old shepherd who cared for the flocks on the east side of the mountain. His cabin was apparently very remote. There was no apprentice shepherd, and Hippolyta suspected there might be a family. This girl may have even been a granddaughter. However, the old man had lived his life. He was ripe for harvest.

"Does he allow visitors out to the pastures? I do love sheep," Hippolyta trilled.

"Oh, sure, ma'am. Old Crosby would love to get some visitors. He always says there aren't enough Cloudies interested in the sheep these days." The freckled young girl flashed her a crooked smile.

This was a great start. She had selected two of her prey. Hippolyta felt she needed at least three to get her, Kei, and the slimes through winter. In just a couple of weeks, the snow would start and eventually block the mountain pass.

Hippolyta was sizing up a plump teenage girl across the square when, all of a sudden, there *she* was. Hippolyta spotted her glimmering lilac robes from across the square. The familiar pale, oval face of Leonna floated above the plain, tanned faces of the townsfolk. She looked as though she had barely aged a day in the ten years since Hippolyta had last seen her. *Damn youth potions.* The sickening smell of gardenia thickened the air in Hippolyta's lungs, causing her to cough unintentionally. She could remember feeling smothered by the flowery odor in every class she had been forced to take with Leonna. The scent now seemed overpowering, even from meters away.

Despite Hippolyta's efforts, she could not stifle the coughs that were racking her body. Her coughing fit drew Leonna's unwanted attention, despite Hippolyta's efforts to control it. The shepherd's shopgirl rushed over as well with a skein of water.

"Are you quite well, ma'am?" Leonna cooed in her high voice.

"She took to coughing after visiting my stall," the shopgirl explained. "Maybe she's allergic to wool?"

"Not to worry, ma'am, I have just the thing," Leonna trilled, beaming. Uninvited, Leonna swooped behind the stall to Hippolyta's side.

Hippolyta's face was still half-hidden by her handkerchief covering her cough. She could not let Leonna see her face. Leonna would definitely recognize Priscilla.

Thinking quickly, Hippolyta faked a violent sneeze and cast a hasty curse upon herself that caused her face to swell as though in anaphylactic shock. As she pulled the handkerchief away, Leonna and the shopgirl both drew back in shock.

"Hurry, take this," said Leonna, placing a vial of violet liquid into her hand. Hippolyta took it compliantly, so as not to draw out the interaction. She knew there was a limited time before Leonna's tonic would take effect and reduce her facial swelling.

"I must go lie down," Hippolyta gasped.

"Yes, you must rest," Leonna agreed.

"I have a room at the Inn. Perhaps the girl can help me." She squeezed the shop girl's hand.

"I can help," the shopgirl agreed.

"Should I come look in on you?" Leonna asked.

"NO!" Hippolyta shouted. Then she cleared her throat. "No, I mean. You've already done so much. Thank you."

Leaning on the shopgirl, Hippolyta hobbled to her feet.

"What about your wares?" Leonna wondered.

"They're perfectly safe," Hippolyta said, waving her hand in dismissal.

"I'm sure they are, but I'll cast a protection spell just in case!" Leonna offered cheerfully.

From her room in the Inn, Hippolyta watched loathingly as Leonna waved her pretty arms gracefully around her stall. The ever-helpful witch had also instructed the shopgirl to feed and water her mule. *How dare she?* Hippolyta thought as her stomach churned.

Leonna's helpfulness had almost ruined all her plans. Now she would have to change the formula for her Priscilla transformation so that Leonna would not recognize her. She had spent so little time with the townsfolk, they were unlikely to notice the change in the droop of her nose or the thickness of her eyebrows. Leonna, however, never forgets a face. Hippolyta hoped it would be enough.

If Kei were here, he would warn her of the danger of fraternizing with an old schoolmate. Someone who was certain to recognize her. But Hippolyta could not let this chance go. This chance to turn the tables! Leonna would never see her coming.

That evening, Hippolyta worked diligently, preparing objects charmed to lure her chosen victims back to her lair. The slimes had not eaten in weeks, and Kei would be anxious for her to get back. For the schoolteacher, she enchanted an elegant quill she had crafted from a peacock feather. She would return to the pub until she met Tobin again and bestow it upon him as a gift. She doubted the man could resist Priscilla's charms.

Next, she cast her spell upon a handsome wooden staff that had been carved from the trunk of a black walnut tree. She had acquired the wood in Hazeltown and paid a fellow tradesperson to carve it, trading them a healing potion for their ailing child. The handsome staff would make an excellent gift for the hermit shepherd.

She thought for a while about how best to entrap Leonna, but then she had it. Leonna had always been a superstitious little witch, bedecking herself with amulets and lucky charms. Hippolyta had a fine collection of rabbits' feet, which had been dyed a myriad of colors. If there was only one lavender rabbit's foot on display, Hippolyta was sure which Leonna would choose. Leonna's goodwilled nature almost ensured she would come back to check on Hippolyta at her stall again.

After her preparations, she meandered out into the garden behind the inn. There was a large aspen tree that she could use to help send her message to Kei. She looked around to make sure no one had followed her outside, and then she sat at the base of the tree. She placed her hands against the trunk and could feel its life force within. She closed her eyes as she searched among its roots for the familiar energy emanating from the strands of fungi, which would help connect her back to the Woods.

The low hum of the mycelium vibrated in her blood. She sent a few pulses of energy out towards the Woods to let Kei know she was safe. It would take a while before he would sense the message and return one back. Hippolyta waited. The moon and stars seemed particularly bright up here in the mountains. She felt closer to the sky and further from the earth, where she felt most at home.

After awaiting a response for almost an hour, she tried again. Another long stretch passed with no reply. Her heart quickened. *They couldn't have*, she thought with panic. Her heart quickened, and beads of sweat formed above her brow. Hippolyta changed strategy and sent a vibration out to her slime molds.

She did not have to wait long for a reply.

They had been hungry. She had waited too long. *I should have killed the mule*, Hippolyta thought, sobbing into her hands. How could she have been so daft? She thought the slimes would still obey her since they had an understanding that she was coming back with more food. *My poor Kei.*

"This is all Leonna's fault," she hissed under her breath. "I-I-I would've reached out to Kei sooner if she hadn't disrupted my plans tonight," Hippolyta mumbled to herself. Leonna would have to pay. Leonna would have to suffer for Kei's death. Hippolyta could no longer abide this world with that flowery witch and her feeble powers. This was her chance to finish Leonna once and for all.

AUTHOR'S NOTE: To find out what happens to Leonna and Hippolyta, be sure to read "Darkbow: Death on Hollow Clouds" in the first installment of the What's in a Name? anthology series, *Once Upon a Name.*

Alex Stubblefield

Alex Stubblefield is a California based author with a full-time career in agriculture. From creative writing classes in school to journaling in her spare time, Alex has been weaving with words from a young age and continues to practice her writing skills in many areas of her life. When not writing, Alex enjoys snuggling her cats, tending her garden, and cooking up fancy meals with her husband, Josh.

Her short story 'Darkbow: Death on Hollow Clouds,' featured in the fantasy anthology *Once Upon a Name*, is her first published piece of fiction. Alex is working on her debut novel, and looks forward to bringing to life more stories in the future. To find out more, follow her writing journey on Instagram (@authoralexstubb)!

The Twin Ambers

Elena Shelest

SEPTEMBER 1596, HUTSUL SETTLEMENT, CARPATHIAN MOUNTAINS

In Yurko's twelve years of life, a real Cossack had never visited their remote settlement. A small crowd gathered around as the white-haired warrior rode through their homestead with a long saber on his hip. The man requested to speak with Yurko's grandfather, Stephan, and stayed in the main house all day. Anyone not old enough to carry a hatchet could not enter their meeting.

Yurko was curious, but Grandfather sent him to take care of the visitor's giant black mare. The stern patriarch never missed a chance to remind his grandson that he had to earn his keep. It seemed every time he looked at Yurko, the old man saw his wayward son-in-law, who everyone blamed for his daughter's untimely passing. With his sturdy build, jet black hair, and dark eyes, Yurko was growing up to look just like his father.

"I'll never *be* like him," he muttered.

The door creaked, and Yurko's twin sister Yana appeared at the entrance to the stables, a newborn lamb cradled in her arms. She always took care of helpless creatures, as if it would hide her own loss. Despite once sharing a womb, the siblings were very different. Yana was smaller and had light brown hair and bright amber eyes—his mother's eyes—that, at times, shone like gold. But unlike their mother's gentle gaze, his sister's always sparkled with mischief.

Yurko frowned above a pile of hay he was carrying. "Why aren't you in the house, helping with dinner?"

Yana pursed her lips. "I came to tell you a secret, and you're ordering me around!"

Yurko paused, pitchfork in hand. "What kind of secret?"

"They were talking about the Nalyvaiko uprising inside the house. I hid in the back storage room and listened." Yana spoke so fast, he could hardly follow. "The leader was killed. That's why the old Cossack came —to warn us. Now we might have to move because the king's troops will be searching for any runaways, including Uncle Ostap. They have a list of names and might go after their families. Then everyone was shouting that they won't submit to the Polish magnates, that they would rather form an *opryshky* brigade to keep them away from our fields, but Grandpa got mad about it."

Yurko stiffened. His father was a leader of such a brigade. He met his mother while on the run and hiding on her family's property. They had married against her family's wishes. Locals supported these high-waymen as they kept the rich landowners from venturing too far into the Hutsul lands, but that lifestyle was hardly fitting for a family. Yurko resented his father for choosing to die as an outlaw over remaining home with them.

"Grandfather will make sure we're safe," Yurko said, resuming his work.

Yana chewed her lower lip. "You won't leave me to go fight when you grow up, will you?"

Yurko frowned. "Never. Forget what you've heard."

But Yana was not so easily deterred. On the following morning, she caught up with Yurko while he was pulling the goat back into the corral.

"The Cossack has been gone all morning gathering herbs in the forest," she said. "Aunt Maria said he's a healer of some sort."

"So what?"

"Things have been upside down since he came. I just want to see what he has in his room."

Yurko narrowed his eyes. "You want to snoop? Your nosiness will get you into big trouble one day."

Yana huffed. "Don't be repeating Grandma. It's not like we'll take anything. One peek."

Yana seemed determined. He could either join or let her venture into their guest's room on her own, which was even worse.

Yana turned as they neared the door. "There is one more thing I didn't tell you. I met the Cossack before he left this morning. He said he knew our father and wanted to talk to us. That's why we have to check things out on our own."

Yurko followed Yana into the dim room, berating himself for going along. The small antechamber had an oven, several benches, and a table. It smelled of bitter herbs. Yana walked to the Cossack's belongings, which he set on the floor near the bed. Everything was out in the open: stacks of books, clothes, and a pile of strange containers.

Yurko gawked at the assortment of weapons on the wall. "See, he has nothing to hide."

Yana walked over to the bed and picked up a small bouquet of Ivan-da-Marya flowers. The bluish-purple petals at the top of the stems and brightly yellow lower ones looked freshly picked.

"Aren't these poisonous?" Yana asked.

"They can be harmful in excess, like a few other things in life." The Cossack's deep voice made the siblings jump and twist around. "Otherwise, this plant is good for healing wounds and calming the heart."

"W-we didn't mean to disturb you. We're leaving." Yurko grabbed his sister's hand. Closeup the man looked even more intimidating. Despite many wrinkles on his face, the stranger seemed robust enough to give them a thrashing.

"I was hoping you would stop by. I am leaving early in the morning and needed to talk to you, but you're hard to catch." The Cossack picked up one of the flowers from the floor. "Do you know the legend about Ivan-da-Marya?"

Yurko stepped in front of his sister. "Everyone has heard the story. Twin brother and sister, Ivan and Marya, did not want to separate, so they were turned into a flower."

"This is why the top is blue and the bottom is yellow." Yana pushed her brother out of the way, anticipation shining in her eyes.

"That's because they were torn apart for years," Yurko said. "When they finally met again, they pretty much died. I don't like this story."

"Long ago, this legend was a little different." The Cossack sat in a chair and twisted the stem between his fingers. "It was about a boy named Kupalo and his sister Kostroma. They were curious, just like you two. One day they ran into the field to listen to the beautiful song of two birds—Sirin and Alkonost, joy and sorrow. Kupalo listened to the song of sorrow as it was closer to his heart, and thus was stolen away into the underworld."

"Why are you telling us all of this?" Yurko demanded.

"Because you will need discernment in the future," the man said. "I promised your father to look after you."

"How do you know our father?" Yana asked, her voice eager.

But Yurko was annoyed, no—angry. Who was this person? Why did he want to talk to them about their deserter of a father and this stupid flower?

"Years ago, I traveled through the mountains, and your father became my guide," the Cossack replied.

"Our father is long dead," Yurko bit out. "And we hardly saw him even when he was alive. He should have been at home protecting us. We don't need your help."

"You're letting your pain speak, young man. Trust me when I say that you'll need support in the future. It would be foolish to decline. Here." The old man opened one of his satchels and placed two cherry-sized amber stones into Yana's hand.

She opened her palm. The golden light swirled within them, dancing as if a pair of firelights were trapped inside.

Yurko had never seen the ones so clear and polished.

"Pretty," Yana gasped.

Yurko frowned. He didn't need these useless trinkets.

"These two ambers came out of one ancient tree," the Cossack said. "They will always be drawn toward each other when separated. Keep them close, and you will find one another no matter what life throws your way."

"Give them back, Yana," Yurko ordered. "I'll never leave you."

"You will be her rock, unless like Kupalo, you let bitter feelings lure you away," the Cossack told him, then turned to Yana with a smile. "You have your father's inquisitive spirit and bravery. Still, you need your brother's steadfastness and sound judgment to stay on the right path. Draw on each other's strengths and don't let your differences separate you. Then you'll avoid the dangers ahead."

Yana thanked him for the gift and placed the stones in her pocket. Yurko didn't want the stranger's uninvited advice or any assistance that was linked to their father. They were doing just fine with relatives to care for them, and as long as Yurko lived, Yana would never be alone or destitute. Still, the Cossack's strange talk left him unsettled.

"I wouldn't let anything bad happen to you," he promised his sister when then stepped outside.

But from that day forward, a heavy stone settled inside his heart.

---

5 YEARS LATER

It was the spring shearing season, and everyone at the homestead was hard at work from morning until nightfall. Yurko's family had moved to a new place, rebuilt, and prospered. Everything they needed was within walking distance: a forest filled with timber and a sparkling river that ran through their green pastures. The only thing that worried Yurko was his sister's restless spirit. She often rode out for hours or explored the forest. Once, she tried to sneak out on the cart filled with the goods for the trip to the Halychyna. He covered for her absences then scolded her in private, and their constant sparring was exhausting.

The old Cossack's words got into Yurko's head, and the fear that something terrible might happen to his sister gripped him like a vice. After another one of Yana's disappearances, he decided to try a new approach.

"Give me one of the amber stones," Yurko demanded.

Yana arched an eyebrow. "I thought you didn't believe the man."

"I'm ready to believe anything if it'll help me know where you are. Having to spin fibs for you is getting tiresome."

Yana pursed her lips, petting the sheepdog at her feet. She named the furry monster Vatra, and it followed her everywhere since she'd mended its injured leg. "Why are you always so worried? Vatra can protect me."

"Why do I worry? Because... because you're the closest person I have left, and I don't want to lose you too!"

Yurko stormed off and stayed all day in the stables, dulling his frustration with work. He didn't come down for dinner. He wished his sister was more reasonable, like her meeker cousins, who spent their days making meals or weaving. The old Cossack said Yana had her father's inquisitive spirit, but the compliment made Yurko grind his teeth. Even in his death, that man wouldn't leave them alone, as if his ghost tried to lure Yana into the untamed forests of the surrounding mountains.

Yurko shook his head, horrified at his own thoughts.

Yana entered the stables and stood by the entrance. Even though his sister was strong of temperament, to him she looked fragile, in need of protection. Yurko grew tall and broad, his body hardened by physical labor, while she remained slender. If the need arose, how would she defend herself?

Yana must have read the gloomy thoughts on his face as her brow furrowed. "You worry too much, brother. Maybe this will ease your mind."

She came closer and opened her hand. Two amber stones glistened like liquid gold. Each had a hole now with a silky string looped through. Yana stood on her tiptoes and tied one around Yurko's neck with an impish smile on her lips.

"I don't need this little rock when I have a big rock like you to hide behind, but if this makes you feel better, I'll wear it all the time."

"Laugh all you want," he grumbled. "If you keep running away, I'll tie a longer string to your ankle and will give another end to Grandma."

"As if I don't own a knife to cut it." Yana stuck her tongue out and ran off.

Immediately, Yurko felt a pull from the amber stone.

After waiting for a few minutes, he followed the nudge and found Yana collecting chicken eggs in the shed.

From that day forward, he always knew where she was. For the first time, Yurko could relax, even if it bothered him to rely on something he couldn't explain. There were still wild animals and overzealous admirers, but at least Yana couldn't venture too far without his knowledge.

When a peddler stopped at the neighboring property, Yana ran off to look at the wares. Yurko didn't think twice about it.

"That man has so many interesting things!" Her eyes shone with excitement when she returned. "He traveled all over and has been to big cities, all the way to the Ottoman Empire. Can you imagine? I wish I was a peddler."

Yurko let go of the horse's hoof he was shoeing. "Peddlers are always separated from their families, and I doubt there's a place more beautiful than our mountains."

Yana pursed her lips. "Don't you get tired of seeing the same thing every day? Doing the same things?"

"No. I love our home, and I am thankful that we are provided for."

"Fine. But can you come with me, please? I've finished a new blanket. Maybe we could trade something for it."

Yana piled several blankets and a weaved basket into Yurko's hands. They walked through the fields to their neighbors' property, where curious locals gathered around a strange-looking wagon. It was made of carved wood, the roof covered by a dirty canvas. One side was open, displaying multiple shelves. A short man showed off his goods. He wore a robe with golden embroidery and a strange hat on his balding head. Yurko was surprised to hear him speak in the broken Hutsul dialect.

The peddler took his time looking over the blankets and praising Yana's work after she made her way to the front of the crowd. Yurko stayed close, glancing over the items for purchase. There were elaborate metal containers, strange tools, foreign weapons, and scarves made of the thinnest thread.

"You won't find this in Halychyna or even in Kyiv." The man unfolded a scarf so light that a gentle breeze picked it off the table. "This silk is from the Far East. The material is the best in the world."

An intricate pattern of trees, flowers, and exotic birds shimmered as the man moved his knobby fingers over the delicate fabric.

Yana clasped her hands. "Please, Yurko, could I have it?"

"I'm afraid what you brought isn't enough," the man said. "But I'm sure your bride deserves such a gift."

"Sister," Yurko corrected. "What do you want for it?"

"Bring me two new bridles for my horses, and then we'll talk. Bring your sister along too with more of her fine handiwork." With that, the man turned toward the next customer.

Once at home, Yana rummaged through her things and brought out several new rugs.

"Keep these," Yurko protested. "The man is already cheating me out of two sturdy bridles. Just take the blankets you showed him earlier."

"Thank you for doing this!" She hugged him and left, humming an upbeat tune.

The familiar sensation of the amber stone tugged inside Yurko. How easy it was to make his sister happy. He swore to never let her suffer as his mother did.

That evening, they loaded the horse and set out to meet the peddler. He had already packed his wagon and readied his horses for the journey.

"I'm glad you decided to come." He looked over the items Yurko and Yana brought, took out the scarf, and wrapped it over Yana's head. "Such a rare beauty hidden in the middle of nowhere. Come. Let me give you some of the Persian tea I just brewed to celebrate your fine purchase."

The man handed them two delicate cups. The dark liquid he poured in was sweet. A moment later, Yurko's vision blurred, and his head swayed. He threw a worried glance at his sister, who seemed unsteady too.

"Did you add spirits to the drink?" Yurko demanded.

The peddler's thin lips spread into a predatory grin. "Not a drop. But I did add a paralyzing potion."

Yana dropped to the ground like reaped grass.

Yurko launched toward her, but his movements were slow, as if treading water.

The man rubbed his unkept beard. "I should have used a bigger dose on you."

Yurko gritted his teeth and pushed forward, but his legs gave out from under him and sent him tumbling to the ground. The peddler lifted Yana into his arms and threw her into his wagon. Yurko growled, reaching for the hatchet at his belt his grandfather gifted, but his fingers were too stiff to grip it.

"I'll take that." The peddler picked up the weapon. "Beautiful handiwork. Just like your sister. She'll make me very rich at the slave market. Her rare eyes and beauty are worth a fortune. I'm willing to give up this trading route for such an opportunity."

"I... e-every... one... will... search," Yurko forced out.

"Not if I make it look like a bear attacked you, left you for dead, and only bloody pieces of clothes remained of your sister. I have plenty of fine dresses to give her instead." He leaned closer and sneered. "I'll take good care of her, don't you worry. She'll be happier in a place of luxury, a harem perhaps, than here with the unwashed herdsmen."

Yurko glowered. He had heard of slave raids that devastated settlements in the valley, but nothing of this sort had reached their home. How had he not recognized the danger? The Cossack thought Yurko could steer his sibling to the right path, but he failed to fulfill his duty and keep her safe. Had the old man known this might happen when he warned them? If only Yurko had told someone about the amber stones' ability so they could take it off his body and track her down, but it was too late now.

Yurko's vision blurred as the peddler raised the hatchet over him, but something knocked him off his feet. Vatra stood between the man and Yurko, its teeth bared in a growl, ready to attack again. The peddler backed away. The dog jumped, and Yurko fell into dark oblivion.

Yurko woke to Vatra licking his face. Bright sunlight made him squint, and his body was sore from lying on the ground. He stretched his legs, trying to remember what happened.

"Yana!"

Yurko jumped to his feet. The world spun and bile rose in his throat as he looked around. There was just Vatra barking and his horse grazing nearby. At least the man hadn't taken it. Maybe he had to run to escape the dog's sharp teeth.

"You saved my life." Yurko rubbed Vatra's ear, then whistled to his horse.

Everything around him swayed as if he teetered on a narrow plank. It took him a while to saddle. He leaned onto the stallion's neck to keep himself from falling over and listened to the pull of the amber pendant. The direction burned through him with urgency, but despite the fog in his head and worry in his heart, Yurko hesitated. He had no weapons or provisions for the journey. Even though the wagon was slower than riding on horseback, the peddler could have been traveling all night and was far ahead of him.

Clenching his jaw, Yurko sent the horse into a gallop toward home, Vatra following close behind. He came upon several of his cousins tending the sheep in the fields and explained what had happened. His relatives pressed food and weapons into his hands, then ran toward the house to gather the search party. Yurko didn't wait for them. There were only so many ways the wagon could get through the mountain passes, and several of his uncles were experienced trackers. They could follow his lead and catch up.

Thankfully, the amber's pull was still strong, and Yurko directed his horse without pause, over the endless hills and through the forest. As Yurko ventured deeper in, he wondered how the peddler took his wagon through the trees. Maybe the amber was showing him a shortcut? He nudged the horse forward but couldn't shake the feeling that someone was watching his every move. Finally, a dark cave hidden in the foliage blocked his way. He jumped off the horse and took one of the knives off his belt. Vatra stiffened and bared its teeth in a low growl.

"Where do you think you're going?"

Yurko twisted around and faced a man in his twenties with a rifle pointed at his chest. He was dressed in a simple but neat Hutsul outfit: wide, black trousers and a long shirt with an embroidered collar.

Yurko eyed the weapons hanging from the young man's leather belt. "I mean no harm, brother. If this is your land, let me pass through."

The stranger didn't lower the firearm. "It seems you've lost your way. Turn around and leave."

Yurko gestured at the cave. "My path lies through here."

"If you insist."

The young man smirked, then whistled. Several burly fellows jumped upon Yurko and pushed his face into the prickly carpet of pine needles, twisting his arms behind his back. Vatra's barks lessened to whimpered.

The young man who first apprehended him crouched in front of Yurko. "Why did you come here? Who sent you?"

"No one sent me! I'm just passing through, as I've told you."

"You're *passing through* right into our hiding place, really? I don't think so. Take him. We'll have to question him."

"No, please!" Yurko tried to dislodge the men who held him on both sides. "I have to go. I'm looking for my sister. She was taken last night. Let me leave! I'll do anything."

The young man halted, and the rest of his crew stopped dragging Yurko.

"Your sister?" He scratched the back of his curly head, displacing his felt brim hat. "How does she look?"

"She's got light brown hair and eyes the color of amber."

His captor grinned. "Those eyes are hard to forget, aren't they?"

Yurko's chest tightened. "You've seen her? Do you know where she is? If you've done anything to harm her—"

The young man put his hand up. "Relax. First, tell me who you are."

"I am her brother, Yurko."

"I've heard of you. My name is Oleksiy. Let him go. Come with me."

Yurko shook the dirt off his clothes and followed, wondering how this person met his sister.

Oleksiy stopped by the cave entrance. "I have to cover your eyes."

"Wait... why?"

He chuckled. "Because we aren't friends. Yet."

A piece of cloth was wrapped around Yurko's head, plunging him into darkness. Was it a mistake to trust these people? But what choice did he have?

He was led forward by the elbow. The temperature dropped and the air stilled, save for the echoes of their steps and the hollow clip-clop of his horse. They twisted and turned for a long time until the sun's warmth hit his face. When their procession stopped and the blindfold was removed, they stood in a clearing, with several temporary dwellings nested among the trees. Men moved about, cleaning their weapons, gathering wood for the fire, stirring food in the large cauldrons.

"Welcome to our lair," Oleksiy announced, his blue eyes smiling but sharp. "If you tell anyone, we'll find you and kill you."

He winked and sauntered ahead.

Yurko pressed his mouth into a hard line, dragging behind Oleksiy. This was no ordinary gathering, but a group of highwaymen. Yurko was right in the middle of the *opryshky* hideout—the last place in the world he wanted to be.

Familiar musical laughter rang through the air.

Yurko grabbed Oleksiy's arm. "My sister! Here? How?"

Oleksiy shrugged. "The peddler got the attention of our men. We usually let them pass and collect what's due for our people from the rich travelers. You know, the landowners and gentry who robbed us first."

"I know who you are and what you do," Yurko said. "What of my sister?"

"Well, the girl managed to free her bonds somehow and yelled for the entire forest to hear. Our people decided to investigate."

"And what of the peddler?"

"The poor bastard put up a fight and was sent to his Creator to answer for all his evil deeds." Oleksiy peeled Yurko's fingers off his sleeve. "Wanna go see her?"

He nodded, unsure whether to feel relieved or worried. Would these people let them go? Demand some sort of payment for all their trouble? He was certain Grandfather would be generous.

All his worries evaporated when he saw Yana adding spices to a cauldron filled with beet soup. A group of men gathered around her as she shared her suggestions on how to make it better, but food was the last thing on their minds. Oleksiy's eyes were on his sister too, a blush coloring his tanned face.

Yurko flexed his fists.

Yana gasped and ran toward him, throwing both arms around his neck.

He hugged her tightly, his throat tightening as her tears dampened his shirt.

"I was worried you got hurt," Yana sobbed. "That evil man kept saying that he killed you, but I didn't believe him. I felt you coming after me." She wrapped her fingers around the pendant on his neck.

"You knew?" Yurko asked.

Yana nodded and smiled, wiping her tears away. "But it doesn't mean you can follow me around all the time. Only if I get abducted again."

Yurko embraced her and kissed the top of her head. "I'll never let that happen again."

Oleksiy cleared his throat and beamed at Oksana. "I'd be happy to assist in the important task of ensuring your safety, especially during travels."

Yurko flexed his jaw and pulled Yana closer. "No."

Yana smiled, deepening his blush and Yurko's frown. "I'd feel much safer with such brave men looking after me. My family would be grateful too. Please, join us for a meal."

"Grandfather won't approve," Yurko whispered.

"I was saved from doom! We need to thank these people properly."

Their argument was forgotten as Vatra jumped into her arms. Yurko threw a wary glance at Oleksiy, who crouched next to Yana and said something that made her laugh. Even Vatra didn't mind him leaning close. It would be better if they left soon.

"I believe this belongs to you." A man in his forties walked over to Yurko and handed him the stolen hatchet. The stranger had the same blue eyes and dark hair as Oleksiy, the same strong features and broad shoulders. Both acted as the leaders of this brigade.

Would Yurko have joined his father too if he were alive? The thought twisted like a knife in his gut.

"Thank you," Yurko said. "For everything. But we should be on our way. Our family is worried." Yurko grabbed the hatchet, but the man didn't let go.

"May I ask where you got it from?"

"It was a gift from my grandfather for my sixteenth birthday."

The man chuckled. "So the old grouch kept it after all. He swore he'd never let you have your father's hatchet. Who knew our paths would cross like this?"

Yurko stiffened. "How do you know my grandfather and... father?"

"Your father and I were friends and comrades. I've met your grandfather once and not under the best circumstances. He never understood why your father wanted to throw himself into danger when he offered him to live peacefully in the wealthy homestead."

"I don't understand it either," Yurko said. "He had a family to take care of, but he left us."

The man put an arm on Yurko's shoulder, his face somber. "There is something you need to understand, lad. He loved you all very much, but he knew that you and your mother would be safer living with her family. And your mother was well aware Petro could never settle down to a life of comfort, but she still wanted to be with him, even if it was for a short time."

"She died of grief!" Yurko snapped.

He wanted to leave this place and never think of the past again. It hurt too much, and after nearly losing his sister, it was not something he was ready to face.

"Your mother died of illness. And yes, she missed your father terribly. We had a chance to talk a few times after his death. Everyone chooses their own path, whether you agree with it or not. Forgive your father for choosing one that took him away from you. His life didn't belong to him but to his people. He was willing to sacrifice it to lessen their suffering. Do you understand this?"

Yana wrapped her dainty hand around Yurko's arm. "I understand. Our father fought for what he felt was right, and our uncle did the same. Hutsuls will never bow to anyone but God."

The man chuckled. "Here is her father's daughter! Petro would've been proud of you both. Now, shall we go see your grandfather? Let's hope he won't try to chase me off his property this time."

That evening, Yurko's grandfather filled the tables with food and invited the highwaymen to partake of his meal. The *opryshoks* redeemed themselves in his eyes. Yurko also forgave his father. He still didn't agree with his decisions but no longer resented him. And after hearing more stories of his selfless bravery, Yurko began to see how his mother had fallen in love.

He also understood what the old Cossack had tried to tell them. Like Kupalo, Yurko chose to listen to the sad songs of sorrow and gave in to fear and bitterness. His overprotectiveness was like the blue-yellow flower—too much of a good thing that turned into poison. The truth was, he couldn't control other people or even some of the circumstances, but he could take responsibility for what was going on inside his heart.

Oleksiy and his father stood out from the crowd in their finer clothes. Yurko discovered that they were noblemen who'd switched sides to fight for the poor and destitute. During the meal, Yana had eyes only for Oleksiy. Yurko decided he wouldn't interfere, despite his concerns about the man's dangerous lifestyle.

Well—maybe he would interfere a little.

"Remember what you told me about the cave?" Yurko asked Oleksiy as he sat next to him at the table, lowering his voice so that others wouldn't hear.

Oleksiy tore his eyes away from Yana, who was laughing at something her cousin said, and patted Yurko on the back with a good-natured grin. "No worries. My father and your family came to an agreement. I trust you."

"Then I'll trust you too, but if you break this trust, I'll break your neck."

Oleksiy rubbed his chin, his smile widening. "I'm willing to risk my neck for your sister's amber eyes. I'll even move back to my father's estate like he wanted and sleep in my own bed instead of the cold forest ground to assure her lovely eyes always sparkle with laughter like they do now."

Yurko's shoulders relaxed, and he smiled back. "I couldn't agree more, brother."

They shook hands, and Yurko looked across the table at Yana. She put her hand to the amber stone on her chest and smiled. As he felt the gentle pull, Yurko knew that no matter where the road took them, they would always find each other.

Their twin ambers made that possible.

Elena Shelest

Elena Shelest is an author of contemporary and historical fantasy stories with lots of heart.

Be the first to read more magical stories about historical Ukraine, get inspirational messages, and find out about free books—sign up for the monthly newsletter: https://www.subscribepage.com/slavic_fantasy

FOR OSIAN

SARINA LANGER

Carys slowly licked the blood off her fingers. Moments like these were to be savored. Every little triumph over the destroyers brought Osian, her beloved brother, closer to peace. It wouldn't be the same once the blood was cold—still good, of course, just not the same. Osian deserved better.

The Wild Elves had given her the name Crimsonfist for the hearts she devoured, and she intended to be worthy of that title. She was their queen, after all. She had to lead by example.

It always surprised her that humans were still stupid enough to wander anywhere near her forest and plains. She hadn't exactly given the stragglers the chance to take back a message to the rest of their vile people, but even the dumbest animal eventually learned not to go where it hurt. More than enough humans had gone missing around these parts that they should have known better by now. That they still found their way here, usually out of curiosity and to make some kind of point about bravery, was proof that they deserved to be killed . . .

For that, and because her kingdom was crumbling at the foundations. Their once-beautiful cities were falling apart because of the war humanity had brought to their doors. Carys's magic kept up the barriers that protected her city from the humans. If they stumbled upon her kingdom anyway, they were trespassing. She wouldn't allow another tragedy to befall her people. Once, she would have loved to reopen the borders. Osian would have wanted her to. But he hadn't seen what she'd seen. As queen, she couldn't risk it. Better to focus on what she could do, and that was killing any humans who entered her protected city uninvited.

Besides, her elves always gave them a night to remember, if they lived long enough to find any pleasure in the memory. Every human who got lost in her kingdom was given a feast and hours of dancing. They had always enjoyed these things when time had still been young, so Carys figured it was a last mercy . . .

Until she couldn't stand the wait anymore. Until the humans couldn't move another step or had lost their minds and didn't know what was happening. Normally, she pulled them out of the celebration before their minds were too far gone or they didn't seem to feel any fear, either, and then where was the fun in that? These parties were meant to be celebrations, victory feasts to celebrate another win over their tormentors, their betrayers, their unworthy—

An elf entered the great hall. Yesterday, a lone human had stumbled into her territory. It had been a while, and perhaps Carys had gone a little overboard, but it had been so long. Once the human hadn't been able to stand upright, she had pulled him away from the dance floor and killed him.

How she lived for those moments.

Arawn, the goddess of vengeance, knew humanity had taken everything else from her, including her twin brother. Even her kingdom wasn't what it had once been, but her people? They were free. Not trapped and cowering in the shadows like the rest of their siblings and cousins. Her subjects had no need to fear her. She made sure they had everything . . . or what that was within her power to give. Peace with humanity? She had given up on that a very long time ago.

The elf cleared her throat. "Sorry to interrupt, my Queen, but we have spotted another human coming this way."

"Oh?" It had been too long since Arawn had blessed them with two kills so close together. "You know what to do."

She'd have to move, bathe herself and dress like the queen she was. Every celebration was so much more satisfying when the humans believed they were safe.

Like Osian had believed himself safe.

Then again, how many humans had been red with the blood of her brothers and sisters? How many had the humans killed? Carys would see to it that every human paid, no matter how long it took. She owed Osian that and so much more.

"There's something you should know, my Queen."

Carys raised an eyebrow and licked more blood off her hands. She'd finish what was left of the heart in her chambers. Just because they had another celebration to plan didn't mean she had to be wasteful.

"Then speak."

"The human isn't alone."

Carys's heart raced. Two humans? Perhaps even a whole group? She closed her eyes and inhaled the scent of blood. Arawn be—

"A male vampire is with her."

Carys stilled. "He must be using her as a blood vassal."

She hadn't ventured out of her kingdom in centuries, but from what she had gathered, some still practiced the old ways. Once, it had been every vampire, but then those idiots had as good as bent the knee to the humans and chosen to hide amongst their hated enemy rather than be free. But not her. Carys and her elves were free in their kingdom, sealed from the humans' view with powerful magic. Not that they'd needed much magic. Humans were so easy to mislead. And still, so many had chosen to—

They would all get what was coming to them.

"See to it that this hall is clean and prepared," Carys said. "I will get myself ready."

The elf inclined her head. "I will see to it personally, my Queen. What shall we do about the vampire?"

Carys smiled. "I'm sure he will see reason when the human's blood flows."

The elf nodded and left Carys to clean herself up.

She took her time finishing the heart, but she wouldn't be wasteful. She even left some in offering to Arawn, Nuada, and the Morrigan. Usually, she just prayed to Arawn for vengeance, but she was in a good mood today. Since there was more blood wandering into her halls, she felt she could spare the extra offering. Once she was done eating, she luxuriated in her bath under the sun. She always bathed outside. The rainwater was cleansing, and the sunshine charged the water with so much joy that even Carys couldn't stay upset for long. Instead, it gave her the energy to push onwards. Until Osian was avenged.

She took her time getting dressed. How long had it been since someone other than a human had walked into her territory? She didn't remember. Perhaps the vampire brought the human as a present, but what might he want? Perhaps he had grown tired of living with the enemy. Yes, that had to be it. He wanted to return to the old ways and ask for a place in Carys's court. The human was a very fitting gift. Her lands weren't what they had once been, but there was always room for another ally and maybe, if he knew the human world so well, he could help lure more humans to her. That would make his joining her court very worthwhile. Something like that deserved her best finery—a dress she'd received as a gift for her coronation. She hadn't worn it in centuries, but then she hadn't had anything to wear it to.

Someone knocked. She looked herself over one more time and, pleased with her appearance, opened the door. One of her elves greeted her.

"So impatient." Carys smiled. "I don't blame you. I feel the shift in the air, too."

But the elf looked . . . baffled? How unexpected. "The human wishes to speak with you, my Queen."

Carys frowned. "The human does? Not the vampire?"

The elf nodded. "He looks calm, but . . . I think he's protecting her, my Queen."

Now this was preposterous. Vampires didn't protect humans.

And humans did not make demands of her.

"I will join you shortly. Please see to it that our guests have all the food and drink they could want."

The elf nodded and hurried off toward the hall.

Just because the human had dared ask to speak with her, Carys would be petty and take another moment. This was her court. She refused to let some human decide what happened when.

After half an hour, she sauntered toward the hall. Usually, she greeted humans with fake smiles and pretend warmth, but for what this prey had dared, she would appear every bit the superior ruler. No human was anything next to her. She would make sure her guest remembered that before she tore this stupid girl's heart out.

Carys took a deep breath to calm herself, then opened the grand doors and sauntered into the hall. By now, the human should have had a serene look in her slightly glazed eyes—a first effect of their food and drink; human minds didn't respond well to magical foods—but this girl looked all too lucid. And the atmosphere in the hall was . . .

Tense.

Her elves were never tense around humans. Not since the war. They had stayed in their kingdom, put up their barriers, specifically so no elf would ever have to fear humanity again.

The woman and the vampire sat at the table, their food untouched. Even the vampire hadn't taken a bite. Carys assumed he hadn't touched his wine, either, even though her servants had spiked it with blood—she smelled the iron tang from the other side of the table. What vampire refused blood? Perhaps she was missing something that would make this absurdity make sense. Maybe the vampire was playing some game to trick the human into a false sense of security? Surely that had to be it.

"By what great fortune have you walked into my court today?"

She enunciated everything sharply, using her voice as a knife to make the first fine incisions. It wasn't blood she wanted to draw just yet. She would cut the threads of the human's nerves, leave frayed edges all over her mind, until she was too afraid to do anything but obey.

But the human blushed, and the vampire smiled at her.

"We, erm . . ." The human cleared her throat. "We wanted to camp."

"We didn't realize we were intruding," the vampire said. "I only sensed the magic when Esta here told me there was a whole city ahead."

Carys scoffed. "Excuse me?" No human saw through the barrier until her elves led them into the hall. What would be the point if anyone could just see through it? "Humans cannot see through our magic."

The vampire chuckled. "I'm afraid your magic didn't stand a chance against hers."

Carys willed her hands to stop shaking. If this woman—she refused to use her name—saw through the magic, then she couldn't be human. There was no other explanation.

But her elves knew the difference. If she wasn't human, her elves would never have prepared another feast.

Carys forced herself to breathe evenly. "You must have traveled far to reach my lands. Please, help yourselves to the food. My best chefs prepared a celebration when we spotted you nearby. It's so very rare we get visitors."

The woman looked at the vampire, and he had the nerve to shake his head.

"My apologies," he said, "but I can't allow it. You know as well as I do that the food would drive her mad."

"How dare you suggest—" Carys cleared her throat. "Music, please!"

Her musicians began to play at once. So what if this human could resist the food? No one resisted the incredible skill of her best musicians. Magic sang along with every note—old magic. The human would not leave her court alive.

"Starve yourself if you must," Carys said. "Sit in silence if that's what you wish, or perhaps join my elves for a dance"—the vampire shook his head at the human again—"but I would like a word with you, vampire. In private."

"Please, my name is Leverett. And there's nothing I might discuss that Esta can't hear as well. We don't keep secrets from each other."

Carys sneered. "Her blood must be special to control you so. You are guests in my court. Surely a word in private isn't too much to ask?"

Leverett whispered something to the human. Carys had half a mind to end it right there, but she needed answers first. She had a feeling Leverett wouldn't be so forthcoming if she hurt his human before she had answers.

The woman nodded, and Leverett touched his forehead to hers. Like they were in *love*. Carys's stomach turned at the thought. Her twin had been in love, too, and it had meant less than dirt to that human. That monster had destroyed Osian in more ways than one.

Finally, Leverett stood, turned to fog, and reappeared in front of her. Carys took him to the side until she was positive the human wouldn't overhear.

"Thank you for hosting us," Leverett said. "We didn't expect—"

"Stop right there. I don't want to hear it. How is this human controlling you? Why are you protecting her?"

Leverett looked taken aback, but only for a moment. "Because I love her."

Carys pushed down the bile. One of their own, with a destroyer? She had made the right choice to keep her court away from those filthy, lying murderers.

"Oh, please," she spat. "I don't believe you. Is it her blood? Stay with us and we will share our victory feasts with you. I'll even let you kill her with me. It'll break whatever foul spell she has put on you."

His eyes darkened. A dangerous glint entered them. "Threaten Esta again and I will end you."

His teeth extended just enough to show his fangs. His nails length-ened too.

He had threatened Carys in her own court.

"Do you really believe," he growled, "that any human could work a spell strong enough to control a vampire? Does your hatred for them run so deep that you can't think straight?"

"I—" She wanted to throw insults at him, but what he said . . . *Did* she believe that? Her kind was superior. Elves, vampires, mermaids, elementals—they were all superior to humans. Of *course* no mortal could control them. But that meant—"You genuinely love her?"

Leverett nodded with a smile. "She is everything to me."

Carys glared at him. "How could you betray your own kind like this?"

His smile disappeared. "The war was a terrible thing. No one will argue with you. But it was a very long time ago. The times are changing. Not every human wants us dead."

Carys scoffed. "You are deluding yourself." She looked past him, and a smile spread on her lips. "It doesn't matter now. Your human belongs to us."

Leverett shot around just in time to see the woman fall into a dance. He flew over to her, begged her to stop, but it was no use.

"She will dance until her feet bleed and she collapses from exhaustion. You should have let her eat our food. It would have masked some of the pain."

But Leverett ignored her. He reached for the woman's wrist, but she danced out of his grasp. He said her name, over and over, but she didn't hear him. All she would hear now was the music.

Carys relaxed. She didn't know how this human had seen through their barrier, but their magic had conquered her weak human mind in the end.

Leverett took the human's hand, put one arm around her waist, and danced with her. Carys huffed. It wouldn't have the same effect on him, but if he wanted one last dance with this vile creature, she supposed she could allow it. It was more than Osian's *lover* had granted him.

Except, Leverett didn't look worried. He touched his forehead to the human's again, and the human *stopped* dancing.

Carys marched over to them and grabbed a knife off the table. "*What did you do!*"

"Put that knife away before I ram it up your throat," Leverett hissed. "I warned you what would happen if you hurt her."

It was hard to stay calm. Twice now he had threatened her. She could kill the human easily enough—one flick of her wrist, and an archer would take her out in one clean shot—but the vampire wouldn't go down as easily. Her elves would try to protect her, and he would likely kill a dozen or two before they overwhelmed him. Carys hated the idea of letting some human go, but she hated the idea of sacrificing her elves because of this woman even more. No more elves would die because of humanity.

"It's okay, Lev," the woman said. She sounded dazed, like she was still coming out of the music's magic or the vampire's coercion, or whichever was affecting her more. "I don't blame her."

Carys spat at her. "A human who doesn't blame us for something? What a treasure you are!"

That Leverett still had his arm around her to help her stand made Carys sick. Once, none of the elder races would have treated humans with such kindness. Had so much time passed that none remembered the mountains of corpses? She hadn't forgotten. She still saw it all.

"I saw the war in a nightmare," the human said. "Or some of it, anyway. I don't blame you for being scared."

"*Scared*? How dare—"

"Esta and her sister have been helping the Veiled. She doesn't—"

"Don't you dare speak that name in my presence! *We are not the Veiled*. You cowards hide amongst the enemy! You work for them!" Carys sneered. "Apparently, you even bed them. It's no miracle our kind is dying. You've forgotten your place. You've forgotten what they did to us. But not my elves and me. Those of us who are left remember the war."

How could this human possibly have seen any parts of it in a dream? And Leverett vouched for her! Whatever dark magic this woman had used to convince him, it wouldn't work on Carys. She wouldn't let it. She didn't want to let this human go, but with Leverett so stupidly, *humanly* doe-eyed for this stupid girl, she didn't see a way of killing the woman without losing her own people in the ensuing fight.

It wasn't worth the bloodshed.

"Is that why you're here?" Carys glared at them. "Because you think we need your *help*?"

Like there was anything a mere mortal could do. What did it matter if she was special somehow? She was still only human.

The woman shook her head. "We honestly didn't know you were here until we arrived. We really did come to camp."

"And I'm supposed to believe that?"

"Well," Leverett said with another infuriating chuckle. "I believe you surmised for yourself what we were going to do."

"Get out," Carys hissed.

The woman blinked. "You're letting us go?"

"Don't think for one second that it will change anything we do here. You humans are monsters. As you leave my kingdom, take a good look at every cracking wall, at every broken roof, at every tear in the magic. It's all your fault."

Leverett pulled the woman away, but she paused and turned to Carys. "You say you're not like the Veiled, that you'd never hide like they do, but the magical barrier you've put up keeps you just as hidden as a simple glamour disguises wings. You're hiding too. And the state of your kingdom?" The woman gave her a sad smile. "You could fix it all, if only you took down the barrier and opened your city to trade again."

Carys watched dumbfounded as Leverett left with an arm still around the woman. No mortal had ever dared accuse her like this. Of course, no human had ever lived long enough. None had ever had the chance to talk to her this long.

No human had ever seen the city–and left again–like this one had, or the horrors of their war.

It haunted her how right the woman was. How sympathetic she looked to her people's pain. If Carys took down the magical barriers, if everyone applied glamours to hide their pointed ears, their wonderful city could thrive once again. Once, centuries ago, her closest advisor had suggested a similar thing: to not even bother with glamours but to simply claim it was part of this city's tradition and charm that everyone pretended they were elves. But to pretend their heritage wasn't really theirs . . . Carys had him killed. Had offered his heart to Arawn as well as to Osian, as proof that she still did anything she had to if it kept her people safe. But now . . .

How marvelous it would be to see her city thrive again. In truth, she had thought so many times over the centuries, but she had never deemed it worth the incalculable risk.

She couldn't remember the last time a human had looked at her without fear. Carys had never given them the chance. But even after her musicians had spelled the woman, even after she had recovered against all odds and realized what might have been, she hadn't shown fear. She said she understood. Carys didn't believe it—no human could understand—but she had never expected a human to communicate so . . . honestly, as much as it pained her to admit.

An odd feeling came over her as clouds briefly covered the sun. Carys was tired. Her hatred was still there and she doubted it would ever go away, but it *was* exhausting. They used to share this forest. And weren't vampires usually good judges of character? He'd said this woman and her sister fought *for* the cowards. Had that ever happened before? A human fighting for the elder races?

Would she have cared enough to pay attention?

Carys followed Leverett and Esta outside. She looked over her dying city. How much longer could they last if nothing changed? Everything she'd done, she'd done for her people. For Osian. They deserved better than permanently being reduced to man-eaters. They had *been* better, once. If there was a chance her kingdom might be restored, that her people might be glorious again.

Carys thought Osian would have wanted her to see that future, that a part of her wanted to see it too, and she wouldn't admit to anyone, certainly not a human, that she *had* been scared. This was the future her twin would have wanted.

She could—she *would*—do this. For Osian.

Sarina Langer

Sarina Langer is a dark fantasy author of epic and urban paranormal novels who lives with her partner and daughter (read: their cat) in the south of England.

She's as obsessed with books and stationery now as she was as a child, when she drowned her box of colour pencils in water so they wouldn't die and scribbled her first stories on corridor walls. ('A first sign of things to come', according to her mother. 'Normal toddler behaviour', according to Sarina.)

In her free time, she reads magical stories with dark plot twists, plays video games, and loves a good breeze. She has a weakness for tea, tarot cards, and pretty words (*specificity*, anyone?).

If you liked her short story and want to read more, check out her series-starter box set: https://books2read.com/worldsofshadowsmythsandmagic

Join her mailing list for free books and monthly updates: https://www.subscribepage.com/sarinasbooks She'd love to have you on board.

TO FIND A QUEEN

SKY SOMMERS

"Where may I find Gretel?" a raven-haired man asked a young girl ushering customers into The Graceful Duchess. He flicked nonexistent lint off the arm of his black velvet suit, and his nostrils flared as he regarded the simple wooden sign of the restaurant.

"I'm Greta, actually," the petite girl said as she craned up and smiled toward the vicinity of his chin. "Welcome to The Duchess, the best and only restaurant of Borough. Do come in, have a seat. The menu will float to you shortly."

Nefarious inclined his head, eyeing the girl's fiery hair. "You're Gretel Crimsonlocks?"

"Still Greta and it's Goodall," the girl smiled.

"You're married?" He paled.

"Not that it matters in terms of feeding you, but no," Greta said. "What'll it be, mister?"

"Whatever you recommend," Nefarious said, swatting away the hovering menu. "Where are the . . ."

"Past the mirror in the hallway, at the back," Greta said and sped off toward the kitchens.

Nefarious had to bite back his order for her to curtsey and address royalty, as per etiquette. He was here incognito.

He spotted a familiar, ornamental silver-framed mirror in the hallway. The elven king had one just like it at the palace. Nefarious tapped the surface and it wobbled once then showed him a tired-looking brunette.

Nefarious hissed, "You were mistaken. That is not Gretel Crimsonlocks, the most feared dragon queen!" He glanced behind him to check that nobody else was around. "That's a bar wench."

"Bar wenches can turn into queens. This one will. It's in her blood. Her older sister Ella is now a princess," the woman in the mirror said.

The elf pinched his nose. "If her relatives are royalty, why is she a pariah serving tables in a roadside tavern? I thought you would send me to a palace to fetch a lady of great standing. I'm in the wrong place, Morgana!"

"Not fetch, but steal, you mean? And I didn't send you to steal. That was all your idea. As it happens, you're a tad early. So, you're not in the wrong place, but at the wrong time."

"I see that! What is she, fourteen?"

"Sixteen."

Nefarious huffed. "The dragon queen I seek was a fair bit older and wiser."

"All older and wiser queens were once sixteen. Take it from *the* Fairy Queen who knows," Morgana said from the mirror.

The elf smirked, glancing at Greta, who circulated among the customers. "It does warm my heart that Eddie will get a much-used human woman for his concubine. If he gets her. We can use the information on Gretel's past indiscretions against Eddie and the dragons if . . . things fail."

"Past indiscretions? She's sixteen!" Morgana huffed.

"And she's a bar wench."

"Don't measure her by your own promiscuity," Morgana leered.

Nefarious narrowed his eyes. "I'm still not convinced she's *the* Gretel Crimsonlocks."

"The auburn hair . . ."

"Can come out of a bottle," the elf said. "Maybe you're purposefully steering me wrong, so I would eliminate some wench for you and then you'll go, 'Oopsie, wrong person!'"

Morgana rolled her eyes. "You are where you need to be, just maybe not when you wanted to be. Or would you prefer to go and try your luck when she's already Queen? There'll be no mistaking her *then*."

Nefarious pursed his lips. "The whole point of this escapade is to prevent her rise to power with the dragons. To prevent Goldencrest from becoming the first Dragon King. Answer me this, Fairy Queen. Is this the future Queen Gretel Crimsonlocks or is this all your fae trickery?"

Morgana sighed. "Where is Queen Gretel Crimsonlocks supposed to have come from, as per your dark elven lore?"

"The Magic Kingdom."

"Well, that's where you are right now. The fact that she's the only one named Greta, a variation of Gretel in this dimension, is a dead giveaway."

"Yes, but if I'm in the right place at the wrong time, how am I supposed to fulfill my mission? I can't just live here for years and years, waiting for things to happen so I could prevent them from happening. I'm leaning toward my original idea of eliminating her."

"Pfft . . . What's the fun in that? Why don't you woo her away before Eddie and Gretel even meet?" Morgana suggested.

"Woo her?" The dark elf gulped.

"Yes, woo. She is going to be a formidable queen one day. Why kill her? Why give her to your dark elven king? Snare her for yourself. Maybe with her by your side, you, the seventh cousin to the king, can become someone of higher standing?" Morgana crooked a smile as Nefarious straightened.

"Not kill her? Wed her? Become the king?"

"Unless you want to leave her to your king and have him prosper instead," Morgana said.

Nefarious threw a glance at the girl bussing tables in the restaurant, adjusting white linen cloths here, laying a hand on a customer's shoulder and laughing with them, waving her hand at the kitchen door, and directing the soaring dishes to the tables. "That child of sixteen looks . . . adequate."

Inside the mirror, Morgana laughed. "You'll have to come up with better adjectives if you are to woo her."

"I don't need to woo her," Nefarious said. "Females always succumb to my charm."

"Well, if you plan to start the wooing sooner rather than later, make sure to stay out of the way of her twin," Morgana said and switched her mirror off.

"I'll start the wooing right now, thank you very much," Nefarious said and exited the restaurant without a backwards glance at Greta. It wasn't until the doors had swished shut that the words of the Fairy Queen caught up to him. "Twin? She has a twin? Morgana *sicced* me on the wrong girl!"

<hr>

Nefarious had to wait until midnight to catch another glimpse of the girl. Who knew abduction business was mostly waiting? It was midnight when Greta finally stepped outside, and she was hauling a basket of trash and using her foot to push the back door open. How very unladylike. *And this is the famous future dragon queen? Not if I can help it!*

157

Nefarious opened his mouth to accost the girl, except she ignored him. When she opened the lid of the green container and upended her basket, there was a faint squeak and a raccoon darted out, almost knocking her over.

"Oy, how did you get in there? The thingamabob is supposed to be airtight!" she mumbled.

They both watched the coon scamper off. The girl emitted an unladylike yawn. "Finally. Sleep."

Nefarious separated himself from the wall and stepped closer and the shadows underneath his boots moved. "Come here," he said, attempting to grab Greta's shoulder. Seconds later, he found himself face down on the ground with his wrist in her grasp. "I knew it! You *are* Gretel Crimsonlocks!" Nefarous's excitement was muffled by the grass.

"Still Greta Goodall," Greta said through gritted teeth.

"But you have warrior reflexes."

"Yes, thanks to my brother teaching me how to defend myself against creeps like you!" Greta said.

"Brother? You have a brother? Nobody ever mentioned a brother!" Nefarious was annoyed, vowing to twist the necks of his spies for doing shoddy research.

"You mustn't be from around here." Greta held him firmly. "Here everybody knows and fears Hans. I'm sure he'll be pleased to make your acquaintance."

According to the annals of the dark elves, Gretel Crimsonlocks never had a brother. He had the wrong girl. Probably. Their annals were sketchy on all things dragon, since the species was secretive and in hiding.

"So, you're not the dragon queen?" Nefarious blurted.

"Dragon queen? I'm not a dragon!"

"You don't need to have dragon powers originally. You can just marry one, you idiot girl," Nefarious enlightened her and bit his lip. *I really shouldn't have said that.*

"I don't know any dragons! Now. Mind. Your. Manners. Apologize!" Greta spat out, tightening her hold and in the process nudged the trash container with her hip.

There was a wild skirmish as Nefarious tried to reach for his wand

and get away all at the same time. He yanked, her grip loosened, and he was finally able to slither from her grasp.

The raccoon peered at them from the top of the container.

Nefarious took a step back, stuck a hand in his wand pocket, and willed himself away into the nearby copse of trees. From the safety of the forest a few hundred yards away, he observed the girl wave her finger at the raccoon, look around, throw her arms in the air, and march straight back into the restaurant.

So much for wooing.

THE DARK ELF RUBBED HIS WRISTS AND CONTEMPLATED HIS options. *That did not go as expected. Why didn't my summoning powers work?* Even with Morgana's tips, he wasn't sure he had the right girl. This Greta seemed to have more brawn than brains. *To overpower me! Me!* Then again, he was looking for a warrior queen.

The wench said she didn't know any dragons, which was good news. She hasn't met Eddie yet! Still, it was strange. With elves, the wooing at aristocracy level took a while. After the abduction, it took time for the bride to stop screaming and then more time for her to come to her senses and abandon any thought of escape. They usually started being nice to the dark elf if they wanted to eat, and eventually, there was a yes in front of the sacred altar. Dragons might be simpler, of course. Eddie in particular.

Is she the right person or is she not?

Fairy Queen Morgana had mentioned a twin at the very last minute. The elven annals never mentioned Gretel having a twin. They didn't mention her background at all, as if before she became queen, she had never existed. He might be here at the wrong time, but Morgana had been convinced the meeting was due any day now.

Maybe he should stick close to Eddie to make sure they never met. As for the twin—in case Greta wasn't the right girl after all—he needed eyes on the ground.

There was movement in the underbrush and Nefarious inhaled sharply. A critter peeked up with telltale bandit stripes across its eyes. That raccoon again. It squeaked and attempted to slink back, but Nefarious whipped out his wand and the animal froze like deer in front of the huntsman.

"You," Nefarious said and smiled. *The girl has a kind heart and a penchant for animals. This could be useful.* "She would never suspect an animal spying on her." He blasted the racoon with a slew of peat sparks. "Follow Greta and report to me. Everything she does. Everyone she sees. Especially if she sees her twin sister. Or a dragon called Eddie. Understand?"

The animal nodded while its paws lived a life of their own, performing washing motions.

"Repeat what I said, so I know you understood me correctly," Nefarious ordered.

The creature chittered but didn't get very far until the elf put up his hand. He blasted the animal with his wand again. "In human speak. Now, tell me."

"Fol-low girl. Tell you what I see," the animal rasped, its vocal cords not adapted to human speech.

"When she sees her twin, tell me immediately!" Nefarious reminded.

The raccoon nodded.

"If you have anything to report, just find a safe place and say, 'Nefarious Russelbulb the Seventh . . .' and then I'll find a way to contact you."

The raccoon looked at him reproachfully.

"Too complex? Fine. Just say, 'Master, I have news.' Can you do that?'

The animal did a quick headshake and repeated, "Mas-ter, I have news."

"And don't let her catch you talking either," the elf admonished. "As for an excuse to wheedle into her confidence if she does spot you tailing her—suit yourself. She mustn't suspect a thing! Now, shoo!" The elf made an imperious gesture and pocketed his wand.

There were smarts in enlisting an animal. The wench would never suspect a hapless critter spying on her. Now that his spy was in place and hopefully the twin situation would soon become clear, he could go after Eddie. All he had to do was find the enchanted border to the Dragon Realm, cross it, and ingest a potion to disguise himself as local flora. He would have to position himself somewhere Eddie and the other princes frequented. Where seven giant multi-headed dragons could land. Eddie had six heads, but reportedly, the eldest prince had twelve. It'd have to be a vast plain that could accommodate all of them. Maybe he could concentrate only on Eddie? Dragons were rumored to be possessive. If one of the other princes met Gretel first, Eddie would probably never get to wed her. Decided, he would keep an eye on Eddie so as to witness the meeting with his future queen.

Nobody would suspect a giant foul-smelling plant of spying, would they?

One week later, Nefarious could have sworn women were the cause of all ills. Women and dragons. The blasted raccoon spy hadn't surfaced. Probably defected to the girl and her twin's side. What was worse, his clever stinky plant disguise hadn't worked. One of Eddie's six heads had taken a whiff and gobbled him up. Now, he was nestled in the belly of a dragon. The only thing that warmed his black heart was that his existence was giving Eddie the indigestion of a lifetime for three days in a row. Nefarious aimed another poke at the wall of the flower he had conjured around himself and hoped it reached the dragon's innards.

One would think that a dragon wouldn't touch a six-foot carnivorous flower that emitted a carrion-like stench? Any sane, normal dragon, that is.

Well, Eddie wasn't normal or sane. He had gobbled the plant Nefarious had been hiding in after one whiff.

One would also think a normal dragon would spit out food that was awful for his taste buds.

No such luck.

And now, three days later, here they were.

Eddie had indigestion and Nefarious had no idea how he was going to get out of . . . well, Eddie.

Nefarious had made his presence known. In the abstract. Never quite introducing himself—maintaining proper etiquette and bowing in the belly of the dragon was rather tiresome, not to mention pointless. Thus, he had merely mentally alerted the dragon that there was a sentient being in his bowels that needed to be let out immediately.

The reply couldn't have been more insulting.

His escape options were to be digested, pooped out, or burnt to a crisp upon regurgitation.

He couldn't use his wand, seeing that his arms were glued to his sides, and he didn't want to open his mouth to cast a spell without getting any bit of the foul-smelling plant anywhere inside.

So, they had both run out of options.

None of this would have happened if he wasn't under strict orders from his king to find and disarm Queen Gretel Crimsonlocks at any cost. Idly, Nefarious considered Morgana's warnings that he had been in the right place at the wrong time to meet Gretel. That's why there was no Gretel to meet. Yet.

But there was an Eddie.

And, by the feel of it, Eddie was taking flight.

Where is the stupid dragon going now and how far from meeting his queen is he? Of all the wicked women, why'd he have to go after some unknown girl?

Nefarious tried to hold on to the slimy walls of the stinky flower. The chance to keep to his dignity was long gone, seeing as his pristine black velvet suit was probably ruined from being encased in the green goo of Eddie's innards for three days. Well, at least the plant was dead.

The dragon's flight was rhythmical. Nefarious found himself nodding off to the steady rocking and faint swish of the wings he could hear even from the inside of his double prison.

Nefarious woke up to the sound of Eddie's voice rumbling through the dragon's body. How long had he been asleep?

Nefarious strained to hear. The sounds Eddie was making were reaching him as if he were underwater—echoing syllables in slow motion.

"Twins."

That was a word he recognised.

Wait, had Eddie finally met up with Gretel Crimsonlocks, Greta's twin?

"Help."

That's another word he recognised.

Was Eddie seeking help on how to get him out of here?

"Cut."

They were going to cut at Eddie?

Nefarious could have shrugged if it weren't for too tight quarters. One less dragon to worry about. More importantly, if they dispatched Eddie, he wouldn't have to worry about him marrying Gretel Crimsonlocks. Worry, over. Mission, accomplished.

The walls of his quite voluntary prison started to shake due to what felt like an earthquake.

It took Nefarious a while to realize Eddie was laughing.

Laughing at the threat of being cut?

Oh, well. This dragon had never been sane to begin with.

The girl Nefarious needed was outside. He hoped. If he didn't locate and disarm Gretel, he could never go back to his dark elven kingdom of Windermere.

"There would be no coming back from that kind of shame," Eddie said in a low whisper, echoing Nefarious' thoughts.

That seemed to be a sobering thought for everyone, as nothing happened for quite a long while until the earthquake.

The elf felt the dragon's insides lurch left and tumble to a standstill. It was a strange, steady swaying. There was no noise but the whoosh of air in and out of Eddie's lungs. Thankfully, all six of his heads had stopped talking.

Had Eddie . . . fallen asleep?

In fact, it was so quiet, Nefarious could now hear the humans outside. He perked up his ears.

"He's asleep?" A female voice said. Nefarious wasn't sure, but it sounded like the bar wench. "But he said he had indigestion! Never mind. Now all we have to do is tell Mister Plant to climb out."

Mister plant? Are they referring to me?

"How do you propose we tell him? Our telepathic conveyor is fast asleep," a low male voice said.

Great, there is a man out there I will have to contend with, vying for the affections of the twin sisters. At least he hoped there was a twin sister nearby.

Eddie emitted a powerful snore.

I better go out and deal with it.

Nefarious summoned his willpower and projected into the mind of whoever was listening. "I can hear you, you know."

"Everyone's a telepath these days?" The female voice grumbled and then whispered directly into his mind, "Well then, you already know what you have to do. You have to exit while the dragon is asleep so as not to get fried in the blast. Start climbing back the way you went down."

The gall of that woman, telling him—an elven prince—what to do!

Stifling his ire, Nefarious climbed out the way he had gone in, which was no picnic. In the last effort at freedom, he pushed against Eddie's tongue with his feet and slithered out of one of the maws, falling to the grass below.

The head he had just exited snorted and licked its nose as Eddie slept on.

Nefarious ambled to stand up, dripping slippery green goo.

"Mister Plant? You're Mister Plant?" It was the wench. Her eyebrows shot up to her hairline as Nefarious took stock of the red-headed warrior by her side. Nefarious also spotted a boy child writing something in a leathery book and dismissed him. Children attempting their first scribblings were no threat to elves. He noticed the raccoon frozen on the porch and arched his eyebrow.

Standing on the porch of a hut, the raccoon promptly lost its bladder. Nefarious smirked. *Be afraid, be very afraid, you traitor. No matter, I'm here now.*

The twin sister was nowhere in sight. Nefarious spotted chicken legs under the hut.

A witch's hut? Is Gretel Crimsonlocks a witch? Is that why the dark elves needed to fear her?

He couldn't ask outright where she was, else they would all get suspicious, but he had to find out.

His gaze returned to the warrior. He was tall, muscular and had weapons strapped to his chest and back. Although Nefarious had his wand, it was somewhere in the nether regions, below all the goo. Diplomacy it would have to be in the first instance. And it better not fail.

"Actually, I'm Nefarious Russelbulb the Seventh. As in the seventh cousin to the ruling elven king of Windermere. Of the Dark Territories, of course." He bowed.

"Mister Russelbulb . . ." the girl started.

"Nefarious to you, dear lady," he said, expecting no introduction from her, but for her to introduce the warrior. The girl did no such thing.

She is no queen. This wench has no idea about proper etiquette!

Greta said something else to him, but thanks to Eddie's stomach goo choosing that moment to run from the top of Nefarious's head and into his ears, he only caught the last bit where she accused him of being a spy.

The warrior crossed his arms, looking straight at him. "Spy, eh? Wait 'til Eddie wakes up. He eats spies for breakfast. So, I guess he was right to gobble you up."

Nefarious needed to consider his next words carefully. If he didn't manage to persuade this oaf that he was no spy, it would be the first thing the dragon heard when he woke up and then back inside Nefarious would go.

Observing the humans bickering, Nefarious had an ingenious idea. If this was the way they preferred to speak, he could adapt. He could act superior, ironic, and condescending any day. Enough with the niceties.

"Are you quite finished?" Nefarious asked, wiping his face with the tip of the dragon's wing. "I'm not a spy. I was experimenting. Testing out a supposition on how carnivorous dragons really are. Turns out, the not eating humans thing . . ."

"You're an elf," Greta pointed out.

Nefarious shrugged. "So? As I was saying. It seems that for dragons, eating humanoids is more of an ethical taboo. If they don't know you're an elf or human . . ."

"Meaning, if you pretend to be something else," Greta interjected.

"Yes," Nefarious ground his teeth. "When I pretended to be a plant, but perchance smelled like an elf, then the dragon still attempted to eat me."

Greta nodded. "Uh-uh, uh-uh. Mister experimenter, how were you planning on getting out of there, given that the two natural ways did not suit Your Highness?"

Nefarious froze, being addressed by his proper title. *How does the girl know? Is everyone aware of the complicated conundrums of the lines of dark elven succession? I thought it was our best kept secret.*

In his confusion he even forgot to point out that the oaf, just like his

—what could the wench be to him; a paramour?—forgot to introduce themselves.

The child continued his calligraphy, but rather animatedly, as if in a hurry.

Nefarious noticed the green goo still dripping from his sleeve. He had been living surrounded by it and spitting at it for the past three days. That was it! "Oh, dear. This just won't do," he said, feeling for the wand in his pocket.

One cleansing spell later, he stood in all his regal glory, wearing his favorite black velvet suit, and flicked back his shoulder-length raven hair.

Greta narrowed her eyes at him. "You look familiar. Have we met?"

Nefarious bowed but didn't utter a word, casting glances at the hut. Still no twin in sight. *I have to stall for time and find out about the twin.* Flattery was part of diplomacy. So, flattery would have to come next.

He smiled his best enigmatic smile and muttered a spell, touching the wand in his pocket. "I owe you my life, sweet maiden, and I'm at your service." He bowed yet again, with a flourish this time, his hair nearly touching the forest floor.

"Please call me Greta," the girl said, looking unimpressed by his charms.

The only ones who could ever resist his enticement were fairies. Like Morgana. And fairy godmothers. Given that the Fairy Queen hadn't mentioned this, Greta was one of hers, logic dictated she could only be . . .

Out loud, Nefarious said, "What an enchanting name for such an enchanting . . . mmm . . . Fairy Godmother, I believe?" He inclined his head and tried to listen to see if he could hear her thoughts. He could always hear the thoughts of humans. Not so with fairies. Or fairy godmothers.

"Godmother already? How do you manage that on top of running a restaurant and an animal shelter?" The warrior smirked.

The girl said something else and then smiled at Nefarious. He could swear the sun lost its spark as a new star emerged to bless him with its warmth. Nefarious blinked away the image and his desire to stand a little closer to the girl.

The warrior took Greta by her chin and Nefarious wanted to slap the smirk off his face. Suddenly, he wished these two were not lovers and he didn't know why. The warrior told Greta, "You look tired. Been working yourself to the bone with studies and everything, have you?" He pointed at the raccoon, who was anxiously washing her paws. "See, even your helper is worried about you."

Helper? So that's how Greta had lured his spy away from performing its duties. She had offered better terms than just an order and a threat. The girl had probably given the critter food as payment. Coons and food.

Nefarious missed some of the conversation but noticed Greta biting her lip and looking at Eddie as if she didn't trust him.

She isn't fond of the dragon? Then Greta can't be Gretel Crimsonlocks!

While that warmed Nefarious's heart, he could still not get over his confusion as to why he cared. But he did care that she was worn down and that her warrior acquaintance—at least he hoped he was just an acquaintance—was blaming her instead of offering support. Clearly, Greta was a kind heart, trying to do all she could to help everyone. Even a wayward dragon with indigestion. Nefarious decided to point out the upside of her good deeds.

"If Eddie hadn't come here and you hadn't rescued me, we would never have met," Nefarious said and took a few involuntary steps towards Greta.

What is with me? Usually, it was the enchanted maidens that would flock to him and paw his lapels. Instead, *he* was feeling drawn to the girl. She *should be running towards* me!

There was a loud snort and one of Eddie's heads opened one eye. "Did someone say my name?" Eddie asked, and all of his heads yawned in unison.

Nefarious increased the pull of his charm and saw that he was making Greta uncomfortable. He let a slow smile spread across his face.

Not a fairy godmother yet, then. The girl was still human. *Soon, she will succumb and tell me all about the location of her twin.*

Greta inhaled sharply.

Nefarious smiled wider. *Any minute now.*

He himself kept edging closer to Greta, attempting to close the gap between them faster.

Now for the final nail in Eddie's coffin, and the girl will be ripe for the taking.

"Considering Eddie nearly ate me, he must be hungry," Nefarious said, hoping this remark would instil fear into Greta like it would to any damsel standing next to an allegedly carnivorous and hungry dragon. "Permit me to assist you in a getaway." The elf bowed low, never taking his eyes off Greta and trying to hide his smirk.

Any minute now.

Instead of taking his arm, Greta backed away, tripping on a tree branch. She would have landed on her bum if one of Eddie's heads hadn't caught her. The rest of them snaked around, sniffing for something.

Leaning on Eddie's scaly neck, Greta said, "You're quite chivalrous for a beast. You know, I wish . . ." Greta said and clapped her hand over her mouth. "Oh no, I'm not wishing for anything."

Two of the heads encircled her, pushing Nefarious away. "Yeeees, but if you could wish, what would you wish for?" they whispered. Nefarious huffed his indignation.

"If I could wish, then I would wish for you to have just one head, not six. It's rather disorienting, you know," Greta said.

Nefarious noticed the boy child smiling at his journal. *Probably proud to have finally mastered a new letter.*

One of Eddie's heads peered over the boy's shoulder and said, "I can do that."

"Do what?" Greta asked.

The dragon disintegrated into a million golden particles that kept condensing until moments later, the particles reassembled into a golden-haired lad in a white shirt and dark blue jeans. "Darius Edward Goldencrest, at your service," the young man said, flashing white teeth on his bronze face.

"You forgot, prince," the warrior said and Nefarious cringed.

Prince. *He best not get to be king.*

"Prince? I think I liked you more when you had six heads and were just Eddie," Greta told the dragon.

Nefarious looked at the dragon prince like he was snot. "Well, well, well."

At least royalty and aristocracy knew how to do a proper introduction. Bows were exchanged, and Nefarious caught himself thinking that for only two members of royalty being present, they had, somehow, been doing a bit too much bowing in this meadow today.

Nefarious noticed Greta looking at him, seemingly fighting with bouts of slack-jawed awe that changed to anger. He saw her balling her hands into fists and remaining where she was.

She is resisting my charms. How marvelous! And annoying.

"I'll have none of your underhanded pheromone seduction ploys, thank you very much," Eddie suddenly waved his hand at Nefarious and Greta's face went slack. The boy child kept scribbling into his leather book, seemingly oblivious to everything and everyone.

Damn that dragon! Why did he have to interfere? How was Nefarious going to learn about the twin now?

"Why did you do that?" Nefarious asked. "Aren't dragons always saying, 'finders, keepers?' So, what if I enhanced my charm a little? In human form, I saw her first," he said haughtily.

"Technically, *I* saw her first," Eddie argued. "You were still food at that point. If only you had had the good sense to be digested when you had the chance, she wouldn't have met you at all."

"And you wouldn't have needed her help, so neither of us would be vying for her attention," the elf retorted.

"Would you please stop it! I'm right here and I'm not interested in either one of you!" Greta shouted at them.

Nefarious turned to look at Greta and felt annoyance and darkness bubbling up in his solar plexus.

"Whyever not?" Darius asked Greta. "Are you not of marriageable age?"

"She is," the warrior replied.

"Which one of her male relatives should be addressed for her hand in marriage, Hans?" Darius asked. The red-headed warrior raised his arm high.

Relatives? The warrior and Greta were related? Oh, thank goodness.

"You can learn magic with me," Darius said and moved closer to Greta, which made Nefarious's stomach turn to knots. *He is offering her something she might want as a fairy godmother apprentice only to lure her away from me. No, no, I can't lose her now.*

"She could learn in the Dark Territories," Nefarious said and moved to Greta's other side.

"Yes, but you'd have to marry her, and even then, she wouldn't be accepted in your kingdom. She's as light as they come. She heals people and creatures," Darius told him, moving yet another inch closer to the woman Nefarious coveted.

Coveted?

I'm coveting her?

Her, not *the information she can supply about her twin?*

If she were my bedmate, I could easily get access to her twin as well.

The decision almost made itself.

"I'd be amenable to marriage if she could keep her sharp tongue in check," Nefarious said. *There. With this caveat, he didn't have to marry her, if he didn't want to.*

Greta huffed and surprised him with her answer. "If you subjugate women, no way I'd marry you even if you begged."

"Me? Beg?" Nefarious felt scandalized. *She dares to reject my almost-marriage proposal?*

"I'd beg," Darius said, stroking Greta's hair. "And marry."

By Darius's besotted look, Nefarious gathered that Eddie wasn't acting to irk him. He really would marry this girl if she said yes right now. *Maybe it is love at first sight, like the lore said about King Golden-crest and Queen Crimsonlocks?*

"Stop that!" Greta swatted at Darius's hand, earning herself a brain-melting smile and being pulled closer into his embrace.

Nefarious opened his mouth to protest but closed it again. *Could Morgana have been right? Was this the real Gretel Crimsonlocks masquerading as a bar wench with a much-shortened name, Greta? Was there even a twin sister or had the Fairy Queen tricked him?*

Nefarious took a good look at the warrior again. Relatives. His flaming hair was the same hue as Greta's. His facial features also resembled Greta's, signaling closer proximity than cousins. A brother? At the restaurant, Greta had mentioned a brother who had taught her how to fight. The only thing that was markedly different was their height.

Can it be that the twin is not a sister, but a brother?

With a warrior twin brother and a fated meeting with the dragon that had already happened progressing to the swiftest meet-to-marry he had ever witnessed, Nefarious felt deflated and defeated. The elven king would have to do his own bidding if he feared the girl so. *She isn't a queen yet. There is still time.*

Out loud he said, "You're right, dragon, as the negotiations have progressed to marriage proposals, I'm bowing out. My king can tame her if he likes. I prefer my women pliant." Nefarious bowed to Greta and vanished by touching his wand, wishing Greta—as queen—would never go against dark elves because deep down, he'd be sorry to see her destroyed.

If you're curious to find out if GRETEL CRIMSONLOCKS ever became the dragon queen and what happened to Greta and Eddie, read *To Steal A Kiss* in ***Enchanted Flames*** (out June 18, 2023).

If you want to follow Greta's & Hans's story, read ***Cinders: Necessary Evil***.

Sky Sommers

For most of her life, Sky has lived and worked in Tallinn, Estonia, with brief escapes all over the world in search of her muse. Penguins and polar bears, beware, she will get there. Eventually. Her debut e-book was about ancient goddesses running amok, trying to get their wilted powers back. Sky has mostly written new takes on fairytales, but also has one dystopian post-Brexit book and one pre-Arthurian fantasy under her belt. A secret eco warrior, Sky has co-authored several charity anthologies, some of them to aid reading, but most to support cleaning up our oceans or retaining our rainforests and helping communities touched by wildfires. All her books are peppered with dry humor, linked by some character or another and sometimes she makes you choose the ending, depending on whether you are an optimist or a pessimist. Sky lives in a house with a small garden with her husband and two, but on occasion plus three kids. No dog.

If you're curious if the dragons ever got a Queen Gretel Crimsonlocks and what happened to Greta and Eddie, read **To Steal A Kiss** in **Enchanted Flames** (out June 18, 2023).

If you want to follow Greta's & Hans' story, read **Cinders: Necessary Evil**.

A FEAST OF WILLS

BEKAH BERGE

It was the kind of evening that spoke of icy winds, chapped skin, and the promise of a biting cold that stung the tips of bare fingers. Draped in piles of fluffy snow, the branches of the forest hung low, and the scent of wet evergreens and pine overwhelmed the senses—a reminder of days spent picking the last of the marionberries from prickly bushes.

Elaxi's wicker basket weighed down her arms as she hustled through the thick snow that Thora had, of course, decided not to clear off the path to her cottage in the Silver Wood. It was the eve of the winter solstice and her mouth watered at the thought of the feast they'd be cooking tonight, their annual tradition.

Both born of parents who did not want them, Elaxi and Thora had grown up together in a shack filled with orphans on the outskirts of the kingdom. Though not blood related, they had been drawn to each other since the moment they'd met at five years of age. Often intrigued by the same strange creatures of the night, they regularly went on dangerous adventures that exposed them to countless nefarious acts that little girls should know nothing about. But who could blame them for being curious?

Not long after their tenth year, the girls began to show an affinity for magic, and their connection solidified into something so deep that they simply started to refer to themselves as sisters. They were witches, oddities, viewed as nothing more than weapons to be abused by men in power.

As the years passed, they continued to hold each other's hands as they grew up, moved out of the shack, and fell in love with men who did not deserve them. Men who would betray them. They were used and discarded, treated as filth. But that would not always be the case. Both witches turned on their kingdom and embraced all the darkest corners of their powers. They delighted in the wicked, and when they'd decided to go their separate ways, the two women vowed to always remain loyal to each other.

But something had shifted between them this past year.

Their correspondence had been less frequent, and Thora was strangely cryptic in her letters. As though she were purposely hiding something.

The creak of hinges groaning startled Elaxi.

"How much longer is it going to take you to trudge through the snow and get inside?" snapped Thora from where she stood with the door wide open and a hand on her hip. Dressed in long black robes with a thick purple scarf wrapped around her neck like a snake, Thora looked every bit the young maiden she often ensnared in her traps. Her skin remained sun-kissed despite her proclivity for only being outside when the moon was high in the night sky, while her black hair glistened with a dash of blue in its depths. Her lips were painted blood-red.

"Perhaps if you had shoveled . . ." Elaxi trailed off as she gave Thora a disapproving glare. She was the exact opposite of Thora in appearance. White hair, dark skin, and eyes the lightest shade of green. She stomped her boots to shake off the excess snow before entering through the open door and dropping her heavy basket on the floor. "What's that smell?"

"I started brewing the cider ages ago," said Thora, slamming the door to lock out the winter chill. The cottage was as it always had been —cozy and warm from the roaring fire. The place was filled with drying herbs hanging from strings tied to wooden beams, while pots and pans decorated every free surface. There were piles of wood, potions in glass vials strewn about, and every poison known to man housed in various vessels. Thora wasn't practical, nor was she organized. In fact, it was a wonder she even knew what was edible and what wasn't, but Elaxi assumed Thora's magic helped with that particular predicament. Otherwise, she would be dead by now.

Many a fair maiden had fallen into the clutches of Thora's enchanted Silver Wood. The bubbling brooks and charming ponds were filled with poisoned waters that swept the maidens into an eternal sleep. Doomed to have their lives bled from them and feed the Silver Wood, to keep the forest healthy and thriving, as the maidens rotted away in the crypts below.

Elaxi's vices were less obvious.

Ruler of Destiny Cove, she enjoyed confusing fishermen and pirates with wild winds, tempestuous seas, and a directionless night sky. When their fates finally brought them to Elaxi's shores, she welcomed them with a grand feast and overflowing pints of ale. The men were so relieved to have finally set foot on land that they never paused to ask who Elaxi was or why she was showing them kindness. Though that hardly mattered. The moment her homemade ale touched their lips, their fates were sealed, and they turned into sea creatures she used to fill her cove with life.

But alas, she had recently stumbled upon a rather strange problem. Her shark spell kept turning the men to stone.

Something was wrong with her spell book.

And there was only one other person who had access to it—her sister.

Elaxi frowned at Thora as her suspicion spiked.

"Don't give me that look." Thora scowled and shook her finger disapprovingly in Elaxi's face.

"I suppose we're skipping over basic pleasantries then." Elaxi rolled her eyes. "And I'm not giving you a look."

"Yes, you are. It oozes betrayal." Thora scoffed. "If anyone should be using that look, it's me."

"What's that supposed to mean?" The accusation made the hairs on the back of Elaxi's neck stand up. Why was Thora acting as though she'd been wronged? Elaxi was the one whose personal spell book was damaged. With a great huff, she yanked the heavy basket off the ground and deposited it onto the cluttered table, smashing dried beetle carcasses in the process.

"I think you know exactly what I mean." Thora raised an eyebrow and gave her a dark smirk. She slammed her knife through a handful of turnips and potatoes, all but hacking into the wood of her table in the process. Pieces of vegetable flew across the room and landed in dusty corners. Subtlety was not one of her strengths. "Strange that my potions have stopped working. I do take such *care* with the plants I cultivate for my brews."

And there it was.

The accusation.

Something happened to Thora's garden, just as something had happened to her spell book. What in all the wild winds was going on?

"Is there something you'd like to say?" asked Elaxi, placing her hands on her hips as she glared at her sister.

Thora simply grinned in return and threw a dead duck on the table between them. "Yes, actually. I need you to pluck and butcher that for the stew."

Elaxi ground her teeth in aggravation as Thora evaded her question.

If that's how she wanted to play this, then fine.

"Only if you make a pie," Elaxi fired back, unloading the goods from her basket. As she set down a bottle of oil, her eyes caught on an empty vial of aconite. She narrowed her eyes at the cauldron of simmering cider over the fire.

Had Thora been so bold as to poison it?

Was she truly that convinced of Elaxi's betrayal?

"Speaking of potions not working properly, my spell book has failed me."

"Really?" drawled Thora, feigning surprise.

Elaxi's nostrils flared. "I wonder how such a thing could happen?"

"Spells can be such finicky things, dear sister."

"Yes, so it seems," Elaxi growled, as she finished cleaning the duck and whipped out a knife of her own to begin the process of butchering it. The blade glimmered in the firelight and Thora's gaze snagged on the sharp edges. "Would you like some bread and liver pâté?"

Thora's smile was downright lethal. "That would be lovely." Reaching behind her, she grabbed an even larger serrated knife and held it up like a prize. "Allow me to slice some bread for us."

"How thoughtful of you."

"I do like to make sure my guests are"—Thora sliced through the loaf with a saccharine smile—"fully taken care of."

"Yes, you're always thinking of *everything*. Would you care for some of that delightful cider you made?" asked Elaxi. If Thora assumed she could best her sister with a bit of aconite, then she had been paying little attention to her powers.

The sisters squared off as they stared each other down. Unease and suspicion wafted in the air around them, as potent as the smell of cinnamon and stewed apples.

It was unusual for their feasts to be so hostile.

Thora narrowed her dark eyes. "I would love some."

"Wonderful." Elaxi grabbed a ceramic mug hanging from a peg on the wall and ladled cider into it. Spinning around, she held the mug out to Thora expectantly.

"Won't you have some with me?" her sister asked, taking the mug with a defiant look in her eyes.

"Of course." Elaxi grinned viciously before filling a mug for herself.

She stood before Thora as they waited for the other to drink first. The wood crackled in the fire beside them as the tension continued to build. And build. And build.

Until finally . . .

"Drink up," said Thora, gesturing with her mug. "I'm curious to hear what you think of the taste."

"Oh?"

Thora nodded, while failing to hide her smirk.

"Why don't you try it first to make sure it's ready?"

Thora's smirk grew. "What a marvelous idea." With a cheeky wink, she took a sip of the hot cider and licked her lips. "Delicious."

Elaxi frowned and took a sip from her own mug. Nothing happened. There was no bitter aftertaste from the poison, no stomach cramping or blood pouring from her eyes. The cider wasn't poisoned. In fact, it really was tasty. Spicy even.

Had she misjudged her sister's mood?

Was this all a game?

Placing her mug of cider on the table, Elaxi finished butchering the duck and fished around for a clean pot to use for the stew. Thora tossed in the vegetables she'd roughly chopped, along with the meat and a jar of broth Elaxi had brought with her.

"Tell me what has been happening with your spells?" asked Thora, slathering a piece of bread with pâté and shoving the whole thing in her mouth.

"My pirates have been turning to stone instead of sharks."

"Who would tamper with your spell book?"

"Yes, who indeed," Elaxi muttered with annoyance as she eyed Thora. "Can you take a look at the spell and see if you notice what's wrong with it?"

"Only if you wash the dishes," Thora replied as she pulled a basket of berries out of her pantry and set them on the table.

Elaxi stilled.

Her eyes narrowed on the little red berries.

"Why do you have harem berries?" she asked, pointing at the basket as distrust reared its ugly head once more. "Those are poisonous."

Thora threw her head back and cackled. "Those aren't harem berries, you fool." She continued to laugh. "You've been around water too long. My forest carries many different types of berries, and harem berries, those are not. They're wickham berries. I'm making a pie, as you requested."

Though she wanted to believe her sister, Elaxi wasn't convinced those were the edible berries her sister claimed them to be. Was this another one of Thora's mind games?

"I haven't had wickham berry pie in years," said Elaxi, as she grabbed a spoon to stir the stew. She glanced behind her to make sure Thora was watching when she ever so slightly waved her hand above the pot, as if casting a spell.

"Did you just add some herbs?" asked Thora, her question laced with accusation and perhaps a tinge of worry.

Elaxi smiled to herself.

She hadn't cast a spell, nor had she added herbs, but Thora didn't need to know that. "I was thinking rosemary and thyme would be lovely in the broth," she said, while adding a healthy dash of salt and pepper.

"Shall we add some garlic as well?" asked Thora, hacking down a bulb from a hanging vine with her enormous knife. She smashed the bulb on the table and cloves shot out in every direction. She grabbed a handful and tossed them into the pot without chopping them up. Her hand still firmly grasped the knife.

"I was thinking we should add some bones into the broth," said Elaxi, grinning at her sister as she continued to stir the pot. "For flavor."

"Excellent suggestion." Thora tightened her hold on the knife. "I have just the thing," she said, turning on her heel and rustling around in her pantry before coming back with a linen sack. She upended the entire contents into the pot with something close to a triumphant harrumph. "Fairy bones. Collected them myself."

Elaxi ran her tongue along her teeth.

Fairy bones could go one of two ways. If they were woodland fairies, the bones wouldn't be poisonous, but if they were river fairies . . .

Elaxi drummed her fingers on the table and decided to bring up something she'd heard at the tavern. "On my way here, I was made aware of the most salacious bit of gossip from the town people."

"Oh?" Thora sliced another piece of bread and slathered it with honey. "Do tell, dear sister."

The stew was bubbling and would be ready shortly. But the real question was, would either of them eat it?

Elaxi took another sip of her cider. "There's a rumor being spread in the taverns that King Henrik has been seen entering the Silver Wood on several occasions. They say he comes to see you. Care to explain?"

"I have nothing to explain," said Thora with a shrug as she mashed the supposed wickham berries before mixing in sugar and lemon juice. With a pointed glance at Elaxi, she plucked a vial from inside her robes and dumped the contents into the bowl. Another bluff? Elaxi couldn't be sure. Thora then set aside the pie filling and began kneading the dough for her crust.

Elaxi snapped her fingers above the chopped mushrooms in response, once again pretending to cast a spell. Giving her sister a pointed look, she scooped up the mushrooms and added them to the stew. "What are you doing having King Henrik in your forest? You know what kind of man he is. Perhaps it was he who cursed your garden."

"To save the life of his dying wife, he struck a bargain with me." Thora rolled out her pie dough before putting it into the tin for baking. "On the day his eldest son takes the crown, we will marry, and I shall become queen."

"Are you mad?" gasped Elaxi, gaping at her sister in horror. "The people will never accept a witch as their queen. And Henrik, he'll have you killed before you even step foot in the castle."

"Do not underestimate my powers. I will simply bewitch the kingdom with my beauty and magic, then they will fall in love with me," she replied casually. "Jealous, dear sister?"

Elaxi wasn't jealous, but she was worried.

It was one thing to do as they wished in the shadows, but to be at the center of the kingdom's attention was asking for misfortune. People would not accept that which they did not understand, and magic was far from understood.

Thora poured the berry mixture into her tin and set it on the grate above the fire to bake. With her back still turned to her sister, she said, "Do not stand in the way of my ambitions. I will not hesitate to act in my own best interest."

Understanding filled Elaxi. All these threats of poison were her sister's way of telling her to not interfere with her plans. Though she wasn't entirely convinced these threats were harmless. Thora had always been motivated by power and if she thought Elaxi would stop her from getting what she wanted, there was no telling how far Thora would go.

Elaxi would not be intimidated by her sister.

And it seemed that Thora needed a reminder of that.

Setting down her knife, Elaxi pointed at her spell book and said, "What did you do to it?"

"I'm not sure I know what you're referring to."

"Do not play coy with me, *dear sister*," she fired back, feeling the heat of her magic begin to boil within her flesh. "You are the only one who has had access to my *private* spell book this past year. I know you did something to it. Fix it now, and all will be well."

"And what did you do to my garden?"

"I never touched your garden, Thora."

"Well, someone did!"

The fire roared within the hearth, reacting to the intensity of their magic as it crackled on the surface. Suddenly, the pie was engulfed in flames.

They were ruining their winter solstice feast.

"Enough of this nonsense," snapped Elaxi, slamming her palms on the table. "I have not and would never interfere with your magic. I did not touch your garden." Cursing to the high heavens, she hurried around the table and grabbed a cloth to wrap around the handle of the pot and save the stew from the raging fire. Her stomach rumbled. The liver pâté had not been nearly enough to satisfy her appetite.

"Then who did?" Thora barked, shoving papers and vials off the table and onto the floor to make room for the stew. She snatched a pair of chipped bowls off a shelf and placed them beside the steaming pot.

"Let me remind you of a certain king who you recently threatened," said Elaxi with a sharp gleam in her eyes as she plucked a ladle off the wall. "I don't imagine King Henrik is too keen to see his heir marry a witch."

"He wouldn't dare cross me."

Elaxi rolled her eyes as she filled their bowls. Despite the potential for poison, it smelled wonderful. "Yes, no powerful man in history would ever try and rid himself of the witch in his woods."

Thora cocked her head to the side and drummed her fingers on the table. "He must know." She rubbed a hand over her heart and cursed. "No. I refuse to believe this."

"Have you learned nothing over the years?" Elaxi hissed. "Your hubris betrays you. King Henrik will never allow you to marry his son. He will do everything in his power to ensure that day never arrives. To think otherwise is asinine."

"But—"

"King Henrik cannot be trusted." Elaxi sighed and hung her head. "Do not ignore the truth that stares you in the face."

Thora pursed her red lips together as the truth began to settle in. Her sudden anger flared and rattled the cottage walls. "I have been a fool!"

"Did you touch my spell book?"

"Yes, I was angry." Thora waved away Elaxi's exasperation. "But I would never tamper with the important spells."

"Oh, how reassuring." She ground her teeth while staring daggers at her sister. Why did Thora always have to cause so much damage when she lost her temper? "I will expect you to fix the spells before I leave."

"Yes, yes, all will be well," Thora replied dismissively, while picking up a spoon and dunking it into the stew. She paused and raised an eyebrow at her sister. "Did you truly poison the soup?"

"Did *you* poison the soup?" Elaxi glared back.

Silence filled the air as they continued to watch each other, waiting for the other to crack first. When it was clear that neither of them was willing to confess the truth, Thora sighed. "We both take a sip on three."

"Fine." Elaxi gripped her spoon. "One."

"Two."

"Three."

They lifted their spoons to their lips and swallowed.

Then waited.

Stared.

And came to the same conclusion.

"I have behaved like the greatest of buffoons," confessed Thora, as she cursed and raged about the cottage. "How could I ever think my own sister would turn her back on me? To think I believed King Henrik when he told me you would be jealous of my position at court." She shook her head in disgust. "I would never poison you."

"Nor I you," Elaxi replied as she ate another spoonful of stew and savored the rich flavors of the broth. She felt ridiculous and angry for thinking Thora would ever want to harm her. She should know better. They both should.

"I must make him pay for clouding my judgment. For whispering lies into my ear."

"What do you plan to do to King Henrik for ruining your garden?" asked Elaxi, as she dipped a piece of bread into the stew before plopping it in her mouth. Revenge was a far more fitting topic of conversation for their winter solstice feast. Much more appetizing than disloyalty.

A wicked smile spread across Thora's face. "I shall poison him."

"*We* shall poison him." Elaxi winked at her sister and reached across the table to squeeze Thora's hand. "Together."

Bekah Berge

Bekah Berge fell in love with all things mystical at a young age. Her love of stories led to her writing her first book in her early twenties, and she's never looked back since. When not scribbling down fantastical tales, she enjoys traveling, gardening, vegan baking, and brewing the perfect cup of tea.

She also suffers from a rare chronic pain condition called CRPS (Complex Regional Pain Syndrome) and to learn more visit: CRPS-Bookshelf.com

Her latest novel, Needlework, follows a group of four musicians as they vie for a spot on the coveted main stage at the illustrious Olive Branch Music and Arts Festival.

Instagram: Bekahbergeauthor
TikTok: Authorbekahberge
Website: CRPSBookshelf.com

Star Dancer

Astrid V.J.

Vega squeezed his fingers against the tiny protrusion in the cliff face and heaved with all his might. His muscles bunched and toes scrabbled against the obsidian wall. After a moment of agony, hanging in the balance and fearing he might have to give up, his foot found purchase on the tiniest of indentations.

Pressing his body to the glass-like rock, Vega scanned the area above him, noting the low slant of the sun's light streaming under a blanket of dark grey clouds. He could just see the lip of the cliff face. It was so close. Just a little too high to jump.

As he failed to find any solution, Vega slumped against the cool surface and glanced at the waters frothing below. Had he really gone through all of this to fail?

Images of Namid taunted Vega's mind, Namid's open smile and sparkling eyes, and his curly hair dancing about his shoulders.

No. Vega couldn't let this sheer wall stop him. Namid needed him, and for that reason alone, Vega refused to look down and search for the sliver of sand from whence he'd climbed. By now, with the rising tide, that last spit of land would have been devoured by the hungry waters of the Endless Sea. He had to move onward. Vega had no time for death, for he had a life to save. One more valuable to him than any other, more precious than his own family, who had been among those to carry Namid up to the cliff as a sacrifice to the sea.

It didn't matter what tradition said—irrespective of the elders' wishes—Vega would stand by Namid through this. He had to. His conscience demanded it.

Ablaze with determined fire, Vega shifted his weight, readjusted the strap holding a spear in place against his back, and felt around until he encountered a crack. A moment later, he pushed himself up to grasp the top lip of the cliff. His hands were slick with blood from the razor sharp obsidian, and as his grip slipped, he called up the image of Namid's face. Flashing eyes filled with humor, full lips quirked in a smile to light up the darkest of days.

Giving up was not an option. With a final heave, he dragged his body over the rim and rolled onto his back. Above him, blue-black thunderheads swirled with softer grey; the clouds seemed to race each other in waves so very similar to the agitated crash of the ocean below.

The shaft of his spear dug into his back as he lay winded and watched the clouds roil.

Namid.

When the discomfort of the weapon grew too much, Vega rolled onto his stomach and pushed himself upright. His legs were shaky, but a few deep breaths steadied them enough to take a step away from the edge of the precipice. Vega's hands stung but didn't seem to be too badly off. He easily brushed away the few trickles of crimson against the rough fabric of his lavalava skirt. He stood on a flat surface a mere five paces wide and six canoe-lengths long. To his right, the obsidian surface came out of the base of a basalt cone. Heat from the mountain counteracted the chill wind coming off the sea, and Vega saw an orange glow— the eternal fire.

On his left, the platform narrowed to nothing as it gave way to air and a plunge four times his height into the black waters below. A few paces away, on a stretcher of wood and palm leaves, sat Namid. His curly hair danced about his face and shoulders. His legs were extended, and Vega's heart squeezed at the sight of muscle-less bone and skin.

"Vega?" Namid's voice carried on the wind. "What are you doing here? And your hands? Did you *climb* the cliff?"

Before he could answer, water rained down. It splashed cool liquid onto Vega's cheek, which chilled the heat of his skin. He looked up, but more water splashed from the left, dousing his short-cropped hair and bare shoulders.

Vega spun around as cold droplets trickled down his back. His eyes widened and breath stuck in his throat. At the end of the obsidian ledge, a mere foot away from Namid, where air had been a moment before, rose a creature so terrifying the mere thought of facing it almost brought Vega to his knees. Its iridescent body rose from the waters below; the serpentine frame was immense, and from its back rose a crest, gleaming pink at times, deep blue at others. A mighty snout curved above Namid, revealing two rows of pointed teeth.

Pulling the whale-bone spear from its holder at his back, Vega considered his options. Bearing in mind no one in living memory had actually defeated a sea serpent, he had very little to go on. There were a few legends, but they were all vague.

Keep away from the razor-infested maw. An obvious thought, but not much help when his spear tip wasn't much larger than one of those mighty teeth. Nothing for it. He had to do something.

Vega shifted his weight and jumped over Namid to face the monster, only to come to a standstill when a dazzling light enveloped its head. The blinding sparkle softened to a shimmering rainbow glow and revealed the upper body of a woman. From her hips down writhed the snake-like form of the beast. Her long, black hair fell to her back, and she was crowned with a leafy headdress of plumeria and hibiscus flowers. The splash of color drew attention to the soft brown of her skin.

She was exposed except for an intense, green item covering her breasts. It was made from the leaves of the paradise plant. Intricately twisted verdant ropes wound about her neck and shoulders, holding everything in place, and a sprig of pink and orange flowers adorned the outfit. The sea serpent with human head and torso leaned forward and Vega took a step back, his calf brushing against the stretcher where Namid reclined.

"What have we here?" the woman's voice boomed, echoing with the depths of the ocean.

Squaring his shoulders, Vega pointed the spear where the creature's heart might be. "You can't have Namid, monster. I will send you back into the ocean's depths where you belong."

"Vega—"

Vega shut off Namid's interjection, for the great serpent-woman brought her face within inches of Vega's. The size of her overwhelmed him, as did the hard stare she gave him. Even more unsettling than her size and the severity radiating from her were the glittering silver-blue markings whorled around her right eye. Reminiscent of a half-mask, the shimmering lines twined over part of her nose and up into her forehead.

The female's broad nostrils flared. "Is it for madness you've been deposited here for me? Or some other ailment?" Her eyes appraised Vega, and it felt like she could see right into his inner self. It made him tremble, but also sparked a flame of angry determination.

"I won't let you have Namid. I refuse to give him up. Since our people betray him and offer him to you, I will defend him."

The sea serpent woman's eyes narrowed. She took in Vega a second time and muttered, "Definitely insane. What am I to do with this one?"

Even though her voice was low, it resounded all the way to Vega's bones, and he quaked under the force of it.

"Vega is not the offering," Namid shouted from behind him.

The beast's eyes widened. "What is this?" She peered over Vega's shoulder and her mouth formed an O.

"You cannot have him!" Vega shouted and drew his arm back. He took aim for what he hoped would be the creature's heart. The air around Vega rippled, but he didn't let it distract him. With a heave, he threw the spear.

Namid spoke, but the wind swallowed his words. Vega focused on the weapon barrelling its way toward the giant woman's torso. Before he could fathom what was happening, the serpent woman shrank, surrounded by a cocoon of rainbow light, and the spear whizzed past above her head, disappearing into the void beyond the cliff. In the twinkling of an eye, the serpentine tail transformed into a pair of legs and the woman, now shorter than Vega, stepped onto the obsidian platform.

Vega stood bewildered and stared at the former sea serpent who marched up to him, the green leaves of her skirt swishing as she moved. "Out of my way, impostor." she jabbed a finger into Vega's chest.

He blinked. "Wha—?"

"Out of my way, I said, you uninitiated lummox! You have no business being here. This is a sacred rite."

From behind him, Namid added, "Just step aside, Vega. Although I appreciate everything you've done for me, you did just climb a cliff to save my life, you're making a fool of yourself."

Vega couldn't move. How was nothing as it should be?

Namid reiterated, "Vega, it's okay. Move over. No harm will come to me."

The woman nudged Vega, and he took a step to the left, his mind reeling with the unexpected development. He'd come here to kill a monster, and now a beautiful woman stood there tapping her foot at him with her arms settled on her hips. She glanced down at Namid, drawing Vega's attention to his friend.

Namid's shoulder muscles bulged, strengthened from dragging around his spindly legs. An intricate design in black ink wound its way up Namid's left arm. Charcoal hair crinkled to his shoulders. Namid held the woman's gaze, determination blazing from his dark eyes, domed by thick and prominent brows. It surprised Vega to see Namid so excited.

Namid's full lips parted, and he addressed the woman. "Lady of Storms, it is I who accepted the honor of being presented to you. I will gladly perform any quest or task you would have me do."

The woman's stern expression softened a little as she took in the withered legs. "You are what I expected. What's this oaf doing here?" She jerked her head toward Vega.

"I don't know, but Vega is definitely no oaf." Namid shrugged and shifted his gaze to Vega. "What gave you the idea this was a sacrifice?"

"This morning, you were called to the shaman while I was out fishing, but when I got there to see what it was all about, the elders refused me entry. They spoke in riddles as they always do and then I had to watch them carry you away. When I found out they were bringing you here, like a sacrifice to the sea gods, I knew I couldn't let that happen. I —" his voice broke, and he turned his head aside to blink away the burning at the back of his eyes.

"Sacrifice?" the woman sputtered. "Whoever said anything about sacrifice?" She shook her head. "Crazy humans."

Vega inhaled sharply and turned back toward her. He'd almost forgotten she was there. The woman's crown of flowers made his nose twitch at the tantalizing scent. A spark of frustration germinated inside him. Who was she to laugh at him after he'd done the impossible, scaling the sheer wall of obsidian rock at Hopāina, this mystical place where land, water, fire, and air met? Her floral headdress stuck up to about eye-level for him. Apart from the glittering silver-blue tattoo around her eye, she appeared human. Vega's fear of her had melted away as smoothly as her beast-like form had.

"What's so funny?" Vega grumbled.

The woman tilted her head back. Once again, it surprised Vega how short she was when the broad leaves on her crown tickled his shoulder. Her eyes glistened, but before his anger could swell, she shook herself. The pleasant smell of flowers enveloped Vega, and he forgot everything else.

"Apologies, boy, but you humans have some pretty messed up ideas." She wiped a hand over her face and sighed. "It is quite impressive that you climbed that wall unscathed. Nevertheless, you ought not to be here."

At the same time, Namid interjected, "I have no idea who gave you the idea I was a sacrifice. The shaman informed me there was an opportunity for me to do good for our people in a way no one else can. I have been . . . A . . . a *burden*. . . for most of my life. Being able to do something meaningful to help my people is a gift I won't decline."

"Still sounds like a sacrifice to me." Vega glared at the woman. "And there is no way I'm leaving without knowing Namid is safe—truly safe."

"Are you trying to say I'm not worth anything better than meeting death, Vega?" He glanced down at his shriveled legs and then met Vega's gaze. Fire blazed in Namid's eyes. "Your words tell me you don't believe I'm capable of anything else. How could you think so little of me?"

There was hurt and a hint of anger in Namid's tone, and his words seared their way into Vega's heart. They burned into his very being and, sinking to his knees, Vega brought his eyes up to meet Namid's dark brown ones.

"That is not true. You are capable of many amazing feats. I believe you are worth more—" Vega's voice faltered when his throat squeezed painfully tight. He took Namid's hand in his. Their touch sent a cascade of memories through his mind. Namid beside him before the hunting accident, tall and strong. Namid in bed, angry and helpless with his legs useless. Namid striving to make something of himself despite the injustices of life. And through it all, Vega pushing down the guilt of his own functional legs while doing everything in his power to help Namid through it. "You mean too much—" He paused again, struggling to sort his thoughts and push aside the memory of Namid at his worst, curled up and refusing food or water. "When the others said you were being brought here, I couldn't stand by." The words didn't do his feelings justice, but Vega couldn't get anything more through the constriction in his throat. He took in a ragged breath and hoped his eyes could better convey everything he felt.

The woman scoffed. "Humans! You're so deranged." Vega glanced at her. She now stood with her arms crossed, foot rapping the rock even faster. "Have you two finished whatever this is?" Her hand waved between him and Namid. "I don't have time to dilly dally."

"Yes, My Lady Stormqueen. I apologize for our rudeness." Namid placed both his palms on his chest in a gesture of deference. Although the motion was gentle, Namid's withdrawal cut Vega deep. The sting remaining from the slight cuts on his palms was nothing compared to this ache.

The woman's fingers wiggled. Dismissive. "Please, there's no need for titles here. I'm Olwen. Plain and simple." Her voice was brisk.

"It is a pleasure to meet you, Olwen." Namid inclined his head. "I am Namid, the cripple, the most useless villager in—"

Frustrated, Vega interjected, "Why do you put yourself down, Namid? You are kind and helpful in ways many of our fellow tribespeople are not. And this is precisely why I object to this whole sacrifice."

Namid shook his head and gestured towards Vega, cutting him off. "And this is Vega, Nakapua's greatest warrior and my unexpected, shall we say. . . erm, *rescuer*."

Olwen took a step forward and tapped her fingers on Vega's right shoulder. "Out of my way, boy. I have work to do."

Vega looked up at her. "Why do you keep calling me 'boy'? I can't be much younger than you."

"Ha!" she scoffed. "Nice try, boyo, but I've been around since before your grandparents were born. Now, move over." Olwen knelt beside the stretcher.

Scratching his head, Vega came to his feet, but only shuffled a little to his left. Nothing was going as he'd expected, and he didn't trust this woman, even if Namid did. Shapeshifters were notorious for being tricksters, and she had been a sea serpent mere moments ago. It was all very hard to fathom, not to mention know what to do. Who had ever come face to face with a beast of that size and lived to share the tale? No one Vega knew of.

"So, Namid, is it?" Olwen said, and Namid nodded. "I come to you today to offer a chance at a life very different from what you have experienced before. Should you choose this path, you will forever be severed from your past and your people, but you will step into a purpose beyond what you have been told is possible. I see in you a powerful spark, and I already feel the ripples of your potential. Should you choose this, you will help reshape many lives."

Namid held the woman's gaze for a moment before nodding his

head. "Being able to do anything meaningful would be a dream come true."

Vega wanted to interrupt, but Olwen held up her hand.

Gesturing at his legs, Namid continued. "Our village shaman was very vague. Will you be able to heal me?"

"No." Olwen shook her head, and the leaves of her flower crown rustled. "The transformation you will undergo has nothing to do with your physical body. It is rooted entirely in the energies of your spirit. From my quick appraisal, it seems you harbor the seed of a harbinger of change: a herald to portend the intersection of extraordinary destinies and the shift between ages."

When Namid's expression crumbled into disillusionment, she reached out a hand and placed it on his chest. "I understand the deep desire for physical regeneration, I really do. It is something that may come in time, but I cannot promise it."

Acid surged from Vega's stomach. *What does she even mean? Harbinger of change? And severed from his people?*

He wanted to lash out, dash this meddlesome woman's hand away from Namid. He bit back his anger and clenched his fists, but couldn't stop himself from gritting out, "So you fill his head with empty promises and meaningless ideas instead. Why does Namid have to leave those of us who love and appreciate him? You trick him with your riddles. It's ridiculous!" Vega turned toward Namid. "You can't possibly go along with this! It's absurd! She's a shifter. They lie and fill your head with silly notions. Don't all stories warn against them?"

Namid's beloved dark brown eyes narrowed and wide nostrils flared. "Vega, it is my decision, not yours. Perhaps you think you're looking out for me, but your beliefs weigh down your thoughts. You would keep me chained to this stretcher: helpless, useless. I know you mean well, but you have not been granted this gift. You aren't even supposed to be here."

Vega took a step back. He had definitely not expected that. His plan had been simple: climb the cliff, kill the beast, save Namid. *How did I become the villain instead of it being the sea serpent?*

Namid turned back to the woman. "How do I do this? Can you help me now or must I go with you?"

Olwen considered Namid for a moment, as if she weighed her

answer. At length, she said, "We stand upon a sacred conjunction of ley lines, an anchor and breathing point for the magic of the earth. Additionally, it is one of very few elemental meeting places and rich in those energies. Your spark is strong. I think—yes, I do believe you could achieve what you desire here and now. Time is of the essence, though. I must be on my way soon. If you can achieve this now, so be it. Otherwise, you must journey with me and try again elsewhere."

"How?" Namid leaned forward. His eyes sparkled.

"You must discard everything that weighs you down. Only by embracing the lightness of being that is your true state, can you become who you are meant to be."

Vega clung to calm as waves of anger surged through him, but he bit his lip. He would not say another thing. *You aren't even supposed to be here.* Namid's words still stung.

Olwen smiled as she continued. "What brings you joy? When you find your delight in life, the ecstasy of living, you will soar. Cast off the worries and the wishes. Embrace what bubbles with unbridled joy within you."

Vega wanted to rail against the absurdity of this, but Olwen once again held up her hand. The motion forestalled his acidic retaliation against this idiocy. In contrast, Namid nodded and gazed off beyond Olwen and Vega, over the expansive ocean. While he drifted, Vega listened to the sound of the waves crashing against the rocks below and the wind whistling around him. He looked into the sky, the clouds were lifting. The sun's last rays glinted orange off the parting wads of gray.

"I've longed to dance again," Namid admitted, blinking away whatever faraway place he'd visited in his mind.

Olwen nodded. "That will most definitely do. How would you feel if you could?"

Closing his eyes, Namid seemed to drift. He looked serene, but Vega couldn't help a restless feeling from surging through his veins. He shifted from one foot to the other and huffed. It wouldn't work and that would crush Namid, the last thing Vega wanted. He folded his arms. Namid shouldn't have to resort to hocus-pocus to achieve a place in the world. It wasn't right. He shouldn't feel this need to prove himself. What did he imagine all this nonsense would achieve?

Olwen put a hand on Vega's shoulder. It was an unexpected weight, and he looked up into her obsidian eyes. They glittered with impatience and unlooked-for compassion. "Vega, you must stop this. Your thoughts are leaden. They are a noose around Namid's neck, dragging him down when his own beliefs wish to see him soar. If you cannot be the supporter he needs, then I think you should go. Believe in him. Trust in his ability to achieve what he longs and dreams to do. Or take the path the villagers took and go your own way."

Vega had to bite back a growl. Who did this woman think she was? Vega wanted what was best for Namid while she teased with the impossible. His spirit would be pulverized when he failed.

Namid opened his eyes with a sigh and looked up at Vega. "She's right, you know. You're holding me back because you believe this is impossible. I know you want what's best for me, but can you, just this once, let me decide what is best for myself? I know I can do this, for me. It is hard. But I know with all my heart it is possible. And then you are here, standing there with your arms crossed and a scowl on your face, and I feel the energy coming off you. It's telling me you do not, for a single heartbeat, believe I can do this."

Namid raised his hands and held them out. Vega accepted the gesture, sinking onto his heels, and Namid continued. "I feel like I'm a kite, ready to fly off on the wind, but you're there with a string, reeling me back in, forcing me to return to the ground. Please let me go so I can reach for and achieve this. I want to be more than broken. Give me the freedom to do this."

Vega's heart squeezed. Namid's impassioned words struck a chord, and he sighed. "I just don't want you to get hurt."

"I know. But all that does is stop me from trying. Give me a chance. If I should stumble and fall, be there to help me back up. Don't stop me from ever setting foot out the door. You cannot protect me from everything. Life has already doled out a bad deal, but that doesn't mean I should be a snail and withdraw into my shell. I want to feel the sun on my face. Please, just let me. Stop keeping me trapped."

With his heart clenching ever more tightly, Vega leaned his forehead against Namid's. The elder's tale of the sea snail hiding in its shell, trapped by fear, swept through Vega's mind. It was a fitting reference.

Deep inside, he knew what Namid said was the truth. It rang like a note from a perfectly crafted flute. Vega brought his arms up and settled his hands on Namid's shoulders. A surge of fear coursed through him. It thrummed at the speed of his heart and twisted in his gut. It was making him draw in on himself, just as the snail did in the story. Closing his eyes, Vega took a deep breath and pushed away at those black wings of fear. Vega would not let them sweep him away. He had to be a rock. Namid was right.

Vega opened his eyes and met Namid's gaze. "You make a fair point. I didn't mean to hold you back. I do believe in you. You are the strongest person I know. Go. Do what you must. I'm here. You have nothing to prove, but I respect that you want this."

Namid's answering smile breathed a warm glow to life in Vega's stomach. This was how he wanted Namid to look, always.

He squeezed Namid's shoulders and straightened. In an attempt to keep his thoughts away from what Namid was attempting, Vega let his mind drift to his favorite memories. Their conversations were always so deep, and the way Namid often looked at him made Vega's heart flutter. He remembered the agony he'd felt earlier that day when he'd interpreted "the cripple is being taken up to the mountain" as an indication of Namid's imminent sacrifice. Vega acknowledged his decision to come to Namid's rescue was born of fear. He dreaded losing Namid. It was also the reason he chose to scale the sheer obsidian cliff, rather than taking the path by which the villagers returned to their homes. He hadn't wanted the villagers to stop him.

Vega sensed Olwen shift beside him, and he snapped his eyes open. She stood still, her eyes fixed on Namid, and Vega turned his attention to him. A speck of golden light shone from Namid's chest. It pulsed and grew until it was about the size of Vega's thumbnail. His breath caught in wonder.

Namid's face was serene. The ball of light pulsed again, and Namid gave a cry of exaltation. His eyes opened, they shone with triumph and delight.

"I can feel it!"

"I can see it," Vega replied. He couldn't stop his smile from spreading.

The golden dot shone more brightly and doubled in size. Inside it, Vega could make out a flicker of flame. His own heart soared in response.

In less time than it took to blink, Namid transformed. One moment, he was sitting there, his atrophied legs stretched out before him, his crinkled hair waving in the wind, and the next, a mighty, flaming bird with brown eyes flickering in the firelight of its own body spread its wings and launched itself into the air with a mighty cry.

Vega stepped back from the searing heat and watched in wonder as the bird with blue and orange feathers, flaring as they burned, soared into the darkening sky. The first stars peeked out and glinted as if laughing with Namid, whose triumphant shrieks echoed as he swooped. Each turn left a trail of afterglow in his wake.

Dazzling light drew Vega's gaze to the edge of the cliff behind him. Olwen towered above him, her legs a serpent's tail once more. He'd forgotten she was more than the short female who'd stood beside him moments before. In her serpentine form, she was quite terrifying, if also majestic.

As Namid traced a flaming arc overhead, Olwen bent forward and held out a hand. "I think I may have a use for you yet, warrior. Would you like an adventure? Come, hop on my back. You can help us bring the change that must be wrought."

Vega looked out over the sea, Namid's glow captivating him from the corner of his eye. With Namid gone from the village, there was nothing to keep Vega there, no reason to stay. The villagers would wage their wars or live in peace, but none of it enticed Vega. He looked at the outstretched hand and reached for it. "Thank you, Olwen. I think that might be just the thing for me."

---

* IF YOU'D LIKE TO FIND OUT MORE ABOUT NAMID'S continued adventures as the phoenix, check out *Golden Apples*, a retelling of The Firebird, releasing in *Enchanted Flames* on June, 18th, 2023. Or if you'd like to find out about Namid's successor, centuries later, you can take a look at *Gisela's Passion*, a retelling of Giselle (please note, this last stays true to the original, tragic tale).

* A note on names. When I was given the scope for *Twice Upon a Name*, "namesakes" was included as a theme and I thought, since I hadn't been able to participate in *Once Upon a Name*, I might play

around with namesakes of my own name. Astrid is a Nordic name meaning star, in some cases extrapolated to 'Divine Light'. When I first started looking for names with meanings related to stars and other heavenly bodies, I came across Vega quite quickly. It is not only the name of a star in the Lyra constellation, but it is also a Latin name meaning 'Fallen Star'. It got me thinking of the concept of a fallen state and a lack of belief in miracles and possibilities. A short while later, I came across the name Namid, a Native American name meaning 'Star Dancer'. At the time, I was also thinking about writing a retelling of The Firebird ballet and suddenly all the parts came together for me, making both characters in this story namesakes.

Astrid V. J.

Award-winning and USA Today Bestselling Author, Astrid V.J., was born in South Africa. She is a trained social anthropologist and certified transformational life coach. She currently resides in Sweden with her husband and their two children. In early childhood, she showed an interest in reading and languages—interests which her family encouraged. Astrid started writing her first novel at age 12 and now writes fantasy in a variety of genres, exploring her passion for cultures and languages. When she isn't writing, Astrid likes to read, take walks in nature, play silly games with her children, do embroidery, and play music.

Astrid writes transformation fiction: incorporating transformation principles in novels, rather than writing another self-help book. She loves exploring the human capacity for transformation and potential to achieve success in the face of adversity. Astrid is interested in minority group questions, considerations on social standards of beauty and the negative consequences these have, and would like to make the fantasy genre accessible to people of non-white, non-Christian backgrounds. Astrid feels the fantasy genre has become too restrictive with limited representations of race, ethnicity and culture. She seeks to explore other paths on this writing journey, incorporating her background in anthropology and psychology to create engaging experiences, which also provide food for thought on the diverse topics she finds most important. These include: racism, minority rights, cultural diversity, culture change, intolerance, humanity's environmental impact, the representation of people on the autism spectrum among the general populace, the human capacity for transformation, and much more.

Linktree: https://linktr.ee/astrid.v.j_author_official

Haunting King Ezra

Susan Stradiotto

iper Jadeflute sat to the right of the empty throne, flute resting on her lap and a chain lashing her ankle to the chair. It ate at her that the king used the artifacts to keep her imprisoned when he'd outlawed artificing and alchemy two autumns prior.

Piper's fingers worked the keys as she scanned the crowd. The Wynthrop Kingdom throne room buzzed with murmuring nobles and the realm's subjects lining the balconies above. Petitioners, guards, and transgressors gathered in the center of the long room. Not for the first time, everyone awaited the king.

Today marked Piper's fifth court since Royden died. She'd never grow accustomed to being inside the keep without the Crown Prince, but this was her prison now. Her music at King Ezra's court, her penance. She should be thankful she didn't suffer the same sentence as her guild peers, life in the oubliettes. At least her choice granted her comfort: a castle suite and a lush bed.

She'd drank the elixir, severing her access to Æther, so she could no longer infuse items with alchemical magic. Part of herself, forever gone. But she experienced peaceful sunrises and the freedom to practice music. The king allowed her to keep the jade flute, though the absence of Æther left it useless beyond making mundane melodies.

A clatter arose from the antechamber, hushing the audience. King Ezra stormed into court. His body swayed with his wide waddle as he dragged himself onto the throne, grumbling and ignoring those gathered.

"Ale!" he shouted.

A serving boy poured and tasted the ale, then paused before proffering it to King Ezra.

The king swiped the tankard and yelled, "Play, bard!" then gulped greedily.

Red-rimmed lids surrounding the king's cloudy eyes made Piper's stomach turn, but she obeyed. Her flute sang the king's favored tune, a melancholy funeral march.

The king wiped froth from his beard. "Move, boy. Serve my guests. Guards!" The king raised his ale. "Bring the first case."

Piper trilled on a high note while an advisor leaned toward the king. With more grumbling, Ezra pushed him away. The king's regard for propriety tarnished as moons passed since his son's death.

Knowing her tune by rote, Piper watched the room as she played. The guards pushed a small man forward. He stumbled, his tattered pants' legs brushing the stones, and he wore the sun on his skin in color and lines. A woman gasped and hugged two skinny girls into her skirts. The man held out an arm to quieten her.

Piper's ribs squeezed, but she played on. The king's herald, Leander, made eye contact with her and pulled a scroll from a bronze cylinder with intricate runework—his own, now useless, artifact. They were kindred souls, both noble peers turned prisoners since the explosion and relegated to mere servants to the throne.

King Ezra held up a crooked finger, and Piper took the cue to stop playing, lowering her flute.

Leander cleared his throat. "Your Majesty. Nobles of Wynthrop. We bring Jonas Verne before you today on charges of tax evasion. He has failed to provide sufficient grain to the crown for two summers."

The nobles mumbled while Piper watched the farmer's wife and daughters.

Leander continued, "Mister Verne, your plea?"

Mister Verne bowed his head. "King Ezra, Your Majesty, the floods . . ." He wrung his hands. "Our fields drowned, and we couldn't produce sufficient grain. During winter, Thomasina and my twins, Nettie and Naomi, fell sick."

Piper hoped how he laced love around their names would touch the king's icy heart.

Verne glanced at his family with a trembling smile, then lifted his chin. "I paid the healer, but I've given you everything since. I beg for one more season to work the land and repay my debt."

Piper's stomach lurched. If artificing weren't treason, one of the guild members could have helped—with either the crops or the sickness. *She* could have done something if she could access the Æther. The lands in Wynthrop prospered with the use of artifacts, but no longer. Everyone had struggled since the decree.

King Ezra slammed down his tankard. "Excuses. Same as last autumn, and you bring them again. No leniency."

"But Your Majesty—"

"No. Leave the Wynthrop kingdom." He slouched in the chair. "Next!"

A bang against Piper's door announced the arrival of the evening meal.

"Are you hungry, Fagini?" Piper scratched her ferret's chin, then went to the small slot where servants delivered food.

"Quail tonight," Piper added, returning with the tray. She sat at the table near her window and split the bird in equal portions for herself and Fagini.

The sable-colored ferret chittered and sank her teeth into the breast.

When they'd both finished, Piper held out a hand. "Come here."

Fagini scurried into her arms and purred as Piper stroked her from head to tail. Thankfully, the king allowed her this small company.

"I was wrong, Fagini, to accept the king's bargain. Royden wouldn't have watched quietly while his father banished a hungry family. Leander looked troubled too. You remember Leander?"

Fagini blinked at Piper twice. *Like Leander. Ferret-like.*

Piper's eyes rounded. "No way!" She hadn't heard Fagini's voice in her head since before she'd drank from that accursed goblet. "How can I hear you?" She ran her hand around the collar that'd once been infused with Æther. Her thumb traced over the green gemstone. Warm. Alive with alchemy.

You. Collar. Words, Fagini answered.

"I gave you words, but I haven't heard your voice in two years."

Fagini nuzzled into Piper's chest, near her heart. *Comes back.*

"The infusion on that goblet was binding. I agreed to give up my connection to Æther for life. How is it returning?"

Not know.

Of course not. How would she?

With closed eyes, Piper sensed the Æther within her. Weaker than before but growing stronger. If Leander's connection to magic was returning too, then . . . then what? His suite-of-a-prison would be somewhere in Wynthrop Keep, but where?

Piper didn't know how, but . . . "I have to reach him!"

Fagini hopped up. *I go?*

Piper tossed and turned, wondering how Fagini fared, and when she felt movement on the bed, she popped upright. "Fagini?"

Here.

Piper reached toward the small voice and found the collar. When her thumb brushed over the second inlaid stone, the cloaking spell released. The air shimmered, and Fagini shook as if she'd just bathed.

"You feel different with magic?" Piper squinted at the ferret.

Yes. Thick. Fagini shivered again.

Curious. Perhaps because her pet couldn't access Æther, whereas Piper began honing her ability before she started walking, thanks to her mother and the Artificer's Guild.

"Did you find him?"

No Leander. Fagini turned in circles and something fell from beneath her arm.

Piper picked up a small trinket. A key. "I can't go . . ." But could she? She reached over and unbuckled the collar from Fagini's neck, then fastened it around her wrist, touching the white gem. Æther flowed in a cool stream from her heart center to the tips of her fingers and toes. When she'd spent enough magic, she lifted her finger. "Can you see me?"

Fagini blinked. However, she no longer wore the artifact. If she sent any thoughts, Piper couldn't perceive them.

Piper padded to her right to see if Fagini tracked her, and after only a second's hesitation, the ferret turned to face Piper. Her nose twitched, so maybe smell rather than sight, but Piper needed to be certain. "If you see me, curl up. If not, stretch out."

Fagini kneaded the bed with her front paws, then stretched out her back legs. Piper clapped and lurched forward to scratch Fagini behind the ears. "Good girl," she said and went to the door, inserting the key.

Click.

Yes.

The hallway torches had died down, so the only light was the scant glow from the moon shining through windows at either end of the corridor. The moon must have been near full with the eerie glow. Piper could find the common areas by feel after the guards' daily escort there and back.

At the center of the castle, near the throne room, she stumbled upon an alcove where she and Royden stole kisses. She turned her back, sucking in a sharp breath, not because she didn't yearn for the memories, but because she couldn't afford to waste the freedom she'd stolen. If someone discovered her, it'd mean the oubliettes. Or death, given she'd broken her oath to King Ezra and used Æther.

She met no one in the silent upper halls or lower ones. The large clockface, once an Æther-powered artifact, overlooked the court. Still. It possessed no mechanical gears, so without the infusion, it stood as a reminder. A memory of the moment—a quarter 'til four—when the explosion obliterated the Alchemical lab and Prince Royden died.

Piper pressed onward as the autumn air filtered inside, carrying a crisp smell. No yeasty warmth permeated the halls, so bakers had yet to begin their bread-making. The night was young.

She crossed the rotunda's marble floors and climbed the western stairs. Everything felt familiar—an inverse image of the eastern floors. At the door that mirrored hers, she tapped her nails.

No reply.

Piper tried again for fear of drawing the guards. She pulled the key from her robe pocket and tried it in the lock. It wouldn't seat.

Her shoulders fell in defeat.

When Piper returned to the rotunda, a breeze brushed inside and lifted her hair. The wind seemed to carry a voice and sent gooseflesh along her arms, beckoning. Instead of returning to Fagini and bed, she crept toward the exit, then left the castle.

The sensation drew her across the courtyard and through the open gates. The town slept as she followed an invisible thread toward the chapel. As she regarded the arched entrance and gabled roof, the pull guided Piper to the left, around the building, and finally to where the eeriness lay.

The cemetery.

Piper hadn't attended Royden's funeral, but she'd watched from her personal prison with Fagini in her lap. She spent nights gazing from her window down at the largest gravestone in the yard. Every night for months, she watched the death marker. Seasons passed, and she hardened her heart, resigned herself to being a prisoner. Instead of pining, she threw her heart and soul into her music.

Piper never said a proper goodbye, but tonight, she stood steps away from Royden's grave. The moon set, but the skies didn't yet brighten with morning's light. Time remained.

Ca-caw!

She jumped, swallowing a squeal. Blood rushed, an angry river in her ears. She gasped for lost breath, then blew it out. Only a crow perched on the iron fence enclosing the graves.

Piper opened the gate.

Bile clawed up her throat with every step she took toward Royden's tomb. She lifted a hand to her face and found her cheeks wet. Tears bottled for too long. The gray stone shimmered, and she leaned against it with both hands. Æther, triggered by her emotions, blanketed her, cocooning her into the stone.

Ca-caw!

Piper sniffed and took her time lifting her head to regard the bird. Atop the gravestone sat, not a crow, but a man with a crown and royal crest gleaming with ethereal light. She stumbled backward, splaying sideways onto the grass.

"I've missed you too." Royden moved his head in jerky, crow-like motions. His eyes were beadier than she recalled and flitted toward her window in the keep. "I've seen you."

Piper stammered. "I... Royden—how..." She plunged her hands into her hair, drew her knees and elbows together, and rocked. Æther could bend the visual spectrum, but create ghosts? She must be mad as a March hare. "No. Not real. Hallucination."

"I'm here, Piper," Royden countered, his familiar baritone deeper than others their age.

She peeked between her fingers as if they'd protect her from the apparition.

The prince's ghost remained. The same Royden she'd known all her life. He wore the tunic and jerkin he'd worn during their last attempt to make the drakeheart elixir.

"I'd help you stand, but . . ." He swiped a hand through the granite gravestone.

So many questions warred for her attention, but none found a voice. She and Royden had once been so close he could almost read her mind.

He did that now too, answering what she couldn't ask. "It's nearing Samhain, Piper. The veil between the spirit world and yours is thin. Your touch draws Æther, allows me to appear as I once was."

"You *are* a spirit?" Piper stood, knees quaking. "W-why are you here?"

"I'm tethered. Something isn't right about my death." Royden's head cocked again.

Piper's hand found her throat. "An accident."

"You didn't come to mourn me." Royden jerked his head to the other side. "And haven't visited?"

"I'm a prisoner. There." She jutted her chin to where Royden looked before, then cast her eyes to the ground. "I chose the more lenient of the punishments. Leander and I agreed to drink an elixir from Mortimer's goblet. You remember the King's Artificer? It severed our connection to Æther. Afterward, King Ezra had Mortimer killed so he couldn't reverse the alchemy he'd wrought on us. Eight seasons, I've served your father as his bard."

Royden's ghostly brow furrowed. "This makes no sense. You used Æther here. Now. To free me from bird form. And a cloaking spell shimmers around you."

Piper chuckled. "Whatever Æther I've conjured has clearly faded now. Otherwise, you wouldn't see through my infusion." She held out her arm with Fagini's collar on display.

The prince glanced at Piper's makeshift bracelet then cocked his head. "I see because I'm not of your world. Æther still flows around you. You say you drank a potion?"

"I did. Tonight is the first time I've been able to . . ." Her throat constricted, strangling her words. She didn't have to say more for him to know, because Royden suffered the worst fate of all.

He narrowed his eyes. "I've heard your flute singing from your rooms."

"It's still an instrument. Only, without Æther, it's useless as an artifact."

He paused, then asked, "What of Almyra? Or Brisco?"

Piper wrung her fingers. "The oubliettes. Almyra didn't survive the first winter. Your father never recovered from the grief of losing you. He took out his sadness on our friends and me at first, but his misery is spreading and affecting all subjects of Wynthrop."

Royden leaped down and paced. "I knew something felt wrong. The people who pass this yard seem weathered." He swiveled his head to stare at Piper. "You must stop him."

She recoiled. "You expect me to stand up to the king? I'll end up in an oubliette. Or worse."

"Now that you can use alchemy again, you can use your skills to convince him."

Piper started toward Royden but halted when he paced so fast his feet left the ground and, still striding, he levitated in the air. What could *she* do? Even with the ability to use her flute, she could only lull people. She'd need other objects to infuse, and even then . . .

"It's almost Samhain!" Royden drifted down to the ground like a bird soaring in the air. The sight made Piper shiver as he floated toward her, beady eyes piercing her soul. "There will be a ball and the fires." He pointed toward the fields near the stables at the end of the lane. "Surely, you'll take part?"

"Yes. My dress arrived earlier for Samhain eve. Your father will have me chained while I play, but I'll be sequestered during the bonfires."

Royden grabbed for her, his hands ghosting through her body and leaving her cold where he'd touched her. He grimaced, but his determination didn't falter. "You have Fagini still?"

Piper gave a cautious nod.

"Send her to the treasure room for gems. Then,"—His eyes twinkled with raw mischievous creativity, the very thing that drew her to him long ago.—"here's what we'll do . . ."

On the morning of Samhain eve, Piper woke before dawn. Fagini returned during the night and slept in a coil at the foot of the bed. Piper scratched her ear, and the ferret stretched her body, revealing a cluster of twinkling jewels. Piper scooped them up as three bangs sounded on her door.

She gasped and swiped her fist behind her back. When a tray slid through the slot near the door, she exhaled. Her stomach flip-flopped. Not much time remained to complete the infusions necessary, but the meal reminded her to follow her routine. She stashed the jewels under her pillow, visited the garderobe, then sat by the window to practice her jade flute.

When she'd rehearsed the tunes for the evening's celebration, she retrieved the jewels.

Fagini good?

"Yes. Amazing," Piper answered. She counted seven gems, more than enough. "Sleep now, Fagini. You'll have a long night."

From the bedpost, Piper lifted a leather thong—the last material token she had from Royden—and left her ferret alone. In a corner out of view through the window, she selected an amber-colored stone from the bunch. It reminded her of Royden's eyes when he'd been alive, so it fit her purpose. She cleared a space and placed the stone on the floor. Then Piper kissed the thong and draped it alongside the gem. In a crouch, her hands hovering over the two items, she closed her eyes and reached for Æther.

It flowed around her, thickly and warmly, until a shape formed behind her eyelids. She poured more magic into the objects, standing as they grew and formed a homunculus. When she opened her eyes, she stared at a replica of Prince Royden, so real none would suspect a fake, save for the lack of sentience in his eyes. She led the doppelgänger into her bedroom and commanded it to remain there until she returned that evening.

"Fagini, watch over it."

The ferret nosed the replica. *Soulless thing.*

Piper ran a hand down the homunculus's face. "For now." She returned to the other stones to complete her task before the guards came to escort her to the king's midday activity—whatever that would be today.

She finished the final infusion, whispering her message into the cloudy white stone, when another knock sounded on her door. Piper hid the gems beneath the bell of the evening gown and straightened.

"His Majesty awaits," a guard's voice announced through the door, followed by a jingling keyring.

When they entered, Piper stood brushing the skirts as if she were admiring the finery. "Where to today?"

"Tea in the garden." The guard glanced at her untouched morning meal as he held out the chain that'd bind her to some inanimate and stationary thing once she joined the king.

Piper sighed and grabbed her flute, joining the guards with a smile.

Fagini watch, the ferret said as they left.

AT THE EVENING'S BALL, PIPER STOOD IN A PULPIT ENCASED by chest-high pillars. A bird in a gilded cage. Only these bars were alabaster rather than gold. Wearing an ostentatious gown of burnt orange with golden accents, Piper played her flute for the subjects gathered. King Ezra sat on his dais, slumped to one side, while the guests danced to Piper's song. She considered allowing the Æther to flow into the jade stones crafted into the flute but feared she'd disrupt the plan.

When the song ended and the audience applauded loudly, Piper bowed. At the deepest point, she whispered, "Fagini, now."

As the ferret moved beneath her skirts, Piper stood, arms wide. "Something faster now?"

The crowd cheered, and no one seemed to notice Fagini slip out behind her.

Piper played a lively tune, and the townspeople clapped. The dance ensued, couples cavorting throughout the hall, until one woman stumbled to King Ezra's feet.

The king glared at her. "Imbecile. Guards! Remove the graceless wench!"

Piper stopped playing and lifted her chin. "Your Majesty?"

Ezra turned to her, his upper lip twitching.

A good distraction, but she was walking a fine line. She searched the crowd for Leander, hoping Fagini would find him and deliver the stone with her message. But she didn't see him. She addressed the king, "Sire, you never would have thrown someone from your parties before."

The king wobbled over to her little jail. "Watch yourself, Bard." He never used her name. Probably because it reminded him too much of

Royden. King Ezra lowered his voice to a level only Piper could hear. "Or it'll be the oubliette for you." Louder, he added, "Play on!"

The partygoers hesitated, then cheered.

When the party ended, the guards delivered Piper to her room. She waited with Fagini, who had delivered the message stone to Leander. Pacing, she glanced outside regularly. Revelers meandered away from Wynthrop Keep, some to houses in town and others rolling away in horse-drawn carriages. The cemetery was still, save for the crow flitting between graves. When all other motion stilled, she woke the homunculus and cloaked them both.

She cradled her flute in one arm, and the key shook as she extended it toward the lock. If the plan didn't work, she'd face the consequences. Life, or the semblance of it, would be over. But if they succeeded . . .

Piper commanded the doppelgänger to mimic her quiet footsteps, and they left the castle. In the cemetery, she whistled softly. The crow perched on the homunculus's shoulder, and Piper held her hands wide, reaching for the Æther. In her mind's eye, a rainbow of light flowed into her, and she redirected it toward them. Red strands wrapped around the bird and shattered it into multi-colored starlight. Blue rays spread from the artifact at the homunculus's heart, reaching for the star cluster. Orange and yellow surrounded their forms as they merged into one, and finally, violet and green hues pulsed around a solitary form.

When the alchemy was spent, Piper sagged, closing her eyes and panting. The air chilled, then a warm touch lifted her chin. In the once lifeless amber eyes, she found Royden. Piper smiled, and her eyes leaked. He was temporary, but if she could bottle the moment and spirit them away, she would. Heedless of the reality behind the alchemical infusions, she fell into his arms and held on. He stroked her hair like he'd done so many times before.

A throat cleared, and they parted to find Leander sauntering toward them. "You've grown strong, Piper, to return the prince from death." He peered down his long nose at her before turning to Royden and offering a small bow. "You look well, Your Highness."

"I . . . ah," Piper stammered, "he's not real. An infusion and a bound soul. It'll be done by the time the veils close after Samhain." She slipped between them, looking up at Leander. Their friend didn't seem surprised. "Has your access to the Æther returned?" she asked.

"Yes . . . but clearly not as strongly as yours." His eyes darted between Piper and Royden. "Why did you call me here?"

Royden squeezed Piper's shoulders. "We must put an end to Father's grief-stricken reign."

<hr>

Piper expected to meet guards along the way to the oubliette hall in the bowels of Wynthrop Keep. It stood to reason that the king and his captain would allow the guards time away for the celebration, as there were no prisoners in the dungeons, save for the one in an oubliette. The deep hole sealed with an iron grate left Brisco no hope of escaping—at least not on his own.

Before entering the dungeon, Leander stopped and held the stone he'd infused with radiance between himself, Piper, and Royden. "Are you . . . that is, are *we* sure about this?"

With a glance at Royden, Piper said, "I'm not returning to my prison, no matter how much comfort I'm afforded. And I refuse to end up in an oubliette. If we don't succeed . . ." She hugged her flute to her body. After she'd infused the gems, she worked on another infusion. One she hoped she wouldn't have to use. "Well, if we fail, I'll face that when the time comes."

Leander pressed his lips together and held out his hand for her to lead the way.

Piper crouched near the only sealed grate on the floor. "Brisco?"

Rustling, then a hoarse voice asked, "Piper?"

"Yes," she hissed, her heart quickening, "and Leander and Royden."

"What? Impossible!" Brisco's voice boomed.

"I'll explain," said Piper, "but we need to free you first. Leander, the grate?"

The king's forced herald tore his eyes from Royden's doppelgänger. "Yeah. Sure." He passed the lit stone to Royden and bent over the oubliette, inhaling, reaching for Æther.

Piper glanced at the second hole, the one where Almyra would have been, and blinked away a tear.

After Leander lifted the grate, Piper peered inside. Utter darkness. "I'm dropping three gems. You'll feel what to do." Piper stood and waited.

Heartbeats passed before Brisco levitated up from the oubliette—fully dressed, clean, and eyes alight with Æther-infused alchemy. He gaped at the prince, and before Piper could explain, Brisco reared back with his left hand.

To Leander, Brisco growled. "Eight seasons, you left me here to rot while you lived in luxury. It's clear by how soft you've grown . . . except for your magic."

Brisco danced on the balls of his feet and lunged forward.

Leander recoiled.

"You were supposed to be stripped of the Æther! Coward." Brisco loosed the punch at the herald.

Leander ducked.

"STOP!" Piper wedged herself in between them, pressing a hand into each of their chests. She pushed them apart with a grunt. "We were prisoners. The same as you, Brisco, and the Æther has only returned in the last few days. We only have until sunup to reach the king. And Brisco, I need you to act as Prince Royden."

"Why?" He flipped a hand toward the homunculus. "You have one already."

Piper rolled shoulders, readying herself, when Royden inserted himself between her and Brisco. All three men's nostrils flared, and energy buzzed in the air.

"Stop!" Piper barked.

Everyone froze.

She breathed, "We have a plan."

They moved from shadow to shadow toward the royal chambers. Three versions of Prince Royden, Brisco leading, the homunculus with Piper, and Leander in the rear. Brisco and Leander wore Æther-infused necklaces to maintain the disguise.

Two guards stood at the king's door, and Piper licked her lips as she lifted the jade flute. With a slow stream of breath, the instrument emitted low, rolling notes. The guards perked, but they wouldn't hear her song thanks to the flute's infusion. When she'd played them into slumber, Piper padded to the doors and opened the royal common room.

She waved the Roydens forward. When only two joined her, she stared questioningly at them, not daring to speak and alert others. The homunculus, she could discern. Brisco and Leander, though, had been identical. She huffed. Two would have to be enough. She shooed them toward the bedchamber and carefully pulled the doors closed. Piper shivered at the haunting double image of Royden ready to throw open the doors to the king's bedchamber. If it spooked her this much, how would the king react?

That, however, was the point . . . haunt the king on Samhain eve, scare him into becoming a better ruler for the people. Piper nodded, and the Roydens opened the doors to reveal an enormous lump in the four-poster bed.

The doppelgängers padded to either side of the bed as Piper looked out the window. The sky brightened on the horizon. Time was almost up.

Piper mouthed, "Go."

The first Royden boomed, "Father!"

Royden crooned, "Faaatheeer," and the ghostliness of the sound lifted Piper's neck hairs.

The king's eyes flew open. He thrashed. The frame groaned.

On one side, a Royden said, "Wake, Father. 'Tis the witching hour."

The king rolled over like a large ox in the stables, squealing like a little girl. When he saw the second version of his son, he gasped. Ezra shook, his jowls flapping, and fumbled for the clock on his night table. He heaved himself upright in the bed and shook the clock. An Æther-laced peal pierced the night, a magical alarm to alert the king's guards.

Piper ground her teeth. "Treason by your decree! Two years, you've used me as a warning to alchemists who would practice in Wynthrop."

"You bring witchcraft into my bedchamber, Piper Jadeflute, and accuse me?" King Ezra threw off the covers, his aged feet reaching for the ground.

The homunculus pushed the king down as the door clattered open. Piper pivoted, flute at her lips.

Leander entered. Undisguised.

Guards appeared behind Leander, and the person Piper had believed a kindred spirit smirked. He pointed. "Capture the traitors."

Piper backed toward the window and played, her fingers dancing over the keys.

The king stared at the Royden homunculus. "Wh-What's the mea-meaning of this?" He turned to the second replica of his son, his eyes glistening in the breaking dawn. "Two? Y-you're not real."

Leander rolled his eyes and sighed. "King Ezra, be at ease." On the scroll, his fingers in a pattern over the runes.

With vigor, Piper played on to counter Leander's magic. The guards' movements froze, but those with access to the Æther resisted her alchemy, only stalling by half.

Brisco lunged toward Leander, who ducked then swung the bronze scroll. He connected with Brisco's cheek and rounded on Piper.

Still playing, she crouched as the air brushed overhead.

With perfect resistance to her song, the herald sneered, "King Ezra and I eliminated the Æther's curse from the realm. You're unraveling the progress we've made." He glared at Piper. "I ridded the world of your tinkering kind. If I hadn't stopped you from making the drakeheart elixir, it would have disrupted the world's balance. The drakes' longevity is not a human's to steal."

She stopped playing. "You killed Royden!" If she had the means, she'd slay him. "Hypocrite! You're using Æther, Leander. How long have you controlled the king?"

Leander drew a sword, something he'd kept hidden. A cloaking infusion, surely. What other secrets did he have?

The blade zinged and Piper leaped backward. A sable-colored blur soared from the windowsill. The flapping of feathers beat the air. "No!" Piper cried as the homunculus disappeared. Fagini latched onto Leander's throat and the raven pecked his eyes.

A whistle came from the bed's direction.

Brisco held a dagger to the king's throat. All present returned to normal speed but froze in the face of the threat to the king's life, save for the animals attacking Leander.

Eventually, Fagini and the raven stopped. Leander clutched bloodied eye sockets and wailed.

Brisco growled at the king, "Tell your guards to seize the traitor. I suggest an oubliette."

The king nodded, his eyes clear now, and the guards muscled Leander from the room.

The raven shifted into the ghost of Royden, the one Piper had met at graveside. Brisco released King Ezra as the prince floated over and addressed his father. "My spirit has been bound to this world for reasons I didn't understand until tonight."

Tears rolled down King Ezra's cheeks. He looked at the ghost, then at Brisco, still disguised as his son. "Who . . .? I don't understand."

Royden continued, "Father, the kingdom has fallen from grace. Our subjects suffer as they walk the city's streets. Æther is not evil. Not the enemy. It sustained our people once."

The king lowered his head, holding his face in both hands.

His son said with finality, "I'd hug you, but I have no form. Rule well so I may rest." Royden reached for Piper.

She grasped at his apparition, eyes prickling.

Brisco rested a muscular arm about her shoulders, lifted the necklace over his head, and resumed his natural form.

"Care for her?" Royden asked.

Brisco's arm tightened on Piper's shoulder. "I never—"

"Perhaps not," Royden interrupted, "but you have a kind heart." The prince's hand ghosted down the side of Piper's face, then he moved as if caressing his father's shoulders. "And Father."

Prince Royden misted into the morning light. On the wind, his voice drifted, "Until we meet again."

Susan Stradiotto

Susan Stradiotto is passionate about the written word, whether it is in her own writing or her editing practice. She is a fan of well-told stories. She spends part of her days honing her own voice and the rest editing or reading. Susan is always searching for unique voices and stories that tell a truth. As Neil Gaiman said in his master class, "Write the truest story you can." She believes that is what makes a story sing.

Susan is an author of fantasy and romance and has professional editorial experience with genres such as memoir, mystery/thriller, cozy mystery, fantasy, and women's fiction. She attended Capella University for her BS in Information Technology and University of Chicago's Graham School for her professional editing certification. She lives in Eden Prairie with her husband, a hoard of Bernese Mountain Dogs, and one Miniature Dachshund.

You can see Susan's other works at https://susanstradiotto.com/susansportfolio/.

BLOODY MARY'S DAY OFF

SOPHIA-ROSE JOHNSON

I stared into the blue flames of the Bunsen burner in chemistry, needing to get through the last few classes of the day and tell Mama that I played the good girl and didn't burn the school to the ground. Fires weren't my thing, but under the right circumstances and given the annoying population of the school, I might make an exception. But I had promised Mama that today would be different. The odds were not in my favor.

"Witch," someone whispered, and I curled my hand around the mechanical pencil. "Witch." The voice was closer.

I pushed the pencil tip into the paper and broke the lead. It skittered off the end of the table. What did Mama know anyway? When was the last time she had been in high school? The same high school with the same rumors swirling around her.

I took Mama's advice and kept my mouth shut because one witch hunt was enough for a family.

"Witch," someone said, louder. Then a chorus of *witch* popped around me, and I glanced at the group of laughing girls opposite my table. One of them had said the word, and they banded together like a mob. Mobs proved to be dangerous for us witches. I dared Regina, Heather, or Megan to say the word while I stared at them. Regina opened her mouth, and I snapped my pencil in half. She gasped.

Each chant of *witch* behind me burst like a bubble, hitting my back, and I twisted with a sneer, magic tickling my skin.

"Back to work!" called the teacher from the front of the room, eyes set on me.

I turned to the worksheet. The chemical compounds melded together until the printed black ink was incomprehensible.

"Witch," someone hissed, and I whipped around, meeting a lit plastic lighter. The heat of the small fire warmed my skin, and I stared into the orange flame that reflected the worst night of my life.

"Penelope Ravensblood burning in a tree, D-E-A-D. Her daughter screaming at the pyre," he whispered, adding his own lyrics to match the beat of a song playing off someone's phone. "Burn the witch, called the men! But they didn't burn Neve. But I say, put her in the tree. D-E-A-D." He tipped his lighter toward me, right under my nose.

Memories of Mama's death sparked in my mind, and heat flew across my skin like wildfire. I blinked and was shrouded in the darkness of my childhood with the orange flames growing on Mama's withering body.

I curled my hands into fists. Wind whipped around the room, and the flames of the lighter and Bunsen burners went out. The worksheets on the tables fluttered to the floor, and the girls at the table across from me scattered with their hair winding around their necks.

The boy in front of me lost his smile and stepped back. Pushing off my stool, I towered over him. He hadn't hit puberty yet, cute, I could pick him up with one arm and toss him like a ragdoll. But that was physical labor, and why do that when I was a witch?

Matching the beat of the song, I sang to the boy, "Burn the witch, called the men, and they burned Penny. D-E-A-D. They kept her daughter alive. Bad choice for them. Drown the men, said N-E-V-E. Their bodies can never be found. No one can prove it. Ask the L-A-K-E."

The boy gulped, and the lighter clattered to the floor. With a sigh, I let my magic go, and the Bunsen burners sputtered blue flames. The lighter remained on the floor beside the boy.

The teacher called, "It's okay, everyone. Just a freak power outage." But his excuse didn't explain the flying paper or the hair. Things like that just happened around here.

Around me.

"Neve, is there a problem?" asked the teacher at the front of the classroom, finally caring after he let many things slide.

Megan behind me cried. Humans always played the victims so well. They started the fight but couldn't finish it.

Magic rushed across my body, and now that it had tasted freedom—and I had tasted revenge—it wanted more. Burning down the school was so 1980s. Choking on jawbreakers was too '90s, and running girls over with a bus wasn't fetch. I liked the '70s theme of drowning them in blood, but blood was hard to come by in a small town. People tended to notice.

I faced the teacher. "I need to use the bathroom." Or else I might've burst with magic.

And Mama would've hated it when I told her what happened. No matter that the humans had it coming.

The teacher pointed to the door. "You know where it is."

Pasting a smile on my face, I weaved through the tables and left the room. The classroom door shut behind me. That flimsy piece of wood wouldn't stop my magic. Several black specks hung in the hallway like volcanic ash, and the souls dug into my mind. When I blinked, I saw flashes of this school and then ancient ground. I opened my eyes to the bright fluorescent lights of the hallway.

My anger rushed through me like a brewing storm on Lake Superior, and I would've taken everything down in my wake. But I told Mama I would try today, so I went to the bathroom and closed the stall door behind me to calm myself.

Eventually, the automated lights timed out. The teacher hadn't come looking for me, so I was fine. For now. The bell beeped for the end of class, and the bathroom door squeaked open. The lights flipped on, and girls' voices filled the bathroom. Seated on the toilet, I curled my legs under me in the stall.

While I walked the line of being expelled from school, it never happened. I had been suspended, but there was never enough proof to expel me. If there was "proof," the humans would have to believe in magic instead of hurling "witch" like an insult. I was no more than a magician from a weird family to them.

The voices came and went like a wave upon a shore, and then they were gone, the bathroom door swinging shut. I released a breath as a high-pitched voice asked, "Do you actually think Neve Ravensblood is a witch?"

"You saw what she did in chemistry class," answered another girl's voice, and I recognized those voices from all the times they had messed with me. Regina and Heather traveled in a pack.

"Yeah, but you heard the teacher," responded the third girl, Megan, and I leaned forward. The toilet seat creaked, and I froze.

I was stuck in the stall with them gossiping at the sinks. Well, not really with magic. Didn't they want to see what I could do?

I held out my hand. Black smokey ink oozed from my fingertips, but then I stopped, slamming my hand against my chest. Revealing myself as a witch would lead to my death, like it had with Mama. I feared humans more than I wanted to admit, but girls in crop tops and miniskirts weren't as terrifying as the men who lit Mama on fire.

Who held me down and forced me to watch her burn.

"Magic doesn't exist," continued Megan. "It's like Santa or the Tooth Fairy. It's something our parents told us because they knew Penelope Ravensblood. And Neve is a freak, like her mom."

"What if magic does exist?" asked Regina, voice pitching up an octave. There was a zip of a backpack and then a shuffle. "I saw something online. Go into a dark room with mirrors and call out Bloody Mary three times."

"That doesn't sound definitive," responded Megan while Heather answered, "Let's do it! Turn off the lights!"

Footsteps slapped the tile floor, and then the lights snapped off. Megan shrieked, and Heather said, "Shut up. You're going to get us caught. We should be in class."

I placed my feet on the floor and stood up from the toilet. Witches used spells and potions and charms, but I relied on brute force.

A light beamed out, and I peeked through the crack between the bathroom stall door and frame. Heather held a cell phone with her screen lit up. The girls stood shoulder-to-shoulder, staring at the mirrors with clasped hands. They wore matching straightened hair down to their small boobs and braces to correct their overbites. Their sweet perfume of some country princess churned my stomach, and I pushed out a shaky breath.

"On the count of three," said Heather, and the two other girls giggled. "Can you not? We need to focus."

"You're taking this very seriously," commented Megan.

"This is how we find out if magic exists," snapped Heather.

"And if Neve is crazy," added Regina. "She probably is. Just like her mom was. Did you hear her mom 'healed' people? Like with crystals and herbs."

These idiots.

I balled my hands into fists and stared at the three girls through the crack. Magic did exist, and revealing it to these girls wouldn't start a witch hunt, right? They wanted to see it! They already thought I was crazy.

They chanted, "Bloody Mary. Bloody Mary. Bloody Mary."

Nothing.

Apparently, Bloody Mary had the day off, but Bloody Neve was just getting started.

Flexing my hands, I called on a power that I had procured from another witch a couple of years ago, after I dug up her body and took her skull. The skull controlled the power and the soul, if the soul was still connected.

My magic shifted, and I cracked my knuckles. The lights flickered overhead like a flash of lightning, and the extra electricity zapped into me. The small jolt ran over my skin, and the hair on my arms stood. The girls gasped.

"Like what the teacher said," Megan muttered. "A power surge. It isn't magic."

"Sure," answered Heather, and I rolled my eyes, pushing another pulse of magic.

The lights flickered for a few seconds, and then the bathroom went dark. Heather dropped her cell phone, and the flashlight pointed toward the ceiling, shining up in a white cone. I smirked through the crack and then reached out my hand. Black smoke oozed like crude oil from a pit. I lowered my hand to the tile floor and pushed the magic out, making sure I didn't open a portal to another place.

Escape was easy, but I was facing my bullies. How could Mama blame me for that?

The black smoke slithered across the floor, and the inkiness reached around the girls' ankles like tentacles of a sea monster. Regina jumped out of the way with a scream, kicking the smokey tendrils, and they slunk away. Using my other hand, I split my energy, and the lights flickered with the diminished magic.

"It's Bloody Mary!"

The girls ran to the door, and I let the electrical surge drop. Sweat beaded at my temples, and my mouth had run dry.

Raising my hand, I pressed my telekinesis power against the door as Regina tried to open it. The other two girls ran over too, and they slammed their fists against the door. "We're stuck! Help!"

This was a small school, and I knew every hiding place. I had done enough hiding from these jerks. Someone would come running for them soon. It was time for my grand finale.

Drawing back my smoking hand, I twisted my wrist until black ink formed a small black door. Beyond it was a portal built without a connection to a specific place, so I could hold the portal open and travel wherever I liked. It was convenient when I was hungry, and I had even aced a Spanish project by traveling to Mexico. But I didn't need to go that far to scare my classmates.

Snapping my fingers, I opened the portal, and sunlight blinded me. I licked salty sweat off my top lip and dipped my hand into the Ravensblood Temple, which was only a few miles away from school but hidden from anyone who didn't have Ravensblood heritage. And those numbers dwindled to only me. Eyeing the girls through the crack in the stall door, I grabbed the nearest skull I could find, but one skull always had a special place in the temple. I gave her the best spot for the sunrises and sunsets, hiding her away from the cold during the harsh Minnesotan winters and letting her outside because she loved the bright colors of spring and the vivid colors of fall.

Her skull looked no different from any other, and though she had died violently, there was no blunt force trauma to the head. It belonged to Mama, and a small black dot blinked between her abysses for eyes. Her soul was connected to her bone. No afterlife or life recycled here.

Guinevere, what's wrong? she asked, her soft voice echoing in my head and vowels long with her accent.

The girls screamed to get out of the bathroom, and that was the answer. I slammed the portal shut and let that magic go. The smoke settled onto the tile floor, and the phone light seeped out.

Guinevere, think about your actions.

I ran my thumbs over the eyebrow bone of the skull, whispering, "Sorry, Mama."

Twisting her skull around, I lifted it with my magic, and the skull hovered over the bathroom stall door. Then I whistled, and the girls whipped toward me and pointed at the floating skull. "Bloody Mary!"

"She's real!" called Regina.

"Magic is real!" added Megan.

Heather yelled, "I told you. Now get the door open!"

Stifling a laugh, I dropped Mama's skull into my hands and smiled at her. I knew what she would say, so I didn't listen. Only I could hear her anyway. With the portal open, I put her back in the temple and closed the door to another part of the world. The sunlight blipped out.

The girls banged on the door. "HELP!"

They were giving me a headache. I released the magic against the door, and the black smoke trickled into the vents and drains.

The girls nearly ripped the door off the hinges to escape the bathroom, screaming "Bloody Mary!" to the rest of the school. It was a good reason for me to get out, too. Leaving the stall, I stepped over the forgotten backpacks and left the bathroom. The girls had taken off one way, so I turned in the opposite direction, running into a chest.

"Do I want to know?" asked Travis, and I looked up at him.

I sighed. "Don't you have better things to be doing instead of sniffing around?"

"I'm the hall monitor." Paired with his smug smile and mountain-high morals, all he needed was a shiny badge, and the nark trifecta was complete.

I snorted. "I have to get to class. I'm running late."

"You're already late."

"I was looking for a tampon. Very bloody."

He crinkled his nose, but before he said anything else, the principal appeared in the hallway. "Guinevere, in my office now."

So close. I smiled at Travis. "Be a good boy and stay here."

He lowered his voice. "Or what? You'll haunt me as Bloody Mary?"

Rolling my eyes, I followed the principal.

While Principal Mauer loved to strut in front of me with her arms crossed over her chest, she didn't have a lot of proof. Magic was cool like that. I was suspended for smoking in the bathroom—*technically*, there was smoke—but nothing else could be pinned on me. I was out of class when I shouldn't have been, but whatever Regina, Heather, and Megan said about Bloody Mary lacked proof.

A floating skull? As if.

Turning the lights on and off? Stop trying to make it happen. It wasn't going to happen.

The principal turned to the secretary, muttering about who to call to pick me up. Mama was dead, and I was basically hatched because no one ever mentioned a dad, including myself. The principal could've called her police chief husband, but usually, a police officer was only called to take me to school, not away from it.

A knock echoed on the office door. My "godfather" had arrived.

"Hello, Guinevere," said Stewart in his *posh* British accent.

"Mr. Powell," said Principal Mauer, and he shook her hand. Before she launched into the complaint, he was already casting a spell under his breath. Her head tilted to the side, jaw dangling open so far that I saw her back teeth, and the whites of her eyes glistened with the trance that encompassed her.

"Principal Mauer, I'll take Guinevere home now," said Stewart, and the principal stumbled back a step before walking away. He turned to me and winked. "A small memory spell. I could teach you. And more, Guinevere, if you used your magic for more than just playing with mortals. I can take you back to my mansion, get you a good meal, and teach you proper magic. As I have always offered. My son, Lee, is a couple of years younger and living with me full time now. You would have someone your own age."

People my own age were the problem, not the solution. In fact, all people were the problem. There were too many of them.

Stewart sat beside me, and the old wood bench groaned as his corduroy suit rubbed against it. "I thought after the last time we talked that you would be keeping out of trouble, Guinevere."

I picked lint off my jeans. "Give me some credit. I lasted a week."

"Your mother won't be very happy."

I rolled my eyes. "Maybe she'll ground me."

He leaned in, and his breath smelled of cigars. His strong cologne couldn't stifle the scent. "Do I need to bring you to the Council?"

"Oh, come on." I laughed. "Why drag me all the way to the Council just to have the same conversation with me again?"

"We've talked about this," he said in a lowered voice that didn't lose any of its threatening tone, "about using your magic on mortals. They are weak and foolish, but they are useful. *And* they outnumber us. I don't think I need to remind you of witch hunts."

"You don't," I muttered through gritted teeth.

"Then I also shouldn't have to remind you that using magic on mortals will get your powers bound, Guinevere." He looked at me from the corner of his eye, waiting for me to shiver, but his threat was lost on me.

I couldn't count how many times I had used magic on humans, yet here I was. Even Stewart sitting beside me, the Council Elder himself, couldn't compare with his fragile two powers. He was more powerful than most witches, but everyone was weak compared to me.

"My name is Neve." Grabbing my backpack, I pushed past him into the hallway.

Students loitered with their after-school practices and clubs. Nothing that concerned me. Leaning against the lockers embedded in the wall was Travis Charleston. He stepped forward as if to speak to me, and then stepped back as Stewart followed me out of the office.

"Shall I take you home?" asked Stewart.

There was no home, and I didn't need Stewart following me around. "No. I'm going to see Mama."

Black smoke seeped into the cracks of the earth, drifting away in the breeze blowing off Lake Superior and whistling through the trees in the woods. Waves crashed against the rocky cliffside, and bugs buzzed around, mixing with the specks of souls that haunted my every step. I swatted them away.

In the middle of the woods was a circular clearing. It looked natural to any hunter that stumbled across it, but it also made any human nervous. It was no wonder why humans didn't like magic when it left a metallic taste on their tongue and stomach in knots. I stepped through the shield, and the Ravensblood Temple appeared with its four walls made of wood and a pointed roof. Piece by piece, it was falling apart until a strong gust of wind would blow it over, but piece by piece, I was rebuilding the temple to create a new place.

A place that was truly mine against the loudness of the world: the Castle of Skulls.

The skulls stared into the temple, the hundred that I had, and the vacant spaces for more to come. I wanted to fill the whole space until it was truly my own. Depending on how my conversation went with Mama, maybe I would be digging up a new skull tonight. How did Paris sound? Last time I tried to get to Paris, I accidentally ended up in eastern Europe, but then again, I got a D+ in geography. When I entered my family's temple, the skulls peered at me with their black, unblinking gazes, and the souls crowded around, wanting to be heard. I ignored them all and picked up Mama's skull.

After throwing her back through the portal, her jaw had come off, and I fit her back together like a puzzle while cleaning the grime out between her teeth.

Guinevere, said Mama, her voice echoing in my head. *You didn't have to do that today. I know they get on your nerves—*

"Is that what we're calling it?" I asked, words clipped.

You're stronger than they are, and it isn't a fair fight. I asked you not to cause trouble at school or with the mortals.

"I won't be going to school for the rest of the week. You won't have to worry about it."

Guinevere. Her voice was tighter. *Those mortals can be your friends.*

"No," I said in the same tight voice. "I don't need them as friends. I have you all." I looked around at my skulls, and their souls pushed closer to me, the black specks hovering around my face.

They wanted to be heard, and only I could listen.

You can be a good girl, Guinevere. Don't hurt the mortals, and don't give into their foolishness. It will only hurt you more.

"I know I can be a good girl, Mama," I said, "but I don't want to be. I'd rather be feared."

What about respect?

I laughed. "Humans don't know anything about that."

Guinevere, she said in a warning tone as I placed her back on the small shelf that I had for her. An amulet red with blood and a singular black raven's feather sat beside her. *Please don't do this.*

"It's already done, Mama." It was done when I got revenge on the men who killed her over ten years ago. "They started it. I'm just ending it." Leaning down, I kissed her skull. "Good night, Mama. I have homework to ignore." And skulls to dig up . . .

And powers to steal.

Sophia-Rose Johnson

Sophia-Rose Johnson, who has also written under S. Johnson, is from Minnesota, USA, and she is a northerner by heart and accent. She graduated from the University of Wisconsin-Superior in 2018 with a writing degree, and she argues about commas constantly. While she first published in 2022, she's been writing since 2011. When not working at her day or night job, she enjoys reading, hanging out with family and friends, playing with her dogs, making sarcastic comments, being a fake blond, chugging energy drinks, and wearing high heels as a tall woman.

Stay up to date with Johnson:
https://www.sjohnsonbooks.com/

In the Fierce Shadows

Jo Holloway

GRIFFEN

The walls blur around me. Ink threatens to stain my freshly penned letter as I sign my name with a shaking hand, so I finish and quickly set the quill down. It settles beside a gilded invitation that still strikes panic through my core. But I'm doing this. My final lines and signature on the letter seal my promise.

Until I see you soon, my love,
I remain yours in heart and soul,
Griffen Fiercebeat

Someone with the moniker Lord Fiercebeat should command armies and respect instead of a meager household staff of three. I should parade the streets of my fiefdom, taking praise from all those who live on my lands. As lord, I should be a fearless leader, a great man. Handsome. Powerful. Confident.

I am none of those things.

Neither tall, nor brawny, nor brave. I am not the son my father wished for, nor the lord my people deserve, especially having taken the title so young. I cope by hiding from it all, and it has been working for me . . . until now.

Until Annaly.

Her letters are all that has ever made me feel desired or strong. Perhaps it is seeing her words on parchment—much more personal than our Anterran water screens—that make me feel closer to her. She knows the real me. Our letter friendship across worlds and over three annums progressed slowly to more, and now she holds my whole heart in hands I've never seen.

In five short days, I will cross worlds to Zocere to change that. My stomach clenches as if it knows I never leave my estate, let alone my world.

Stamping the envelope with my seal is the bravest thing I've done, which should perhaps not be such a point of pride, but here we are.

Only the promise of meeting Annaly at long last could lure me to something as horrific as Zocere's Season Ball. My heart thumps at the images flooding my imagination: the crowds, a cavernous space thrumming with people, myself lost in the chaos, drowning.

No. Stop. Annaly will be there for me. She promised, and I trust her.

The door to my study swings open to reveal the stern face of my butler.

"Lord Fiercebeat."

"For skies' sake, Darcy, how many times have I said to call me Griffen?"

"I'm afraid I lost count several annums past, my Lord."

"And what does that tell you?"

I swear, he almost smiles. "Only that I should keep better count."

He's impossible. My gaze catches on the gold foiled invitation that will take me to Zocere, and I shove it hastily beneath other correspondences on my desk, trying to ignore the panic a little longer. Then I fight my nerves and hand Annaly's letter to Darcy to send out.

"Are you all right, my Lord?"

I give him a tight nod, not trusting my voice while my throat feels padded in wool.

"Good, because you have a visitor."

Oh, no. I cannot possibly meet anyone right now. "Handle it please, Darcy. If one of the farmers is here about the Mist encroaching their lands, tell them taxes will be forgiven for all lost land, as I have done for others."

"Your generosity knows no bounds, my Lord."

I give him a sharp look.

He appears sincere, if slightly smug. "Unfortunately, the visitor is not one of your subjects. He's a Keeper."

My eyes dart to Annaly's letter in his hand, but this mustn't be about a simple mail Keeper, here to pick up post for other worlds. The invitation hidden on my desk is a looming presence behind me. Travel between worlds requires a Keeper's accompaniment, so perhaps this is about arrangements for the ball.

I suppose I must go see. Now, if only my hands would stop shaking. A Fiercebeat should not tremble.

LOCKE

Lord Fiercebeat looks nothing like his name. Lord Fearful-Feet maybe? Lord Faints-Easily? The guy looks like he's meeting a ghost instead of a Keeper at his door. I give him a quick assessment, finding him shorter and blonder than me. Nothing that will be an issue since he's such a recluse that no one ever sees him.

I give my little spiel about searching for someone traveling illegally between Anterra and Havannsar. Shocker: he has no information. Probably because I made it up.

"Thank you for your assistance, Lord Fiercebeat," I say, mustering the formality Anterrans prefer. I hide my amusement at feeling like I've stepped into a historical drama whenever I come to this world, and then put the rest of my plan into action.

I shift, acting antsy and lingering on his threshold. *Hook . . .*

"If there's anything else we can do—" he starts.

Line . . . "Actually, could I make use of your facilities? It's been a long day." Now paint some embarrassment on my face . . . *And, sinker.*

"Of course. The closest is up the stairs on your left."

I already know that from the blueprints I examined earlier. Also, the study is three doors down on the right and that's my best bet for this mission. One sneaky trip down the corridor later, I find exactly what I'm looking for on the desk and, five minutes after that, I'm out the front door with a gilded invitation lining the inside of my jacket. I hurry back to the nearest gate to Zocere, returning to Juliet's smithy less than an hour after leaving.

"Locke, you're back already." Jules looks up from her anvil at my entrance, and sneers at the fancy parchment in my hand. "Success, I see."

"Did you doubt me?"

When Juliet contacted me about this job, I had concerns. Stealing crown jewels is a little high profile for my taste. I prefer to operate in the nice dark shadows where no one knows my name or how I do what I do. Plus, I'm a smuggler, not a thief. Fortunately, my part is only to get the silver scepter out of Zocere after the theft is over. Attending the ball where the theft will occur is for my own purposes. I like getting into places I don't belong.

Besides, I'm not comfortable without knowing every detail of the jobs I take. I do my research, I learn my targets, I plan my routes and backup routes and backup-backup routes.

Rule number one: plan for everything.

In this case, I don't know the thief, but I trust Jules, even when she eyes the invitation with a strange look. I hold it up. "This Lord Fierce-beat really was the quivering recluse you said. There's no way he's going to the Season Ball."

GRIFFEN

I can't believe I'm going to the Season Ball. My heart has been racing since I woke, and now that it's time, I've forgotten how to breathe. The promise of Annaly is the only thing keeping my body upright.

The two lorcans drawing my coach may be ugly beasts with their shaggy humps and large horns, but they're steady, and I'm grateful for the smooth ride. I'll need all my energy later to deal with people. I'm already stressed after losing track of my invitation somehow, and I've been rehearsing for days what I'm going to say to explain its absence.

When we stop too soon, anxiety tightens my throat. A glimpse outside reveals Timothy jumping down to lead the lorcans through a stretch of thick Mist.

"Small delay, my Lord," he calls, as the beasts dig their hooves in.

Delay. Wonderful. I wanted to be early, but animals don't like the Mist any better than the rest of us. Its spread is one more thing for me to worry about alongside the crop failures.

Annaly. Annaly. I'm going for Annaly.

With any luck, she will agree to marry me and return with me, and then I will have a partner with whom to face all of this. The calm confidence in her letters is exactly what my fief needs in these times. That *I* need. Ever since my family died, that anchor has been missing from my life. I crave her company like my next breath.

When we finally reach the gate, I join the queue.

The Keeper takes my arm at my turn, and she's kind about my

obvious fear. "I recommend closing your eyes and counting to ten. By then, the new world will have re-formed around you. Ready?"

I'm normally uncomfortable with strangers touching me, but her solid grasp is the least of my concerns. The vice tightens around my ribs as I nod.

She smiles. "Relax. In a moment, you'll see stars again. At the edge of the Mist here, you must not see the sky often. Shame you won't be there during the day to enjoy real sunshine."

I nod with a last glance up to where swirls of Mist obscure any chance of seeing stars. *Blue skies*, I'm really about to travel between worlds with a Keeper! When she nudges me forward, I close my eyes and count to ten. *For Annaly.*

When my eyelids open, I'm in a flagstone courtyard with a towering château looming over me. Voices assault me from all sides. Chatter. Greetings. Laughter. Instructions being barked out. Smells join in. Perfumes. Colognes. A whiff of mint nearby. Fainter, there's a scent of meat being roasted and something sweet like spun sugar.

Dizziness swirls over me.

The Keeper releases my arm and heads back for her next guest. Efficient. Gone.

I'm jostled from behind and stumble. How I wish my plan to be early had worked out and I could have arrived before the crowds. I wanted to be inside, staking out a quiet corner to watch the staircase. I didn't want to deal with the expectant gazes of a packed room. I wanted to be there waiting to hear Annaly's name, to know I could not have missed her. I wanted to feel in control.

The ground swirls and tilts, making the château walls feel like they're falling away from me. I might tumble into the sky, which—*oh!*—is indeed full of stars. How are there so many? How can I feel so unmoored, so small, so—

"*Allo.*" A guard in an official uniform of blue velvet with brass buttons waves a hand in front of my face. Then he holds it out expectantly. "Your invitation, *Monsyr*?"

"Invitation. Uh, yes." Breathlessly, I stutter out the explanation I rehearsed. I remember shoving it under other papers on my desk, but when I next entered my study two days later, it was nowhere to be found. *Please let him understand.*

"I cannot admit you without your invitation."

My voice shakes and my legs quiver, but I've come this far. "I'm Lord Fiercebeat. My fief is the fifth largest in Anterra. Please check the guest list." I ignore his skeptical look because I know I look too young to have inherited a lordship already, but I didn't ask for my parents to die.

I'm sweating as he insists, and I beg.

"There's a woman . . . I'm to meet her here." Desperation tinges my choked words.

Then my throat fills, the quiver in my legs intensifies, and my heart races to flutter with the shaking. I should have known I couldn't do this. Black night and bright stars swirl together, exploding, fading, until I fall into the darkness.

***

LOCKE

The courtyard of Château Mont drips in lavish blue draperies, with twisting topiaries lit by blue fairy lights stationed along low walls. Live peacocks strut between them. Pretentious much? Even the outdated British monarchy in my world isn't this bad. I have new appreciation for the way Juliet scoffed at the invitation.

Gates from multiple worlds all open to this courtyard, and it thrums with activity as people emerge in all manner of dress. Stone arches have been built around each gate to give them substance since only Keepers can see the colorful shimmering lights of each world.

Me, I see a rainbow. On my left is the gleaming silver gate to my world, good ol' Terra, or Earth . . . whatever you want to call it. To my right is the red of Rustak, the purple of Havannsar, and more. In the center is the one I should have come through if I were truly the Lord I'm impersonating tonight, the shimmering green of Anterra. There seems to be some sort of commotion there, and since I don't want any undue attention in my direction, I move to an entrance farther away and show my pilfered invitation to a guard.

I'm dressed in Anterran fashion for my role tonight. Black trousers, black shirt, black stand-collar tailcoat. Even a black cravat. Hey, it worked for Zorro. The Dread Pirate Roberts, too.

The truth is, I'm worried about a cut on my arm opening up, and black will hide any bleeding. Serves me right for sparring with Juliet earlier today, but I was falling out of practice with my blade work. Of course, Jules showed me my weak points with the business end of a saber, but that's Jules for you.

The still-fresh wound pulses with dull heat.

Château guards give each guest a quick wave of a magic wand—like a metal detector that alerts to magic. I pass easily and move inside to hand the invitation to the herald at the top of a sweeping staircase. I also pull out a pewter flask and take a small swig.

"*Non confia bev que non fay,*" I say in Zoceriene with a wink, telling him I don't trust drinks I didn't make myself.

While he reads the name and prepares to announce me as Lord Griffen Fiercebeat, I use the distraction to flick the hidden catch on the flask and let the ruby within fall into my palm.

Pewter naturally blocks witch-magic, hiding this little enchantment from the wands. Now that it's out, the spell I bought from the Ruby Witch will start working. Nothing nefarious of course. It'll only make me less interesting. This ball is a golden opportunity to gather useful intel from all the important people gathered here. The more I fade away, the better.

The spell is about to be tested because I can't avoid being announced, no matter how reclusive I'm supposed to be, or how much the real me prefers to work in the shadows.

"Lord Griffen Fiercebeat," the herald bellows to the room below.

A few heads turn as I make a careful descent down the stairs like the timid Lord Fiercebeat would, and their eyes skip past me to find something—*anything*—more intriguing. I'm smug about the Ruby Witch's spell right up until I spot a woman near the back whose gaze is locked on me. *Huh.* That shouldn't happen.

I take in the room, the decorations, the dancing couples, the dignitaries. At one side, a raised dais boasts four lavish seats for the royal family, two of which are occupied. I recognize the Mont'Ag, the ruler of Zocere. The younger man beside him must be his eldest son, the Mont'Ague. Zocere's crown prince wears a cape trimmed by brilliant red feathers jutting up behind his head like a flaming crown.

Personally, I think it makes him look like an overgrown bird on fire.

I can picture Juliet's disgust if she could see it. To be fair, he doesn't look pleased about it either.

I'm even less pleased when my quick scan finds that woman still staring at me. *Seriously, lady*? Why isn't she ignoring me like everyone else? *What the hell, spell*?

When she heads my way, it's time to get lost in a crowd.

Dignitaries from different worlds mingle together. Lucrative trade deals are being arranged alongside advantageous marriage pairings. It's networking on steroids, and I'm here for it, eavesdropping everywhere I can. An informed smuggler is a good smuggler, and I'm the best, so I'm all for soaking up everything I can.

No one pays me any attention, and my wandering finally shakes my stalker woman. It also brings me to an offshoot room where I lay eyes on tonight's prize.

The silver scepter rests on a burgundy pillow atop a pedestal. A pair of guards watch over it, not letting anyone too close. We wouldn't want any overeager guests getting fingerprints on our precious heirlooms, now would we? I take a moment to appreciate the symbols cast in silver that probably mean something to Prince Flaming Peacock back there, but not to me, then I test the security. Despite my *not-the-droids-you're-looking-for* spell, the guard on the right steps forward as soon as I lean in. I have no idea how the thief is going to pull this off.

"Griffen?"

Distracted by the scepter, I fail to turn to the voice behind me.

"Lord Fiercebeat?"

Right. That's me! I'm Griffen Fiercebeat. I spin.

"It's me. Annaly." It's the woman again, and the expectant way she introduces herself has me getting a case of the uh-ohs.

She's clearly Zoceriene with that copper skin and sleek black ponytail, so she can't know me . . . know Griffen, that is. I made absolutely sure he'd never left Anterra before. He barely leaves his estate. But Spidey senses tell me something's wrong.

"Yes, hi. I'm Griffen. But, I guess, uh, I guess you know that."

For some reason, she smiles at my deliberately dorky, fumbled introduction. "I heard you announced."

"Ah, of course." It doesn't explain why she's still here despite my attention repelling charms, both magical and otherwise. "Well, I should be going."

"But, you just got here. I . . . we . . . did I do something wrong?"

"Of course not."

"You're not what I expected," she says.

"Expected?" Like I said . . . uh-oh.

"The way you described yourself wasn't so . . . tall."

She doesn't know Griffen by sight, obviously. "Sorry to disappoint you."

"No, I'm being rude. You're, um, fine." After a pause, she continues. "I envisioned this differently."

Her gaze cycles from upset to angry to confused, and when she fixes on the guards, I need a distraction. "Shall we dance?"

I guess I'll be putting more of my Griffen Fiercebeat research to the test until I can ditch this Annaly person somewhere, preferably far from the scepter. It's a good thing I know how to dance like a lord.

GRIFFEN

If I never attend another ball, it will be too soon. Any lingering hope of finding Annaly amidst the dancers is fading. The ballroom is even more crowded than the courtyard, and the herald flat out refused to announce me without my invitation, so Annaly won't be finding me either. He even claimed he'd announced me already, which is absurd.

Then again, I'm lucky to be inside at all. Fainting may not have been my proudest moment, however it did have the advantage of making some well-intentioned meddling women sympathetic to my plight. One of them pleaded with a guard to let me through because it was, "For love. Isn't it romantic?"

A woman about my parents' age was kneeling beside me when I came to. "Griffen?" She must have overheard me giving the guards my title, and she vouched for me. "I knew your parents, dear. I'm terribly sorry for your loss."

That explained why she believed me in spite of my age. I was barely a man when my parents lost their lives, barely old enough to legally take on the lordship. It has been two annums since then, and I doubt I look much older now, no matter how ancient I feel under the pressures of the fief and the curse of the Mist. The only bright spot has been Annaly. She helped me through my grief and to cope with the rest.

I must find her.

I can't come this far to give up now.

The hope of hearing Annaly announced is a dream long lost, as I must be one of the final guests to enter. Wherever she is, she is already here. Does she assume I failed to come? Did I disappoint her? That intolerable thought drives me into the mayhem of the dance floor.

Dance lessons were torture growing up, and I skipped as many as I could rather than suffer the nauseating mix of girls laughing and boys competing to earn their attention. Thoughts of dancing are still enough to make me sweat, even though I would try for Annaly.

Blue skies, must it be so hot?

It's hard to focus with the pulse hammering at my neck. The trouble is, many Zocerienes share the same features. Everywhere I turn there are women with black hair and copper skin. They're spinning and passing me too quickly to search for the brown eyes and smile I feel I will somehow recognize. I know her. I can feel that she is close. She has to be.

"*Monsyr.*" A hand appears in front of me with a tray of tall flutes filled with bubbling amber drink.

Grateful, I pluck one from the offering and down its contents. The delicious burn steadies me and opens my throat. There! I spot a woman wearing a sleek dress of mahogany fabric, close enough to the brown Annaly said she'd be wearing. Alas, this woman is already dancing with a partner, a man all in black who looks vaguely familiar. She's also far too beautiful, although I know my Annaly will be much prettier than she describes. She's too humble, cleverer than she will credit herself, funnier than she imagines, too kind to put into words.

Much as I would like for the striking woman to be her, it must not be, for that woman is engrossed in her partner and not searching the room or looking disappointed that I did not show. Maybe I give myself too much credit. Perhaps she simply moved on when I did not appear.

The idea pains my heart.

That settles it. I must find the courage to ask after her. It's an effort to force my feet toward a group of Zoceriene nobility conversing together, but I manage.

"*Escuzay*. Pardon. Would you happen to know Annaly Forsayn?"

The first group gives me contemptuous glares for the interruption and deny knowing Annaly before returning to their quick language I cannot hope to understand. *Sunny skies*, I hate people.

"I saw her *la*," a woman in the next group says with a vague wave in the direction of the open doors where the orchestra plays.

Heart in my throat, I head that way, keeping my eyes open for more brown dresses on black-haired women. Gold. Tawny. Bronze. That one's brown, but on a blonde woman who looks Anterran like me. Nothing that fits. Until . . .

It's her again. The same woman, dancing with the man in black. She looks less enchanted now, and more . . . studious? I cast about for anyone from Zocere who might know the woman's name.

"*Monsyr, escuzay*. Do you know—"

That's as far as I get before the far end of the room erupts in chaos.

LOCKE

"You severely undersold your dancing ability, Griffen," the woman named Annaly says.

I've run out of safe distractions like the weather or the dresses and tunics of the people nearby. She's persistent, this one.

"A lord must know his way about the dance floor." I don't know what to make of her endless questions. I did my research, and I know Griffen Fiercebeat took dancing lessons growing up, like all nobles in Anterra. I've carefully stuck to Anterran dance styles, so what gives?

"I knew you were modest in your letters, but your skill is impressive." Her words say impressive. Her face says suspicious.

Yeah, I've gathered these two are some sort of pen pals. She actually expects the most reclusive lord in all of Anterra to travel through a gate with a stranger, come to another world, to a ball full of important dignitaries, where he would certainly be uncomfortable at best . . . all to see her. Well, . . . *blue skies*, as the Anterrans would say. What if he is here?

"You're too kind."

At that, she smiles. "You always say so."

Phew. Got one right. It would be difficult for Griffen to come without his invitation, but not impossible. If he was determined enough. If he cared enough.

The guy I met looked like he might hurl just from having to greet me at his front door. That guy wouldn't go to all this effort to meet a pen pal across worlds. Unless . . .

She's looking up at me with dark, intelligent eyes, sparking with something softer, something longing. I spin her to pull her closer, and her cheeks flush.

Aw, hell. She's in love with him. *They're* in love. I can practically hear my old mentor reminding me, *"Count on something unexpected going wrong."* Yep. Nailed it.

"You dance well,"—she slides her hand along my biceps—"but you hold this arm too low." She squeezes.

I can't hide the flinch at the stab of pain from the cut there.

"You're hurt."

"I—" I need a believable reason, and fast, because she is stiffer than she was a moment ago, and her eyes lack the softness they held before. "Small sparring accident. Nothing to worry about, darling."

I can tell the words are wrong before she speaks. "Sparring? You? And, *darling*? I think not. You dance. You haven't asked after my sister's health or commented on my wren-feather headpiece. Who are you, and where's Griffen?"

Ugh. Women. Too smart for their own good. Exit strategy— engaged. "Don't know what you're talking about, *sweetums*. I call all the ladies darling. Or honey. Baby. I've been known to use pumpkin on occasion." With a wink, I spin her again to set her off kilter.

Before I can slip away, the music screeches, warbles, and stops. Someone shrieks. Someone else curses. People yell, and Annaly and I get thrust together into a mass of pushing and shoving. The crowd surges from the open doors to escape whatever uninvited mayhem just crashed the party, and I get a look over the tops of frightened heads. I almost laugh.

Why is there a goat in the ballroom?

Hey, don't look a gift goat in the teeth, I always say.

I drop my grasp on Annaly and make the best of a perfect distraction. Unfortunately, she stumbles right into the clearing opening up.

"Griffen!" she shouts indignantly.

Even if I feel a brief flash of guilt at leaving her to her fate, I'm out of here. She might get a few bumps and bruises, but she'll live.

Besides, I have a keen suspicion about the reason for this random goat-triggered mayhem. Curiosity returns me to the scepter just in time to see the crowd jostle the pedestal. For a single breath, the scepter disappears as it rolls off the top. A moment later, a guard rises with it clutched in his fist. His partner clears the crowd from around them, and they hover over their royal family's treasure.

Only someone who has spent as much time in a smithy, seen as many pieces forged with the precise technique used by my old mentor—which he taught to Juliet, who then perfected it—would be able to detect a subtle dark luster to the silver that wasn't there before. I smile.

Cheeky thief.

I'm chuckling under my breath as I exit. Whoever the thief is, they made an impressive switch, meaning now it's my turn. I head for our arranged drop point without a glance back for Annaly. Part of me hopes that if the real Griffen Fiercebeat is indeed here somewhere, that those two find each other. Maybe someday they'll tell their grandkids about this crazy night.

As for me, I'm Locke again, and the job comes first. All that's left is to smuggle one shiny object back to my world and hand it off. The stars are out. It's a beautiful night to get paid.

GRIFFEN

I've been thrust into my worst nightmare. Touching, shoving, shouting, crushing . . . I can't breathe.

Somehow, I claw my way to the crowd's edge only to find the commotion being caused by a single sun-forsaken goat of all things. Sure, it's running through party guests, but it's only an animal. People are the problem.

I'm shoved into the opening, hardly caring, though, because there's that woman again. She falls away from her partner, directly into the goat's path.

Surely, the man in black will pull her from harm's way. My stomach gives a jolt at the almost familiar calculating expression on his face, but before I can get a better look, he flees. The goat sends a group staggering into one another with shouts of surprise and pain, and then there's nothing left between it and her.

"Griffen!" she shouts after the man who abandons her to her fate.

My name shocks my feet into motion, no matter that it's not me she's watching.

Whether it is my name or basic decency that drives me, I dart across the opening. It's not elegant or smooth. I crash into her and loop an arm around her waist to pull us both out of the way. Hooves clatter on the marble and a barnyard stench brushes by. The fabric of her dress is buttery soft against my palm and the texture soothes me, calms my thoughts, stills my trembling. A soft *ouf* escapes her as she thuds against my chest.

I cannot believe her partner left her. Scoundrel! I want to yell at everyone around us as to why no one tried to help. I don't even realize the way I'm blocking people with an arm outstretched and my body between her and the crowd until soft pressure pushes against my chest. *Oh*. I'm still holding her.

My hands drop to my sides, tingling with the loss of that silken sensation against them.

"Sorry. I'm terribly sorry."

"You're sorry you saved me?" Her smile is bemused. She's stunning.

"No, I . . . that is I . . . I didn't mean to grab you."

"Well, I'm certainly glad you did. It beats the alternative, *non*?"

"I suppose so." The fact that she called my name has not slipped my mind. Could this be? Her brown dress, the black hair, and dark, warm eyes . . . "Your dance partner left in a hurry. Who was he?"

She scowls in the direction taken by the man in black, and I suddenly realize the feathers she wears are those of a wren. My favorite bird. She remembered.

"Lord Griffen Fiercebeat," she replies bitterly, and then adds, "apparently."

"Annaly?" I hold my breath.

Her eyes refocus on me, and she blinks. "I am. But . . ." She drops her gaze and takes me in properly.

Sun save me. I take her hand. "I don't know who that man was, but he was neither lord nor your Griffen." I muster my best smile, which is admittedly tentative. "I'm sorry I'm late, my love."

Her expression would be funny if I weren't trying to breathe through a tightening throat, awaiting her reaction. The surprised O of her mouth closes to a tight line and her eyes go hard. "I knew it! That man. I knew you would never . . . *ooh*!"

A squeeze on her hand brings her back to me.

She's frowning. "You have no idea the terrible things I've been thinking."

My heart stutters. Is it ruined? Have I lost my chance?

"Oh, *cher*. You should see your face." Her other hand comes up to caress my cheek and the room falls away. "We ought to see that imposter hanged for putting such stress on my beloved's face."

"Beloved?" My chest squeezes. Is that hope?

"Come, we must catch him."

I should probably be angry at whoever stole my invitation and my name for the night, for *this* of all nights, but with Annaly finally in my arms, I find I don't care. "He's long gone. Look around."

She does, taking in the chaos, and her scowl softens to concern. "Are you all right, *cher*?"

All I can do is beam at her. I must look daft.

Annaly knows me well. "Shall we get you out of all this bustle?"

"*Sunbeams*, yes. You have no idea how wonderful it is to hear your words lifted from the pages at last."

"I have some idea." She gifts me her stunning smile and takes my hand.

We weave through the crowd to the terrace doors. Outside, I can breathe again, though my heart doesn't slow its mad fluttering.

"Better?" Annaly asks, turning to face me.

Did I say I could breathe? I was wrong. So very wrong. She is even more beautiful in the light of the stars than she was inside. They sparkle in her eyes. I am leagues beyond my depths.

Her mouth quirks into a sly smile. "You know, he may not have been you, but that man was a very good dancer."

"Oh. I—" Does she have regrets now that she has seen the real me? "I'm afraid you'll be disappointed, then."

"I'm not. It was part of what made me suspicious." She tosses me a grin and my entire stomach flips over. "But I do regret not dancing with you." She nods to where the orchestra is striking up again as the royals and various important people struggle to get the ball under way again.

From the corner of my eye, I spot a guard walking a surly-looking goat out on a length of rope.

Annaly bursts out laughing.

Before I know it, I've joined her. "Your royal family certainly knows how to entertain."

That only makes Annaly laugh harder. "Oh, the Mont'Ag will be furious if his son's party is ruined. How ever did a goat get into the ball?"

"Perhaps it was possessed. Mischievous spirit?"

She looks up at me, checking whether I'm serious, then her laugh rings out again. "I'm glad I almost got trampled."

"You are?"

"It brought me to you. The real you," she adds. "Now about that dance . . . Let's stay out here to enjoy the stars. I won't be seeing them much after tonight."

"Does that mean . . . are you saying you would still do me the honor of accompanying me back to Anterra? I didn't get a chance to properly ask you, or speak the romantic things I wanted to say, and you were nearly trampled, plus I should explain about my fief, and there are things to arrange, and—"

She stops me with a finger on my lips. "Griffen, what do you think these past seasons of letters were for? I already know you. I already love you. Not even possessed goats will change my mind now."

My stomach swoops. I step in to cup her cheek. "I love you, my Annaly. You are more perfect, more kind, more . . . *more* than I ever imagined. But are you sure? Are you not . . . disappointed . . . having met me?"

Her smile is a tease. "That depends. I'm still waiting for that dance. But I do believe I'll keep you in the end."

"Even if I tread on your toes?"

"Especially then. Because I'll know you're really you." And she lifts onto those precious toes to press her lips to mine.

The kiss melts into an embrace and then we're dancing on the stone terrace beneath the stars in a world all our own. We hold each other, swaying and talking softly about everything from her sister's recovery to my fainting earlier, to what she will experience in Anterra. She has ideas to help the fief. We'll have a lot to face together, and for once, it doesn't scare me.

With the strings of the orchestra soft beneath the velvet sky, we dance to the sound of our beginning.

Jo Holloway

Jo Holloway is a Canadian author of fantasy books for young adults and fantasy-loving readers of all ages. *In The Fierce Shadows* is a short story set in two of the worlds from her upcoming series, *The Cursed Globe*. Her completed YA fantasy series, *The Immortal Voices*, features a unique hidden species known as the Pyx, the rare humans who can hear them, and the incredible bonds they form.

Jo refuses to choose between cheese and chocolate and believes that soup can't be trusted, and that animals are better than people. If she's not lost in a fantasy world, you might find her out walking her beautiful, quirky dog.

For a free book and a complete list of Jo's published works, visit johollowaybooks.com/books

A Polite Thief

D.M. Taylor

K ianna Waywardforger was born into a royal family at the end of a succession of three brothers.

"I'm a girl not a porcelain doll. I want to play outside with my brothers," Kianna cried to her father.

"I don't like you in the mud clinking wooden sticks and shields with those boys."

"But father, I'm a strong opponent. I beat Richard twice yesterday," she said demonstrating her quick footed abilities.

"Furthermore, I don't like to see you jousting on horseback with them either," her father said pushing his glasses up the bridge of his nose with his index finger.

Kianna's scowled at her father's disapproval. "I do my etiquette lessons learning to ride as a young lady, but I prefer riding no handed alongside my brothers." The balance and muscle she'd developed during her ballet lessons also afforded her strength when jousting.

"I don't know what to do with you, Kianna. You need more female influences in your life. We must get you a nan."

Kianna wasn't against the idea of having a nanny, but she was dismayed that her father wanted her to become a lady and leave behind the fun she'd always had with her brothers.

Mere days later, Kianna hid behind the drapes in her father's study. She spied on the parade of women that her mother and father interviewed to help her become a proper lady.

The prospects left her feeling hopeless. She disliked each one more than the one before, for each seemed more stuffy and strict. Kianna would never forget the air of magic that fell upon the room when the woman who'd become her nan finally arrived. She'd worn an oversized bonnet and full-length dress of green velvet. The sway of her bustle captured Kianna's attention. She answered each question Kianna's parents asked with a convincingly firm tone on the methods of how a young lady should behave. But Kianna could've sworn that Nan had glanced her way more than once winking and offering Kianna a sly smile. When her mother set the tea tray out for their guest, she was certain she witnessed her future nan slip half a dozen cookies into her handbag right under her parent's noses and they had not even noticed. How had she done that? Kianna wondered.

"Darling you can come out," the nan said.

Kianna's mother and father were surprised that their daughter had been hiding in the room with them.

Nan offered her hand to Kianna, "Pleasure to make your acquaintance, young miss."

Kianna abandoned her hiding spot to accept the woman's hand vigorously shaking it. Nan placed her left hand over their improper handshake, quietly correcting Kianna's greeting. Kianna was captivated by the contrast of the woman's red lips and her bright white teeth as she smiled. Kianna was more than happy to receive the woman's correction of how to properly greet a guest.

As Kianna grew, her time was spent mostly with her Nan. She showed Kianna how to be a lady and make her parents proud. She also introduced Kianna to the world outside of the privilege she was granted with birth.

Often as a little girl, she'd journey to the shire where her nan's family lived. No one treated her like she was the baby sister there. She had friends that would play with her at the riverbank the whole day.

"Let's build mounds, Kianna!" The children would squeal as they scooped the wet dirt piling it as high as they could before the water would wash it away. Day after day, she joined them to investigate which mud worked the best to withstand the water's power and then Kianna would listen to stories from the folk who gathered by the river for its earthly riches. These activities carried Kianna into her early adolescence.

One day while Kianna was interacting among the shire folk, she overheard Nan speaking with one of her friends. "The girl has a talent for seeing," Nan said.

"Do you think she's worthy of training?" her friend asked.

Nan nodded. "Indeed, I do."

Kianna didn't know what her Nan had meant about seeing or the training her friend spoke of, but she felt a spark in her belly. She knew better than to reveal that'd she been eavesdropping and so she waited for her Nan to approach her about the training.

Over the years, Kianna watched many privileged people around her complain and waste their hours, while the oppressed people she knew worked hard and enjoyed their time with friends and family when not working. Witnessing and interacting with both sides of life influenced young Kianna's belief that many people had too much and others did not have enough.

One day, Kianna asked, "Nan, can I give the toys that my brothers don't play with to Jamsie?"

"Those are not your toys to give, my girl."

"But they were complaining to mother about how boring they were and that they did not want them anymore." Kianna pushed the box of toys she had gathered from her closet. "Jamsie doesn't own a single toy. He only plays with what is outside in nature."

Nan's brow lifted. "If you give those toys to Jamsie without asking your brothers for permission, they could be upset with you for taking their things."

"Should I ask them first?" Kianna said.

Nan nodded and Kianna was out the door, down the hall in search of her brothers. A quarter of an hour later, Kianna, eyes red and puffy, returned to the room where her Nan waited.

"What happened? Nan asked.

"They said no. They told me those toys belonged to them and they didn't want to give them away."

Nan comforted Kianna, wrapping her in an embrace. "I'm proud of you for wanting to give Jamsie toys when you saw he didn't have any. It was a kind thing for you to see his need and want to give him something. I'm sorry that it didn't work out."

"I don't understand my brothers, Nan. They didn't want those toys earlier. Now they do. I bet they won't ever play with them either."

Nan patted Kianna's back and said no more. But Kianna felt that her nan agreed. She did not say the words but Kianna sensed them.

Kianna's involvement as a polite thief began right under the nose of her parents. She'd swipe a treasure from their sitting room and deliver it to the stoop of a family she'd followed home. The family had caught her eye as they carried meager supplies from their trip to the market. Kianna found a thrill from each part of the act: first the seizing of things and then releasing them. She'd collect a surplus of food from her pantry blaming her brothers for increased appetites and would then pass out the food to hungry children at the schoolhouse in town.

She developed an ability to really see people for who they were. Both inside and outside of her coddled world. Learning to value the fact that birthright didn't determine the true nature of a person wasn't an easy lesson for Kianna. It had come to feel simple that the people of the world who struggled inherently deserved more than they'd been given. The simple line seemed to blur a bit the day she'd lifted a loaf of bread from a vendor with her eye on a man sitting hungry in the shadows.

"Stop," the vendor raised his voice and reached toward Kianna. "I saw you take a loaf of my bread."

Kianna froze, she'd never been caught red handed before. "Sir, I apologize, but there are people who are starving."

"How do you think I feed my family?" the man asked her.

"You have plenty of food. Look at all this bread."

"You think it is that easy? I sell this bread and use the money I make to buy what my family needs. My family doesn't eat bread this fine. We eat what we can manage from my sales." His eyes burned into Kianna as he spat the words.

"What about the people who have nothing to eat?" Kianna asked.

"I can't feed the world on my bread alone. If you are stealing bread from me to give to another, give them the bread and tell them I have work they can do to guarantee food in their belly."

Kianna nodded, grateful to the breadman. But as she turned to leave, the breadman added, "And girl, if you ever steal from me again, I'll turn you over to the council. They will cut off your hand for thievery."

Kianna's eyes grew. She'd never thought of herself as a criminal until that moment. With her heart still racing, she increased her speed toward the hungry man. Reaching into her wrap she revealed the loaf of bread to him. He stared at her with disdain.

"What do you want, girl?" The hungry man asked.

"I've brought you food. Here," she said lifting it to him.

"I don't want your bread," he said.

She set the bread near his feet and pulled her hand back to her chest. "Why not? Aren't you hungry?"

"That is none of your business." He folded his arms and leaned his head against the brick wall.

"I'm sorry sir. I didn't mean to offend you," Kianna said. The man gave no response. She nodded to the bread at his feet and told him of the bread man's job offer. The man kicked the bread away and closed his eyes until Kianna left him alone.

As her nan brushed Kianna's hair before bed, Kianna told her about the day's events. "Nan," she said, "I tried to help someone at the market today and he was unhappy with my offer."

"Did this man ask for your help?"

Kianna shook her head. "I could tell he was tired and hungry. He looked like the many others I've given food to before," Kianna replied.

"So, you judged the situation without knowing the details?" Nan asked.

Kianna shrugged. "I thought I had enough details."

"And did it turn out that you did?"

Kianna again shook her head.

"Not everyone wants their weaknesses up for public interference. That man might not have been hungry at all. He may have been struggling with something altogether different. Something he did not want you to be a part of."

Kianna began to understand that her simple notions of people might need to be refined.

"Nan, I want to help people when I see them struggling. How will I know when to help and when to stay away?"

Nan finished brushing Kianna's hair and settled her in bed for the night. "I think you're ready to meet someone. We will go to him soon, but get some rest tonight. Goodnight sweet girl."

Days later, Kianna could barely contain herself as she waited for Nan to take her to the meeting she had mentioned the night of the bread market incident.

"I can't wait any longer, Nan."

The woman chuckled. "What do you mean?"

"Please! You said there was someone I was ready to meet. I would like to know more!" Kianna pleaded.

Her Nan smiled knowingly. "For the next several weeks your daily schooling will be transferred to my friend. You will meet him two days from now."

Kianna's eyes grew wide.

Nan leaned closer. "You will not be permitted to speak of him with anyone."

Bursting with excitement, Kianna wrapped her arms around her nan.

The anticipation she felt on the day she met Nan's cloaked friend, the Mage, would stay with her as they spent the next several weeks together. Kianna, acutely aware that the Mage was observing her, testing her, and likely deciding what skills he would impart to her, wanted to prove herself.

It was torture waiting outside as the Mage shared his decisions about Kianna with Nan. Try as she might, she could not hear a word that passed between them.

"Kianna, you may come in now," Nan said, opening the door.

The girl made her way to the corner of the room where the Mage sat in a grand chair fashioned from branches and twigs. She lowered her head in respect and patiently waited for the Mage to speak.

"Only some are perceptive enough to see the elemental beings," he told her.

Kianna had no idea what he meant, but she knew better than to interrupt with her many questions. Instead she continued to wait in silence as the Mage explained, in his own timing. "I feel that with the proper training to harness your perceptibility, you will be able to see the unseen friends of our world."

Kianna swallowed hard. Eyes wide, she remained silent.

He looked deep into Kianna's eyes. "Friendships with the elementals can be an avenue that you might take to be of help for those in need."

A long silence passed among them, which Kianna could barely contain herself.

"What do you want to ask me, child?" The Mage said.

"I have so many questions that I don't know where to begin." Kianna paused in thought. "All questions will be anwered in time, the Mage said. He nodded to Kianna. "I will see you tomorrow and we will begin your training."

Throughout the months of her time with the Mage, Kianna's sensitivities not only allowed her to quickly discover gnomes, but she also discovered mermaids quite early on. As her discernment grew, the salamanders and nymphs revealed themselves.

Where Kianna excelled most was the cunning skill she'd developed as a child, the art of being a polite thief. She no longer only lifted treasures from her home.

"Good day Sir," she said, curtseying to her father's best friend and his son.

"How do you do, Miss Kianna?" he asked, tilting his hat.

"We are having a lovely stroll," she said nodding in the direction of her Nan. Kianna had noticed his willful disregard of the woman she loved so dearly. She'd made up her mind in that instant he would be her target and she spotted the gleam from his golden pocket watch reflecting in the sunlight. She'd also noticed the nymph fluttering nearby and had gotten its attention.

"Ohhh, Sir Shepard, your top hat certainly needs a touch of charm and I have just the trimming." Kianna reached into her bag retrieving a feather she'd purchased from a vendor that morning. Holding the beauty out for the family friend to approve of, she could tell from the curve of his lips that he agreed it was a nice addition. "May I?" she asked gesturing to his top hat.

"Indeed, and thank you! I shall tell your father what a delight it was to see you at market today."

Kianna was pleased by his appreciation of the feather in his cap, but she was more pleased with the golden pocket watch her nymph friend had lifted from him and dropped into Kianna's bag.

She knew exactly how she'd trade this treasure on her next leg of the day's services. Her working knowledge of the market led her to the watch repairman, who would trade her coins for this piece. He would trade the unused gold to the goldsmith for future assistance with watch repairs that might require the goldsmith's skills. The goldsmith would melt the remaining gold of the watch and form it into something new to sell for profit to feed his family. Kianna would give the coins she received for the watch to the family of the farmer whose bean crop had not yielded as promising of a harvest this year. She glanced over her shoulder to share approving eyes with the nymph.

Kianna and her Nan curtseyed once more and continued their journey through the market. Nan whispered, "You are bold young one. Be careful that you don't get careless in your pursuit."

"Noted. I will remain careful in my pursuits." The girl promised her nan.

As they strolled, Nan asked, "What have you learned in your studies of the history of the elementals thus far?"

"Each of the elementals kings and queens possess a ring of power which denotes their specialty."

"How do they ensure the safety of these powerful rings?" Nan asked.

"Each ring is impossible to remove from the hand of its elemental. The uniting powers of an elemental with its ring creates a hold not to be undone by any magic save a rare metal."

"What do you know of this metal?" Nan asked.

"It is called Dimeritium and the elementals live with an awareness of their vulnerability paying mind to its possible treachery at every turn."

"Do you know of the incident with the mermaids?"

Kianna nodded. "It was Dimeritium and deceit which led to the merfolk king losing his ring of power." Kianna inhaled before launching into the retelling of the story. "Asleep in the arms of the woman he loved, she cast him in a net of Dimeritium. Her plot revealed a sinister grab for the throne, while he hung magic-less and heartbroken in the metal net. She'd made a deal with a seawitch for the ring in exchange for reign of the open waters. The seawitch has not been successful in wielding the ring."

"Has the Mage yet shared your part in this story?"

The girl nodded. "The mermaids have made a plea for help in restoring the ring to the king, its rightful owner, so that he might have the strength to regain his kingdom. In his absence, the queen has undone the peace treaties among the merfolk and the humans, resulting in many vicious deaths on both sides."

"And have you accepted a part in this quarrel?" Nan asked with concern.

"I have." She paused. "I think the underwater battle is a new skill I can master. I've been training in the water elements and made many mermaid friendships.

Nan squeezed the girl's hand. "If you feel ready and the Mage believes you are ready. I know you are ready."

Kianna waited for the moon to shine before she dipped her head below the surface receiving gifts of underwater breathing abilities from her mermaid friends on her way to retrieve the king's ring. The cunning plan meant that Kianna would go directly to the seawitch herself. Although the mermaids would not accompany Kianna past the boundary that existed between their kingdom and the witch's dark underwater forest, they granted Kianna enough breathing magic to continue her quest.

Kianna finally found the seawitch and was surprised her theory had come to pass. The witch had become weighed down by the glowing ring of power, unable to remove it, unwilling to part from it if she could.

Kianna's blood pumped faster and she patted the blade tucked into the band around her thigh to calm herself.

Kianna had requested a sword of Dimeritium from her goldsmith friend. She'd been given the Dimeritium from The Mage and set it down at the goldsmith's counter. He asked no questions and went to work smithing a mini version of the storied Roman Gladius.

She remembered her first gaze upon it as her smith friend held the sword explaining its features. "It packs as much punch as its bigger cousin, it has a tough Dimeritium double edged blade with black finish. Its textured handle is slip resistant and I've included a reinforced belt sheath."

Summoning courage from the blade, Kianna addressed the seawitch who was in obvious distress over her ring. "I can help you master your ring of power," Kianna told the witch.

The witch flailed in fury at the intruder but found herself recoiled by the ring. "I will not accept the treacherous offer of a human child." The witch continued muttering incantations on the ring in her desperate attempts to harness its magnificence.

Kianna watched in amusement for a time before she became bored and inserted her advice against the witch's will. "In order to wield the king's elemental ring, you must perform a test of wisdom that the ring sets before you."

The seawitch flinched at the reveal. Hoping Kianna hadn't seen her reaction, she regained her composure and turned upon the girl. "Remind me what the king's test was, child."

Kianna smirked at how easy this was to be. She bobbed through the water closer to the witch. "I was told a story of how he proved his trust and courage so that he would be deemed worthy by the ring and it would divinely protect him."

The seawitch screwed up her face. "Speak plainly child."

"Once he proved he was a servant of the ring, the ring granted him the ability to harness its power," Kianna said.

"You haven't told me what the mermaid king had to do!" The seawitch snapped.

Kianna's lips curled. She delighted telling the seawitch, "He allowed himself to be stabbed in the heart."

The seawitch scoffed. "Who are you? Do you think me a fool?"

"Once the knife was in his chest, he fell from his throne and his life began to fade. The king's knight slipped the ring onto his finger and pulled the knife from his chest. The king instantly floated to his throne grasping his chest with the newly ringed hand. Before their eyes, his wound had healed, and he had returned to health." Kianna cleared her throat. "If it wasn't enough of a miracle that the ring had granted the King immortality, he was henceforth able to wield its powers."

The seawitch was thoughtful a moment. She looked Kianna over. "If you are lying to me girl, I will put a hex on your entire family."

Kianna raised her hand to demonstrate she told the truth. The seawitch cast her eyes upon the ring which weighed her down.

"If you'd like me to do the honor, I will humbly oblige," Kianna said. "But I would like something in return."

"Ha. I knew you were after something," the seawitch said. "What do you hope to gain?"

"I request that you make me your apprentice," Kianna requested knowing full well she had no intentions of being this silly seawitch's apprentice.

"Fine. Do what must be done."

Kianna slid the blade from her thigh and plunged it into the witch's chest before the seawitch had a second thought. The metal began its work, blocking all magic the witch possessed. As life passed from the seawitch, Kianna made haste slipping on gloves made of the same Dimertium threads before removing the ring of power from the seawitch's lifeless hand. Dropping it into a small metal box, she tucked the trinket into her vest pocket and swam from the seawitch's cave. At the boundary where the mermaids anxiously waited for her return, Kianna offered the box containing the MerKing's ring to his loyal guard and wished them well in their pursuit of restoring his majesty. Kianna named her blade *The Seawitch* to commemorate its first just act.

Word spread among the elementals of Kianna's bravery, and she quickly became a ranger of the realm. Her cunning and skill in both fighting and science proved to demonstrate her good character and friendship of the elementals.

Many years had passed and Kianna, now a woman who'd helped countless humans and elementals alike, received a request from the gnomes to sit among their council who were gathering to discuss how to defeat a ghostly giant tormenting the Sun Mountains every night after the sun fell to slumber.

"What does this giant do, exactly?" Kianna asked of the gnomes.

"He eats the children who play outside at dusk," said one rather perturbed old gnome with a beard that cascaded along the floor.

"Isn't he a ghost? How does he eat them?" Kianna asked.

"First, he chases them. Let's them run around terrorized like little mice," continued the old gnome. He folded his hands on top of his cane and pursed his lips in disapproval. "Then he dangles them above his mouth and drops them into his ghostly cavernous belly to which they fall through and die from the trauma of the fall."

Kianna winced. "Is he just playing with them?"

"He has been nefarious with many other unpleasant actions, and he must be held accountable," snapped another gnome.

"Indeed," Kianna agreed. "Have you called me to the council because you wish me to subdue the giant?"

"Your family is royalty." The gnome paused. "But because you were born both too far down the line and as a female, you will not likely succeed your brothers."

Kianna was well aware of her standing. Up to this point in her young life, she was satisfied with her ranger lifestyle. Something of the way the gnome had delivered this fact, inferred an offer.

"I'm listening," she said.

"The Sun Mountains need leadership. Not only to be freed of the ghostly giant, but to represent our monarchy. It has been lawless and barren. We believe you are skilled in the elements of earth and can replenish the land and bring order."

"I accept," Kianna told the council. "I will leave at first light."

Kianna arrived in the Sun Mountains to find the land parched. The people inhabiting the valleys, were starving and well below their means.

She'd witnessed vile behavior and crude exchanges among the folk. That night, as Kianna lay next to a fire, she watched the stars dance in the crisp night sky.

"Will you join me at the summit of the Sun Mountains tomorrow?" she asked her fiery friend.

"What will you have me do?" asked the salamander.

"I think that you and your love should dance upon the mountains," Kianna suggested.

The salamander smiled. "You've seen the blaze her wind can ignite from my flames."

Kianna nodded. "I have. It is exactly what these mountains need." She fell silent for a few moments before adding, "Start your dance slow, move anyone lingering out of the way and then let your love explode." Kianna winked at the salamander.

"It has been a long time since the two of us have been able to let go and get swept up in the movement of things," said the salamander.

"Enjoy each other and know that you are helping to replenish the mountains with your love," Kianna said before she drifted off to sleep.

She awoke in the light of morning. Standing, she brushed the dirt from her body and started on foot, clearing the inhabitants. By late morning the sun beat down on the mountains emphasizing the dry air.

"Well, hello, Wind Nymph," Kianna said. "You're right on time."

The nymph gracefully glided around Kianna. "Has my love arrived yet?" she asked.

"I haven't seen any signs of him," Kianna replied just as she caught his scent carried from the nymph's last sweep near her. The nymph caught his cologne as well and disappeared after him without even a goodbye.

The fire swept across the mountains engulfing everything in their path. Kianna kept watch over the displaced townsfolk who looked to her for guidance.

She'd rescued them from their untimely demise of a forest fire and for that they were grateful. She led them to a clearing where they built a temporary habitation and Kianna got to work governing.

In the weeks passing, her visits to the Sun Mountains demonstrated what she'd learned from the Mage was true, the fire would replenish the land. The nutrients fell into the soil from the tree ash fueling rapid new growth. The creatures that had fled the mountains in the night during the fire had almost immediately returned. Some sensing the heat from a distance came in search of the feast on burnt plant matter. Low feeding insects lured back the chirping birds and small rabbits, beavers, and voles.

Kianna watched the wonder unfold in the early dark morning hours. By the time the sun hung high, she witnessed the sequoia and flower seeds begin the long awaited germination they could not begin without the heat the fire brought.

In the months that followed, she'd taught the folk how to care for the soil and organize a government.

Once the gnomes had come to see what Kianna had done in their mountains, they were deeply pleased and coronated Kianna Wayward-forger Viceroy of the Sun Mountains.

D.M. Taylor

D.M. Taylor is a writer of science fiction thrillers. She has a constant desire to be at the beach or as close to a combination of: water, sand, and sunshine as she can. You can tell by looking at all of the freckles she has collected as evidence.

If she's not writing in her tiny cottage by the lake, then it's not summer. The rest of the year, she's writing on her couch under blankets near a giant bay window. On the less romantic days of writing, and let's be real--most of them, her pages come together while waiting in a car for one of her kids--as part of her chauffeur gig.

Her gravitational pull to science fiction developed throughout her teacher training; where she concentrated on science education. Graduating from Michigan Tech with an Applied Science Master's Degree jump started her geeky interests. An obsession of time travel pushed through her romantic notions of the world and the easy fear she holds of anything frightening. Together, these elements created a writer of: sci-fi thrillers who sprinkles in a bit of slow burn romance.

Accruing in her head is a checklist of places to travel, items to accomplish, and book ideas to write.

She regenerates from deep conversation, laughter, and dancing.

Instagram, Facebook & TikTok: @authordmtaylor

THE HUMMINGBIRD

C.C. SULLIVAN

I *f that bitter northern wind hadn't blasted through her garden,
Claire's life might have remained unchanged.*

She knelt in the dirt, snipping off the shoots on the row of hydrangeas. One last errant stem caught her attention when a dragonfly rested upon it. She leaned forward to clip it when a spasm rippled through her chest, rattling her diaphragm. The pruning shears slipped through her fingers to the ground.

Coldness crept up the middle of her back like a snake slithering along her vertebra. Dampness clung to her like morning dew on moss. She shivered, and gooseflesh rippled upon her arms. A cerulean October sky, the betraying kind, hung over her.

The distant chime of her phone drifted from the house to the garden. She propped herself up with her elbow and rolled onto her knees. Pushing herself to stand, she hobbled inside to answer the call. A crackling sound filtered through the speaker.

"Hello?" she said over the poor connection.

A low, gravelly voice spoke. "Hello?"

She pushed the receiver closer to her ear. "Daniel?"

"I'm calling regarding your son."

"My son? Daniel? Has something happened to him?" Her voice wavered as worst-case scenarios played through her mind.

"No, this is about your other son."

Her mind went blank for a second.

"You must have the wrong number."

"I'm certain I've dialed correctly. This is about Christian."

"Christian died thirty years ago, two days after he was born—" Claire choked on her words. "What kind of sick joke is this?"

A throbbing began beneath her temples.

"Ma'am, I'm sorry, but I have some information about Christian that you might find interesting." The voice on the other end of the line paused. "I need to explain—"

"I don't know who you are or what you need. Don't call again!"

With her index finger, she hung up and threw her cell phone on the table. Who could be so cruel? She didn't socialize, and the friends she had, she could count on one hand. The phone rang again, making her jump. The name 'Christian' appeared on her screen, and her pulse quickened. She tapped her fingers on the table. *I will not answer that call.* She turned to walk away, then stopped. The ringing continued. Clenching her fists, she swiveled on her heels and grabbed the phone, putting it to her ear.

"Please stay on the line. I only have a bit of time," he said.

Claire sucked in her breath, reproaching herself for getting drawn back into this conversation. "You're trying my patience."

"There's too much to explain over the phone. May I come to your house?"

"*My* home?" She looked about her house. "Absolutely *not.*"

Claire should have hung up; he'd already reeled her in when he mentioned he had information about Christian. Though she burned with curiosity, she'd lost faith long ago in ever getting any actual signs. Brian has once suggested they visit a medium, but she'd rejected the idea. She was not a fool. How could people believe in all that stuff?

"What's your name? I'm not naïve, you know; I've heard all about scammers."

"They call me Christian, but never mind that. This is about *your* son. Not me."

She wandered to her living room. "Why should I believe you?"

"Your son, Christian, was born on the 17th of October 1991, at eight thirty in the morning, in Battle Mountain, Nevada, to Claire and Brian Baine. Correct?"

A tingle crawled under her cheekbones. *Brian* . . . if only he was here. With her thumb, she twirled the band on her ring finger and glanced at the urn in the display case.

"You could have searched the registry for those details," she said, proud she'd stood up for herself. That's how Brian would have handled things.

"I could have," he agreed, a little too fast for her liking.

Her stomach churned, and a vague malaise seized her. "What do you want from me?"

His tone softened. "Nothing. I can explain everything in person. We'll meet wherever you want."

She rubbed her forehead, knowing she wouldn't be able to let this go unless she saw it through.

"Fine. Let's meet at ten at the Dragonfly Cafe in town."

"I'll be there. Thank you."

"Bye—"

The phone call ended before she could say more. She stared at the butterflies in the garden landscape painting before her—one of her favorites. The colored brushstrokes of their wings warped and blended together. Unsteady on her feet, she shook off the dizziness and headed back outside to her pruning.

A sense of déjà vu coursed through her as she bent down to pick up her clippers. Traces of vertigo made her head spin as she clapped her gardening gloves together to shake off the earth. She stretched and gazed at her trimmed shrubs, pleased with her work.

Whispers stirred in the wind, and she cocked her head to listen to their message. Her shirt flapped, and her loose, salt-and-pepper hair caressed her cheeks. A few shrubs down, a hummingbird hovered in mid-air, motionless except for the blur of its wings. *A straggler.* Why was it still here? It should have already flown south. Another gust of cold air rushed through her garden, and the leaves on the surrounding maples twisted and turned. She squinted to observe their movements.

"Great. Just as I was getting my garden in shape."

She packed up her gardening tools while storm clouds rolled in. The burlap would have to wait for next weekend. Water droplets pelted down as she stumbled across the yard. The mudroom's screen door slammed shut behind her. She threw her tools into the mud-spattered utility sink and shook off her rubber boots.

The short hallway led to her conservatory, where she spent her mornings. Its glass walls, separated by metal girders, curved toward the sky. Light filled the room, which made a perfect environment for rescuing ailing plants from A Petal in Time, her garden shop in town.

Claire's inspiration came from giving new life to distressed florae and saving living things from an uncertain death. Whenever a fresh shoot emerged, it infused her with a sense of renewal and transformation. Years ago, she'd been powerless to protect her baby, her own flesh and blood. But in this sacred space, she influenced the outcome, served penance, and sought asylum.

Rivulets trickled down the windowpanes, and the patter of rain-drops faded into the background. Her bones ached as if she was wasting away from hopelessness, but the scents of rosemary, mint, and lavender helped chase away the thick cloud of claustrophobia. These gloomy mid-October days always threatened to expose the bleak memories she kept locked away in her subconscious.

A few years ago, she'd begun taking this month off, letting her manager run the shop. It had been a futile attempt at releasing her perennial sadness. Dreams of breaking away from her quiet life, filled with regrets and reminders, occupied her mind. But how could she leave her children or her store behind? What if they needed her? And each year, her heels dug in deeper. Resisting, denying, avoiding.

Now, this dubious phone call threatened to topple her delicate fortress.

On her way to the front door, Claire stopped at the console table. Her eyes scanned across framed photos of her children, Sylvia and Daniel as toddlers, teenagers, and into their college years. She picked up a photo hidden behind all the others where a fair-haired boy sat between Sylvia and Daniel. *The Three Musketeers.* She'd almost forgotten about Dylan. He'd taken on the role of their missing brother, and the three had played together almost every day. When he moved away, her two children had suffered a terrible void. On his last day, he'd hugged her and placed a coin in her hand. "It's a lucky penny," he said.

Just then, another spasm quivered in Claire's diaphragm. Her chest tightened, and she struggled to breathe. The living room walls spun around her, and she leaned against the table to steady herself.

By the time she stepped outside, the storm had passed. Claire left her home and arrived early at the Dragonfly Cafe for her rendezvous with the mysterious caller. The cafe was empty, so she ordered her coffee and waited near the front entrance. The phone call continued to play in her mind. There'd been something else in the stranger's voice. Fear. Was he in some kind of trouble? She tapped her foot and picked at a loose hangnail until it bled, then glanced at her watch. He was late.

Moments later, a young man in his early thirties with tousled hair and a timid expression entered, glancing over his shoulder as he walked in. She followed his gaze out the door but saw nothing. He stepped forward and threw his arms around her.

"I can't believe I've found you." His voice became muffled by her sweater as he hugged her tight.

He held on to her as if he'd never let go. Claire froze. A feeling scratched at the walls of her heart, itching to crawl out of the vault where she'd locked away her pain. She wriggled out from under his grasp.

"Chris—" The rest of his name splintered inside her mind. There was nothing familiar about this young man; he was *not* her son. She recoiled and put some distance between them. When she reached the counter, she half-turned to him. "Do you drink coffee?"

"No, I don't."

She grabbed the cup with her name scribbled on it and crossed the vacant coffee shop. An unusual sensation of floating followed her as she lowered herself onto a seat. Christian settled into the chair opposite her. Despite the warm coziness of the cafe, a dampness sent chills down her spine, like moist earth pressing against the nape of her neck. She waited for him to start.

"I had to come in person," he started to say.

She clenched her jaw. "I still don't know what you want from me?"

"Nothing. I'm simply here to bring you a message."

"A message? From whom?"

He pointed to the sky. She raised her eyes to the ceiling as he leaned forward and lowered his voice.

"I've found out something extraordinary, life changing, about your son. *And* me, by proxy."

"Something you learned up there?"

"Yes."

Tears pricked her eyes. She drew a sharp breath, and a torrent of words spilled out. "I've spent years waiting for a sign, and forgive me, but I find it a little ironic that it has come from someone bearing *his* name." She pressed her fingers to her eyes, and like a waterspout, rage burst out of her. She leaned forward. "Why come now?"

Christian placed his hand on her forearm, and she flinched. "I can't do this . . ." she said, squeezing her eyes shut. If she kept them closed long enough, perhaps she'd wake up from this nightmare. Despite her resolve to reject him, his warmth radiated through her, calming her nerves. She heard his chair creak, and he whispered, "I'm not supposed to be here."

Her eyes flew open. "Stop! You need to explain yourself before we go any further."

"It took me a while to figure things out *and* to find you. At first, it was confusing without having all the details. But when I discovered who I was, I knew I had to tell you what had happened."

Doubtful, she pursed her lips. "You didn't know who you were?"

His mouth tightened into a flat line. "You still don't believe me."

Her eyebrows twitched, and she shrugged. "You must admit, this sounds a little far-fetched."

He sighed. "Under usual circumstances, there's no reason for a baby to know. However, they keep a ledger with every entry. So, I went snooping and found a note written next to my name . . . about an error."

"An error? And who do you mean by *they*?"

"They . . . they are the firm." Again, he pointed upward.

She stared at him, numb with disbelief. Her neck hairs raised, but she remained focused on him.

"The firm made the error?"

"No. *They* don't make mistakes."

Mistakes. She'd made plenty of them. When Sylvia and Daniel were little, they never once forgot to include Christian. If someone asked how many children she had, she'd answer, "Two." One or the other would scowl with fists on hips and announce, "No! You have three children. Why do you always forget Christian?" She never forgot her little boy. It just shattered her to be reminded of him each time. Had she been wrong to exclude him?

Drawn back to the man sitting opposite her, she said, "So, someone else made an error."

"That's correct."

She clenched her hands together and glanced out the window. A man and woman in crisp charcoal suits sat on a bench near the cafe.

"Are those people looking for you?"

"Inconspicuous lot, aren't they?"

"Yes, they fit right in."

They both laughed, and she cleared her throat. Clearly, he'd escaped from an institution.

"Are they here to take you back?"

"Yes." And with a faint nod, he murmured, "Angels."

Her eyes widened and darted back to the window. They bore no resemblance to the angels she'd always imagined.

"The angel on the left is Castiel, Servant of the Order of Lost Children. He works for Naarai, the Archangel of All Children," Christian explained. "And the one with the scowl on her face—that's Muyre. She's a Spirit Sentinel—a psychopomp who works for Yehudiah, the Caretaker of Souls. Muyre's role is to retrieve and guard souls who are in transition and deliver them to him. She's a little resentful because she does all the dirty work, and Yehudiah gets to help those souls celebrate their lives."

"Are you an angel?"

"No, I'm not."

She clasped her hands together. "And you only have a short time?"

"Two days. I lost time trying to find you."

"Why two days?"

"The veil closes again this afternoon at my hour of death," he explained.

She swallowed the burr caught in the back of her throat.

At her baby's hour of death, a doctor had brought her loosely swaddled baby and placed him in the crook of her arm. The blanket barely swelled from his shallow breaths, and his eyes were closed. His skin was pale and cool to the touch, and bruises covered the back of his frail hands. He wore a small blue knit hat. Caressing his cheeks, she kissed his forehead. Prayer had not helped him, no matter how much she had bargained for his life. Tears blurred her vision, and she brought him close to her chest to whisper goodbye. When she handed him back to the doctor, her heart cracked.

Movement brought her back to the coffee shop. Christian fiddled with the hem of his jacket.

"Is there another way out of here?" he asked.

She shook off the unbearable memory and glanced out the window at the suits. "We can leave out the back door. I'm parked there." Even though this situation seemed absurd, her natural tendency was to help. But who was she fooling? It was more than that. Every cell in her body was desperate to find out about her son.

In the car, she asked, "Are you going to tell me about Christian?"

He nodded but kept quiet and stared straight ahead. As she drove, Claire chatted about the flowers and plants she grew in her garden to fill the awkward silence. She didn't ask him why he'd needed to escape.

Instead, she tried, "I'd like to stop by my daughter's shop." It would provide her with an opportunity to get away. He shrugged and peered out the back window.

When they arrived at Sylvia's botanica spa, Claire parked under a tree near the entrance. As they walked through the parking lot, he stopped her. "There's something I must explain. My name isn't—" When he tried to finish his sentence, he wheezed, struggling for breath. He straightened his body and stared at her, his eyes wide with terror.

She stood frozen, watching as his throat and jaw contorted in unimaginable ways. His mouth opened wide and a hummingbird flew out. Claire screamed. She wanted to flee, but her feet stayed rooted to the ground. The tiny bird hummed and hovered in front of her before flying off.

Christian bent down, his hands resting on his knees. "I'm sorry you had to witness that."

Repulsed, yet fascinated, she found her voice. "What the hell was *that*?"

With her heart beating against her ribcage, she looked at him, unable to erase the horrid image of the emerging hummingbird from her mind. She was already regretting her decision to help him. For all she knew, he was going to kill her and dump her body somewhere. A niggle in the back of her knees threatened to defeat her, and she glanced at Sylvia's shop.

"Please don't run off," he said.

"Or what? What'll happen if I do?"

"Nothing. It's just . . . I can't verbalize the information I want you to have."

"So that's why the bird flew out of your mouth? Was it the angel who stopped—"

"No, Castiel's only job is to take me back. It . . . it's a heavenly decree that states we can't share certain knowledge with the living. So . . . *that* happened. However, I must try to share my discovery with you before I advance to the next realm. It's for my peace of mind."

Claire's determination to run away faded. "So, you took time out of your heavenly schedule to bring me a message, yet you can't speak a word of it?"

He pursed his lips. "Something like that."

Another question hovered in the periphery of her thoughts, but she brushed off the foreboding sensation that lurked.

"Come on." She walked toward the store. "Please keep these shenanigans to a minimum."

He sheepishly bobbed his head as they made their way to the entrance. The door swung open as a customer left, allowing them to enter. Sylvia glanced at the door and frowned. A crowd of patrons browsed the shelves, and even though Sylvia stared in her direction, she hardly acknowledged Claire.

"That's my daughter," she said, pointing toward Sylvia.

They approached the counter when a bustling group of young girls brushed past them. One of the girls jostled a flower-filled vase sitting on the countertop. The ceramic container wobbled, and one flower's corolla exploded in a burst of colors, lover's blush and lavender. As the petals wafted through the air in slow motion, Claire gaped at them, fascinated by this moment's chaos.

A sharp, bristly sensation crawled up the back of Claire's arms like tiny needles poking her skin. To remove the awful sting, she rubbed them and tried to get Sylvia's attention. But her daughter stared at the mess scattered across the countertop with a strange expression. Sylvia pulled her phone out of her pocket, tapped its screen, and pressed it to her ear.

"This is the third message I'm leaving. Please call me back. I'm getting worried." Sylvia hung up and cleared the mess.

Christian said, "She seems pretty busy, and we don't have time to waste. We should leave her to it."

Despite this young man's earnestness, Claire resisted. Why should she trust him?

As if he'd read her mind, he said, "You have your doubts. I assure you, when I find what I need to show you, you'll understand."

"You don't know what you're looking for, do you?" she said. He looked down at his hands, and she tucked her hair behind her ears. "Fine. What do we do now?"

"We need to drive around town."

She knitted her brows. "Any place in particular?"

"No, but I'll recognize it when I see it."

Claire's car tires squealed as she pulled out of the lot. In her rear-view mirror, she spied the two suits near Sylvia's shop. Again, she shook away the nagging question scratching at the back of her mind.

They'd driven twice around town when she lost her patience. "Any luck?"

Christian bit down on his bottom lip. "Not yet." He rubbed his eyes. "Maybe I've got it all wrong." He paused, then started again, "The error happened on the day I was born—" His words became stifled by an obstruction. When he exhaled, a kaleidoscope of butterflies rushed out of his mouth. Claire yelped and slammed on her brakes as colorful flapping wings filled the front seats. "Roll down your window," she cried out. After the butterflies escaped, she gave him a stern look. "Are you trying to give me a heart attack?"

"No . . . " He looked away, avoiding any eye contact. "I'm so sorry. Let's keep going."

She huffed. "We'll go around one last time, and I'll try a different route."

With utter desolation in his eyes, he agreed. The late afternoon sun crested the tip of the tree line bordering the newer section of town. How strange that it was already so late.

As they followed the ring road back toward town, a notion flitted through her mind. *Butterflies!*

"I might have figured out what you're looking for."

Moments later, she pointed to a pub nestled within a small building on the right.

He straightened in his seat. "That's gotta be it!"

She steered the car to the bar's full lot and parked under its sign. Was she enabling this poor fellow? He slid out of the front seat and cocked his head.

"The Kaleidoscope," he said and chuckled. "What a splendid name!"

When they reached the door, she stopped him before they entered. "The suits reached Sylvia's store as we were leaving."

"Yeah, I saw them too."

When they entered the Kaleidoscope, patrons crowded around and sat at the bar. Others ate and drank in groups at tables. The place buzzed with conversation. She followed behind Christian, still indulging him in this hopeless pursuit. To her right, a towering blond-haired man in his thirties burst through the kitchen doorway, helping a server carry her order. Claire did a double take. *Daniel?* She shook her head. The bartender could have been his doppelgänger.

A peculiar sensation prickled at her fingertips, and she peered down at her hands. Filament-like roots had sprouted from under her fingernails, curled around her fingers, and wormed their way up her arms. In the middle of this utter chaos, her breath hitched. When she tried to scream, something tightened and pushed against her neck. She must have made a sound because Christian turned toward her and his face blanched.

She shouted above the noise. "What's happening to me?"

He took hold of her hands. "I thought we'd have more time."

At that moment, Claire became distracted by a glint above her and looked up. The bartender's gaze went up as well. A sparkling object dropped from the ceiling onto the bar top with a loud crack, startling the clientele. Where it had landed, a copper penny twirled and spun on its vertical axis. The crowd became mesmerized by the sudden spectacle. When the coin drummed to a stop, a lull fell across the room.

Then, someone hollered, "Nice parlor trick, Dylan!"

Behind the bar, Dylan laughed. "Another round for everyone!"

The place erupted in a noisy cheer, and the crowd's banter continued as if nothing had happened. *Dylan?* She stared open-mouthed at him. Could this be the same boy who'd played with her children? She'd never noticed the uncanny resemblance, he had Daniel's eyes and smile and Sylvia's fluid movements.

She nudged Christian. "I believe he was my children's friend when they were kids," she said, still awestruck by his likeness. "He must've moved back into town."

Christian looked from Claire to Dylan. "Look at his arm. He's the message!"

On his forearm, the bartender wore a hummingbird tattoo. With a blur, its wings fluttered. Claire's eyes widened.

Christian blurted out, "Dylan Murphy was born on the same day as Christian, thirty years ago. At the same hospital."

"What? I don't understand—"

Behind Claire, the bar's front door opened, cutting off the end of her thought. A bright ray of sunlight entered, slicing the shadowed room in half. When the door closed with a thud, the beam disappeared as if sucked back out in a vacuum. A shivering nested itself between her shoulder blades. Christian's expression peaked, and she turned to find the two angels behind her.

Castiel stepped forward. "Your time's up."

Christian shook his head. Above the noise of the bar, he yelled, "Claire, you must go home."

She balked. "Why?"

"I don't have time to explain. Please trust me," he said. "Come on!"

Confused, she followed him down the darkened hallway to her car. They drove off, careening through the streets to her house.

"Why are the angels after you?" When he remained silent, she tried again. "Are you sure someone made a mistake?"

"Yes, I read about it in the Akashic Records."

"Akashic—?"

"The firm keeps a record of everyone's life and death. The life story I read for Christian Baine was not mine; it was *his*."

She gave him a quick glance while keeping her eyes on the road. "Whose life?"

"The bartender," he explained. "*I'm* Dylan."

"I don't understand... Are you saying *he's* Chris—?"

A sob escaped her throat, and she couldn't finish. Tears blurred her view. Her heart exploded into a million shards. All those years, it was Christian who'd lived next door and played with Sylvia and Daniel. Their brother had been with them all along. When she wiped her eyes to clear her vision, Castiel and Muyre appeared in the middle of the road. She slammed on the brakes, and the car slid to a screeching halt. Castiel tapped the back of his wrist.

Dylan clicked his tongue. "He's calling me back."

A tickling sensation on her forearms made her glance down. Her veins moved like slithering snakes.

"What's happening to me?"

"Drive around them. Now!"

"What about you?"

"Just drive!"

Claire pushed down on the gas pedal and squealed past them. Her mind whirred with images from the hospital, and she squeezed the steering wheel until her knuckles went white. "When my son was born, he was a healthy baby. I couldn't understand what happened." She paused when a motorcycle overtook them. "I spent years blaming myself. The doctors told me they'd taken him off the ventilator, and I became confused because he hadn't needed one. They didn't believe me when I told them. They even brought him to me to say goodbye." Her tears streamed down her cheeks. "What kind of mother doesn't recognize her own son?" she cried out. "I should have asked more questions, pushed harder."

"It was the hospital's fault. Not yours. The nurses switched us by accident, placing us into the wrong bassinets before they put on our hospital bracelets."

"I can't seem to wrap my head around all this..." she murmured as she pulled into her driveway.

"Now Claire, please listen to me. The angels are almost here. Run to your backyard!"

"What?"

"Go!"

She unlocked her front door, dashed past the photos of her children, and sped down the hallway past her living room, kitchen, and conservatory. When she arrived at the back door, she stopped in her tracks. Staring out her screen door, her gaze stopped on the silhouette laying near the hydrangeas. Shock skittered up her spine.

"Is that—"

Dylan came up behind her and said, "You must rejoin your physical body before they arrive."

He opened the door for her, and she walked out. Before reaching the hydrangeas, she tripped and stumbled into the gloom.

Claire struggled, thrashing against the roots and stalks that held her down by her wrists and ankles. Creepers latched themselves onto her clothes and skin. Vines snaked around her neck and torso, tightening with each breath she took. And flowers bloomed as she lost breath. The plants she'd once brought back to life snuffed the air out of her . . . and she stopped breathing.

Far away, she heard a scream. *Sylvia?* Claire's frame quivered, the way the leaves had shaken in the wind just before the storm.

"Mom, you can't leave us. Not yet!"

In the dense fog, a door slammed.

"Daniel!" Sylvia cried. "Do something!"

Muffled voices crowded around her. Hands pulled at the roots, ripping away at the vines. But the creepers intensified their hold on her, and the cool, moist ground swallowed her, burying her deeper. The thumping grew stronger. And her chest shuddered.

She let out an audible gasp, drawing in a long breath.

A brilliant white light beamed on Claire's face, and she lifted her arm to shield her eyes. Her children looked down at her with red-rimmed eyes, and behind them hung a brilliant cerulean sky. She shifted and struggled to sit.

"Mom, just lie still," Daniel ordered her.

"Hel . . . Help me up!" she demanded.

In the far corner of her garden, three figures stood watching her. Castiel, Dylan, and Muyre. She now understood why the psychopomp had accompanied Castiel.

Claire wiped away the mist from her eyes. "Thank you, Dylan."

The corners of Dylan's mouth curled up. Castiel's wings unfolded and encircled him, and they vanished in a resplendent display of lights. Only Muyre remained.

"You've come for me, haven't you?"

"Not today, it seems," the angel said with a crooked smile. "Make the most of what you've learned."

"Mom, who are you talking to?" Sylvia asked.

Claire smiled as Muyre spread her wings and disappeared, leaving a trail of iridescence in her wake.

CC Sullivan

CC Sullivan is a writer from Toronto, Canada who writes in the fantasy, magical realism, and women's fiction genres.

She writes screenplays, short stories, and has published Book 1 of her *Masters of the Elements* series, *A Storm of Doubt*. She is working on the second book of the Elements series, and on a women's fiction novel.

CC has also designed a set of journals as part of her *Intuitive Journey* series.

You can find all of her ebooks, paperbacks, and journals on Amazon. Her ebooks are also available at other distributors (nook books, Apple iBooks, and Rakuten Kobo). Digital files of her journals are also sold at ccsullivan.me.

Check out her shop, *The Write Shelf*, at ccsullivan.me where you can find tools to help writers get started with writing.

In her spare time, she reads tarot cards and astrology charts, and enjoys painting, traveling, and reading.

Find out more:
https://linktr.ee/ccsullivan_writer

TERROR & TWILIGHT

N. D. T. CASALE

This is the last place I ever envisioned myself to be. Even my people would not set foot in the Twilight Forest. I never imagined I would have to venture here. No one who enters here ever returns to tell their story.

Mahfood and Dawood warn me repeatedly to turn back, but I stand here nevertheless, at the place where I might die. I have to confront the terrors that lay beyond this mist.

I face the entrance to the Twilight Forest. The woods border the edge of my kingdom, Jerdaj. Secrets hover among the trees, shrubbery, and bushes where death lies quietly in sinister, calculating treachery. This is a place of mystery, pain, and intense horror.

Do not enter! Wind from The Twilight Forest whispers to me.

I must! This holds the key to saving my husband!

Engraved in my mind, I see Kamal's decimated body among the blankets of our bed where his flesh is hot as the illness spreads through him like a river in flames. Having been bitten by a Helltrie, a small mosquito-like creature that carries the Kiss of Death, he has lost consciousness and all knowledge of his surroundings. His mind is drifting into insanity.

Helltrie are not beasts that roam in the wild. They are created in the Twilight Forest and bewitched in order to poison their victims. Someone within this dense foliage, within this place of horror, within this portal of agony wants Kamal dead. My suspicions have led me to this threshold from which I may never return. There is evil here that is born of the muck and mire of this place combined with deep heavy mist in which a breath is nearly impossible. I can barely breathe. Mahfood and Dawood counsel me; their words ring true, but my love is stronger than my fear.

Gray swirls before me, a barrier, an impediment, and an insubstantial illusion that carries the whiff of poison. The movement of the fog is like an old friend waving for me to come chat for a while, but this friend twists in the mist, as if it is smiling at us. I see it through the darkness, smirking in quiet triumph. I hear whispers call my name.

Ria Sultana of Jerdaj.

Murmurs are more foe than friend.

Legends among my people state the only cure for a Helltrie bite requires an antidote which comes from a Grelez, a plant that grows in the darkest shadows. According to the wise women in our village, the sap from the leaves reverses the effect of the toxin and restores life. Without the antidote, the victim suffers until death.

I look at the silvery smoke. It twists before me, and within its swirls, I see a vision of my husband lying in his chamber within the safety of the palace walls.

What trickery is this?

I remember the words of my handmaiden, Nabilia, who told me that such illusions are probable when one is about to embark on a journey into the Twilight Forest. The woods manipulate the mind to make one delusional.

My heart is in my throat and anxiety gnaws in the pit of my stomach. In the apparition, Kamal looks the same as when I left him. His skin is blotchy with a greenish tinge. His breath comes in shallow gasps. A year ago, I had brought him back from the dead and now I fear I will lose him again. His soul is on the brink of eternity. My only hope is there will be enough time to save him.

Slowly, the hallucination fades. I clench my fists and grit my teeth as I stare at the mist that whirls in lackadaisical spirals, anticipating my next move. Trickery is manifested here. I must listen to the voices of reason.

My lips part as I struggle for air that is thick with the taint of rotting vegetation. Taking a step forward, I cross through the mist and into the terrors.

Fog hangs low like a covering. It is not completely dark but not completely light. Gaps in the canopy of trees filter illumination. Skeletal limbs reach out, as if to grab an unsuspecting victim. Shadows stalk the dark corners of the wood. We hear sounds unfamiliar and full of menace. My heart is in my throat, but I must persevere.

"Maybe we should turn back," Mahfood calls. The little frog pokes his head from the inside pocket of my cloak. He crawls until he is sitting on my shoulder.

"We are already here, and Kamal needs us," Mahfood's twin brother Dawood hops onto my other shoulder.

"Brothers, this is no time to argue." I run my fingers over the hilt of the sword attached to my hip. The blade is a comfort to me.

"Dawood, do you know what direction we are going in?" I ask as I pull out my compass. It is made of brass on a long chain. The nautical sundial makes up the cover that shields the crystal of the complex mechanism. For no known reason, the directional spins at a chaotic rate, going around and around with no sense of purpose. I am lost. Now is the time I must call upon my instincts as a warrior. This is the reward for training among my people. Preparation is a key to victory in a battle with evil. I may be lost but I am not forsaken.

"According to ancient lore, I believe we must keep going north until we find the shadiest part of the forest. There we will find what we seek," replies Dawood, nestling in my hair.

"It is dark everywhere. How will we know what the shadiest part looks like?" asks Mahfood.

"That is what the book told me," Dawood answers.

"I thought you said you spent time in the Twilight Forest?" I ask.

"Well, not exactly," replies Dawood sheepishly.

"Dawood!" I yell.

Embarrassed, the little frog scurries deeper into my thick curls. "I knew you wouldn't bring me if I didn't say I knew something. But I have done research on the forest. Danger lurks in every corner," he whispers into my hair.

"I told you we should have hired an actual guide," replies Mahfood.

I shake my head. "I do not wish to put anyone else at risk."

Playing with the lush locks of my dark hair, the wind moves the bushes and shrubs while branches bob and weave like sentinels in battle.

A tingle on the back of my neck signals danger, and I jump to the side as something that looks like a head jerks forward from the bushes.

I stumble back and grab a nearby branch, which snaps like an icicle. I look at the perished gnarly object in my hand and throw it to the ground.

My eyes widen as I spy the monster who tried to make me its dinner. A serpent-like beast slithers forward from its hiding place and raises itself to full height. It is three times my size. The beast's forked tongue flicks as it tastes my scent on the breeze. Yellow with red stripes, the serpentine creature stares at me through closed eyes.

"It's a Selchnuerm!" Mahfood cries.

"What is that?" I ask, baffled and terrified at the same time.

"A type of snake, but the good news is, it has no sight. It relies on scent and movements. Stay where you are. Do not move a muscle. Do not even breathe."

I lean against the trunk of a nearby tree and feel the gnarled bark dig into the middle of my back. The Selchnuerm moves its head back and forth, its nostrils flare. I look down at the compass in my hand. Useless until now, the little tool might prove its navigational worth after all.

Moving my hand back in line with my ear, I thrust my arm forward, launching the compass into the air. It falls into the bushes, creating a loud rustle as it hits each leaf and branch before plopping onto the ground.

The Selchnuerm lunges forward and scoops the compass into its mouth. This allows us to slip away in the opposite direction.

Branches thrash in my face as I stumble down a narrow pathway between the outgrowth and fronds. I feel the boughs pull at my skirt as if trying to take me captive.

"Stop!" cries Dawood.

I halt. We are in a small clearing with bony trees surrounding us. Uneasiness wells in my chest. To the right of us is a grove of mangrove trees. Their sharp limbs interlock with one another, creating a blanket of darkness. Nestled into the boughs is a rock wall. I squint. It is hard to make out the shape for the darkness that surrounds it. Since we are in a permanent state of twilight, objects appear more ghostly than they really are.

"What is that?" I ask.

"That must be the shadiest part of the forest," replies Dawood.

"That cannot be the shadiest part of the woods."

I take a step closer. Partially hidden beneath the tangle of mangroves, there is a faint glow from the rocks that resembles green eyes. The illumination casts a dim light on a small plant that is growing in front of a hidden wall. My eyes fall upon the leaves, as my intuition strikes a chord of discovery.

Could this be the Grelez plant?

I crouch down and reach my hand forward. As I wrap my fingers around the base of the shrub to pull it out from its roots, my palm feels wet and sticky. I look at the stem and see a small crack in the structure. Orange liquid oozes out and spills across the dirt. As more of the fluid leaks, the plant shrinks until it disappears.

"What just happened?" I whisper. My chest tightens. Have I just lost the antidote that will save my husband's life? I cannot have come this far and be so close, only to lose. Without the antidote, Kamal will certainly die.

"The plant is not real. It is bewitched," cries Mahfood. "We have been tricked."

"I think it is a trap," replies Dawood.

Rumbles beneath my feet unsettle our balance. I fall. Grasping the mangrove boughs, I feel prongs puncture my palm. I wince and look down at the dirt.

My eyes widen as the soil parts before me. I see a fist but it is all bone. More skeletal hands rise from the ground and encircle us.

I see osseous fingers, then an emaciated arm, then a spindly body. Before I can blink, skeletons emerge and stand before us. An army in soldier attire. Like knights with sunken faces and holes for eye sockets, they present a portrait of terror.

Mahfood and Dawood tremble at the back of my neck. Their webbed toes cool my heated flesh. I look around for an escape route but we are surrounded. My breath comes in shallow gasps. My eyes fall to the skeletons' bony hips, for each has a scabbard where a shiny sword rests.

Dawood was right. It is a trap.

I reach for my weapon but a whisper makes me stop.

I expect the soldiers to attack us, but instead, they stare at us for a few minutes with their hollow eyes. Then they point down the path. They wave their hands, commanding us into a quick pace. We are marching to a new location, and I have a hunch where we are going.

***

WE ARE IN THE PALACE OF TWILIGHT, MY ENEMY'S DOMAIN.

She stands before us, the leader of this villainous clan.

A fellow member of royalty, she specializes in death.

Her hair is dark like mine. Her olive skin glistens in the illumination of the candles from the chandelier. A gown of navy clothes her body, and a crown is perched on her head.

It is Rabhya, Sultana of the Skull Soldiers.

"Ria, Sultana of Jerdaj," hisses Rabhya

We are in the throne room of her gothic castle. The vaulted ceiling and large windows spread a chill that sends shivers up and down my spine.

The Sultana of Death rises from her throne and saunters toward me. I feel Dawood and Mahfood shutter. I look into the evil queen's brown eyes. Her red lips curl back to reveal her pointy teeth as she snickers.

"You are dying aren't you, Ria? The Grelez plant is your only hope."

I furrow my brow. *Dying?*

"What you seek, you will not find in the Twilight Forest. I have had all my men bring every last species to the castle. The only path to the antidote is through me."

I glance around the circular room as I lay my eyes on the many skull soldiers who lean against the wall, watching us intently, their eyes vacant, their scabbards shiny.

I turn back to Rabhya, her translucent veil falling delicately on either side of her face. She is beautiful yet smug. Cruelty crosses her face like a shadow.

"I am not dying," I reply.

"What do you mean?" Rabhya pauses. A realization seems to descend upon her mind as she stares at me. "Wait a minute." She circles me like a panther stalking its prey. "Fair skin . . . pink nails..no greenish tinge..no wrinkled lips . . . no gasping for breath."

Her eyes widen. "You were not bitten."

"You're saying the Helltrie was meant for me?" I ask.

"Of course it was meant for you! How is it possible my potion failed? Why are you here? Why are you trying to retrieve the Grelez plant?"

"To save the person who suffered the bite of your hellish messenger," I reply.

"Who?" sneers Rabhya. "How is it possible Helltrie disobeyed my command?"

We lock eyes and a moment of clarity passes between us. Rabhya gasps as she realizes who is the victim of her curse.

"Kamal!" She pales and sinks into her throne. "No, not Kamal! Not my Kamal!"

"He is not your Kamal," I hiss.

Rabhya's eyes grow dark, and she grips the handles of her regal chair. "Then he will die. It serves him right for his stupidity and poor choice of wife."

"What is she talking about?" whispers Mahfood.

Rabhya stands up from her throne and paces the floor. "This is all your fault, Ria," she hisses.

"My fault!" I shriek. "How is it my fault?"

"You two should have never met." Rabhya folds her arms and glares at me. "A long time ago, Kamal's parents had bargained with me that in exchange for a continuous supply of the Grelez plant to their kingdom, they would give me their son in matrimony. Your kingdom keeps a storehouse of medicine and antidotes to be used against poisons and toxins that may harm the people, but they lack the Grelez plant. Exchanging medicine for matrimony seemed an acceptable bargain for Kamal's family. However, Kamal believed that marriage should be based on love and not used as a contractual agreement. When Kamal became sultan, he broke our arrangement. I was angry and kept my Grelez plants. I believed he would change his mind once he saw how vital the antidote would be to his people. But then you were discovered posing as a man in order to fight in the castle army. You were recognized by the kingdom for your bravery, and Kamal fell in love with you. This ruined my plans.

"I think she is crazy," whispered Mahfood.

"The only way you will get the antidote now is if you go through me." Rabhya reaches into the armrest of her royal chair and pulls out a double-edged sword. She holds it out before her, the blade shimmering in the shadows.

Immediately, I pull my sword out and ready myself for battle.

"You want me to fight you with all of these skull soldiers ready to come to your aid?" I inquire.

Rabhya clicks her tongue. "They won't move until I summon them. Do not worry. I do not need them. I can dispatch you with one thrust of my sword."

"I do not trust her. It is a trap," hisses Mahfood.

"Go and see if you can figure out a way to eliminate these soldiers," I mutter through clenched teeth, not trying to move my lips.

She extends her sword outward with the tip pointed at my heart. "Are you ready, Sultana of Jerdaj?"

I lift my blade to accept her invitation.

She steps toward me. We glare at each other as we move in a circular motion. Our elbows are bent and our weapons are high, waiting for the moment to strike.

I swing. The blade whistles as it cuts through the air. I am not close to hitting my intended target, but my abrupt action distracts Rabhya, which allows Mahfood and Dawood to scurry into the shadows of the room.

"You fool," cries Rabhya. "You don't even know how to fight."

She moves her weapon towards my ankle, but with rapid speed, I block her advance. A look of shock passes over her face as she stumbles backward but composes herself.

Apparently, she has no knowledge that I am the descendant of a proud warrior family.

She thrusts forward, but I move back. I raise my weapon over my head and bring it down, but I am blocked.

I move low and the sultana jumps over my blade. I advance, backing Rabhya to the wall. At the last second, she turns and runs to the opposite wall, going up the side and somersaulting over me. I turn and clash weapons with her.

My shoulders ache, but I do not feel anything except the rush of emotions flowing through my blood.

The room is silent, save for the banging of our swords, her yells, and my grunts. Our blades clang so hard, sparks fly. I stumble backward and fall to the floor. Rabhya brings her sword down towards my face, but I roll out of the way and her sword dents the floor.

I spring to my feet.

As we fight, I think about Kamal and how time is running out. I cannot lose my husband. I arc my sword with all my strength. My blade hits Rabhya's weapon with such force that her saber snaps in half. The Sultana of the Skull Soldiers stands before me, holding half a weapon with a jagged edge.

My fingers grip the hilt of my blade, my hands shake, and my breath comes in ragged gasps. I have no idea how I shattered her weapon. Rabhya and I stare into each other's eyes. Slowly I lower my advantage. I do not wish to kill her.

In my moment of compassion, Rabhya lunges forward and slices my arm. I gasp and drop my sword as I clutch my wound. I step back and expect the sultana to finish me, but she is frozen. Her eyes are wide as she drops to the ground in front of me. Her eyes close.

The skull soldiers stand tall and look at one another with their expressionless faces, as if inquiring what has happened to their leader. They raise their sabers and advance on me. However, before they can get closer, they freeze like their sultana. One by one, they turn into puffs of dust until I am all alone in the room.

"I told you it would work," I hear a voice shout behind me.

I turn to see Mahfood and Dawood hopping towards me.

I hear a buzz in my ear, quick and loud. Then the noise becomes silent.

"What did you two do?" I ask.

"While you were fighting, we made our way into Rabhya's secret room," replies Mahfood. "It turns out that she is breeding Helltrie. We decided to set the insects loose with some intended targets in mind."

"The Helltrie attacked the skull soldiers?" I ask.

"Yes," answers Dawood. "Because the skeletons are not real humans, they turn to dust when a Helltrie bites their bones. And then we sent a lovely one to the sultana over there, and I believe our gesture came at just the right time."

"You two are the best companions a sultana could ask for. Thank you." I look over at Rabhya's still frame. I crouch beside her and feel her wrist. There is a pulse.

"Come on, Ria!" calls Mahfood. "We found it."

"Found what?"

"You will see."

I follow the two frogs into a secret lair adjacent to the throne room. Before me, is a solarium with rows upon rows of Grelez plants.

I clasp my hand to my chest. Thank the gods! I grab one of the potted plants then bend down for Mahfood and Dawood to jump onto my palm and into my pockets. As we emerge from the solarium, I see Rabhya lying on the floor with my sword nearby.

I walk over and pick up my scimitar, which I return to my scabbard at my hip. I stare at the fallen sultana. Her breath comes in shallow gasps.

"What are you doing, Ria? We must hurry." Mahfood cries.

I look at the Grelez plant with its many green leaves. I wrap my fingers around some of them and pull them from the stems. Bending down, I place leaves on Rabhya's face, chest, and palms. Immediately, the color returns to her face, and her breathing grows normal. By the time she wakes, we will be far away.

Turning on my heel, I run out of the castle. The frog brothers and I take the quickest path through the forest until the swirling mist stares at us. No Selchnuerm crosses our path. The way home is now safe.

"Ria, you saved Rabhya. Why?" asks Dawood. "You know, if it was the other way around, she would have killed you."

I look down at the frogs' heads poking out from the pockets of my cloak.

"Maybe so," I reply. "But I am not the Sultana of the Skull Soldiers. I am the Sultana of Jerdaj. It is not my place to take a life."

Inhaling a deep breath, I step through the smokey fog. My feet touch Jeradj soil, and I see the turrets of my home in the distance. An intuition in my soul tells me everything will be alright. As I head towards the castle, I feel joy spreading through my heart. I cannot wait to be back in my husband's arms and see him healthy again.

In another time and place, I will battle Rabhya again. Right now, I have a life to save.

N.D.T. Casale

N.D.T. Casale is an Italian-American author who lives in the United States. She creates magical realms for others to escape to and enjoy. Her goal is to write stories that bring joy, happiness, and hope to the lives of many.

When she is not hard at work writing, N.D.T. Casale spends her time riding horses, working out, traveling, snowboarding, and looking for her next adventure. She is fluent in multiple languages, loves animals, and is obsessed with fashion and fitness. She always ends her day with a cup of tea.

N.D.T. Casale also writes under the pen name N.D. Testa.

Games Egyptians Play

Donna White

Pax Bellona watched a mongoose slip through a patch of tall grass in the garden that once belonged to Cleopatra, the last ruling descendant of the Ptolemaic Dynasty. The sound of gurgling water and birdsong filled the air. A duck quacked out of annoyance as it drifted along the soft currents of the pond fed by a rocky waterfall. Beds of roses lined the water's edge, some of the climbing flowers twirled around the trunks of the sycamore and palm trees. Her chaperone, Diana Fortunato, was sniffing all the delicate scents of the flowers. Pax chuckled to herself while watching this tall, blond adventuress enjoy such a pretty pastime. It was a very different activity for her than hunting treasure and fighting cutthroat villains.

The women were dressed in long tunics with their finest embroidered shawls, draped in the elegant fashion denoting their Roman family status.

A well-dressed Egyptian man ascended the steps that led to the private garden. He opened his arms wide as he walked on the path meandering through the roses. "Welcome to Egypt. I am Onnophris, servant to your host."

Pax skipped out of the shade and greeted him. She heard a loud crack and a swish and turned in time to see Diana standing under the tree looking at the palm frond dropping down at a great speed. Diana had only a second before the heavy branch made contact with her head.

***

"Oh, that hurts." Diana fluttered her eyes open and reached for her head. Her arms and hands were wrapped in gauze. "Ugh!" She glared at the room. "Where am I and why is there two of everything?"

Pax bit her lip and looked at Onnophris with wide eyes.

"Noble lady, you are in the house of my master, Pa-neck. You are under the care of the finest physician in all of Egypt.

"Who is Pa-neck?"

"Diana, don't you remember? Pa-neck paid for our trip. He brought you here to help him with a task. You brought me to learn about the architecture and practice the language."

Diana stared at Pax for a few seconds. "Who are you?"

Pax was saved from answering the question by the physician walking in with a tray of potions. "Ah, you're awake." He spent a few moments questioning and examining Diana. "The branch hit your head with great force and your arms are battered from the thorns. You'll need to be under my observation until you're well."

"I suppose that's fine because I don't know where I am, or who any of you are. Come to think of it, I don't know who I am." With that, she eased her head on the pillow and closed her eyes.

The physician turned to Pax and Onnophris. "We have a problem. Pa-neck wants to see the adventuress in an hour. She will not be ready. Our dear master is not a patient man, and if he is inconvenienced someone could end up locked in a tomb."

Pax burst out laughing. She gripped her sides at the ridiculous joke and caught sight of the men's pained faces. "What? Are you serious?"

"Young lady, Pa-neck's family line is that of an ancient dynasty. He has never accepted the rule of any of the new dynasties. He is one of the most powerful men on this continent, save for our newly installed Augustus." He gave a conciliatory nod to Pax. "Roman occupation does not sit well with him. Why he called forth a Roman treasure hunter is beyond me. He does not seem rational. I'm sure you've heard the saying, 'He who has the gold, makes the rules.' That means we play his game by his rules," said the physician.

"She's in no shape to meet with him. I will go talk to him and ask for some more time."

"You don't understand. If he does not see Diana Fortunato in less than an hour, someone's going in that tomb!"

"What if I pretend to be Diana Fortunato, the great adventuress?"

The physician slapped his thigh and laughed. "You?! You look like a mouse. Don't be ridiculous."

Onnophris stood. "She is small, but she has courage. I can feel it." At that moment, Pax's heart skipped a beat as a spark ran throughout her body. She gave him a shy grin. He flashed her a smile of admiration.

The physician shrugged. "It looks like our only chance. Take her to the wardrobe and have her dressed as an Egyptian noblewoman. Pa-neck hates Roman style clothing."

PAX ARRIVED ON TIME AT A SET OF COPPER DOUBLE DOORS. Her Roman look was replaced with a black, straight haired wig and a long, white linen dress. She could have passed for Cleopatra herself. Pax lacked the ornate jewelry, but she knew that Diana did not fuss with fancy items unless they could be used as a weapon. She knocked on the door.

"Enter," a deep voice commanded from behind the copper.

Pax pushed through the heavy doors. She was met with . . . more copper. Copper walls and copper accessories glowed from the light of the copper braziers. Various animal skins were draped across the floor and dark wooden chairs.. An obsidian colored snake moved over the black marble floor shot with veins of gold. Although not a fan of reptiles, she showed no fear.

"Come. Sit."

The voice startled Pax. What she had originally taken as another piece of furniture was a man. His skin and shaved head blended with the metallic orangish glow of the room. He was wearing one of the animal skins across his bare chest like a sash and a shendyt that matched. A thick gold chain completed his look. Onnophris warned her to expect theatrics from this man. She was determined to act as hard and cool as she had observed Diana Fortunato, the legendary adventuress, do on many occasions. He placed two bronze goblets on a dark table as Pax seated herself.

Pa-neck approached her with a jug of wine. She covered the top of the goblet with her hand. He stepped back, raised his eyebrow, and smirked. He poured wine for himself and sat across from her.

"I am touched by your gesture of donning Egyptian attire. You are undoubtedly politically astute, or Onnophris warned you of my abhorrence of Roman dress."

Pax spoke without smiling. "You need my services. Tell me what you want."

"I like you, Fortunato. You get to the point. In return, I will get to the point. An important family heirloom went missing centuries ago. Romans are in charge now that Cleopatra is dead, and I fear they will find my heirloom and destroy it."

"What's its significance?"

With mock surprise, he put his hand to his chest revealing fingers wrapped in thick gold dotted with jewels sparkling from the brazier light. "History, culture, art, my link to my ancestry."

"Do you have any leads?"

He sipped his wine. "I have a library."

"Is anyone else working on this?"

"You, alone. My scholars will give you their pieces of the puzzle. They can't go any further without you."

"What am I looking for?"

"A gold scepter shaped like a snake's head. It is graced with exquisite rubies for eyes."

"Do you know how many objects look like that in this area?"

"You'll feel it before you see it."

Pax pushed her chair back and folded her arms. "Oh, I see. It's imbued with power."

Pa-neck dropped a pouch of gold on the table.

"Am I correct in assuming there are hidden traps surrounding it?"

A second pouch of gold hit the table.

"And let's not forget my favorite, it's guarded by some deadly creature waiting to devour the marrow out of my bones," Pax described.

Gold coins tumbled onto the table from the third pouch.

Pa-neck rose and pushed a copper panel aside, revealing a window. A light breeze blew into the room.

"My library is the round building surrounded by the red roses. Use it."

Pax peered out the window. "It's beautiful, but unusual for Egyptians to use that style of architecture."

Pa-neck whipped around and frowned at her with a calculating gaze. "Since when does the great Fortunato care about building design?"

Pax blushed and stammered. "Oh, um, well every great treasure hunter studies architecture. We have to break into buildings sometimes."

He stared at her in silence until she started to fidget underneath his glare. She was flubbing her acting and she guessed he knew something was amiss. She cleared her throat and put on a brave swagger. "Triple the amount of gold, and I want that emerald ring on your finger."

Without removing his gaze from her face, he smirked and touched his ring. "This will never leave my finger. Onnophris will pay for any expenses. You get six bags of gold and your life. Failure means I will seal you up in one of my wine cellars, Fortunato."

A chill ran down her spine and it took her a moment to reply in a shaky voice. "I never fail." She turned, pushed the bronze doors open, and fled back to Diana's side.

***

DIANA GAVE A GROGGY SMILE TO THE YOUNG WOMAN WHO dashed into her room. "Pax, I'm so glad to see you."

Pax was happy to see that Diana was regaining her memory, but there was no time for chatting. She needed help.

"That man is insane! I can tell he plans on killing me!" Pax said to the groggy Diana.

"Don't worry. I'll be back to normal tomorrow." Then she fell back on her pillow and snored.

***

THE ROUND LIBRARY WAS STOCKED WITH SHELVES OF scrolls and heavy tables. The scholar attending Pax brought her an armload of scrolls that contained Pa-neck's family history and their treasures. She read for hours about Pa-neck's line, whose family name was blotted out on the papyrus. She supposed it meant that his ancestor's successors did this. It wasn't until the late afternoon when she came across a passage that stated, "The twin ruby scepter was taken by force by the Good Ones." She stared at the hieroglyphs.

"Aaaargh! I figured out what a Good One is! Scholar! Why didn't you tell me? Alright, have locations on the Good Ones on this table early in the morning, please." She thanked him and went back to Diana's room for dinner.

Diana was looking much better, but she was quite sore and battered. "I can't wield a sword with these arms."

"Fish is great for getting wounds to heal. Eat up." Pax said to Diana as she shoveled the lentil and onion stew into her own mouth and washed it down with date-sweetened beer.

The physician walked in for his evening visit. "Onnophris will be gone on an errand for a few days. He did not have time to say goodbye, but he wishes for you to stay cautious until he returns."

Pax blew out a big breath and slumped in her chair. "So that means I have to deal with Pa-neck on my own. Fine. I've got an early morning at the library. I'm going to bed. Goodnight."

Pax tried to mimic Diana's bold walk, but her stride came out like a sassy mouse on her way to pull out the cat's whiskers. She climbed the steps to the library and passed through the doors. A scroll was waiting for her on the table. Hours later, Pax was reading amongst several curling scrolls at her elbow. Locations for Good Ones could best be described as cryptic. Her head hurt and her eyes crossed. She was preparing to take her leave because the scholars were shutting the library down for a few hours. Egyptians took sleep breaks on occasion, but the librarians were serious nappers.

"Where can I find a Good One?" she asked.

"They are in plain sight, if you know their names."

"Yes, I figured that out by reading the scrolls. I know one, but I need another."

"I cannot help you with that."

"Oh fine! I'll figure it out myself." She sped out of the library and back to Diana's room. The room was empty, as was the rest of the home. *Where is everyone?*

After some time, Pax wandered up to a rooftop garden covered in palm trees and jasmine flowers. The smell of myrrh tucked away in hidden places was dreamy, but she kept her head about her. Pa-neck reclined in a gold chair cushioned in leopard furs. His feet rested on a matching ottoman. A slender, graceful woman was giving him a pedicure, two others were feeding him bites of a small roasted bird and sliced melon. "What brings you here, Fortunato?"

Pax inclined her head in greeting. "I'm looking for a Good One. If I can find one, I'm sure I can find your heirloom."

He smiled. "I cannot help you with that."

Pax gritted her teeth at the arrogant oaf. She was already annoyed at the scholar for telling her the exact same thing. "Then what can you help me with?"

"I can hurry you along with your quest." He took a long sip of his wine. "I suppose you've noticed your blonde friend is missing?" He held up his hand. "Not to worry. She is in cozy quarters here on my estate. I'll release her as soon as you hand over the scepter."

Fear squeezed her chest. "I . . . I . . . I need my assistant . . . she . . ."

"You are Diana Fortunato! You need no one! Get on with your quest before I tire of you!"

Pax thought this was rude behavior, but she was smart enough to realize that Pa-neck was not an oaf to cross. She turned and headed downstairs. *Fine, I'll go back to the library when they open. My stomach is growling. Maybe I need some stew first.*

She took a detour through the kitchen to grab something to eat. An apprentice was grinding some pork in a mortar with a pestle. She didn't even have to say a word. The young man pointed to a tray with peculiar, thin-sliced meat. Pax popped a piece into her mouth. "This is delicious! What is it?" The taste was salty and peppery with a hint of garlic and fenugreek.

The apprentice smiled with pride, and she watched his process of grinding the meat, mixing it with spices, and shaping it into a tight loaf. Pax was amazed. For a moment, she forgot about Diana. She munched on a chunk of bread with the meat delicacy. She loved it, and soaked up everything the apprentice told her about the recipe. "Do you mind if I take this recipe back to Rome. I'm Pa . . . Diana."

"Diana Fortunato?"

Pax looked at her sandals.

"Wow! I would be honored if you'd share my recipe with the Roman world! You don't look anything like all the legendary stories say you look like. I didn't think a Roman adventuress would go around dressed like an Egyptian noblewoman. Anyway, I'd do anything to go on a quest. Pa-neck wants your task to be secret, which means everyone knows about it." He laughed.

"Maybe you can help me!"

"Yes! What can I do?"

"I need the help of a Good One."

The apprentice frowned and dithered about for a moment. "The Good Ones are a super- secret society of architects devoted to the preservation of treasures that exhibit unusual powers, specifically from Pa-neck."

Pax raised her eyebrows. "A society to thwart Pa-neck's quest for magical or supernatural objects? I knew they protected treasures. I didn't know it was from Pa-neck."

"Yes. Pa-neck has too long of a history for me to tell you. The Good Ones designed hidden chambers in the pyramids, sometimes for the royals, sometimes hidden from the royals."

"Do they only work with pyramids?"

"Oh, no! They work with any distinctive structure. Why, there're hidden chambers and vaults all over Egypt, and even on Pa-neck's estate."

Pax mulled this over for a few minutes while the apprentice wrapped up some bread, dried figs, and the thinly sliced, pressed meat. He put the food in two pouches with straps and gave one to Pax.

"You'll have to excuse me, Lady Fortunato. I have to deliver this food to Onnophris."

"Onnophris is on a mission."

The apprentice gave her a hard look and stared for a long time into her eyes until it dawned on her. *He's not allowed to help me, so he's giving me a hint. Stupid games these Egyptians play!* She nodded in understanding.

He left the kitchen without a word more.

She watched him hurry down the hallway, and followed him at a distance. He went outside and jogged down to the stables. Two horses were being led away by the stable boy. Onnophris stepped down from an ornate chariot fit for a pharaoh. Pax watched the scene from behind a rather pokey hedge. She was too far away to hear them. The apprentice handed Onnophris the package of food, which he ate standing by the chariot as the young man gestured and spoke. Onnophris nodded on occasion. He swallowed the last bite and gulped down something from a flask. He slung a pack across his shoulder, bid the apprentice goodbye, and hurried through the estate.

Pax followed him into, of all possible places, the library. She scratched her head and thought that was an odd place to go. The scholars paid him no attention as he whipped past the tables and shelves of scrolls. A few curious souls glanced at her as she walked into the building.

Onnophris descended a broad, curving staircase, and Pax followed him into the cool cellars. She chased him through a maze of doorways adorned with paintings of deities, all illuminated with the lights from braziers. He moved out of her sight, but she followed the sound of his footsteps until she found herself alone in a large, octagon-shaped tomb surrounded by eight gold sarcophagi.

She scanned the room hoping to see an exit or an alcove, anywhere Onnophris could be hiding. The only place she could think of would be one of the sarcophagi. She shook her head. *Highly doubtful.*

At that moment, one of the heavy sarcophagi lids opened with that creaking sound associated with everything that goes bump in the night. She ducked behind another sarcophagus and peered around the side. Pax was very aware that she had no defensive fighting skills as two arms and a head appeared. Like an idiot, she screamed, "Aaaaagh!" and fell over.

Onnophris climbed out of the sarcophagus and closed the lid. Pax scooted across the floor as he jogged up to her. "Pax! What are you doing here?"

Before Pax could respond, a voice came from above. "Aha! Well done, little spy! You discovered my game room."

Pax and Onnophris looked up at the gallery on the second floor.

Pa-neck was clapping. "You are no Diana Fortunato! Even though I never met the great adventuress, I heard tales of the tall, blonde Roman-Barbarian. I figured you were a spy, little mouse. Perhaps you are one of the assassins that Fortunato trains."

Assassins? Pax wondered what on earth he was talking about.

"I've studied Diana Fortunato from afar. When I threatened to wall you up in my cellar, you blanched with fear. The real Fortunato would have split my skull and used it as a candle holder over that mere threat."

"So why didn't you kill me, if you thought I was an imposter?"

"I like games. Games make a life interesting. Many years ago, my spies found Onnophris as a junior manager of Cleopatra's holdings. I offered him the top position for my estate, and he jumped at the chance." Pa-neck sipped from a goblet. "Now, put the pieces together."

Pax glanced around the room searching for an escape.

"Come, come. You only leave this room if you play the game."

Pax sighed and gathered her courage. "Onnophris means *He who is good*. You put him in your household because you knew he was a part of a secret architectural society sworn to thwart your plans of gaining the mysterious powers stored in the treasures hidden in Egypt."

Pa-neck choked on his drink. "Of the world, girl! Treasures of the world. Onnophris thought of me as grasping, cutthroat, and theatrical, with a large ego. All true! But underneath all the bravado was cunning," he winked at the astonished couple before him. "I saw in that young man a thirst to prove himself. Patience and caution were for lesser mortals. He, himself, thought he clawed his way up the ranks in Cleopatra's court. It was his name alone that singled him out to the usurper queen. She put him where he was, but after a while she had no need of his hidden treasures. Her mind turned to Marc Antony, Caesar, building empires of gold! She let him pass to me. He thought he was a clever star, and that I was a relic to spy on in my own illustrious home," he flashed a sinister grin. "Well guess again, Onnophris-the-egotistical-architect! You brought my ancestor's scepter straight to my humble abode, thinking I was too daft to know what you were doing. Ha! It is I who have played you!"

Onnophris did not hide the shock on his face. "You're right. My pride in my achievements led to my failure. You and Cleopatra manipulated me through the pride I embraced through the prestige of my position. I let my guard down, thinking I was smarter than two of the cleverest people in the world.

Pa-neck laughed, "Letting even one set of ears on this grand estate hear the words *ruby-eyed snake scepter* would ensure that every human, camel, horse, dog, cat, koi, fruit bat, and snake under my dominion would know all the details of my quest by sundown."

Pax and Onnophris looked at each other and nodded. It did sound like an accurate assessment.

"Yes I, the Great Pa-neck, can squash armies of enemies, but can't keep my servant's tongues from wagging. Brilliant, if you know how to manage it. So, with the word that I planted in, what did he call you . . . Pax? In Pax's head. An eavesdropping servant overheard our conversation, and word got around to Onnophris. He took off immediately to secure my family's lost scepter. My spies followed him. They lost him in a most curious way but found him as he returned with what I believe is the scepter."

Onnophris, looking pale and faint, steadied himself against a sarcophagus.

"Pax, grab the iron rod and open that sarcophagus." Pa-neck bellowed.

Scared but obedient, she opened one of the heavy lids with the help of the lever. Inside, Pax found a bound and gagged Diana. Pax removed the gag with shaking fingers and started to untie the ropes binding Diana's wrists.

Diana whispered to Pax, "Turn your back so Pa-neck can't see us. Now remove the large comb from my hair. Press the middle crystal . . . No, the *middle* crystal . . . you have to press it hard . . . harder than that. Good, now slide the comb away from the crystal and it will reveal a slender knife blade. Good, now cut the ropes on my hands."

With a jerk of her head and a shift of her eyes towards Pa-neck, Pax indicated to Onnophris to distract him.

"The scepter is safe. Let it stay hidden from your enemies," Onnophris said.

"Ha! Nice try."

Diana took the comb-knife from Pax and sliced through the ropes binding her feet.

Pa-neck clapped. "Oh well done! Now look across the room to the Sarcophagus of the Scorpions."

Without notice from anyone, Diana threw the comb-knife. It whistled through the air, grazing Pa-neck's scalp as he ducked. Blood spurted and he howled with pain and rage. His panther-fast movement saved him from a plunged knife to the chest.

Diana grabbed Pax and tossed her into a nearby sarcophagus that Onnophris popped open. Matte black scorpions as large as dinner plates were falling out of their ornate coffin by the hundreds. Diana and Onnophris followed Pax. The three of them hit a slick slide and moved at great speed down a darkening tunnel. The air was cold and damp. It didn't smell like the normal baked, floral scents of Egypt. It smelled of cheese, and not in a good way. Pax felt her body level out and stop.

"Move, ladies."

Pax and Diana scrambled out of the way as Onnophris slid towards them.

"Stay here. I'm going to find some light," Onnophris said. He returned within minutes with a torch in his hand.

"Where did you find that?" Pax asked.

"I'm an architect. I've studied the lighting style in Pa-neck's buildings." He raised the torch to show the women the immense slide they just rode. It was supported by stone columns, and the slide itself was hammered metal with sides that curved upward. They could not see the light from Pa-neck's distant game room.

"Let's move. There should be many exits from this cave, and they may be guarded after the great Pa-neck was cut by an assassin of a house-guest, no offence to you, Diana. Only a madman invites the Queen of Spies to stay under his roof."

"I'll ignore that remark." Diana stalked away from him. "Where is the scepter?"

"Secured."

"It will need to be moved. I will accompany you and provide protection."

"I am Onnophris. My society is more than adequate for the concealment of the scepter."

Diana shrugged. "So be it."

They walked on until they found a waterfall pouring from the top of the cave, where a fissure let in ample light. A stream flowed from the pool of water that formed under the waterfall.

"If we follow the stream, we will find our way out of the cave," Onnophris said.

Diana pointed to what appeared to be the end of the cave. "The stream flows through a small passage underneath that wall. It doesn't mean there's a safe passage."

Onnophris frowned. "That stream vanishes beneath a secret vault, a rare room of mystery and enlightenment meant only for those wise enough to be initiated with the knowledge of the powers-that-be."

A tawny colored form moved around the hidden corner of what seemed to be a flat wall.

Pax clapped a hand to her mouth to keep from shrieking. Diana pulled two well-hidden blades from only Horus—the god of secrets and son of Isis—knew where.

The form was a majestic lion with the head of a flawless human man. It wore a nemes, a striped head cloth worn by pharaohs that covered the crown and fell down to the neck. A pair of long, tan wings sprouted from its shoulders. It was a fine example of the rare male Egyptian sphinx.

It padded in front of the secret vault and addressed the three astonished visitors, "Greetings. I can tell by the surprised look on your faces that you are not here to learn the mysteries."

Onnophris opened his mouth to speak, but the sphinx shut him down. "You are not ready to answer the riddle that lets you peer behind these doors. You would fail, and then I'd have to eat you. Neither one of us wants that. Human flesh is too soft and tastes of perfumed oils. I believe you want out of this cave, so give me a payment and I'll send you on your way."

The three humans went to immediate action patting down their pockets looking for coins. Diana was busy pulling out various tiny weapons.

"I have something," Pax said. She opened the pouch that the chef's apprentice gave her earlier in the day. She pulled out the pressed meat and extended it towards the sphinx. He moved towards her and nibbled it from her fingers. He sat back on his haunches and closed his eyes.

"This is divine. Your payment is more than satisfactory. Around the corner is a tunnel that leads to a secret door. Do not return to Pa-neck's estate. Diana has enraged him more than usual with that cut to his royal scalp. If he catches any of you, the punishment will be severe. Pax, I will send good fortune to you and your descendants for your delicious payment. You will return to your homeland and your children will make this food you have shared with me. Many centuries later, they will perfect it and humans around the world will savor it, not knowing the history we are making."

Onnophris shuffled his feet. "Um, Good Sphinx, you say I'm not ready for the mysteries, yet I opened the Sarcophagus of Safety and hid the scepter in the void. Only those of us who would not use the treasures can enter that sarcophagus. It is one of the few places that is safe from Pa-neck."

"You are correct."

"So why can't I learn of the mysteries that my society protects?"

"Pride has a way of growing stronger over time. At some point, you would feel capable of using the treasures in the pursuit of what you perceive as noble. It would end in disaster with Pa-neck running amok. Remember, he plays a long game. He was feeding your pride in order to lay hands on that scepter. Pax's search for it set the game in motion. In time you may return, but you have finished your part as a Good One in Egypt by removing the scepter from Pa-neck. Now you must be a Good One in a place that needs you. You will accompany Pax back to Rome and learn humility from this humble mouse." The sphinx smiled down at Pax.

Both Onnophris and Pax blushed. They gave each other a shy smile.

"Do me a favor though." The sphinx stepped out of the way so the hand-holding couple and Diana could pass. "Make sure your descendants send me a basket of bread and this tasty meat, or I will curse the name of Bellona to mean foolish."

"Please respect my name. If a descendant should ever forget you, change the spelling of *their* name to Bologna."

Onniphris popped a leftover bite of the delicacy into his mouth. "Or how about Baloney?"

Donna White

Donna White is the author of The Whitmere Legacy series and The Enchanted Anthologies. She was born and raised in the South and moved to Southern California as a young adult. Donna splits her time between her husband, children, large dogs, and her passion for nature photography. She writes epic paranormal and action/adventure stories of gracious women with enhanced martial arts skills in exotic locations. Charm and humor are her trademarks while keeping the scare factor at bay.

You can catch Donna on Instagram @donnawhiteauthor.

ALLIE AND THE FOX

EURELIA WINTERS

ALLIE

Allie shuffled towards the master bedroom. Willow was probably still sleeping soundly. *Getting Willow up in the mornings is as easy as getting an unwilling donkey to move.* With a deep breath to steel herself for the morning battle, Allie opened the door to her bedroom. "Maiden, are you ready to . . . eh . . . Willow?" Allie's words stilled at the sight of the unmade empty bed. Looking around, she noticed that the clothes that were usually found on the floor beside the bed were missing. Well, wherever Willow was, at least she was clothed. "Willow?" Allie raised her voice as loud as she dared while walking back out into the hallway, but there was no answer.

Allie sighed. If she didn't get Willow to her lessons for the day, Allie would be the one facing the repercussions. The clergy overseeing the maiden had chosen her as Willow's aide due to Allie's responsible nature and the fact that Allie was only a few years older than Willow. The clergy wanted Willow to follow Allie's good example. *I'm not sure how I feel about their reasoning, but I do wish I could be of help to her. Being the Maiden of Death must be taxing, especially since there's only one born in every generation of her bloodline.* Allie sighed. *I thought we were getting along well, so where is she? Why didn't she tell me if she went somewhere? The ghost problem is pretty big and Willow is the only one who can deal with sending the dead to their eternal slumber. It would be really bad if she disappeared.*

As the maiden's residence wasn't very big, searching it didn't take long. In the ceremony hall and reception area, the only person to be found was the clerk. He was busy noting down the newest requests for the maiden's services.

"Have you seen Willow today?" Allie asked, but the clerk just shook his head, so she continued to the garden. *Willow usually never leaves the house except for enjoying her private garden, and I have not seen her show much interest in going anywhere else. Could it be because Willow has grown up so sheltered?* After Willow's mom died during labor, her dad had managed to keep Willow's gift a secret for several years before the clergy found out and took her away. *Maybe the expectations people have of Willow and the overwhelming attention she gets whenever she ventures outside overwhelmed her*, Allie thought. Combing through the garden unfortunately yielded the same result—no Willow. *I hope Willow isn't lost and alone, or something even worse.* Allie was getting worried, but she didn't know where else to look. She sat down, trying to think of anything that Willow had said or done in the last few days which might give a clue to her disappearance.

Allie must have been sitting there for longer than she thought, or maybe looking for Willow had been more time consuming than it felt.

Allie suddenly heard the voice of Willow's teacher. "Why is my student not ready for her lessons yet?"

Turning around, Allie could see the old cleric's face. Somehow, it was more disgustingly sour than his usual displeased grimace, and she just wanted to shy away. She barely managed to compose herself. "I am terribly sorry, Your Excellency, but when I went to wake the honorable maiden earlier, she was nowhere to be found. I have searched the entirety of the premises to no avail, so I am trying to remember if there has been anything she's said or done these past few days that could possibly give a clue as to where she might be." Holding her breath, Allie hoped her answer was satisfactory. His cold, disappointed glare made her truly worried about what would happen next.

"The maiden is your responsibility," he said in a terribly unfeeling voice that matched him perfectly. "I expect you to have her ready for her lessons tomorrow. If you can't handle your duty, we can have you brought up on charges of neglect and have you judged to work with the gatherers instead. I presume you would rather handle a teenager than hunt down malevolent spirits? Find her." With that he turned around and left, leaving Allie rooted to the spot. *Me? A gatherer?*

To Allie, her granny's story about her great grandma being chased around by a tiny, possessed chicken didn't seem as funny anymore. Back then, the ghost problems in this country were even worse. Spirits possessing the farm animals were one of the milder issues. The longer the ghosts were without bodies, the more corrupt they got. In some of the more chill-inducing stories, entire villages were wiped out and the uninhabitable areas were overrun by these possessed beings. This was when the first Maiden of Death was born. She was able to send the spirits to the afterlife. Hunting down runaway malicious spirits and delivering them to the maiden for cleansing became a task usually given to felons and others who had made grave mistakes to redeem themselves. They were assigned a set number of malevolent spirits to bring in depending on the transgression. Since the closest thing to combat training Allie had was beating the dust out of an old carpet with a carpet beater, this task was equivalent to a death sentence.

Just as Allie got ready to go inside and look through Willow's chambers for any clues, she heard a yelp. A fox emerged from the bushes, its red fur somewhat matted. It approached carefully, hesitating a bit.

"Are you a spirit?" Allie asked. She let her breath out when the fox nodded its head eagerly. The reaction meant the spirit had not been outside a body very long and that it was still in possession of its full faculties. "Are you Willow?" A decisive shake of its head confirmed that at least the maiden wasn't dead and had come back in the form of a fox.

The fox pawed at its ear with one of its front paws.

Allie hazarded a guess, "You heard that, didn't you?" There was another excited nod from the fox. "What should I do? I have no idea where the maiden is." She sighed.

The fox, carefully walking closer and then grabbing hold of her dress, started to pull her towards an opening in the hedge.

"Do you know where she went?" Allie asked. When the fox let go and nodded eagerly, she decided to take a chance. "Will you show me?" As the fox nodded again, relief flooded over Allie. She still had a chance of not ending up as a gatherer, although trusting a stranger was also a risk.

"Let me just pack something to eat and we can be on our way," Allie said, while making a beeline for the kitchen. Thinking for a bit, she picked up a loaf of bread and some cheese; then went and got a small satchel, which she loaded with the food and a bottle of water. She also put a kitchen knife in there, just in case. Then, Allie followed the fox back through the garden to the gap in the hedge it had come from. After slipping through to the other side they came upon a small clearing, which they crossed. The fox showed her a path leading into the woods, looking back several times to make sure Allie was keeping up.

For the six months that Allie had been Willow's caretaker, this was the farthest from the dwelling that she'd been. As they walked through the woods on the small path, Allie wondered what might have inspired Willow to go this far when she had never shown an interest in doing so before. Despite her worries, Allie was enjoying the walk through the forest. She had been too busy taking care of Willow to have time for leisure walks.

Her traveling companion didn't have the means to respond to her questions other than nodding and shaking its head. That communication problem was solved by asking yes or no questions, so they managed to have something resembling a conversation.

The forest was beautiful with the trees not too closely gathered, making it an easy walk. On their way, Allie found out that the spirit had been a farmer who lived alone just a few miles from there. It had been late when he encountered his demise, but it was too difficult to figure out exactly how it happened. Luckily, a fox had been nearby, so he'd borrowed the creature's body for a while to go see the maiden. "That's why you were in the garden?" Allie asked and got a nod in return. "Did you know where she went because you saw her leave?" Another nod. "Did she go alone?" The fox shook his head. "So, she went with someone. Did it look like she was forced to go?" Relief slipped through her when the fox shook his head again. "Thank you for taking me there." Yipping, the fox started walking faster, apparently done communicating.

After a few hours of walking, Allie plopped down on a fallen tree. She ate a few mouthfuls of bread and cheese, sharing some with the fox too. Allie thought of how odd it was to go looking for Willow with the help of a spirit. It was like something out of a fairy tale. Swearing to herself that she would find some way to reward the fox, she slid off the log and then they got back on the trail. Allie wondered about the person who'd had the posting before her. She'd been told the woman wasn't suited for the task and hadn't thought more of it. Could something like this happen to her too?

Allie's musings were interrupted by the fox's snarl. Looking up, Allie could see the fox, its tail twitching from side to side like an annoyed cat, staring toward some bushes up ahead.. She noticed a low growling that wasn't coming from the fox. After that came some rustling, and a huge wolf stepped out from between the bushes, blocking their way. Allie stared at the beast, wondering what to do. She had never seen a wolf before, only drawings and paintings of them, and this one was way too close for her comfort. *This one seems to act like an actual animal and not like one taken over by a spirit, so it can't be Willow,* Allie thought. With the help of the fox, maybe she could take the wolf on, but they would definitely not get away unscathed. What other choice did she have? Slowly slipping her hand towards the opening of the satchel, Allie tried to reach for the knife. Her fingers found the food first. *Could that work?* Her voice was barely audible when Allie asked, "Are you hungry?" The wolf replied with something between a bark and another growl, deep and threatening, but so far it hadn't attacked them yet. Hoping she wasn't about to make the dumbest mistake of her life, Allie tossed the bread as far towards the wolf as she could.

The beast jolted and snarled loudly but didn't attack, and she could see its curiosity about what had landed between them. *Please take the bait,* she thought, praying to whatever being that would listen in on her thoughts. The fox bristled, looking like it was trying to make itself as big and intimidating as it could. Slowly, the wolf took one step toward Allie and the fox, then another, keeping its eyes firmly on them. Allie didn't dare move. Its nose kept sniffing and the growls had gotten a bit lower in volume. Though, that could be her own imagination and wishes. It was almost at the place where the bread had landed. *Please take it and leave us alone,* Allie thought, regretting her musings of this trip being like a fairy tale. Fairy tales usually had scary foes in them, and Allie didn't think herself capable of being a heroine.

With one last step, the wolf lowered its head and sniffed at the bread while still watching the pair with its yellow eyes. Having the wolf close enough to see the color of its eyes was frightening. Allie held her breath, hoping the bread would be enough. Luckily, the wolf snatched it up and then darted off so fast she barely had time to blink before it was gone. Her heart raced as if she had run for miles, she could sense the fox pushing his nose against her hand and then lick it as if to ask if she was all right. "Thank you for worrying about me, I'm all right now," she said to the fox. "But let's get out of here fast. I don't want it coming back for another go at us." The fox barked its agreement and trotted on along the path at a pace where Allie almost had to jog to keep up with it.

They kept the speed up for probably half an hour before settling back into a more sustainable walking pace. After a while, they came upon a small but sturdy looking timber building that looked like a woodcutter's shack. Looking inside through a small hole that served as a window, Allie saw a room big enough to fit a triple bunk bed, three chairs and a table in addition to a chest for the necessities. Allie lowered herself onto a bench outside and leaned against the building, resting her still shaking legs. Then she shared the last piece of cheese with the fox. Thinking the chest inside could contain some food, Allie walked to the door and drew the huge bolt keeping it shut aside. Just after she had pried the door open, Allie heard the fox snarl again and a sense of dread settled in her stomach.

Turning her head slowly, Allie expected to see the wolf having followed them, probably in the hopes of a fast meal, but what she saw was even worse. A huge brown bear had just walked into the clearing. It let out a loud roar and started running towards them. Allie hurriedly yelled at the fox, "Get inside!" and then shut the door behind them, slamming a sturdy bolt in place. It was not a moment too soon and the thud against the door was the last straw. Her legs gave out under her and she landed on the bed. "We might be safe for now, but we're not going to find Willow while being stuck here, are we?" Allie looked over at the fox, wondering how to escape her current predicament. Ironically, this little hut could easily have belonged to the three bears from that fairy tale. Though, those bears would probably be a bit less aggressive. *This is way above my paygrade. I'm definitely not some heroine. The cleric's threats as well as being attacked by a wolf and a bear in one day are a bit much*, Allie thought. A furious roar outside made her flinch and remember she had to find a way out of the shack and soon. *Doing this on a daily basis is a definite no.*

Looking around, Allie couldn't see anything she could use to deal with the bear. She opened the lid of the chest but was disappointed to find only a saw and an axe without its handle. *Well, this was not helpful at all.* Allie kept pondering while looking out the window, and slowly a crazy idea formed. She should question her sanity for thinking of it, but could she fool the bear? Another roar sounded outside and the thuds against the small cabin were getting louder and more frenzied. Considering the way it was attacking the cabin, this was probably a malevolent spirit having taken residence in a bear. *An ordinary bear would probably have given up by now, and a new spirit wouldn't be that aggressive, so this one can't be Willow either,* Allie thought. Meanwhile, the beast did not seem to be letting up any time soon.

Allie looked at the fox, "Would you be able to outrun a bear for a short while? I know it's a lot to ask." The fox seemed to ponder it for a bit, but then gave a short nod, leaning in as if it was waiting to hear what the plan would be. Allie explained while she pushed and pulled at the chest to get it in place below the window, making some loud scraping sounds. The thuds ceased, making Allie worry about where the bear had gotten off to. She found out soon enough as she had to duck when the bear's paw came through the small opening in the wall. Luckily, it was not big enough for the beast to reach her.

As the bear gave up on the window to try to break through the door again, Allie and the fox nodded at each other. "Good luck, and thank you," Allie said as the fox jumped on the chest and then outside before it yipped loudly. Allie heard a bone-chilling roar and the sound of thumping footsteps moving away from the hut. She dared to peek out the window and as soon as Allie saw them disappear into the woods, she got the bolt open and forced her legs to take her back outside. Opening the door wide and hiding behind it, she prayed the bear would be frenzied enough to follow the fox wherever it ran. It didn't take the fox very long to make a wide arch. By the sound of yips and thundering thuds getting louder, Allie reckoned the fox was still running with the bear in tow, straight toward the door she was hiding behind. The sound of the bear's heavy paws thumping on the ground was getting closer and closer and it had Allie's heart racing madly. She thought she might faint from sheer fright, but she forced herself to stay still. Her plan hinged on avoiding notice.

With a deafening roar, the bear followed the fox into the cabin. At once, Allie slammed the door shut and slid the bolt in place. Inside, there was a crash and then silence. The bear must have hit the wall and was probably dizzy from the impact. Hopefully.

The fox came trotting around the cabin. Seconds later, the door shook as the bear tried to get back out. Allie took a few steps backward, scared the bolt wouldn't hold. Luckily it did, at least for now. "Best not to stay here long," Allie said, then started jogging in the direction they had been going earlier. It didn't take more than a few steps until the fox passed her, taking the lead. Knowing the bear would break free eventually, they kept a brisk pace to put as much distance between them as they could. "Will we get there soon?" Allie asked the fox, but it shook its head as if it wasn't sure. "I'm worried about Willow and I just hope she isn't hurt," she explained. Allie figured she would just have to wait and see when she found Willow what the answer would be.

After maybe an hour of switching between walking and jogging, suddenly the fox yipped excitedly, and increased the speed a bit. Finally, Allie and the fox came upon a small, wooden cabin with stone stairs and grass growing on the roof. Outside it, sitting on two small logs, were two smiling teenagers playing cards. Allie sighed in relief at finding Willow and recognizing the kid sitting next to her as one of the kids from the local orphanage. The maiden had enough sense to at least look embarrassed when she saw Allie. As she got closer, she could see the feelings on Willow's face change from embarrassment and shame to disappointment and finally resolve. *Getting Willow to come back with me is going to be a challenge,* Allie thought.

WILLOW

When Willow saw her aide walking towards her in the company of a fox of all things, she knew that she had been found out. Her friend, Dex, had come across her in her garden a few years back after having snuck through an opening in the hedge. Instead of the usual reverence, he had spoken to Willow as if she was just a regular girl. Quickly convincing her to go on an adventure with him. After that first time they found this cabin, twice a year they ran away here together. She had finally been able to try being herself instead of the person everyone expected her to be.

These small breaks from the constant pressure to be perfect, dignified, and selflessly serve everybody were probably over now. To help dead people cross over into the afterlife day after day, with no end in sight, and the expectation that she would happily do this was Willow's lot in life. *I wish they had never found out about my powers.* Even the lectures with that dreadfully stuck up, holier than thou, tutor of hers were only designed to make her into the perfect maiden. Nobody cared about her wanting to know more about life outside of her duties. Every time Willow escaped, the clergy would swap out her aide, sending them back to wherever they came from, so she'd learned not to knit any close bonds with any of them. Willow had felt a bit bad about them losing out on the salary, since she knew it was more than most of that station would get elsewhere. The only one she had felt guilty for getting sacked was Allie, who had treated her the same way Dex did. Though it seems Allie was a bit more crafty and stubborn than the others since she had managed to find her.

"You're so dead," Dex whispered to Willow before the aide could get close enough to hear.

"Yup, I know," Willow whispered back. The knit brows on her aide's face did not bode well. Willow was pretty sure she was in for a reprimand when Allie could get close enough to give her one. Willow prepared herself for the talking-to she felt was coming. There was no use in running. Their secret hideaway had been found, so this would probably be her last escape. Willow could feel her throat constrict at the thought of losing her small amount of freedom. It wasn't Allie's fault. Willow knew the clergy had probably ordered Allie to find her and they could scare anybody. But she wouldn't go back without a fight.

What happened next was not what Willow expected. "Thank the spirits you're fine!" Allie said as she grabbed Willow and hugged her close. "I was really worried when I couldn't find you this morning, you know. I thought you had gotten kidnapped, or worse. You're fine, right?"

Released from the hug, Willow nodded when she saw Allie giving her a once-over, making sure Willow really was all right. *What just happened?*

"Why did you leave without telling me? Aren't we friends?"

The question from Allie came as a surprise. *This is not the scolding I expected.* "I needed to get away for a while," Willow replied, hoping that maybe she could make Allie understand.

"Then can you tell me why you needed to get away?" Allie asked.

Allie's responses gave Willow the courage to explain. "I wanted to be a normal person just for a little while, without all the pressure of being the perfect maiden," Willow said. *Please let her understand.*

ALLIE

"I get that it can be hard with all the expectations people have of you, Willow, but if you want some more freedom, this is not the way to do so. How many times have you two run away before?" Allie looked over at the two youths. She felt bad for Willow, but at the same time, Allie needed her to understand the consequences of her actions and return.

The two of them shared a look before Dex admitted it "Maybe two or three times every year for a few years now?" The answer sounded more like a question.

Allie looked over at Willow, who confirmed it with a nod, still looking a bit tense. "Every action has consequences, Willow. Do you know what happened to the aides you had before me?"

After a short pause, Willow spoke. "I was told they were demoted and sent back to their previous jobs. I'm not going back just so you can keep yours. You've already had it for half a year."

Allie shook her head. "They're most likely dead, Willow. They probably faced what I was threatened with earlier today. I was told I'd be judged for neglecting my duty and then get sent to the gatherers. A regular person will die doing that job." It was a harsh truth to take in, and Allie could see both Willow and Dex blanching at the thought, so she kept going. "I can understand wanting to get some days off to just be a normal human being, but will you come back with me today, so I won't have to get sent to the gatherers? We can plan your next getaway together in a way where I can cover for you without risking the same fate as the others."

Still looking shocked, Willow replied, "I didn't know. I never would have escaped like this if I did. Those poor women. I can't believe the clergy would do something like that."

Allie could see Willow struggling with the information, so she let her be until she managed to get a hold of herself again.

"I'll go back, of course, just in case it wasn't just a threat they gave you. But did you truly mean that you'd help me get some free time now and then if I go back today?" A tentative smile started spreading on Willow's face, and when Allie nodded, a true smile lit up her face instead. "I'm sorry, Dex, but it looks like our stay this time will have to be cut short," Willow said, and both teenagers hurriedly began packing the few things they'd brought with them.

Waiting for them to finish, Allie sat down at the makeshift table. *I better get some rest before we start the trek back again,* she thought. "Thank you for helping me find them," she said to the fox who had plopped down on the ground next to where she was sitting, getting a nod in return. She could hear the two runaways talking while packing.

"I knew you were some kind of important person, I could tell by your clothes, but I didn't know you were the actual maiden," Dex said.

"Yeah, I didn't want to tell you at first because I was afraid you would treat me weirdly and then I forgot about it," came Willow's reply.

"It's all right, everybody has secrets," Dex said with a shrug.

That's the kind of friendship that'll last a lifetime, Allie thought and smiled. Soon, Dex and Willow were done gathering what they had with them, and there was only one thing left to do before leaving. Allie gave the farmer, turned fox, a big hug. It was time for him to get the reward for helping her find Willow. "Have a safe crossing," Allie told him and then let Willow put her hands on the fox to perform the chant of release. *Is that a faint glow?* Allie narrowed her eyes as the prayer neared its end. It was only there for a second, then the fox seemed to fall asleep.

"We need to go before the fox wakes up." Willow said, while getting up and brushing some grass off her dress. Soon after, they left for home.

On the way back, Allie talked a bit with Dex, knowing he tended to run away from the local orphanage based on what the villagers at the market had said about him. He apparently did the odd juggling, some card tricks, and performing for the passersby to earn money for food. *At least it is better than stealing,* Allie thought. Apparently, after one of those escapes, he'd come across Willow in the garden and that's how they got to know each other.

"You know Dex, the people running the orphanage would probably ground you for good if they knew you kept running off with the maiden," Allie snickered, making both youths laugh while imagining the situation.

It was pretty late when they got back and said their farewells with Dex by the opening in the hedge. Both Allie and Willow went straight to bed after a quick bite in the kitchen. Collapsing on her own bed,

Allie hoped that she would never have such an eventful day ever again before exhaustion finally dragged her under. The next morning, to Allie's surprise, Willow was up and already eating by the time Allie got out of her bedroom.

With a smile, Willow asked, "So, how will we do this?"

Eurelia Winters

Eurelia is the pen name of some kind of nocturnal creature from the land of the Vikings. Usually, she spends her days studying, being pestered by her two cats, and chatting with her long-distance hubby in the evenings.

After finishing obligatory schooling, she has worked a number of odd jobs before finally deciding to try getting that university degree in Norse language and literature. She is a new author and debuting with a short story in the anthology Twice Upon a Name after being challenged to do so by one of the other authors. Some other works might be in the planning stages, although being a university student takes up most of her time, so there is no set date as to when those might get written.

Writing is a hobby, and she also does a number of arts, crafts, and cosplay, reads way too much, and plays some games every once in a while. One can say that if there is an artistic side to something, she's probably tried it at least once.

For now, she'll stay an elusive creature, but if she ever manages to finish her other scribblings, she might set up some sort of account where people can get in touch with her to discuss her works. If you're in dire need of reaching her, you can stop by the what's in a name fan group on Facebook and hope that she remembers that she has an account on that platform: https://www.facebook.com/groups/whatsinanamefans.

Cursed Destiny

M.S. Weaver

on't fear the monsters, fear the circumstances that created them.
I hated the dark. I hated the mines. The way the coal stuck to my skin. How I scrubbed myself raw and still couldn't see *me*. I hated the way Robin whistled his merry tune, even when we hadn't eaten all day. After a year of living and working with the six dwarves in their cramped little hovel and this bottomless mine, I even missed that bloody snake, Nagini, and her drafty cave.

My pickaxe wavered as I contemplated the unexpected thought, then I drove it into the rock in front of me with renewed force, willing myself not to look at the black veins mapping my hands and arms beneath the filth. No, I didn't miss the golden-haired devil. She made me like this.

Pestilent.

Cursed.

Damned.

Guilt gnawed at my conscience, but I forced it down. Being angry and hating everyone was easier. It made simply existing bearable.

"Watch out!" The warning echoed from above.

Dirt and small rocks rained down on my head. I barely had time to cram my body into an indent in the rocky wall before an enormous boulder thundered past and took out the torch next to me. Coughing, I wiped the dust from my eyes and reached for my half-buried pickaxe. I would have shared its fate if I had still been six feet tall. I scoffed. It was hard to believe that there was a silver lining to my curse at the bottom of a mine.

"Hey grumpy, did you think a rock to the head would make you forget the girl who rejected you?" Lynx taunted. He jumped down from the rope ladder and shouldered me as he walked past.

"Don't," I ground out, glaring at his back.

A familiar heat roared to life inside my chest at the mere mention of the name Nagini cursed me with as punishment for my sins, just to shift into red-hot claws around my heart. For once, my churning thoughts weren't consumed by tortured blue eyes, but that brief moment was gone now.

Bear made his way through the others with his pickaxe slung over one shoulder. His shirt clung to his broad chest in a drenched V-shape after another long day down in this furnace the dwarves all felt so comfortable in. "Leave Blaine alone. He is just grumpy about losing his girl to a faun."

Bear flashed me his lazy smile, a thousand devils dancing in his hazel eyes, and my knuckles cracked under the pressure. He knew me, knew the darkness that bubbled beneath the surface of my skin, yet he never stopped poking the beast.

"There are worse things than being a dwarf as penance for your sins, Blaine," Robin piped in, hooking his thumbs into his belt and smiling so wide his teeth formed a moonstone bridge between his round, coal-stained cheeks.

"Aye," Fox chuckled, sniffed, and then wiped his nose with his sleeve. "Nagini could have turned ya into one of them fish folk. Now that would have been a shame."

"I heard Correena also changed. A spriggan told me she now has horns," Badger whispered to Fox, but as always, his deep voice carried through the tunnel. With only one good ear, he was the loudest, no matter what he did.

Anger scorched my insides. I had to get out. Had to breathe. Barreling through the laughing dwarves, I headed for the light. Mouse tried to hold me back, making feeble excuses for the others, but I shrugged him off. I knew they meant well, but this wound would never heal. It had been three years since the only person I ever allowed myself to love tore out my heart and stomped it into the ground until there was nothing left besides the raw, pounding emptiness that now occupied the spot where it once beat. And one year since I had to watch her choose him over me all over again.

I crashed through the underbrush, blind and deaf to the beauty of the forest, a single name echoing through my mind with each step I took.

Correena. Correena. Correena.

There was so much hate inside me. So much hurt that my ribcage wanted to explode and splatter my shredded heart for the world to see. And still, it wouldn't be enough to purge my soul of the all-consuming grief. My fingers wrapped around the molded steel resting against my chest, and I tugged, the thin leather strap biting into the skin at the back of my neck.

"Don't be stupid, boy." The gravelly voice of my father played in my head, and I stopped walking. My knuckles turned white around the dark edges of the amulet as the memory swept through me.

I was fifteen again, laboring away in the hell that had been the only home I ever knew. Father slurred his words, swaying as he brought the cup of ale to his lips. "A woman isn't worth the sweat on a man's back."

The heat from the forge had burned my eyes, and the sweat running down my nose sizzled as it hit the red-hot arrow tip I hammered away at. I couldn't wait to see Correena's brilliant blue eyes light up when I gave her the new bow and arrows I had crafted for her.

"Correena isn't Mother," I muttered and immediately bit my tongue.

The cup had slammed against the wooden workbench, sending ale splashing everywhere as Father lurched forward. The sting of his fist against my jaw rocked my brain before the back of the chair touched the ground. Even staggering drunk, he never missed a single blow.

"Don't you dare mention that woman in my house!" he roared, eyes wild with rage.

He fisted the front of my shirt, drawing my face so close to his I could count each red vein that crisscrossed his cheeks.

"If you think that girl won't crush your bleeding little heart the first chance she gets, then you are a bigger fool than I thought, boy. And I ain't raising no fool." Father tugged at the thick leather strap he wore around his waist with his free hand, and I steeled my spine. Showing pain was a weakness in his eyes.

The loud caw of a raven wrenched me back to the present, and I inhaled deeply to slow my ragged breathing, willing the last wisps of the memory to fade.

Blood trickled from my nose, black as the cursed organ that pumped it, and I wiped it away with the back of my hand. The metallic tang drowned out the scent of rotting leaves and damp soil as my knees hit the ground. I was a fool.

A fool for believing Correena could ever love a ruined soul whose own mother didn't even want him, and the biggest fool when I became my father.

A twig snapped beneath a boot, and I rubbed my aching eyes. Bear couldn't stalk a deaf boar if he tried. He sat down next to me, and I felt his gaze roaming the side of my face. Observing. Seeing more than I ever wanted him to see.

Picking up a withered leaf, he crumbled it between his thumb and forefinger, staring off into the trees. "We each battle our own demons, Blaine." He shifted, leaning closer. "That is why we are here, digging up coal instead of mining ore back home in Nidavellir."

"At least you have a home." I flexed my blackened fingers and watched the darkness pulse beneath my skin. Hands that vowed to protect but ended up harming instead.

His hand gripped my shoulder, squeezing hard before letting go. "You have one as well, brother. With us."

"No, I don't. When the time comes, you will go back, and I cannot follow."

"You have that amulet," Lynx said, and it startled me to find him leaning against a tree a few feet from us, tapping the tip of his dagger against his bottom lip.

Lynx was as stealthy as the predator whose name he shared. He stalked toward us, my eyes following the blade as it sliced through the air while he whirled it between his fingers. Crouching in front of me, he pointed the tip at my chest, his green eyes narrowed to slits. "You never told us how you got your grubby little paws on the royal seal of The House of Draconai."

Tucking the amulet back into my shirt, I met Lynx's glare and answered, "It was a gift." The only connection I had to the life I lost.

"You know humans don't know much about the dökkálfar, Lynx, and until a year ago Blaine was still human," Bear said.

Lynx opened his mouth to argue, but a loud crash coming from our home had us all up and running. Weaving through the underbrush, I heard Mouse scream. The anxious lilt to his voice and the sound of pottery shattering gave my feet wings.

We stopped and crouched behind some bushes a few feet from our home. A soldier in gleaming armor ducked out of the door, dragging a struggling Mouse behind him, and walked to where six more soldiers crowded around a kneeling Robin. The horse nearest to us stomped around, kicking up dust. Someone sneezed. Locating the familiar sound, I tapped Bear on the shoulder and pointed at the tree to the left of the group of soldiers. Fox and Badger dangled upside down from a sturdy branch, their ankles and wrists tied together with rope. Fox wiggled his nose beneath his upturned red beard and sneezed again. He and dust didn't get along.

"Now I will ask for the last time," a soldier with a crimson sash across his breastplate, marking him as a noble, bellowed as they shoved Mouse to his knees next to Robin. "Where is your princess?"

"We don't have a princess," Mouse sniveled, shying away from the sword at his neck. My fingers clenched into fists, and I bit down hard.

Images of Correena, her hands tied above her head and her back a bloody mess, assaulted me. The elders demanded information about the fae, and they were relentless in getting it. At first, my scorned heart rejoiced in her punishment, but later and every day after that, I had to drown out the memory of her wails with a few jugs of ale. I wanted to scream that this was wrong, that just like Correena, Mouse was the gentlest, most innocent soul I knew.

"You are dwarves, aren't you?" The leader leaned forward, and the soldier holding the sword grabbed Mouse's hair, tilting his head back. "And we all know the dwarves serve the dark elves down in Svartalfheim."

He uttered the last part with such malice, a shudder crawled down my spine. I had failed to protect the woman I loved and lost her, but I was done with being a coward. I needed to rescue them, and fast.

There was movement in the tree Fox and Badger hung from, and my shudder grew icy tentacles as I watched Lynx's curly mop of blond hair pop from the leaves right above their tied ankles. Lynx and I barely got along on good days, but no matter how hard I fought against it, these dwarves meant more to me than my father ever did.

I searched for a rock, anything, to create a big enough distraction for him to free Fox and Badger while Bear and I went for Mouse and Robin. It was ironic how I was planning to fight the very soldiers I spent most of my life training to join.

My fingers curled around a fist-sized rock, and Bear's gaze locked with mine. It would not be a fair fight. They were more than twice our size, had armor and gleaming swords, and lots of scars betrayed their battle experience. We only had our pickaxes but working the mines had made us strong. And we were motivated.

He nodded, and I leaned back, putting all my strength into that throw. The rock sailed into the bushes behind our house, thunked against a tree, and rolled away in a rustle of leaves.

Silence fell over the group in front of us. The leader held up his hand. No one made a move while they surveyed the surrounding forest. At the drop of his hand, five of the soldiers disappeared into the trees, leaving him and the one who manhandled Mouse behind. They moved to cover each other's backs, and we saw our chance.

Bear and I rushed forward, our battle cry splintering the silence. Robin threw his entire weight against the legs of the soldier behind him, knocking him off balance and into the leader.

Something whooshed along the ground, scattering leaves into the air, and my world tumbled head over heels. Bear's elbow drove into my ribs as he landed half on top of me, and my cheek burned. I opened my eyes to a swaying forest floor and curled my fingers through the rough woven net caging us.

No! I should have expected this. Setting traps was the first thing the huntsmen taught us.

I twisted my neck to see my friends. Maybe Mouse and Robin got away, but a pair of armor-clad thighs obstructed my view.

"The fae are so predictable," the leader laughed. "Make one squeal like a pig and the rest come running."

Anger and shame clashed in my chest. I was once just like these men. Hunting the fae, hating them for being different. I never once tried to get to know them or stopped to question why we were at war with them.

Footsteps approached from all sides, and a soldier stopped next to me. "We can't find any more of them, sire."

"Keep looking," he barked at the man. "The old crone said there were seven of them in her vision. And one of them has a connection to the missing princess the king seeks."

"Not to be disrespectful, sire, but this is the same witch who swore her snake killed the half-blood princess eleven years ago."

"Do you want me to mention to the king that a soldier is questioning his oracle?" the leader asked, his voice low.

The soldier took a nervous step back towards the woods. "N-no, sire. We will search again."

Crouching, the leader tilted his head to look at Bear and me. His lip lifted in a sneer as he gave a loud sniff. "Filthy animals."

My skin crawled under his stare; he reminded me of a viper just before it struck.

Leaning closer, the leader turned the net to follow the black lines along my arms, and I felt Bear stiffen, his body shifting to cover more of mine.

"Well, what do we have here?" My stomach turned to stone as the look of disgust on the man's face shifted into a diabolical smile and he shouted over his shoulder. "Bring the wagon with the cage! I think I've found what we're looking for."

Was he talking about me?

Bear's fingers dug into my arm. "No, you leave him alone." His voice shook, his grip turning painful.

The leader stood, swinging us away from him with a rumbling laugh that made every hair on my body stand on end. Correena once called me a heartless monster. I wonder what she would have said about him.

Correena.

My insides twisted. Lokheth would have taken her deeper into the Darkwood Forest, away from any trails the soldiers traveled, but did he know the king was sending his men further in than they had ever gone? As a human living among fae, she would be seen as a traitor and executed. But if she now had horns, the soldiers would burn her at the stake, as they did with all the fae they captured. Like they were going to burn us.

Nagini had turned me into a fae against my will, but that didn't matter. Once they discovered I wasn't the dwarf they were looking for, my life would be worthless. My eyes followed the soldiers, who were dragging my friends across the ground and tossing them into a pile a few feet from where Bear and I were hanging, and I realized something. If this was what man had become, I would rather die a dwarf.

A goose flew into the clearing. Snow-white feathers extended. It knocked into a soldier, poking the man next to him in the eye with its wing. The injured soldier uttered a disgruntled "ouch" while the first soldier took a swing at it. The goose stagger-flapped and, with a skull-pounding whack, sent a third soldier stumbling over Badger's legs. Grabbing onto his teary-eyed friend, they both went down in a tangle of limbs. Honking, almost as if laughing, the goose ducked and swerved around their heads. Two more soldiers rushed in to help, shouting and hitting at the feathered menace, and chaos erupted.

The leader headed towards his men, pulling his sword from his side. "It is a bird, fools. Kill it."

I caught a flash of darker green shifting through the leaves of the tree a few feet behind the commotion and something sharp nicked my side.

"Shh," a whisper came from behind us. "Brace yourselves."

Relief flooded through me as I recognized Lynx's voice. The net beneath us gave way with a soft whoosh, and Bear and I hit the ground, hard. We rose to our feet, our eyes fixed on the soldiers, who were all too busy dodging blows from the goose.

There was movement in the tree again. A hooded figure jumped from branch to branch, tossing something at the soldier's feet. I frowned as one of the red orbs bumped against a soldier's shoe and rolled toward a wide-eyed Mouse. An apple? Mesmerized, I watched as black mold formed all over it. Wisps of sick green vapor seeped from its rotten skin, trapping us all in a malignant cloud.

"We need to get to the others," Bear said and shuffled ahead, his nose and mouth buried in the crook of his elbow. Lynx and I followed, staying close to the ground. The soldiers shouted slurred curses, disoriented by the green smoke. Then they started falling. We dodged. One landed half on top of me, snoring like a wood saw. I struggled to get out from under him and lost sight of Lynx.

A hand wrapped around my arm, pulling me to the side, and I jumped. The small form motioned for me to follow, and we snuck away from the noise. Through the thinning haze, I glimpsed a dark green cloak, a bow and quiver slung across one slender shoulder, and a single strand of long midnight black hair spilling from beneath the hood.

I froze. Fear, so powerful it stole the air from my lungs, seized my heart. She couldn't be here. It wasn't safe. I wasn't safe.

She turned around. "Come on, the others are waiting for us." Her voice sounded different, but it had been a year since I last saw Correena, and much longer since she willingly talked to me.

The neigh of a horse ripped me from my dazed thoughts, and I spun around. A flash of light sparked off the tip of a soldier's drawn arrow, aimed directly at the one person I loved more than life itself, and my world slowed. I didn't think as death sped toward her; I just jumped.

Pain exploded between my shoulder blades, and my feet left the ground. I hit the dirt with such force it wrenched the last bit of air from my lungs. I couldn't breathe. The pain in my back and chest was excruciating. Spreading throughout my body in bolts of lightning. I never thought dying would feel like being roasted alive.

Hands tugged at me. "Help him," Lynx pleaded, but his words sounded muffled, as if he was standing on the other side of a roaring fire. I tried to hold on, but I could feel my soul slipping away.

Hues of bright orange, yellow, and flaming red swallowed me.

I was soaring. Tumbling and falling through the air. A wave of heat rolled through my chest and exploded from my mouth in a burst of flame. Closing my eyes, I plummeted through the plume of fire.

PECK, PECK, PECK.

There was an incessant hammering against my skull. I forced one eyelid to open and then the other. Fiery shadows danced along scorched stone walls and the familiar scent of burning coal clogged my nose. I should have known I would end up in Hel.

An orange beak shifted into view, followed by a curious, light blue eye. A goose? Hmph. Correena used to call them feathered demons whenever she had to gather them for her mother.

A heaviness settled in my chest. I never got to tell her . . .

"Gus, leave him alone."

That voice.

Delicate fingers brushed against my face, and I pressed my cheek into the soft touch. "I-I'm sorry, C-Correena." My throat felt as dry as a tanned hide. A cup pushed against my bottom lip, and I gulped down the cool water, quenching the burn.

"Kai." Big gray eyes peered down at me. Gray, not blue. Her skin was the lightest shade of ash, and when she tucked her raven hair behind her ear, I noticed they were pointed. "My name is Kai and thank you for saving my life."

A part of me was disappointed, but the tension coiled around my heart left me in exhaled relief. Correena wasn't here. She was safe. That was all that mattered. I couldn't hold Kai's gaze. No matter what she thought, I wasn't an honorable man.

"You saved us from the soldiers, and for that, I thank you."

My eyes searched the dim light of what I now recognized as a part of the mine. My friends were all there. Bear was stoking the small fire. Lynx hacked away at a piece of wood, a considerable pile already next to him, and Robin stirred a pot while Mouse added herbs to it. Fox sat further away, puffs of smoke rising from his pipe while he stared into the fire. Badger was lying next to him, fast asleep.

A smile tugged at my lips. Mouse and I always joked that Badger's snoring could wake the dead. My hand swiped over my chest; I felt no pain.

Turning back to the beautiful fae girl still hovering over me, I asked, "What happened?"

"You died," Lynx blurted out before Kai could answer, and I nearly swallowed my tongue.

She rolled her eyes, letting out an exaggerated sigh. "I should have left you in the soldiers' delightful company." She hooked an arm around my shoulders, patted me on the back, and said, "Ignore him."

Lynx huffed and grumbled something under his breath about not needing a whisper and her annoying animal before the sound of splintering wood drowned out the rest of his tirade.

And Nagini called *me* grumpy.

Bear sat down next to Kai, worry etched into his soulful eyes, and Mouse scuttled around them to sit on my other side, offering me a bowl of the broth Robin made. Sitting up, I took it with a grateful smile. Almost dying sure hadn't dampened my appetite. I could have eaten a horse.

Silence stretched around me, and I looked up from the near-empty bowl to find a half-asleep Badger and pensive Fox sitting near my feet. When did they move closer? I shifted, all the attention warming my cheeks. "What?"

Bear cleared his throat. "How do you feel?"

He kept his eyes locked on my chest, and I knew.

"Lynx wasn't exaggerating, was he?" I grabbed Kai's hand as she reached for my bowl, demanding, "Did you use magic to bring me back?"

"No." She shook her head. "Dragonsbreath is more powerful than any magic a whisper, like me, can ever conjure."

She had a point. Many fae distrusted whispers for their incredible control over animals, or even feared them when their manipulation extended to fae and humans, but they did not revere them for their magic.

Pulling her hand from mine, she pressed her palm against the warm steel resting against my chest. I held my breath, expecting the ever-present grief and anger I felt at the loss of Correena's love and friendship to rise to the surface, but there was none. Air trickled from my lungs as I studied my body. Still short and stocky, but the violent black veins that marred my skin with the evil that had once ruled my soul were gone, replaced by a single mark resembling a flame across my heart.

Correena might have carried the scar on her wrist, but the day she almost died had been seared into my soul forever. We were seven. Correena's eyes had been feverish below the wild midnight black locks stuck to her forehead in sweat-drenched tangles. Her small, clammy hand clung to mine; the frosty steel of the amulet encased between our palms. Her once rosy lips were cracked, the venom of the deathbringer wreaking havoc as it spread from her arm throughout her tiny body. She wheezed, straining to speak, and I tried to silence her, but her blue eyes grew even wider, and her other hand grabbed onto the front of my shirt.

"Take it."

"No," I rasped.

Each intake of breath had hurt. Whether it was from the beating I took from my father for not gathering enough wood for the forge, or the grief of seeing the life slipping from my only friend, I didn't know.

"I don't want your amulet. I need you. You are the only good thing in my life. Without you, I am nothing."

A tear had slipped from the corner of her eye as her lips stretched in a weak smile, causing small droplets of blood to pool in the cracks. "You are not nothing. You are my warrior."

Her hand fell from my shirt and rested against the back of mine, where our fingers were still entwined. "This will keep you safe . . ." her eyelids drooped, then closed, her voice nothing but a whisper, "until you can protect us."

I had pressed my forehead to hers, eyes squeezed shut to block out the world. "I will train every day until I am the strongest huntsman in our village. Nothing will ever hurt you again."

"The royal who gave you this saved your life."

"Royal?" I frowned as my attention returned to Kai, still hovering in front of me.

She nodded. "Yes, only someone from the royal Draconai bloodline can invoke the powerful magic of a dragon, for they are the only fae able to bond with them."

The words of the soldiers rang in my ears, and everything fell into place: Correena surviving the bite of the deathbringer, her love for the forest, Nagini following her like a second shadow, her father's reaction when I told him I saw her with a faun . . .

My hand found Correena's amulet, where my heart threatened to break through bone. She was the half-blood princess the king was searching for. And if the amulet brought me back to life, it could only mean one thing—I had a second chance at being the warrior she needed.

"I . . ." I tried to push myself to my feet, but a hand on my shoulder held me back. Gazing into Bear's eyes, I breathed, "I need to go."

I pushed against him harder, my voice mirroring the urgency growing in the pit of my stomach. "A long time ago, I promised to protect Correena and failed, but I will allow no one, especially someone as evil as the king, to get his hands on her."

A loud whack echoed through the room, followed by a curse from Lynx. A piece of wood arched through the air and landed with a thud in front of an unsuspecting Gus, who was chasing after a spider in the dim corner. The goose fluttered backward with a squawk, bumped into the pot hanging over the fire, and sent a wave of boiling stew in our direction.

"Are you insane?" Lynx shouted, jumping up from the spot where he was chopping wood. He closed the distance between us without giving the mess on the floor a single glance. "The last time you tried to be a hero, you died."

He waved the axe in my face, so close I could smell the sweet scent of the sap sticking to the blade, but I held firm. "We don't know if that amulet will bring you back again."

Kai began, "I think it—" Lynx glowered at her, cutting off her sentence, and then turned to Bear.

"You're our leader. Talk some sense into this fool. One dwarf against the king and his entire army is madness."

Bear looked at everyone in the room before turning back to me. A grin spread across his face till it danced in his hazel eyes.

"There is only one solution to this problem." He held out his hand to me. "We are the Dwarves of the Darkwood Forest. We protect our own. Where one goes, the others follow."

Badger leaned forward, cupping his good ear. "Where are they off to?"

Fox slapped him on the shoulder and grinned. "Pack ya bag, old friend. We're all going on an adventure."

I took Bear's hand, and one after another the rest of the dwarves joined in, even Lynx. He glared at me, but there was a glint of something other than anger in his eyes. "If I die on this crazy quest of yours, I will come back from the dead and drag you to Niflheim myself."

Smirking, I said, "Deal."

"Do you have space for one more?" Kai said, her lips set in a stubborn line as she placed her delicate hand on top of our calloused ones. "The soldiers destroyed my home and everything I cared about. And who knows, you lot might need me to save you again."

I nodded, unable to speak past the lump forming in my throat. She was just as lost as we were.

Gus scrambled into Kai's lap with a low hiss aimed at Lynx, and she wrapped her arms around the pesky bird. He nuzzled her neck, dragging a lopsided smile from her. "You are coming too, silly. I would never forget about you."

I looked at the coal-smeared faces surrounding me, and my once-shattered heart felt so full it spilled over into my soul and drove out the last wisps of darkness that had consumed me for so long.

For the first time, I understood the words my mother whispered into my ear before she disappeared into the night. "Trust your heart, lítill dreki. It will guide you home."

MS Weaver

Once Upon a time MS Weaver was the girl who walked through life with her nose buried in a book. After countless bumps and bruises, she decided to open the secret portal to her imagination and invite readers into her world where magic is real and mythical creatures come to life.

She spends her time in the mundane world on a farm in South Africa with her husband and three children. There, she once had to nurse a python back to health after he wrestled with a porcupine. But the moments she cherishes most are the ones passed staring up at the stars with her children while she encourages them to follow their dreams. Because why would you want to be ordinary when you were born to be extraordinary?

If you want to know more about this bookworm and the peculiar worlds that inhabit her mind, click on the link and hop on through. Just avoid the shadows. They might conceal a villain or two.

Find out more:
https://www.linktr.ee/Sneakymewriter/

ABOUT THE CHARITY

Room to Read is a global non-profit headquartered in California. The organization strives to create a world free from illiteracy and gender inequality in education.

With the core belief that "World change starts with educated children", Room to Read helps children around the world develop literacy skills and a habit of reading, and particularly supports under-priviledged girls to build skills and succeed in school.

Thanks to you, we're helping more children access learning and literacy, and working to lift the next generation out of poverty.

WHAT'S NEXT?

Once Upon a Name, Twice Upon a Name and now Third Name's a Charm! Tales of Trios and Triple Threats coming April 2024.

If you want to make sure you get the next volume you can pre-order now at **books2read.com/thirdnamesacharm**! As always, all proceeds donated to charity in support of reading and literacy.